SPLINTER

SPLINTER

SARAH FINE

47NORTH

Published by 47North, Seattle

www.apub.com

Amazon, the Amazon logo, and 47North are trademarks of Amazon.com, Inc., or its affiliates.

ISBN-13: 9781503936423
ISBN-10: 1503936422

Cover design by Faceout Studio

Printed in the United States of America

For Brigid Kemmerer, of whom I am constantly in awe.
You didn't force me to be your friend, lady—I was ready to beg.
And tackle you if necessary.

CHAPTER ONE

There are two kinds of knowing. The kind that resides in your brain, with straight edges and smooth planes, and fits tidily between memories like a book on a shelf. The kind that matches your hopes and tells you everything is as it should be.

But then there's the knowing that comes for you at night, after layers of consciousness have been peeled off by the exhaustion of the day. It lives in that pit in your stomach, jagged and dark. The kind of knowing that won't let you rest until you finally surrender and let it, in all its ferocious and hideous glory, step into the light.

The kind that changes everything.

"We're going to have to change everything, Mattie," the seamstress announced. "This fit you perfectly last summer, but now . . ." Her gaze met mine in the mirror and slid away.

But not before I saw the accusation in her eyes. "I didn't do this on purpose," I said quietly, looking down at the wedding dress hanging from my frame, held up only by my mother's hands grasping a fold of material at my back.

"Well, you're not the first bride to go overboard with dieting." Her papery skin tickled mine as she flattened the material along my chest and pinned it under my armpit.

I gritted my teeth. This was supposed to be a magical time in my life. I was supposed to be glowing. But one look at my mom and at Chelsea, my maid of honor, told me I was failing miserably. "I haven't been dieting."

"Doesn't exactly look like you've been carb-loading, either," said Chelsea, who stood off to the side, her black hair swept up in a voluminous twist—a test run for the style she'd wear on my big day. We were best friends from college, but now we got to see each other only a few times a year. She'd driven down from Green Bay just for the fitting and the styling, and she still seemed unsettled by how different I looked.

"Just a case of wedding jitters," my mother said from behind me, her voice full of false cheer, so chirpy it made me wince.

"Fifteen pounds' worth of jitters?" Chelsea asked, turning to my mom. "You'd think she'd be emptied out by now."

"I'm standing right here," I said, then gasped as pain lanced through my chest.

After nine months, I should have gotten used to it, but it caught me by surprise every single time. I hunched forward, bracing one palm on my thigh, my other hand rising to rub my chest. It didn't help the pain, but it did make me feel a tad less helpless. Pins stabbed my side, but that was nothing compared to the slice of hurt right in the center of my breastbone. I tried to suppress a whimper.

"Oh, dear. It's happening again," my mother said, letting go of my dress to hold on to my waist.

"What's wrong?" Chelsea asked, stepping out of the way as my mother helped me off the little platform where I'd been standing. My feet tangled in the train of my dress and I nearly went down, but my mother held me tight, her auburn hair tickling the side of my face as she guided me to a chair.

The seamstress pulled out her phone. "Does she need an ambulance?"

"No, no, Mattie has these little panic attacks," Mom said breezily, rubbing my back as I bowed my head over my knees and focused on breathing through the pain. "Probably stress. We're trying to convince her to take some time off for herself before the wedding, but she's just work, work, work all the time!"

If I hadn't needed her so badly in that moment, I would have screamed at her. Work was the only place where I felt like myself, where I was busy enough to be distracted from all the things I was trying not to think about—including the pain. "Mom, I'm okay, really."

I avoided their gazes as the agony faded, a hit-and-run, like it just needed to remind me that I shouldn't get too comfortable. Summoning all my energy and pep, I sat up straight and forced a smile. But my dress, the gorgeous taffeta-and-lace mermaid-cut sheath made to emphasize my curves and help me look taller, gaped at my chest, giving me a view straight down to my hollow belly. I was down to a hundred pounds, a few pounds lighter than I had been as a Red Squad cheerleader at University of Wisconsin. Now I barely had any curves left to emphasize.

My smile faded as I glanced up at my face in the mirror. My hair, strawberry blond and relentlessly thick and curly, had been carefully styled at the salon this morning for our little dry run, but all the product in the world couldn't hide its dull, dry texture. My eyes were rimmed with dark circles. My skin, freckled and fair, had taken on a gray undertone that no amount of makeup seemed able to conceal. "God, I look awful," I choked out, my eyes filling with tears.

"Oh, no, baby, you don't," Mom said, the cheerfulness taking on a shaky edge.

"Stop lying, Mom!" I stood up, clawing at the buttons on the back of my dress. "Get this off me."

"I still have to pin the back," yelped the seamstress, lunging toward me as her pins started popping from the sides of the dress, casualties of my frantic tugs.

"I-I think maybe we should reschedule," Mom said. Chelsea was already unfastening the trail of pearly buttons down my back. Mom pulled me forward, supporting me as I stepped over the crumpled pile of dress that fell around my calves, but I yanked myself out of her grip as soon as I had my balance again.

"I just need a minute, all right?" I turned my face away so they couldn't see the tears. "I'll be right out." I fled to the dressing room, the roaring in my ears drowning out anything they might have said.

Once in there, I slid down the wall and laid my forehead on my knees. My wedding was six weeks away. My life, derailed so abruptly and completely the summer before, was back on track. My fiancé was healthy, his faulty heart permanently healed with magic owned by the very mob boss who had ordered his violent kidnapping in the first place. And Ben had worked so hard to set things right since we'd gotten home.

I'd worked hard, too, but with less success.

"*Stop it*, Mattie," I whispered for probably the tenth time that day, like every other day.

Especially every time I thought of Asa Ward. Every time his face, his crooked nose, and his knife-blade smile crept to the front of my thoughts. Every time his voice slid into my head.

I jerked like I'd been shocked, and pushed myself to my feet. "Dammit." I swiped my hands across my cheeks.

A knock at the door made me turn to see Chelsea's face as she opened it. "You okay?" she asked as she came inside. She scooped my bra from the floor and nodded toward the strapless one I'd donned for the fitting.

I unfastened it and let it fall, then put on my regular one, trying to ignore the way my breasts didn't really fill the C-cups anymore. I'd put off buying new bras, or any clothes for that matter, telling myself

I'd regain my appetite soon, that the weight would stop melting away and I'd be myself again. I hastily pulled my loose-fitting shirt over my head before smiling at Chelsea. "I'm all right. I just wasn't in the mood to stand still today, I guess."

Chelsea arched an eyebrow. "Maybe because your feet have become two giant blocks of ice?"

I rolled my eyes as I pulled on my yoga pants. "I don't have cold feet, lady. I'm nervous, sure, but that's not the same thing."

"Uh-huh. You always ate like a freak when you were nervous, Mattie. This right here?" She gestured up and down my body. "I don't know this girl."

"Well, it's been a while since you were down—"

"We text at least once a day," she snapped. "You might have mentioned that you were falling apart. I'd have been at your door with a barrel of Häagen-Dazs in a matter of hours."

It wouldn't have helped. "What do you want me to say?"

"How about something honest? You haven't been the same since the thing with Ben last year."

"It was kind of stressful." Understatement of the century. "He could have been killed, Chelsea. I nearly lost him." And I'd traveled halfway around the world to save him. I'd risked my life and sanity to pay his ransom—I'd carried an ancient, invaluable magic inside me in an attempt to hide it from the scores of dangerous mobsters out to claim it. I'd survived only because Ben's estranged brother had been willing to go to the same lengths despite the fact that he had every reason to walk away. But we never talked about Asa. He didn't fit into the story Ben and I told. The truth was too unbelievable, too wild, too secret. Too dangerous.

I shivered, trying to shed the memories. "I'm over it, though— that's all behind us. Lately it's just all the little details of the wedding. I want it to be perfect for everyone. It's a lot of pressure."

Unfortunately, Chelsea always called BS when she smelled it—part of the reason I'd avoided telling her how I was really doing. "So you're having panic attacks? You used to be the top flyer off our human pyramids in front of eighty thousand people, and you barely batted an eyelash. You loved it, in fact. This just doesn't sound like you."

I knelt to tie my sneakers. "Things change, and the doctors all agree that's what it is." I'd been subjected to every medical test under the sun. I'd been seen by a cardiologist. A gastroenterologist. A pulmonologist. An endocrinologist. A neurologist. And of course, the last stop—a psychiatrist. Panic attacks were the only explanation for the stabbing pains that awakened me every night, that interrupted my days and stole my appetite. "There's nothing physically wrong with me, so it's all in my head, right?" I let out a weak laugh.

She looked me up and down. "Nothing physically wrong? Are you freaking serious?"

I threw my shoulders back. "It's nothing a positive attitude can't squelch."

"Maybe your body's trying to tell you something." She inclined her head toward the door. "You don't have to do all this, you know. It's never too late to call it all off."

"What have I said to give you the impression I'd want to call it off? I love Ben!"

"I know. And I know you've wanted this for a long time. I'm just saying—"

"Stop." It came out of me so loudly that my mom let out a surprised yip from the fitting room.

"Everything okay, baby?" she called. "You need any help?"

"I'm fine!" I gave Chelsea a warning look, and she clamped her mouth shut, crimping her full lips over her disapproval. "Chelsea just threatened to tell embarrassing stories about me during her maid-of-honor toast, that's all."

"Oh, Chelsea," Mom said, laughing. Even through the door, I could feel her relief. "Save it for the big day."

"If you insist, Mrs. Carver," Chelsea replied, adopting a cringe-worthy fake-enthusiastic tone while she stared me down. "But I've got some good ones."

"Thank you," I said quietly, reaching for the doorknob.

"Don't." She stepped closer and leaned in. "You've been lying to me for months, Mattie. But fine, whatever, I get it. Just don't lie to yourself, okay? Ask yourself if this is what you really want, or if you're just barreling forward like you always do while your body tries to put on the brakes."

She put her hand over mine and pulled open the door, then walked out ahead of me. I took a moment to hitch a cheerful smile onto my face, pinning it into place with happy thoughts of flowers and lace and Ben standing at the end of the altar, waiting for me to meet him there. Then I exited the room to sail through the rest of my day.

By the time I reached the front door of the cottage, I could already smell dinner. Onions, garlic, bacon. "Ben?"

"Kitchen," he called. "My afternoon splenectomy got canceled."

I frowned. The patient, a nine-year-old schnauzer mix named Gordon Lightfoot, had been diagnosed with cancer of the spleen just a few days before. "Why?"

"They decided they wanted to put him down instead," Ben said as I joined him in our kitchen. He handed me a glass of merlot. "They took him home and are spending the weekend with him. He'll come back on Monday."

My throat got tight at the news, but Ben looked unruffled. He'd had longer to process the decision. "You could have saved him."

He nodded. "But it would have been expensive. They said they couldn't afford it."

"Couldn't you have . . ." I took a quick sip of my wine. I'd been about to suggest he offer to do it for free, or for a much lower fee, something he used to do all the time. But we were still repaying the debt he'd racked up with his addiction to Ekstazo pleasure magic . . . and to other types of magic as well.

He used Knedas juice on you, didn't he? Asa whispered in my memories.

I squeezed my eyes shut. "That's too bad. Are you okay?"

"Just part of the job." His fingers caressed my cheek. "You look tired, babe."

I let out a weary chuckle and set my wineglass on the counter. "Isn't that a socially acceptable way of telling someone she looks terrible?"

He took my face in his large, warm hands. "You look as beautiful to me as you ever have, Mattie."

Liar, I thought. But I stayed quiet.

He kissed my forehead. "I came home early to cook dinner for you. Bucatini with bacon, tomato, and onions. Something hearty to put some meat back on your bones."

I pulled away from him. "My mom called you, didn't she?"

"Am I not allowed to talk to my future mother-in-law? She wanted to make sure you had a nice, relaxing evening. Said you'd had a busy day filled with hair and dresses and tricky flower arrangements."

That *would* be what my mom told him. No matter how bad things were, she'd embroider the edges of the truth with a pretty silver lining. It was like she believed that naming a bad thing gave it power, but if we just talked around it, maybe it would simply go away. "Yeah. Who knew wedding planning was so exhausting?"

Hey, I'd learned from the best.

Ben ushered me onto the screened porch, where we could see the emerald buds dotting the branches of the trees that lined our yard, the daffodils poking their little green heads through the soil in the flower beds. We ate our dinner in near silence, him gobbling down pasta while

I picked at my food. It smelled good, but I already felt full, like my stomach had been stuffed with something huge and brittle and too much weight would cause it to splinter.

After we were finished, we did the dishes together. Ben's hands snaked around my waist as I dried my hands with a towel. He bowed his face into my hair. "You didn't believe me when I told you that you were beautiful to me."

I folded the towel over the edge of the dish rack. "I never said that."

"You don't think I know you well enough to tell? Come on, Mattie." His fingers spread, stroking across my ribs.

I fought the urge to pull away, knowing he could probably feel each one. "I never said that, either."

A breath of laughter warmed the top of my head. "Because you don't say much of anything these days."

"I'm stressed out. It's no big deal, just a lot of details to manage."

"Then let me help. I'll take time off—"

"You can't, and you know that."

He sighed. "I know." He was determined to pay off the debt to the contractor who'd renovated the vet clinic, and he wanted to get it done before the wedding. "But I want to do something for you." He tilted his head and kissed the side of my neck. "I love you so much, and I just want to make you happy." His hand slid around to my stomach and began to dip into my pants.

I grabbed his wrist. "Not tonight, okay? I've had a really long day."

His hand stilled, but he continued to nuzzle the side of my throat. "I'd be happy to relax you."

I closed my eyes and tried to summon my desire, but all I could find was a wary exhaustion. "You're so sweet, Ben, but I'm just not up to it."

"I'll do all the work—I promise."

While I lay like a rag doll beneath him? The idea—just another reminder of how much I'd changed—made my stomach turn. "No."

His tongue slipped along my skin. "Come on. It's been months . . ."

I leaned away from him. "It hasn't been that long."

He pulled me against him, letting me feel his arousal. "It's been twelve weeks and three days."

"You've been counting?" I ducked under his arm and took a few steps back, crossing my arms over my chest.

He ran his hands through his light-brown hair, shot through with golden strands. "Can you blame me? I'm dying here, Mattie."

"You're *dying*? Way to make me feel guilty."

He let out a long breath. "I only meant that I want you. I miss you. I love you, and I want to be close to you. Can you blame me for *that*?"

"No," I said quietly. "I love you, too. But I haven't felt like myself lately, okay? Just give me a little time to pull myself together. I'm getting there. And you deserve the best of me."

"I deserve all of you!" He moved toward me, his arms out as if to enfold me, but I put my hands up to keep him back. He stopped and his expression hardened. "Goddammit, Mattie, what the hell is wrong with you? It's like you *want* to be sick. Like you're using it to keep me at a distance. Why don't you just admit it?"

"Because it's not true! I'm trying to get better."

"Oh, really?" His honey-brown eyes flared, and he walked over and opened the cabinet above the coffeemaker. He reached in and took out a pill bottle. "I counted these. You haven't taken a single one in the last two weeks."

"Because they don't help. The attacks still come. And they make my thoughts all fuzzy."

He slammed the bottle onto the counter. "Don't tell me you're trying to get better if you're not even willing to follow your doctor's advice." He grimaced. "Especially after what we've spent on copays and prescriptions over the last nine months." When he saw my stunned look, his shoulders slumped. "I'm sorry. That came out all wrong."

"Or maybe you said exactly what you meant."

"I'm just tired. Maybe we can talk about this tomorrow when my head's on straight." He turned and trudged toward our room, but paused and looked back before he entered. "I'm going to make it an early night. Join me?"

"I'll be there soon."

His jaw clenched, but he nodded and disappeared into the room, leaving me standing in the kitchen. I carried the pills into the living room and sank into the couch, cradling the gently rattling bottle to my chest. The eerily familiar noise was like a fuse sparking to life, burning down until it triggered the explosion of memories.

Pockets full of magic disguised as the most mundane things—floss, baby oil, Pez. They rattled when he walked, when he ran, when his legs flopped to the bed the one time he was too sick to take care of himself and let me do it for him.

Come with me, Mattie. We're a good team. We can figure this out. Together.

I hadn't asked him just what he wanted to figure out. How to get away from Frank Brindle, the boss of the West Coast? How to get Ben free without giving up our freedom in return?

Or how to figure out the tangled, messed-up, inevitably doomed *thing* the two of us were together?

"You know very well what I meant, Mattie," Asa whispered.

My eyes flew open, and there he was, sitting on the rug, a lean arm slung around his bent knee, looking relaxed even though he'd apparently just broken into my house.

"I don't have any idea," I replied. "And how did you get in here?"

"You let me in." He rolled his eyes. "How is it that you can deal with a shitload of ancient Strikon pain magic inside your chest but not be able to deal with your own heart?"

"You helped me with the magic. This is different."

He crawled toward me, predatory and smooth in the darkened room. My heart lurched as he came closer, but I was like prey, paralyzed by the look in his eyes. He stopped only when his face was an inch from mine. "No, Mattie. It's exactly the same."

His mouth descended on mine, and a flash of relief lit me up.

But the moment our lips touched, the pain stabbed straight through my chest, from my breastbone to my spine and everywhere in between. I gasped, jerking up, my eyes flying open, air squeaking from my throat in hitching breaths.

I was alone in the room, alone with myself, alone with so much hurtful truth that I couldn't contain it all. I doubled over, desperate to stay quiet so Ben wouldn't hear. But it was all I could do not to scream as the agony radiated down my spine and up my neck, threading searing pain across my breasts. I clamped my hand over my mouth and drew my knees to my chest as a dark knowledge shifted and turned inside me, cutting my insides with its jagged edges, forcing me to look, as much as I wanted to go on pretending it didn't exist.

I hadn't let go of Asa. Somehow, he'd stayed with me, haunting me. Because I'd let him. Because a part of me missed him, wondered where he was and what he was doing, wondered if he ever thought of me, wondered if the life he'd offered was something I should have explored. And it was ruining me, body and soul.

I managed to sit up. Fumbling, I unscrewed the cap of the pill bottle and let two pale blue ovals fall onto my palm. I tossed them into my mouth and swallowed, then winced as they slowly slid down my dry throat. "I made my choice," I whispered.

Yes, it had been tempting. And *yes*, so was Asa himself. Painfully so.

But I was never meant for a life like that or for a man like him, both endlessly complicated in ways I'd only just begun to understand. And if I didn't move on, I was going to lose the life I had.

"I'm not going to let that happen." I pushed myself off the couch and headed for the bedroom.

CHAPTER TWO

Ben pulled in behind my father's Volvo and squeezed my hand. "You think Grandpa's forgiven me yet?"

I squeezed back and held on, loving the solid feel of him. "I'm more worried about whether he's forgiven me. I haven't come to visit him in weeks." I hadn't wanted to scare him.

"It's kind of amazing he's held on this long. He's obviously a strong old man."

"That he is," I murmured. And way too perceptive for my comfort. "I told him you're clean, by the way—that you hadn't touched magic in months."

"Did he believe you?"

"Why wouldn't he?"

Ben paused with his fingers wrapped around the door handle. "I know it takes time to rebuild trust. But I can accept that, as long as I know there's still a chance."

I leaned over and kissed his cheek, inhaling the astringent scent of his aftershave. "Thanks for holding on this long, then."

"Worth it," he said with a smile.

We got out and headed inside, where Mom was rolling out dough in the kitchen. "Come on in," she said, her tone ever cheerful. "Grandpa just ate some lunch, and his nurse will be here in a bit to bathe him, so it's a good time."

Ben walked over to give my Mom a one-armed hug. "Mattie, do you want to have some time with him before I come in? There's something I want to talk to Kat about."

Mom saw me narrow my eyes and laughed. "Oh, get in there, Mattie. I promise we're not scheming."

Ben arched an eyebrow. "Well, maybe a little. All good stuff, though."

"Okay." I pulled my cardigan tighter around my body as a gust of cool wind came in off Lake Michigan. "But for the record, I'm not in the mood for surprises these days . . ." I swallowed, my toes curling in my sandals, and then pasted a smile on my face. "Never mind. Surprise me!"

Reclaiming my life, dammit. I whirled around and headed for the library, Grandpa's domain. My heart kicked into a higher gear, a hammer pounding splinters of glass a little deeper into my chest wall. I rubbed at the pain and was wondering if I should take another Xanax when Grandpa's frail voice reached me.

"Kat told me you were coming today. I said I'd believe it when I saw it." He turned his head. His eyes were watery, red rimmed, and he was thinner than when I'd last seen him, but otherwise, he looked nearly the same, though he was months past his predicted expiration date.

"I know it's been too long, and I'm sorry."

He frowned. "You look nearly as bad as I do, Mattie." He returned his gaze to the view of the lake beyond the window.

I leaned my forehead against the steel railing of his bed. "It's been a bit rough lately."

His shaking hand settled on my nest of curls. "Is that boy treating you all right?"

"Ben's been great. *I'm* the problem."

"I suspect you're being way too hard on yourself. You risked everything to save him. Are you sure you aren't having buyer's remorse?"

"I made my choice!" I raised my head to find him looking at me. "I risked everything because I love him. I just . . ." I sagged a little. "Grandpa, was it hard to leave *that* world, once you knew about it?"

"Ah. Well, I was in *that* world for nearly fifty years. And as for my retirement"—he chuckled, a rattling, phlegmy sound—"let's just say it was only partial."

"What do you mean?"

He laid his knobby hand on his chest. "Ever carried a secret inside you for so long that it eats away at you? Physically, I mean." His gaze skimmed over my face, and I wondered if he could see past the under-eye concealer, the luminizer, the powder, or if he could just tell that my cheeks were less round, my collarbones a little sharper. "Looks like you might know what I'm talking about."

"Pretend I don't."

"I don't really have cancer."

My mouth dropped open. "You mean you're not—"

"Oh, I'm dying. No doubt about that. But it's the magic that's killing me. Lung cancer just seemed like an easier explanation. A little Knedas juice was all it took to convince the docs."

"Working as a reliquary for all those years made you sick?"

"Oh, no. Never had a problem. Pretty easy job, apart from a few Strikon relic transactions. Those were the worst."

"Tell me about it," I whispered, even as the memory of Asa rose, leaning over me, his eyes hard on mine. *Focus on what you have to do, because you know I'm handling the rest.* And he had, and I was grateful, and I'd let him go. End of story. "So what happened then? After all those years of jet-setting and doing your thing, how did it all end?"

"Jack and I were in Russia, and we'd gotten ourselves into a bit of trouble."

A lump formed in my throat at the mention of Jack. The old conduit had helped me and Asa out of a dire situation—at the cost of his own life. "Jack seemed like he could handle just about anything," I said quietly. Right up until the moment a sniper's bullet shattered his skull.

"Oh, we were old hands by that time. It was hard to surprise us. But Volodya, the Russian boss, was a crafty bastard who employed even craftier henchmen. Crazy time in Russia, less than ten years after the fall of the Soviet Union. We were trying to smuggle a valuable relic full of Ekstazo healing out of the country to save the life of a client's daughter, and we got caught by the nastiest pair you'd ever want to meet." He shuddered. "Lishka—she was a Strikon—and Arkady, a Knedas. I'd heard of them, of course, but meeting them . . ."

While Grandpa wrestled with his memories, so did I. I'd met a couple of nasty operators myself last summer, and I'd felt what they could do. "Did they torture you?" I whispered.

Grandpa started, like I'd just wrenched him from a dream. "Oh, they were going to, but all of a sudden, in walks Theresa. She was a pretty young thing, but always sweating like she was in Death Valley. Still, she acted like she owned the place. Claimed Volodya wanted us to take the Ekstazo magic as a gesture of goodwill, and if those two interfered, they'd have to deal with him. Moment I saw her, I knew we were saved."

"So they believed her?"

He nodded. "Practically left a smoke trail, they cleared out so fast. They'd probably been trying to skim some off the top, you know? Going into business for themselves. That was happening a lot."

"So, Theresa . . ." I bit my lip. "You've mentioned her before—she was a magic sensor."

Even if I hadn't recognized the name, Grandpa's description of her would have given it away. Every time Asa had been close to powerful magic, he'd sweated like crazy, his body reacting violently. I had ached for him.

I was aching *now*.

"Yeah," said Grandpa, his tone turning wistful. "I think I told you how hard it is for those magic sensors to survive in this business. And Theresa was one of the best. We'd worked together in the past. She belonged to Volodya. He depended on her."

"Was she . . . *normal*? I thought that magic sensors couldn't hang on for very long when they're constantly surrounded by magic." Asa had been willing to die rather than let himself be captured by either of the two mob bosses who wanted to force him into their employ.

"Normal?" Grandpa shook his head. "Heartbroken, more like. Saddest lady I ever did meet. She wouldn't talk much about her past, but I had the impression she'd lost someone she loved. Maybe she was even trying to get back to him. She was determined to escape Volodya. In fact, she asked for our help. And considering that she'd just saved our skins, Jack and I were happy to step up." Grandpa let out a rattling laugh. "Had no idea what I was in for. Original magic is nothing to mess with."

It felt like all my blood had drained to my feet as I remembered what Jack had said before he'd helped extract original Strikon magic from the little vault I had inside me—*this isn't my first original-relic rodeo.* "She wanted help getting one of the four relics?"

Grandpa's filmy eyes widened. "How do you know about the original four?"

"That's what I had to exchange for Ben's safety. I smuggled it out of Thailand and delivered it to the West Coast boss." And Frank Brindle had kept up his end of the bargain, thank God.

Grandpa blinked at me. "And did you—?" His fingers clutched at the front of his undershirt, right over his heart.

I nodded. "It went okay." Because Asa had gotten me through it. I'd had to give him a little piece of my soul in exchange, though, one I now knew would be forever his. "I got through it."

"Which one was it?"

I gave Grandpa a tremulous smile. "Strikon."

He looked me over. "And is *this* the result?"

"No, it's not that at all. It wasn't inside me for even twenty-four hours before we got it back into the relic, thanks to Jack."

"Good thing," Grandpa said quietly, now rubbing his chest. "A very good thing."

"What did Theresa want you to do?" I was eager to shift the topic away from myself.

"What? Oh! Oh, yes. She wanted to get out. And to do that, she had to pull off the biggest theft in the history of thefts . . ." He chuckled again. "Until the one you pulled off yourself, that is. She wanted to steal the Sensilo relic from Volodya—and replace it with a fake."

"Why?"

"She wanted to exchange it for her own safety. She never said what she was going to do with it—maybe sell it to the highest bidder, maybe hand it over to the Headsmen in exchange for protection from Volodya. All she asked of me and Jack was to help her get it out of the country."

"So you know what it feels like."

Grandpa closed his eyes. "Jack had to carry me out of the safe house where we did the transaction. Never felt such an overwhelming sensation in all my life. But I was back on my feet quickly, and it was a good thing. We were only about two steps ahead of Volodya's people. Theresa covered for us yet again. She'd told us to meet her in Saint Petersburg, at a club right on the Neva. We planned to sneak out of the country and travel together back to the US."

"I take it something went wrong?"

"I guess you could say that. She never showed. Jack and I waited as long as we could, but the relic was so hot that we knew we had to get out." Grandpa sighed, bowing his head to stare at his own bony, concave chest. "I kept it hidden for her, just in case, but she was gone for good. Never saw her again. No idea what happened to her."

My heart dropped. "Are you telling me the magic is still *inside* you?"

"Yes, the magic is still with me." He reached over and picked up the small locked wooden box he kept by his bedside, bringing it over to cradle in his lap. One of the few things he'd brought with him from his home in Arizona, it was about six inches on a side, and its top was an exquisite riot of carving: twisting branches and leaves, with an elephant's head at the center. "But the relic itself is in here—"

I made a face at the box. "Which body part is it?"

"Viscera."

I grimaced. "Like, guts?"

"Preserved and covered in gold. All of them are. Blood for Ekstazo, bone for Strikon, brain for Knedas, viscera for Sensilo."

"So gross," I muttered.

His unsteady hand closed over mine, his touch cool and dry. "When I'm gone, I want you to take the empty relic to the Headsmen. Let them know the magic died with me."

"Grandpa, this is what's killing you?"

"Magic has a cost, Mattie," he said quietly, his eyes meeting mine. "Especially magic like this."

"But—"

His fingers tightened while he laid his other hand over the wooden box. "It's best this way. Too much power, too dangerous if it falls into the wrong hands. I didn't want to endanger my family by trying to off-load it, no matter how much money was involved. It's going to die with me. You understand?"

Whether I did or not, it was too late. Grandpa was so frail, and I knew from experience that the magic inside him was huge and brutal. "Yeah," I said.

A sudden knock startled me, and I spun around to see Ben in the doorway. "Hey." He took a hesitant step toward us. "Is this a bad time?"

"No," I said—at the same time Grandpa said, "Yes."

"Oh," said Ben, looking crestfallen.

Grandpa set the carved wooden box back on the shelf and stared stonily out the window. "Wanda's going to be here any minute to get me cleaned up. She's never late."

I sandwiched Grandpa's hand between my own. "Can't you give him a chance to make amends?" I whispered.

Grandpa crimped his lips.

"It would mean the world to me if you'd give us your blessing before the wedding," said Ben, coming forward to lay his hands on my shoulders. "I know I messed up, sir, but I've spent the last nine months trying to fix it."

"If you say so," Grandpa muttered.

"Can I come back in a day or two to talk to you, man to man?" Ben asked. "Please."

Grandpa gave me a long, hard stare, and I looked back at him, silently pleading. He rolled his eyes. "Never could resist that face," he said, his lips twitching into a begrudging smile. "I guess I can find room in my busy schedule."

Ben grinned, and then, very slowly and deliberately, leaned forward and offered Grandpa his hand to shake. I held my breath—the last time Ben had touched Grandpa, the old man had realized Ben had been using magic. He'd recognized Ben as an addict even before I knew what magic was. But today, Ben and Grandpa shook, and . . . Grandpa looked down at their clasped hands, and then nodded. "Okay, then."

I kissed Grandpa on the forehead and smiled as Ben slid his arm around my waist, so grateful to have yet another confirmation that Ben was clean. Especially because of what I'd just learned about Grandpa: magic was killing him. Slowly. Painfully. It was deadly, and I needed to stay as far away from it as I could, for the rest of my life.

Looking back, it's a little funny how naive I was. I actually thought I had a choice.

CHAPTER THREE

After leaving Grandpa we drove to the clinic. I was happy they'd seemed to have made up, but I could tell Ben was thinking about something, because he was chewing the inside of his cheek. Finally, he asked, "Do you ever miss that world?"

"What world?"

"Magic."

"Why would you ask me that?"

He shrugged one shoulder. "Just thinking about it. I mean, it's part of your history, maybe even part of your heritage, you know? Your grandpa could tell I was using the night of the engagement party. I knew it as soon as I saw the look on his face."

"And yet you denied having secrets only a few hours later."

"I was scared of losing you, Mattie. I still am." He leaned his head back against the headrest. "The ironic thing is that I'd decided to tell you the next day. If Reza Tavana hadn't shown up, things would have gone differently."

I snorted, even as a chill went down my spine as I remembered Frank Brindle's Strikon assassin. "And after all that, you'd actually ask me if I miss it?"

Ben sighed as we pulled up behind the clinic. "Crazy, right? But remember that Brindle put me up in a pretty swank hotel suite after that. I got a sense of how much money some of his staff made."

"Yeah, so?"

He crossed his arms over his broad chest and stared out the windshield at the building. "I've been working my ass off the last nine months. You know that."

I touched his knee. "And I'm really proud of you."

"I'm not sure we're going to make it, though, Mattie."

"What?" I whispered.

He ran his hands through his hair. "I've been getting up in the middle of the night and running the numbers, hoping they'll somehow magically shift in my favor. But there's a balloon payment due to the contractor in less than a month, and my credit is shot because of the mess I made last summer. I can't get a loan."

"I'm sure my parents could—"

"I don't want their charity," he snapped.

"But my parents love you—"

"I've pushed them to the limit, and you know it. They might have believed the whole mistaken-identity kidnapping lie we told them, but that doesn't excuse the lien on the clinic and the fact that I'd been spending all our money on my addiction. They may not know it was an addiction to magic, but does that matter? And if I go crawling to them now . . ."

"So what's the alternative? We can't lose this place, Ben! This is our future." My heart had picked up a nasty stabbing rhythm that was making it hard to breathe. "I love this clinic," I said lamely. "It's been a bright spot for me these last few months."

Ben turned his face away. "I wanted to be that bright spot."

"You're part of it! But the clinic and the animals make me feel . . . well, normal. And I haven't felt very normal since we got back."

"I know. And I know it's my fault, which is why I hadn't wanted to tell you how bad the situation has gotten. I wanted to protect you from it." He reached over and took my hand. "Then I realized I was underestimating you. You're a strong woman, Mattie, even when you're struggling. And you're going to be my wife, which means I have to be honest with you. I almost lost you before because I was trying to protect you from the truth, and I won't risk it again."

"What do you want to do, then?"

He blew out a long breath. "What if . . ." His voice trailed off, then he cursed and flung the door open. "Never mind."

I grabbed his arm and tugged him back. "Tell me."

"This isn't fair to even ask, Mattie. But Brindle told me how valuable a good reliquary's skills are. Even one job would make us enough money to handle this balloon payment and then some."

A cold tingling sensation crept up across my chest and collarbones. "Even if I thought I could, Ben, I don't know anyone in that world. Not anymore. I wouldn't even know where to start."

"But you would consider it, if it could be arranged?"

My eyes burned with tears as I let go of his hands and sat back in my seat. "There has to be another way." I shut my eyes, remembering the pain, the blood, the bullets, and the death that accompanied the last job in my brief career as a reliquary. The only thing that had gotten me through it was Asa.

And he was long gone.

"There has to be something else we can do," I said, more firmly this time. "We can brainstorm. We'll figure it out." I smiled, though it was pretty shaky. "Together."

"We'll figure it out," he murmured, then tilted his head, his gaze sliding over my face. "I love you, Mattie." He leaned forward, and I met him in the middle, my smile solidifying as our lips touched. "And I'd better get in there. Got myself a whole slate of Saturday appointments to see."

"I'll join you in a minute," I murmured, waving him toward the back door of the clinic.

He grinned and headed inside, and I hunched over the searing pain in my chest.

Come with me, Mattie, Asa whispered. *We can figure this out. Together.*

"I made the right decision." I panted, waiting for the attack to subside. "And I'm making the right decision now."

When the agony faded, I stumbled out of the car and went inside.

Ben didn't mention our finances over the next few days, but that didn't mean I forgot about it. Quite the contrary—I spent every waking moment trying to find a fix. I investigated whether my own credit rating was good enough to secure a loan. Pathetically, it turned out that because I'd let my parents shoulder the big financial burdens for me over the past few years, I would need a cosigner to get that kind of money—and Ben had specifically forbidden me to mention it to Mom and Dad. I looked into bankruptcy and all types of financing, but none of it looked hopeful. Still, I compiled all my findings in a little folder, hoping to present it to Ben by the next weekend.

On Wednesday, Ben announced that he was going over to my parents' house to see Grandpa in the afternoon after his morning appointments. "I'm going to try to clear the air with him," he said, looking adorably nervous.

"You made a start last weekend," I said. "And he might be a grumpy old man, but he knows this is important. And I know that you'll win him over."

"I'll let you know how it goes."

"Oh, I'll come with you. I've been awful about going to visit him over the last few months." I struggled to maintain my smile as the ever-present shard of pain in my chest twisted.

Ben shoved his hands into the pockets of his khakis. "I was kind of picturing talking to him alone."

"That's fine. I'll just hang out with my mom until you're done."

He gave me a tight smile. "Okay."

"You're really nervous, aren't you?"

"Yeah." He pulled me close. "It feels like there's a whole lot riding on this. Part of me wants to avoid it, but I'm sure this is the right thing."

I laughed. "I think Grandpa would get a kick out of knowing you're practically shaking in your boots."

"Well, let's not tell him until after I convince him I'm a good guy, all right?"

"My lips are sealed."

Hand in hand, we headed for the car, and in only ten minutes we were at my parents'. As we pulled up, I noticed an unfamiliar car in the driveway with Illinois plates.

"I wonder who that is?" I muttered as we climbed the porch steps.

"Look who's here!" my mother said as she pulled the door open. She had her auburn hair pulled back and a smear of flour on her blouse. "Grandpa's in a bit of a mood—apparently Wanda's sick today. They sent a new girl over, though."

We walked through the entryway to find the fill-in nurse standing in the hallway, her arms folded over her middle. Her scrubs were a size too big on her petite frame, and by the edgy look on her face, I suddenly wondered if she was brand-new to the job. "Is everything all right, Debbie?" Mom asked her. "Do you need anything?"

Debbie smiled at Ben as he moved to stand next to me. "I think I'm good. I was just waiting for Mr. Carver to wake up from his nap, but he's up now."

Ben squeezed my arm. "Maybe I should take advantage of the moment and go talk to him?"

"I just have to check his vitals and . . . yeah, stuff like that," said Debbie. "You won't be in the way."

"Tell him I'll be in after you two have a chance to talk," I said as they walked down the hall together. "And good luck!"

Ben gave me a tense smile over his shoulder and disappeared into the library. I followed my mom back into the kitchen, where she had a whole assembly line set up—dozens of vanilla cupcakes, bags full of different shades of frosting, and four kinds of sprinkles. "It's a fundraiser for the Sheboygan County Cancer Care Fund," Mom explained. "Want to give me a hand?"

"Sure, why not?" I washed my hands in the sink and grabbed a bag of frosting. Heaven knows my mom had saved my butt about a thousand times when I'd taken on big fund-raising projects for school—some payback was warranted.

"You look better today," Mom said as she lined up cupcakes for me to frost. "I mean, you're always my beautiful girl, but—"

"It's okay, Mom. I know what you're saying. But I'm on the mend. I promise. By May fifteenth, I'll be back to normal."

"Really?" Her eyes had glazed over with tears. "Oh, honey. I'm so glad to hear you say that. I've been so worried." She bowed her head and stifled a sob, and I put down my frosting bag and rushed over to her. She wrapped me in a tight hug, her arms shaking.

"Mom, I had no idea," I said, my throat getting tight. "You always seemed so—"

"I know I always wear my happy face," she said, her voice thick with tears, "but that doesn't mean I don't constantly fret about my baby girl. Your dad is the same way. We just want you to be happy and healthy, Mattie, no matter what it takes."

She leaned back and took me by the shoulders. Her eye makeup had smudged, creating dark flecks and blotches beneath her eyes. "*Are you happy, baby?*"

I blinked at her. "What? Yeah, of course. I just had some stuff to work through."

"Really?" Her face crumpled. "Because I've hated to see you suffering, not knowing how to help—"

"You *have* helped, Mom! Without you and Dad this wedding would have happened at Bob's Sip 'N' Bowl."

She let out a sniffly laugh. "That's not what I meant. I know you and Ben have been together awhile . . . I just want you to know that . . . it's okay to change your mind."

"Whoa." I pulled out of her grasp. "Is this about his money problems?"

"Well, your dad was pretty upset about that. But—" She paused as a loud thunk came from the library. "Is everything okay?" she called down the hallway.

"Oh, yeah," answered Ben. "Just me, being clumsy." His voice was unsteady—I wondered if the conversation wasn't going as well as he'd hoped.

"He really wanted Grandpa to be happy for us," I said.

"Your grandpa loves you. You've always been special to him. When he called us to say he was sick, he admitted to your dad that he wanted to spend his last days here, and to have a closer relationship with you."

Probably because he suspected I was a reliquary, too. "That's why I'm here. I shouldn't have avoided him before." I smiled as I looked down the hall. "He's a pretty fascinating old dude."

She laughed, and it was a relief that the bright note had returned to her voice. She looked down at her mascara-smeared paper towel. "Oh, gosh, I should go to the powder room and freshen up before anyone sees me like this!"

"Yes, heaven forbid they realize Kat Carver cries sometimes!"

She gave me an exasperated look and disappeared into the bathroom in the hallway. I smiled and walked back to the kitchen island, where I picked up my pastry bag full of violet frosting.

A strangled scream made me drop it, and I turned toward the sound of heavy footsteps. "Call 911, Mattie," shouted Ben as he came into view, his hair wild and his eyes frantic.

My mom came bursting out of the bathroom just as I grabbed for the phone, my heart ramming so hard against my chest that it felt as if an ice pick were being hammered through my rib cage.

"Is it Grandpa?" she asked, grabbing the phone from my sweat-slick hand.

But Ben had already run back down the hall to the library, so I followed at a jog, my palms sliding over the wall as I tried to stay steady. The sound of choked sobs reached me an instant before I burst into the library.

Debbie the nurse was curled up on the floor next to Grandpa's bed, crying so hard that it sounded like her lungs were trying to turn themselves inside out. Ben had his hands in his hair, staring down at her and Grandpa like he didn't know what to do. Behind me, I could hear my mom on the phone with 911, her voice quavering as she tried to tell them to send an ambulance.

Almost deafened by a sudden roaring in my ears, slowed by my trembling legs, I stepped around Ben and the wailing nurse to look at my grandpa.

He lay on his back in his bed, his mouth slack, his eyes wide open and staring at the ceiling, his bony chest completely still.

"Is he—" Ben started.

"Dead," I whispered as I sank to my knees, barely able to breathe. "Grandpa's gone."

CHAPTER FOUR

He had a do-not-resuscitate order, but we ended up needing the ambulance anyway—to transport poor Debbie to the ER for a psychiatric evaluation. According to Ben, when Grandpa went into cardiac arrest, practically midsentence, Debbie completely lost her cool, falling apart instead of taking action to save him. Ben didn't know what to do, either, because he was afraid of hurting the fragile old man by doing CPR. It ended up not mattering. He was dead pretty much instantly, his weary, magic-worn heart simply sputtering to a stop.

And a week later, the day after the funeral, I stood in the hallway and prepared myself to enter the room where he'd died. The past few days had been veiled in grief, which I'd felt as a physical pain, the ever-present knife in my chest twisting mercilessly every time I remembered something I wished I had said, every time I thought of all the time I'd wasted.

My parents had done all the work of arranging his memorial, so I volunteered to go through his things. I had a promise to keep. The original Sensilo magic, a power that would allow its user to sense feelings, bodily sensations, intentions, and even magic itself, was extinct. It had died with my grandpa. I had no idea what that actually meant for the magical world, whether it would affect people like Asa who possessed this type of magic, whether they'd notice it was gone. And now I didn't really have anyone to ask, because my grandpa was gone, too. But the relic that had once housed it—the gold-plated guts from the original sorcerer—had to be taken to the Headsmen. It was the last thing he'd ever asked me to do for him, and there was no way I was going to let him down.

Steeling myself, I marched into the library. His bed was still there, stripped of its sheets and pillows. Next to it were the built-in bookshelves my dad had cleared to make way for the few possessions Grandpa had brought with him from Arizona, including the small, locked wooden box. It sat forlorn amid a few John le Carré paperbacks. I traced my finger over the carved designs on the box's lid. He'd told me he'd gotten it in Thailand, and the ornate elephant's head, tusks entwined with a pattern of leaves and flowers, reminded me of the ornate objects I'd seen when I was there. The wood was a rich golden brown, and I wondered if Grandpa had run his hands over the design, if the magic inside him had called out for what I suspected lay within. I touched the tiny padlock over the latch, wondering where the key was. But as I pulled on the little lock, I realized it was broken. Heart pounding, I flipped the lid open.

The box was empty.

Staring at the dark wood grain within, I ran my fingers over the space as my mouth went dry. "Hey, Dad?"

"Yeah, honey?" His heavy footsteps reached me from the hallway. "What do you need?"

I turned to see him hovering in the doorway. He hadn't entered this room since Grandpa had been carried out of it, his body enclosed in a gray vinyl shroud. "Sorry—I know I said I'd handle this, but—" I held out the open box. "Do you know what happened to whatever was in this box?"

"I've never seen it open before. Maybe it was already empty?"

I lowered the box to my lap, biting my lip. "No, there was definitely something in here. Do you trust Wanda?" His nurse had visited him nearly every day since last spring. She'd been at his funeral and cried her eyes out.

Dad's brow furrowed. "She never seemed like the type to steal an old man's things. She took great care of him. What about that replacement nurse who was here the day he died?"

"I wouldn't have thought she'd had the time," I murmured. "She and Ben were only in here for a few minutes before . . ." I sighed and rubbed my stinging eyes. Maybe he'd decided to hide the relic somewhere else. "Did Grandpa have any other stuff?"

"I have a few boxes of old books and letters of his in my office." He bowed his head, revealing his bald spot. "I haven't been able to bring myself to go through them."

"I can do it, Dad." I got up and walked over to hug him.

"He was such a cool old guy," Dad said with a pained chuckle. "Much cooler than I ever was."

"He was definitely cool." I squeezed my dad's paunchy middle and laid my head on his shoulder. "But so are you."

He kissed the top of my head. "Only because I can claim you as my daughter."

We walked down the hallway with his arm around me, and I cradled that empty box, my thoughts spinning. Dad went out to mow his expansive lawn by the lake while I sat down to go through the boxes. But a few hours later, I was coated in dust and hadn't found anything except a packet of letters and postcards my grandpa and grandma had written to each other while Grandpa was traveling the world for "business." Apparently my grandma had never known her husband's true occupation, and Grandpa had never told my dad, either. I was the only one who had known his secret, and now I was alone in it.

•••

I trudged up the front steps to our cottage and pushed open the door to find Ben standing in our living room, a packed bag on the couch. My stomach dropped. "If you're breaking up with me, can you do it tomorrow?" I said, my voice cracking. "I don't think I can—"

"What? No!" Ben had me in his arms before I could draw another breath. "Oh my God, Mattie. I'm so sorry. Here I thought I was being romantic, and I've already screwed it up."

I sniffled and looked up at him. "Romantic?"

He stroked my cheek. "You've been through hell this past week, and I was hoping I could lift your spirits. This was what I was talking to your mom about while you talked with Grandpa a few weeks ago. What do you say to a weekend in Chicago?" He held up his phone and I read the screen.

"The Waldorf Astoria? Ben, that's got to be hundreds of dollars a night!"

"I know. Your parents kicked in some of it."

"I thought you didn't want to ask them for money."

"This was small. I'll pay them back."

"But you couldn't pay them back for a loan to save the clinic?"

He let me go and stepped back, his jaw set. "So much for the romantic part of things. I'll go unpack this." With his shoulders slumped, he went to pick up the bag.

Feeling like a jerk, I held up my hands. "Wait. I'm sorry. It's just been a tough day."

He set the bag down. "Any reason apart from the obvious?"

"No." I didn't want to bring up anything remotely associated with the magical world with Ben for fear of another fight. "It was just hard. I went through Grandpa's things. He led a really interesting life." My voice grew strained. "And I'm sad that it's over." The tears welled up, streaking down my face. "I wasted my last few months with him."

Ben pulled me down onto the couch. "Grandpa told me he wanted me to take care of you, Mattie. He told me to give you a good life. It was the last thing he said to me." He guided my head to his shoulder. "And that's what I'm determined to do. I'm going to take care of both of us. Do you trust me to do that?"

You trust me, Mattie Carver, Asa murmured. *Just admit it.*

I shivered. "Yeah," I whispered, clinging to Ben's solid body as if it were a buoy in a storm. "I do."

"Wow," said Ben as we walked through the revolving front doors and into the lobby of the Waldorf.

"Definitely wow," I said, glancing up at the giant chandelier, which looked like needles of ice that had skewered dozens of glass snowflakes midair. It was supposed to be beautiful and impressive, but to me it was just a painful reminder of the lingering shard of agony in my chest. I'd wanted to believe it was getting better, but since Grandpa's death it had taken on a sharper edge. I didn't want Ben to know, though. It was so obvious he'd planned our weekend down to the last detail, all with an eye toward cheering me up.

"—massage for you," he was saying as he led me toward the elevator.

"What? Sorry. I spaced out." I gestured back at the murderous-looking chandelier. "Kind of dazzled."

"So you like it?"

"Nah. I hate luxury in any form. Are you kidding?"

He entwined his fingers with mine and pulled me onto the elevator. "Good."

Our room was on the fourth floor, a study in white and gray, but still pretty cozy. I plopped down on the bed and spread my arms. "So what's on our agenda?"

The mattress sank as he sat down next to me. "I got us reservations at Shanghai Terrace."

"Chinese food? Not in actual Chinatown, though, right?"

He blinked at the sharp note of panic in my voice. "No. The restaurant's less than a ten-minute walk from here. Why?"

Because the magic boss of Chinatown, Zhong Lei, was one bad dude who I hoped would respect the fragile truce in the magical mob war Asa and I had basically caused. I'd also almost killed one of Zhong's Ekstazo henchmen, but in my defense, he had been trying to murder me with orgasms at the time. "No reason. It's just far."

"I packed you some walking shoes, but that doesn't mean you have to use them. Hell, if you want to stay in and order room service, just say the word." He checked his watch. "The masseur should be here any minute." He threw me a nervous glance. "And there's something I need to talk to you about before he arrives."

I sat up. "What's wrong?"

He got to his feet, suddenly fidgety. "You said you trusted me."

"Yeah . . ."

"Okay, I need you to remember that. I've been doing a lot of thinking, Mattie." He rubbed his hands along his thighs, and I wondered if he was missing his lucky agate, the one that had been infused with Ekstazo magic. "I've barely slept the last few weeks. I've researched every possibility to save the clinic, and I came up empty."

"Me too," I said softly.

"I could do work in another clinic, but I know how much the place means to you. The way your face lit up when Mrs. Chang brought in her new vizsla puppy the other day—"

"His name is Rudy."

He gave me a sad smile. "See? You know all their names without checking the charts. You know exactly where they like to be scratched, exactly what their families need to hear. And I can't bear to take that from you."

"I'll be okay, Ben."

"No. We can't lose this place, Mattie. I won't be able to live with myself if we do."

"So you're going to borrow from my—"

"No! We can do this on our own if you'll just keep an open mind!"

I tensed at the strident edge in his voice. "Okay," I said slowly. "My mind is open."

His hands fell away from his hair, and he let out a breath. "Thank you. I promise I'll get us through this."

"Ben, you're starting to scare me."

"You don't have to be scared. It's nothing you haven't done before."

Just then someone knocked on our door. Ben walked swiftly over and opened it, and in walked a man toting a thin black rectangular case. The guy was slender with pale, ashy skin and a steel-gray buzz cut, and his arms were covered in thick, dark hair flecked with silver. He was wearing an untucked white polo shirt that bore the overlapping *W* and *A* of the hotel logo.

"Where are we gonna do this?" he asked in an accent that pegged him as Australian. Or from New Zealand. Or South Africa. I wasn't exactly a woman of the world at that point.

"Um, here?" Ben gestured at a space between the bed and the window. "What do you think, Mattie?"

"Are you getting the massage, or am I?"

The masseur's eyebrows shot up and he looked at Ben, but then his face relaxed into a friendly grin. "You are, sweetheart." He unfolded the case, and it turned out to be a portable massage table.

I looked down at my skirt and sweater set. I *was* feeling kind of tense—Ben and I hadn't finished our conversation, but maybe if I were more relaxed, I could keep an open mind. "Give me a chance to change."

I went into the bathroom and put on a fluffy white hotel robe. When I came out, Ben and the masseur were chatting in low tones. They stopped when I approached the table. "Just discussing our plans for the weekend," Ben said. "Marcus here knows the city really well."

Marcus gestured at the massage table. "Up you go, my lady."

I sat up on the table. "Do you have a sheet I can cover myself with?" I glanced around, but the table was all he'd brought into the room.

Ben pulled the blackout curtains shut. "Mattie, this is what I needed to talk to you about." His eyes crinkled—his apologetic look. "Marcus is a conduit."

"*What?*"

"Calm down," he said, coming forward to take me by the shoulders. "I told you I'd been thinking, and I wasn't kidding. Mattie, this could be all we need."

I struggled to escape his grip, but he held me to the table. "If you're suggesting what I think you are, the answer is *no*."

"You said you trusted me. We're going to do this together."

Raw panic was making my muscles twitch. "Ben, if you're asking me to transport magic to avoid detection, it must be big, and if it's big, then it's—"

"Fucking valuable," said Marcus, wedging himself in next to Ben. "Your fiancé told me you've worked for Frank before, and I checked into it. You've got a bit of a reputation, Mattie. Lots of people interested in what you can do."

I stared at Ben. "Where did you get the magic, Ben?"

His cheeks darkened. "I don't want you to worry about that."

"Let me go!"

"Not before you hear me out. I've come into possession of a relic," Ben said, his fingers still clamped around my upper arms. "And I know it's worth a lot of money. But we have to get it into the hands of the right buyer, and that means transporting it across the country. I checked into it—a reliquary's the only way to do it without being caught. Forget about saving the clinic—we could be set for life, Mattie. We could have ten clinics if you wanted."

"And I'll get a sweet commission," said Marcus. "Just relax, sweetheart."

"I'm not your sweetheart," I snapped. "You can't do this to me. Let. Me. Go." I glared at Ben. "I can't believe you set this up without telling me. You lied. *Again*."

"I didn't lie. I just left a few things out, but I was trying to tell you."

"Semantics!" Now I understood why Asa hated them so much.

Ben sighed. "Mattie, this would save us."

My chest felt brittle and thin, the walls of my vault scraped away by months of jagged pain. "I can't do it."

"You did it when you were with my brother." The bitterness in his voice made me want to slap him.

"To save *your* life."

He looked down, and then his arms fell away from me. I quickly sat up. "You're right." He looked over at Marcus. "I'm sorry. She doesn't want to do this."

"Yeah?" Marcus rolled his eyes. Then he pulled a gun from beneath his shirt and aimed it at Ben's head. "How about now?"

Ben's hands rose from his sides. "Come on. This isn't the way to resolve this."

"Fuck yeah it is, mate. Get your girl on the fucking table before I paint this place red. *She* is necessary. *You* are not."

"Mattie . . . ," Ben said in a shaky voice.

I glanced around for anything I could use as a weapon, but the nearest option was a clay vase about ten feet away. "Who do you work for?" I asked Marcus.

"Freelancer."

"This is Zhong's territory."

"And don't I know it, sweetheart. If we don't get this magic into you real soon, his people are gonna know it's here. He owns a sniffer."

"Chinatown is miles away."

"But this relic is hot. Already done my research."

"It's worth millions, Mattie," Ben said, taking a step to the side. His gaze darted to the vase for a split second before returning to me. "So let's get this done and make sure Marcus gets what he deserves."

I forced myself to keep a straight face, but part of me wanted to cheer. Ben was on my side. I could practically see his thoughts. "Okay. I trust you."

He held my gaze with his honey-brown eyes. "I'm going to be worthy of it."

Marcus groaned. "Lie down, would you? I wasn't joking about Zhong's people. He's got spies everywhere looking for side deals going on in his territory, and all they have to do is call in his sensor to find us. If anyone spotted me, they'll be paying us a visit. So with all due respect, let's move the fuck along." His voice had risen steadily until he was nearly yelling.

Trembling, I lay on my back, deliberately not looking in Ben's direction. As soon as my head hit the headrest, Marcus leaned over me and pulled a set of straps around my arms, awkwardly fastening me into place with one hand as he kept the gun aimed in Ben's general direction.

"You got the relic?" he asked Ben.

"Yeah, it's right here." From behind Marcus, I heard a faint clinking sound.

He looked over his shoulder at Ben and nodded. "Good. Bring it over, and when I give the signal, hand it to me."

As Marcus turned back to me, Ben slammed him in the side of the head with the vase. I clamped my eyes shut as it shattered, then opened them to grope for the straps holding me to the table. Grunts punctuated the struggle, but then Ben managed to strip the gun from Marcus and clock him with it.

The conduit slumped over on top of me, his bare arm across my throat. "Ben," I gasped.

Ben leaned over me, his face sheening with sweat. "Did you hear him, Mattie? Zhong's people could be here any minute."

He had something grasped in his free hand. The other held the gun.
"Then let's get out of here. Get me off this table."

"I don't think we should risk it." His jaw was rigid. "We have to
do it this way."

"Ben?" I began to struggle in earnest, desperate to wiggle out from
under Marcus's dead weight.

"We'll be safer if we do this. Marcus said it would only take a minute." Ben opened his fingers to show me what he was holding.

I stared at the golf ball–size locket on its thick gold chain and held
my breath as he flicked the latch, revealing what was inside.

And then I started to laugh and cry at the same time. "That's my
Grandpa's relic," I said as he slid the knobby lump of gold onto his
palm. It looked so similar to the original Strikon relic, only a slightly
different shape, rounder, fewer edges. And now I knew who had taken
it from Grandpa's wooden box. "But it's empty, Ben. You set all this up
for nothing—the magic that goes with that relic died with Grandpa."

Ben tilted his head. His eyes were shining with emotion. "I'll
explain everything once we're safe. I promise."

And with that, he pressed the hunk of gold to the back of Marcus's
neck, and every cell in my body exploded with agony.

CHAPTER FIVE

Considering that I'd gone through this already with the original Strikon relic, which housed the most powerful pain magic in existence, you would think that I could handle the Sensilo relic.

And you'd be wrong.

My mind shattered as all my muscles locked and my teeth clamped together so tightly that I was lucky I didn't bite off my tongue. All the emotions of every single person nearby came at me at once, a hurricane of joy and rage and jealousy and despair and so much raw feeling that I couldn't tell one mood from the other, only that it was overwhelming, crushing, punishing. I felt everything they felt. I sensed everything they were going through, everything they were intending to do. From somewhere inside the brutal storm, a shard of magic sliced across my raw, torn soul, telling me there were naturals nearby. I tried to hold on to it but couldn't—the magic picked me up and twisted me, wringing me out, and it felt like a thousand knives were being driven into every part of my body.

And then just my chest.

And then just my heart.

Until only one knife remained, twisting mercilessly.

"I've got you," said a deep voice echoing through the hollowed-out cavern of my skull.

"Oh thank God," I murmured.

Firm hands hoisted me up, and I was pressed to a hard chest. "I'm getting you out of here."

"I've missed you so much," I mumbled, but the words were garbled and weak. I tried to open my eyes, but the dizziness was so overwhelming that I clamped them shut again. "I didn't want to, but I did."

"Hang on for me, baby."

I couldn't get my fingers or hands or arms to work. In fact, all of me was numb except the knife in my chest. "It hurts." The only thing that felt right was knowing Asa would handle it.

"Is that what was supposed to happen?"

The pain cut my foggy confusion right down the middle and parted it like a curtain. "Ben?"

"Yeah, I've got you." I was in his arms, my head lolling against his shoulder.

I'm honestly not sure how Ben got us out of that hotel. I had the impression of footsteps on carpet, then metal clanking, then my head bumping against his chest as he lugged me down a long bright-white hallway. I caught the muffled echo of shouts behind us and the frantic rush of Ben's breath from his throat as he ran with me in his arms.

The next thing I knew, I was in our car and he was buckling my seat belt. "What are you doing?"

"It wasn't safe to stay there."

I clutched at my head and gasped as the sharp pain in my chest intensified. "Something's wrong."

"You can say that again." He put the car in gear and peeled out of the parking garage, tossing money at the gatekeeper and shouting for him to let us out because I needed to get to the hospital.

"We can't go to the hospital." Memories of the Sensilo magic were coming back to me. "There were naturals in the hotel. They might have been—"

"Zhong's spies. Marcus was right to be cautious."

"If they find him, they'll question him."

"He wasn't in any state to answer questions. And don't worry, we're not going to the hospital."

I cracked an eyelid open to see that Ben was driving quickly down a busy thoroughfare. Night was falling fast, and the city was streaked with neon. I squinted to read a road sign through the glare of a street-light. State Street. I closed my eyes again as harsh reality hit me like a wrecking ball. "Now I know how Grandpa died. Debbie wasn't really a nurse, was she? She was a conduit like Marcus."

"I know how this looks, but I was only thinking of our future. And that's all I'm thinking about right now."

"You overheard him telling me about the relic."

"It was too valuable to throw away. Grandpa agreed. He wanted you to have it."

"You're lying. That's the opposite of what he wanted."

"He changed his mind!"

"You killed him!" I shrieked, but it came out as a broken squawk.

"I had no idea it was that powerful, all right? Please, Mattie. Debbie made it sound easy, and I had no idea what would happen. I was just so desperate—"

"Not desperate enough to swallow your pride and borrow from my parents." The pain of the betrayal on top of the magic made me draw my knees up to my chest, which is when I realized I was barefoot and clad only in the hotel robe. "I can't believe you did this. You killed my grandfather. You broke two conduits. And even after you saw what happened to Grandpa, even after you knew how dangerous it was, you forced this magic into me!"

"Mattie, your grandpa was nearly ninety years old and in the last days of his life—a stiff wind could have killed him. And you—you're strong. I knew you could handle it, and you trusted me to make the decision. So I did. You needed me to be strong for you. So I was."

It was such twisted reasoning that I couldn't even think around it, especially because it was all I could do to cope with the pain. "You weren't strong. You were greedy."

"I'm not! I just wanted us to be able to—"

"There is no 'us,' Ben. You've made sure of that." Something was very wrong inside me. What had been an annoying stab before the transaction now felt as if someone were trying to tear my lungs to shreds. "You don't even understand what you've done."

"I can fix it. I swear. I'll get us through this!"

"Stop saying that," I mumbled, but every word hurt.

His fingers were tight over the wheel. "I've arranged a meeting for tomorrow morning just outside of the city. Mr. Brindle's best people will be there to escort us to Vegas. Whatever you need, they'll get it for you. You'll feel better soon."

The betrayals just kept coming. "You're taking me to *Brindle*?"

"We'll get that magic out of you, Mattie. And we'll walk out of there with millions. Reza said if it was the real deal, we're talking eight figures."

Reza. My stomach felt like I'd swallowed nails. "Maybe I do need a hospital," I muttered, glancing again at the street signs, which were blurred by my tears. Disbelief was clawing at my thoughts, making it hard to form a coherent plan or sentence.

But I had to try. "Ben, I'm not joking. There's really something wrong with me. That magic—it's not like normal magic."

"You've carried stuff like that before. Reza told me so before he left to go rescue you and Asa in Utah. He really respects you. So does Frank. You're one of the strongest known reliquaries in existence." He reached over to touch my leg, but I scooted away. "Mattie, I have confidence in you. You can do this."

"I'm not the same person I was last year." I winced as I rubbed at my chest. "And circumstances were different then."

Ben glanced over at me as he breezed through a yellow light. "Which circumstances?"

My fingers closed around the door handle as I recognized the silhouette of a building a block away. I *knew* this area. "Too many to name."

"How about I name *one*," he suggested, his voice hard. "Because you already have. You were saying it over and over again as I carried you out of the hotel." He ran his tongue over his teeth. "Not for the first time, by the way. You say it in your sleep sometimes."

"Don't you dare go there right now." The pain nearly made me retch. My muscles were knotted, adrenaline coursing through my veins.

"Is there a better time to ask if you're in love with my brother?" he yelled.

I groaned. It felt as if my rib cage were about to explode, and the pressure pushed all my words right out of my head.

He glanced over at me, and his grimace softened. "We'll get you some healing magic when we meet our contacts. It's amazing how well it works. *Shit!*" He braked and laid on the horn as a delivery truck double-parked right in front of us, blocking an entire lane of traffic.

Just what I needed.

I flung open the door and jumped out. Rough, warm asphalt scraped my feet as I sprinted to the sidewalk. Ben shouted my name, but I didn't stop. I had only one thought, one hope. Wide-eyed stares hit me left and right as I staggered down a side street and kept running, stumbling every few steps as my legs threatened to give out. I glanced over my shoulder to see Ben trying to steer around the truck and follow me. Panic propelled me forward. I hooked left onto another side street, went up a block, turned right and right again. My thoughts were those of a reptilian brain—survival, escape. No room for anything else. I aimed my body toward safety.

I was panting and wheezing by the time I reached it. My palms hit the glass doors of the building and slid along the surface to tug at the handle. It swung open, but the inner doors were locked. My fingers fumbled at the intercom. Which floor was it? Five? Six? I started punching the buttons. "Daria?" I asked as soon as anyone answered, and over and over again the person on the other end hung up on me.

"Daria?" I asked for maybe the twentieth time as a low female voice answered, just as I was starting to wonder if I was wrong about the building. It had been almost a year. For all I knew she could have moved. "Daria?"

"She's 514, honey," the lady said, then hung up.

Sagging against the wall, I punched in "514." My head was spinning and my lips were tingling. A tiny voice in the back of my head whispered that I was about to faint.

"Hello," said a familiar voice.

"Daria. It's Mattie Carver. We met—"

The door buzzed open, and I stumbled through it, noticing with numb dread that I was leaving dirty, blood-smeared footprints on the tile behind me. I summoned the elevator, working hard to catch my breath. I shrank against the wall as a dark shape passed by outside, but the man just kept walking.

"He can't find me here," I whispered as I dove into the elevator.

By the time I staggered into the fifth-floor hallway, a familiar face was already poking out of apartment 514. "Jesus, Mary, and Joseph, what happened to you?" Daria cried as she ran forward and caught me against her lean, hard body. Her hair smelled of strawberries and coconuts when it brushed across my face. She half carried, half dragged me through her front door. "I can feel every single one of your ribs, girl."

"I'm in trouble."

"No shit, darling. I'm actually not sure I want to know." She flipped her wavy black hair over her shoulder and guided me onto her couch. Even though my vision was sort of blurry, I could tell that she was wearing makeup, perfect cat eyes accentuated by thick black lashes, blush on her hollow cheeks, contouring to soften the hard edge of her jaw. She was probably getting ready to go out, and here I was ruining her Friday night.

"Then I won't give you details. But I need your help."

She gave me a wary look, and I suddenly felt bad for bringing this to her doorstep. "What is it?"

"I need—" I nearly screamed as another bolt of pain zipped through my chest. My fingers clutched at Daria's forearms, balling in the silky sleeves of her dress. Part of me didn't want to do this. It was dangerous, for so many reasons.

But the rest of me knew what it needed to survive. Or, to be precise, *who* it needed.

My eyes met hers. "Asa."

CHAPTER SIX

Daria looked me over. "He's not an easy one to reach, honey."

"But can you try?"

"Haven't heard from him in months. I think he's been out of the country."

I grabbed a tissue from her end table and pressed it over my eyes, embarrassed to be losing it in front of her. "Please," I whispered. "I need him."

"He said you'd gone back to your fiancé. That you were done with our happy little underworld for good."

"I suppose you could say I was forced out of retirement." I pulled the tear-soaked tissue away from my face.

Daria's immaculately plucked eyebrows went halfway to her forehead. "You're loaded up?"

I nodded.

"Something big?"

I winced. "The biggest."

Her eyes went round, and she looked me over again. "Who's chasing you?" she said, her voice sharp with alarm. "Did anyone see you come here?" She cursed and threw up her hands. "Do you have any idea what Zhong would do to me if he caught me with stolen magic?"

Crap. The last thing I wanted was to put someone else in danger. "I'll leave," I said hoarsely, pushing myself up off the couch. "But—can you try to reach Asa? Or tell me how I can?"

Daria caught me as I swayed. "Oh, damn it all. My heart is too freaking soft." Her sigh was full of exasperation. "You stay put while I make a few arrangements."

She lowered me back onto the couch, where I floated in my little bubble of agony until she returned. It hurt to move. It hurt to stay still. It hurt to breathe and it hurt to hold my breath. And most of all—it hurt to think.

I jerked as Daria plopped a shabby satchel down next to me. "I don't have much that will fit you, but I tried," she said. "There's a tooth-brush in there, too. And some moisturizer and eye cream, because baby, you need it."

"Um, thanks. And did you reach—"

"I called a friend of a friend who worked with Asa a few months ago up in Alaska. He said he would try to get a message to him."

"Because of course he doesn't have a permanent number."

Daria let out a squawk of laughter. "Oh, honey. That's cute."

"E-mail address?"

Daria gave me an amused look.

I swallowed the urge to start sobbing again. "Okay," I whispered. "Thanks for trying."

She knelt next to the couch and nudged my chin up. "If it's any consolation, I think he'll come if he knows it's you."

"What makes you say that? Did he say something about me?" And why did my heart have to kick into high gear at the thought?

"Nothing apart from what I just told you. He's not exactly an open book."

"Oh, so you're just guessing."

"I've known him a long time, honey. Trust me."

Gratitude and hope dampened the pain for a moment. "Where should I go now?"

"I got you a room at the Amber. It's down in the South Side and a little rough, but well clear of Chinatown." She gripped my elbows and pulled me up, letting me lean against her. "If there's even a chance they know you've got something hot, they'll be on you."

"I think they already are," I mumbled apologetically. "I never should have come here."

She squeezed me. "We girls have to help each other."

I smiled as she pressed some clothing into my hands. "Thanks, lady."

Daria let me use her bathroom to change and wash the smeared makeup off my face. I scrubbed myself clean and tried not to stare at the blue-black circles under my eyes, the sallow tint of my freckled cheeks. Slowly, gasping with every stab and slice of the knife in my chest, I changed into what she had given me—probably a short dress on her, but it hit me midcalf and hung from my now-scrawny frame. I looked like a child trying on her mother's clothes. A terminally ill child.

She'd given me flip-flops, too, which were several sizes too big. I wore a size six, and Daria had to be . . . jeez. She was well over six feet tall, and her shoes probably had to be custom-made. But I was grateful as I cleaned off my scraped-up feet. At least I wouldn't be barefoot anymore.

I emerged from the bathroom to hear Daria talking sharply into the phone. "Thanks for the heads-up. Yeah. We're leaving now."

"What is it?" I asked as she ended the call.

"You were right. Zhong's after you. Apparently because you left a freelance conduit for dead in the Waldorf. Marcus," she hissed. "Zhong's people found him before police did."

"Oh."

Daria strode to the door. "No idea what happened there, darling, but can I give you some advice?"

"Sure."

"You should have killed him."

I blinked at her. "But . . . you're a conduit. I would have thought— don't you guys have a code of loyalty or a union or something?"

"Most of us protect each other, yeah. Marcus, though . . . how did you get mixed up with him? He's a pit viper, honey."

A wave of nausea crashed over me. Marcus's face rose in my mind, him leaning over me, strapping me down, his dead weight crushing me to the table . . . Saliva filled my mouth and I rushed for the bathroom, making it just in time to retch into the toilet. Sweat prickled along the back of my neck. Daria pulled my hair away from my face and offered me a glass of water. "I guess that subject is off-limits, then," she said quietly. "We'd better get going. Marcus must have given Zhong some info about what you were up to, because Zhong has alerted all his agents."

"Crap," I whispered. If he got hold of me, he would find a way to tear the magic out of me whether I wanted to give it up or not. And with the way I was feeling, I was pretty sure I would end up like Grandpa if that happened.

"So here we go. Just a quick ride on the El."

With her arm hard around me, we made it all the way to the closest station. As she made to walk in with me, though, I pushed away from her. "You've done so much for me, and I'm so grateful," I said. "But I can't ask you to do more."

"Don't be silly."

"No," I said firmly. "I was stupid enough to get myself into this." Because I had loved. Because I had trusted. And apparently I was the worst judge of character on the planet. "If you got hurt because of me, I couldn't live with myself."

Daria bit her lip. "Mattie, you look bad. Are you sure you can make it on your own?"

"Absolutely." I sounded more confident than I was.

She reached into her bag and pulled out a phone, then punched something in before handing it to me. "Just texted myself, so you have a number to reach me."

I looked down at the flip phone. "Is this a—"

"Burner phone. Won't be traced back to me. Just toss it when you're done."

"For real?" I'd seen this kind of thing on TV, but never in real life.

"We all have to stay safe, honey. If I reach Asa, I'll make sure he has the number to reach you. And don't worry about calling me—it's a burner, too."

My fingers closed over the phone. "You're amazing."

"There's enough cash in the bag for a few nights at the Amber. The room is under the name Karen Funkhouse."

I couldn't help but smile at the alias—it reminded me of some of Asa's. "Perfect."

She enfolded me in a tight hug. "Be careful."

"You too. I'm sorry for ruining your night."

"Oh, honey. A little excitement never killed nobody." She let me go and glanced around nervously. "Good luck. Call if you need me. I'll do what I can on my end." She gave me a quick wave, then walked briskly away.

I watched her go with a lump in my throat. "You're a big girl, Mattie," I whispered. "You can do this."

I shouldered the satchel, trudged into the station, bought a ticket with Daria's money, and caught the Green Line heading south. I leaned my forehead against the window as I counted down the stops. I tried to stay on the lookout for possible agents, but I had to keep closing my eyes to keep from puking on the shoes of the guy next to me. Fortunately, the train wasn't all that crowded—it was pretty late. Normally, I would have been nervous about getting mugged or something, since I hadn't taken the train very many times before, but tonight I had bigger worries.

The Amber was a classic cheap motel, with a little parking lot surrounded by a U-shaped building with two floors of walk-up rooms. All the doors were painted a cheerful shade of teal that didn't quite make up for the dingy feel of the place, but I was still grateful when the drowsy manager who smelled like mothballs and gin handed me a key.

After a laborious climb to the second floor, I found my sanctuary for the night. Lugging my bag inside, I closed the door to my room and leaned on it, nearly sinking to the floor with exhaustion.

Moaning as the pain radiated over my shoulder and across my back, I crawled to the bed and under the covers, pulling them up to my chin. And then I let out a wheezy laugh.

This was not how I'd expected to spend my evening. Somehow, over the course of the last few hours, my life, the one I'd chosen, the one I'd committed to, had completely fallen apart. The man I loved, the one I had planned to pledge my life to in a matter of weeks, had deceived me in ways that I hadn't begun to process and killed my grandpa with his stupid greed. I had no idea where Ben was or if he was still looking for me. I had no idea who he was talking to or what he'd told them. I turned the diamond of my engagement ring inward and clenched my fist, letting it dig into my flesh, but nothing could match the pain of Ben's betrayal.

I was alone. Asa was unreachable. He might be in Tokyo or Sydney or Rio for all I knew.

Or, a worse thought, he was close but didn't think I was worth the trouble. Daria had seemed confident, but Asa hadn't told her what had happened between us, and I had no real idea how he felt about it. We'd only known each other for a few weeks of his crazy, adrenaline-fueled life. Had he thought about me at all since we'd parted? Had I mattered to him once he'd had a few months to think about it? Or had he decided I was that simple, narrow-minded, small-town girl he'd accused me of being when we first met?

Who could blame him, since that's exactly what I turned out to be?

I reached over and pulled the burner phone out of the bag. Fighting tears, I clutched it to my chest. Every part of me hurt now, and exhaustion was like a vise, holding me to the bed.

At the thought, I shifted restlessly, hating the memories of straps and dead weight and the look on Ben's face as he decided to force the original Sensilo magic into my body. I wrapped my arms around myself, hoping I was strong enough to hold it in. If I wasn't, if the magic leaked out of my little magical reliquary vault, would it drive me insane? Would it break me like it had broken Debbie?

The throbbing in my head kept time with my weary heartbeat, lulling me into a state of half sleep. All I knew was that the pain dulled a bit. I drifted, stabbed occasionally back to consciousness, but lay suspended in time, no future, no past, no present.

A digital chime jerked me out of my stupor. With shaking hands, I flipped the phone open, joy and hope hammering inside me. "Asa?"

"You have to get out of there," Daria said in a frantic whisper. "Zhong knows you're there!"

"What?" I flipped the covers off my legs, tensing as the pain in my chest returned.

"I'm so sorry, honey. I trusted the wrong person." She sounded terrified.

"Are you okay?"

"I will be. Gonna go dark for a little bit. You get yourself out of there, okay? Don't tell me where you're going. Just go." The line clicked. She'd ended the connection.

Gritting my teeth, I pushed myself up and fumbled for the light in the blackness. Daria had said they knew where I was, and I couldn't just sit around and wait for them to find me.

I stumbled back as my door splintered and swung inward. Spinning around, I tried to crawl over the bed to get away, but someone landed on my back, crushing me to the mattress, his hand clamped over my mouth.

"You will stay quiet," he murmured in my ear. I inhaled the scent of garlic and breath mints. "And you'll do exactly what I tell you to. Now relax. Stop fighting."

Mindfucker, Asa whispered in my memories. Knedas magic would normally have made me as pliable as putty, but the ever-present pain in my chest made it easy to see right through the manipulation. Still, since this Knedas was holding me down, it wasn't going to do any good to struggle.

I forced myself to go limp, closing my eyes as a tear streaked down my cheek.

He let go of me. "Get up and turn around." His weight lifted from my body, and I pushed myself up and turned over as he turned on the lamp. My captor was an Asian guy about my age, dressed in slacks and a neatly pressed gray button-up, his black hair slicked back from his face. And he wasn't alone. The Ekstazo agent who'd nearly taken me out in Utah with his sex magic—a pretty boy with fabulous eyebrows and a wicked look in his dark eyes—gave me a neat little bow. "Good to see you again, Mattie. I don't think we ever truly formally met. My name is Shan. You'll be screaming it later."

My stomach turned. "Your social skills could use some work, Shan."

He chuckled as he looked at his Knedas pal, who didn't seem even half as amused. "Adorable, isn't she?"

Shan's smile was bitter, and in his eyes I saw a hunger for payback. "I look forward to continuing where we left off, Mattie, but we'd better find ourselves someplace more private first. We have another transaction to complete." He looked over his shoulder toward the splintered door. "Let's get her to the car."

The Knedas agent nodded. "Stand up, Mattie. Where are your shoes?"

I walked over to where I'd left my flip-flops and slid them onto my feet with a disappointed sigh. Was there some unwritten law of the universe that decreed I would never have proper shoes when I needed to run for my life?

"Mattie, you will stay next to me. You will tell anyone who asks that you're with us and are leaving willingly. Do you understand?"

"I understand." My whole body was screaming at me to run, but I walked slowly to the door with the Knedas in front of me and Shan behind me. As long as he didn't touch me, I had a chance. I wiped my clammy palms on my dress as we entered the cool night air. The parking lot was not even half-full, and apart from a couple screwing loudly and enthusiastically a few doors down, no one was making much noise. I saw a few curtains twitch as we walked past on our way to the stairs and hoped someone inside might have heard them break the door and called the police, but I knew it wasn't likely.

I had to save myself. If they got me in a car, it was all over.

I eyed the railing and the set of stairs maybe a hundred yards ahead. I had to time this just right and pray that my body wouldn't give out right when I needed it most. It had been ages since I'd asked it to do anything remotely like this, and the pain was still crippling me.

"Mr. Zhong is very eager to meet you in person," Shan said. "He means you no harm."

"Uh-huh. Nothing says 'I mean you no harm' like kicking down a girl's door in the middle of the night."

"He would like to know what happened at the Waldorf," the Knedas said. "You left quite a mess behind. Marcus could only give us a few details, but he was not very clear."

Probably because he'd been hit in the head—twice—and then had his body used as a superhighway for one of the four most powerful pieces of magic in the entire world. "Served him right," I muttered, bracing as I spotted my chance. "Oh, I forgot my phone in the room!"

"You won't need it," said Shan.

"It has some texts on it that Mr. Zhong will want to see," I said, wishing my voice weren't shaking.

The Knedas sighed. "Go get it, Shan. Just in case. Mattie, you will stay with me."

"I'll stay with you," I said in the blank, dreamy voice I'd found myself using when actually under the influence of Knedas magic.

The Knedas nodded and stepped away from me, pulling a pack of cigarettes from his pocket. Shan turned to go back to the room.

It was now or never. Death or glory.

Or possibly several broken bones and a head injury.

I dove over the edge of the railing, drawing on sixteen years of gymnastics training. Before the Knedas could get to me, my fingers closed tight around the horizontal railing and I flipped as if I were back on the parallel bars, ending up hanging just a few feet over the roof of an SUV parked below. As the Knedas shouted and reached for my hands, I let go.

My legs gave out as I landed, my knees slamming into the roof. The car alarm began to shriek, echoing the alarms going off in my head. *Move. Move.* I slid over the edge of the vehicle and kicked off my flip-flops. Above me, I could hear the Knedas shouting at me to stop. I glanced over my shoulder to see Shan sprinting for the steps as the other agent climbed over the railing.

"Fire," I screamed as I tore through the parking lot. "Fire!"

It was the only thing I could think of that might bring people out of their rooms instead of making them lock their doors. I sprinted for the street, still shouting, even as I scanned my surroundings for a place to hide. I wasn't kidding myself. I was fast over short distances, but anything more than that and I wouldn't make it. Already each breath was a searing pain and my feet were faltering. But as much as I was hurting, I couldn't give up. I wasn't about to let Shan put his stupid Ekstazo hands on me, and I was terrified of being strapped to a table while someone tried to force the Sensilo magic out of me.

Basically, I wasn't ready to die.

So I ran. And screamed. Because I could hear Shan and his buddy behind me, and I knew they were going to catch me and punish me for escaping. "Help," I shrieked as I scrambled across South Michigan Avenue and hit the sidewalk again, hoping the trees lining the road would obstruct the agents' view long enough for me to duck out of sight when the opportunity arose. But the block was taken up by one long building, with no alleys or doorways in sight.

Somewhere behind me, a siren sounded, but we were in South Chicago and I was guessing that was a regular occurrence. Knowing I was risking hitting a dead end, I swung a sharp right as soon as I reached the corner of the building—and ran straight into the arms of a man lurking in the shadows.

I yelped as he swung me around and shoved me against the wall. I got my hands out just before I collided with brick, and stumbled backward, landing on my butt in the grass. Movement to my right made me scoot back as fast as I could. Not six feet away, shadowy figures were struggling in the darkness. I heard grunts and the hard slap of fists against flesh, and then saw the flash of a streetlight reflecting off metal—an extendable baton. One of the men went down. The man holding the baton staggered back and pulled something from his belt. At first I thought it was a gun, but then he fired it at his remaining opponent, and it made a crackling sound instead of a bang.

A Taser.

The man he'd aimed at fell to his knees and began scraping at his arms, his fingers clawed and desperate, and I knew whatever was affecting him wasn't electricity. By the looks of it, those prongs had been soaked in some kind of magic, either Strikon or Sensilo. When he began to whimper, I realized it was Shan.

Which meant . . .

The winner of the fight dropped the Taser thingy and turned around, the extendable baton hanging from his other fist.

Tall and lean. Snake hips and dark hair. Crooked nose and smile like a knife.

I stared at the man I'd been trying not to think about for the past nine months. "Asa." My voice cracked as I said his name.

Asa Ward stepped into a slant of light. "Been a while, Mattie." His honey-brown eyes looked me up and down. He arched an eyebrow. "You look like shit."

CHAPTER SEVEN

And just like that, I was transported back to the first night I ever laid eyes on him. I groaned. "Social skills. Get some."

"Social skills weren't what saved your ass from two of Zhong's thugs," he said, grabbing my upper arm and hoisting me up from the ground. He pulled his hand back quickly and shook it like I'd burned him. "What the fuck?"

"What's wrong? What did you feel?"

He shook his head. "Daria said you were loaded up, but with you that shouldn't matter." He looked down at his hand.

Dread ran like icy water across my skin. "And?"

He wiped his palm on his pant leg. "We need to get you out of here." He glanced over at the two incapacitated agents. Shan was still clawing at his skin like there were bugs crawling all over him, and his Knedas partner was out cold. "Come on."

He headed for the back of the building, the pockets of his cargo pants rattling and sloshing and clanking softly with each step. I nearly asked him what he had in there, but the steely tension in Asa's shoulders kept me quiet. The strangest feeling swirled inside me—giddiness, disappointment, wistfulness, frustration . . . my heart couldn't decide where to land. I kept looking up at him as we passed beneath streetlamps, trying to figure it out. He'd let his dark hair grow a bit since I'd last seen him; now it curled at the nape of his neck and against his temples. It was the only soft thing about him, though. Asa was still all angles and edges. Part of me wanted to touch him, to see if he would melt a little, and the rest of me shied away, for fear he would cut me.

We ended up on a potholed access road that ran between the building and a rail yard on the other side. A black van bearing a bumper sticker that said, "Pit bulls are better than people" was parked against the fence. As we approached, I heard a very familiar bark. "Gracie," I said with a smile.

Asa pulled out a clicker and unlocked the doors. "She hasn't seen you in a while, so be careful—"

I slid open the passenger door. "Hey, girl," I said, and in an instant my face was covered in sloppy pit bull kisses. I ran my hands along her silky flanks as she frantically sniffed at me, her entire butt wagging with excitement. But then my fingers flexed as a sudden pulse of searing pain made me tense up, and she whined and withdrew to the backseat. I leaned on the van to catch my breath as Asa hopped into the driver's seat.

"Don't have all day," he said curtly.

I don't know what I'd been hoping for when I imagined him coming to my aid, but this wasn't it. Wincing as the pain sliced along my rib cage, I closed the back door and dragged myself into the passenger seat. "I'm worried about Daria."

"She's fine. Leaving town until this settles down, though."

"I've caused her so much trouble."

"Yeah, you did," said Asa, so harshly it made me cringe. "What did you think would happen?"

I blinked at him. "What?"

"You just charged in like you always do, right? God forbid you stop to think." His fingers were so tight around the steering wheel that I was surprised it didn't crumple under the pressure.

"That's not fair."

"I don't give a shit about fair. How'd you manage to hook up with Marcus? He's a fucking bottom-feeder."

I clung to my seat belt as he executed a sharp right. "Um," I said in a raspy voice. "I didn't really. Ben was the one who—"

"And there we go. Why didn't I think of that? Let me guess— you two needed money for some sweet McMansion in suburban Cardboardville, and you had the bright idea to jump back in and score some quick cash. I'm sure Ben was fucking thrilled when you offered to be his piggy bank." He glared at me, his lip curled into a snarl. "Is that why you look so fucking strung out? You've been at this for a while, am I right?"

His words, the way he was so ready to believe the worst, made a deep gash that hurt as badly as the magic inside me did. "No. You're actually completely wrong."

"Yeah, right. You're pretty fucking predictable, Mattie. But I'll give you a few extra points for having the balls to try to break into the big leagues. How in hell did you get ahold of the relic?"

Fury swelled inside me, pressing against the fragile walls of my vault. I could almost feel it cracking. So I closed my eyes and breathed, praying my body could hold out—but I didn't have the energy to defend myself against someone so convinced I was the villain. "It's none of your business."

"You made it my business about five hours ago, baby."

"Then I'll tell you some other time. But I can't right now—" I gasped as Asa braked suddenly when another car cut him off, and a pulse of agony stole my breath.

His hand closed gently over my wrist. "You okay?"

I squeezed my eyes even more tightly shut, refusing to let the tears come. I hated the unexpected caress of his voice—the one I'd been dreaming about for months, the one that meant safety, the one that meant I could let go and know down to my bones that he would carry me through. Hearing it now, and knowing how Asa really felt about me . . . it was too much. I tore my arm out of his grip. "No, you jerk. It feels like this magic is going to shatter inside me at any minute, and I need it gone."

"I can feel it," he said quietly. "Something's not right in there. Strikon?"

"Sensilo."

His brow furrowed. "What?" He reached for me again, but I dodged his hand. He let out an impatient sigh. "Maybe I was just picking up the pain as part of the overall sensing magic . . . ," he muttered, then seemed to shake himself out of his confusion. "Either way, I shouldn't be able to feel it. Not when it's in *you*. Daria said you told her it was big, but—"

"It's an original, Asa."

For a moment he looked like he'd been clocked with a tire iron. "That's impossible. You do *not* have the original Sensilo magic inside of you."

"I think I do," I whispered. "I know what original magic feels like."

"But the Sensilo relic is in Russia. Volodya—the Russian boss—has it. I've been doing some digging."

"It's a fake."

"How the fuck do you know all this?"

I couldn't talk about my grandpa. Even thinking about him and what Ben had done to him threatened to send me into complete emotional meltdown, something I couldn't afford right now. "You can sense it inside me. Does that mean other magic sensors will be able to find me?"

"They'd have to be really close. I can't feel it unless I'm touching you."

I glanced over to see the glint of sweat at his temple. "Hands off, then."

"Don't flatter yourself," he snapped.

I flinched. "Did I do anything particular to piss you off, or had I just forgotten what an a-hole you are?" I glanced at a sign for I-90. "And where are we going?"

"You want to get the magic out, and that's what we're gonna do. On one condition, though: I get to keep it once it's back in the relic. That's the payment for my help, and if you whine about it—"

"I don't have the relic."

The tires squealed as he pulled over to the side of the road. "What the fuck, Mattie? Where is it?"

"Ben has it. He—"

"Of course he does," Asa said, his voice dripping with contempt. "And where were you gonna meet him?"

"Meet him?" My eyes burned with tears. "You think you've got it all figured out, don't you?"

"Look who's talking."

I'm not a violent person, but it was really tempting to smack him. The only thing that stopped me was the brittle feeling inside my chest, as if my rib cage were about to splinter under the pressure of the magic and the storm of emotions surrounding it. "I don't know where he is, Asa. After it happened, I—"

"You got separated when Zhong's thugs found you?"

I buried my head in my hands. He wouldn't even let me get a word in edgewise—he was too busy making up his own story.

"You'd better find him," Asa said. "I want the relic whole, and magic flows best into bodies."

"But the relic isn't a—"

"You said it was the original, and the original is a body part, right? With something this huge, I don't want to risk trying to transfer it into a vessel that can't contain it. Dangerous for everyone."

And especially him. If the magic was unleashed, Asa would feel it the most. Considering how he was treating me, it was kind of tempting to tell him we'd have to risk it, but I didn't know what would happen to *me* in that scenario, either. "Let me use your phone. I'll try to call him."

Asa fished what looked like a disposable phone out of his pocket and handed it to me without comment. I punched in Ben's number, but it went straight to voice mail. I started pressing keys to text him.

"Don't," said Asa. "If they have him, we don't want them to know what we're up to."

"I'll see if he left me a message." He knew I didn't have my phone, but it would be the quickest way to communicate with me. I dialed my own voice mail while Asa nervously checked the van's side and rearview mirrors, his fingers drumming on the wheel.

"Mattie," said Ben's voice a moment later. "I don't know when you'll get this, but I need to talk to you. I'm in trouble." He sounded out of breath, and I could hear the noise of the city in the background—and the clang and rattle of a nearby train. "I know I messed up big-time, but if you ever loved me at all, you'll put that aside until this is over. Brindle's people are going to kill me if I show up with an empty relic and no magic. And if I don't show up at all, they might go after our family, just like they went after me to get to Asa. Please." Here, he cursed and I could hear the sounds of sirens wailing as they passed by wherever he was. "I ditched the car because someone was following me, and I'm at Union Station. I'm supposed to meet Brindle's people at the DuPage Airport by eight. I'm begging you. For the sake of your mom and dad, if not for me."

My mouth had gone completely dry. "Ben's at Union Station. Brindle is expecting him at the DuPage Airport in"—I glanced at the clock on the dash—"three hours."

Asa slammed the car into gear and pulled a U-turn that nearly resulted in a collision with a taxi. Gracie whined from the backseat.

"Sorry, girl," he said in that voice reserved only for her. And then it went flinty again as he gave me a sidelong glance. "Brindle, Mattie? Really?"

"I didn't set this up, Asa!"

"So Ben's your fucking pimp now?"

"My *pimp*? That's low, even for you."

"Well, I'd hate to disappoint."

"Are you angry at Ben, or at me?"

"You're gonna force me to choose?"

Hurt and bitterness welled up like acid at the back of my tongue. "He said they'd go after my family if we didn't give them the relic."

"And that surprises you?"

"No," I said, my voice hoarse. "But—" I winced and rubbed at my chest.

"I'll figure it out." We were now speeding along I-90 North, back toward downtown. "But if Brindle's people find Ben first, all bets are off. Especially if Reza's there."

"So you'll just let them have Ben now, after all you did to save him?"

"You think I still give a fuck?"

"I *know* you do. You're here, aren't you?"

"You don't know shit, Mattie." His jaw was rigid as he took the exit at top speed. "I'm gonna make a lot of money off this, and I deserve every penny."

"What happened to you?" I blurted out.

He chuckled, dry as the Las Vegas desert. "Let's just get this done so you and Ben can go live happily ever after. Again."

I couldn't breathe past my sadness. My treasured happily-ever-after had been blown to pieces. And the part about it that hurt most? It had happened days ago. I hadn't even realized the truth until it was literally forced into me.

"Right," I choked out, clenching my fist over my diamond ring once again. "Let's get this done."

"Daria's gonna hide out in Joliet, but I think she can help us get the magic back into the relic, since it's Sensilo."

"She did say it was her favorite. But this stuff . . . Asa, it's already broken at least one conduit, and maybe two." I wasn't sure about Marcus.

He gave me a sharp glance out of the corner of his eye. "Two?"

"Just trust me. I'm not sure I'd want her to risk this for me."

"We might not have a choice. Not many conduits are strong enough. I only know of one or two others who could take it." He turned a corner, and the columned facade of Union Station loomed ahead. "But we can—" He pulled over abruptly and stared at the building. "Fuck me," he muttered.

"What's wrong?"

"At the moment, finding the right conduit's the least of our problems."

I peered at the front of the station, wishing Ben were just there in plain sight. "Just tell me."

"You sure Ben's in there?"

"I only know what he said in his message."

Asa shifted in his seat and wiped his sweaty forehead with the sleeve of his shirt. "Then this is not gonna be fun."

"Was it *ever* going to be fun?"

"Point taken." He turned to me. "But that building is crawling with naturals, Mattie. And I'm guessing every single one of them belongs to Zhong Lei."

CHAPTER EIGHT

I looked down at my bare feet, my ill-fitting dress, my skinny limbs that had already gone above and beyond tonight. I rubbed at the brittle, sharp pain in my chest. *Save yourself, Ben.* He'd burned me so badly that in that moment, it wouldn't have been hard to walk away. But Asa had said that the best receptacle for the magic inside me was the original relic—the gold-plated gallbladder or whatever of the original sorcerer. "What are the odds they already have it, and him?" I asked.

"Decent. There are at least four of them in there. One of them's a sensor. Probably Tao."

"But Ben isn't a natural, and the relic itself is empty right now. Tao probably couldn't sense him."

Asa frowned at the building. "Fair enough. You want to go in?"

"What are you going to do?"

"I'll be there."

I arched one eyebrow, and his smile managed to be both feral and cocky. "You're gonna have to trust me," he said.

I shuddered. "I don't think I trust anyone right now."

Asa's smile disappeared, and he gave me a searching look. It was so intense that I had to turn away. I didn't want him to see how badly I was hurting, how close I was to losing it right there in his passenger seat. I'd lost enough tonight—my understanding of Ben, my secret fantasy of Asa. Both men had betrayed me in their own way. But only one of those men had done it intentionally and callously. And Asa was just . . . Asa. This wasn't his problem.

Asa leaned forward to catch my eye. "Hey. Look at me."

I sighed and obeyed.

"I'm not going to leave you behind, okay? You go in there and find Ben. Gracie and I will do the rest."

I laughed as I glanced back at the pit bull. Her ragged ears were perked as she watched Asa for instructions. "I guess I'm in good hands, then."

When I looked back at Asa, something had shifted behind his eyes. He muttered something unintelligible, then reached across me and opened my door. He was staring out the window as I climbed out.

I gritted my teeth as my bare, scraped feet carried me across the city street, past the parking barriers and bike racks, between the columns, and into the cavernous great hall of the station. It was around five in the morning, and there were no passengers around. I scanned the room for people lurking behind the long wooden benches on either side of me as I trudged up the center of the space, headed for the concourse. I wanted to call Ben's name, but I figured that might be kind of a giveaway.

I was just passing an alcove that housed an ATM when a hand shot out and pulled me inside. Ben was pale and his hair was mussed. His hands were shaking as he released me. "Are you okay?" he whispered.

"Do I look okay?"

He blinked at me and then made the wise decision not to answer the question. "I wasn't sure you'd come. The way you took off . . ."

"Do you have the relic?"

He patted his pocket and gave me a hopeful smile. "I knew you'd change your mind after you had the chance to think about it. I bet we can rent a—"

"That's not how it's going to go, Ben," I said quietly, peeking out of the alcove before returning to him. "I called Asa."

"What? You can't be serious."

His contemptuous tone spurred a rush of anger inside me that had me doubling over in pain. "Serious as the heart attack it feels like I'm having right now," I snapped. I slapped his arm away as he tried to help me upright again.

"I should have guessed you'd go running straight to him. But we don't need him, Mattie. If you really feel like you want a magic sensor, Mr. Brindle could probably find a freelancer, and when we get to Vegas—"

"We're not going to Vegas, Ben! We're getting out of here, and then we're going to get this magic out of me and go home. Asa knows a conduit in Joliet who can help us. He's going to take the relic once the magic is back inside it. He'll know what to do with it, and he's taking it as payment for helping. End of story."

"What? That's bullshit! We've come this far, Mattie. We can't give up now," he said, coming forward to take me by the arms again.

I backed up so fast that my head hit the wall. "You want the magic? Come and get it." I whirled around and marched out of the alcove. I hadn't seen any sign of Zhong's agents, but the longer I hung out in one place, the more chance Tao would have to sense my presence. Asa had said he would have to be very close, but the way my chest was feeling, I didn't trust myself to contain it.

I pulled up short when I saw that three people were now sitting on the bench facing the alcove. Two of them looked familiar. One was Zhi, an Ekstazo healer and Zhong's mistress. Asa and I had smuggled a relic full of her magic out to Zhi's ailing mother in Colorado last year, in exchange for information about Ben's whereabouts. Next to her was Tao, looking even more sickly and strained than he had the year before. Daria had told me he stayed high on Ekstazo pleasure magic just to keep him going, and I knew from a brief encounter with magic-sensing power that it felt like needles working their way along my skin. Asa had his own way of dealing with it, but Tao looked as if it were slowly killing him. Still, his dark eyes focused on me the minute I stepped into the open. The man sitting next to him, a short, stocky guy with bright-blue hair, stood up as Tao muttered something in his ear.

"The two of you will come with us," Blue Hair said with a smile, sauntering toward us.

I glanced behind me to see Ben at my shoulder. "Don't listen to him," I started to say, but Ben stepped forward and threw a punch at the guy as soon as he was within reach.

For a split second, I was impressed that Ben had been able to throw off the influence of Knedas magic—until I realized Blue Hair wasn't a mindfucker; he was a Strikon. The guy caught Ben's punch in midair, and Ben cried out as if he'd been stabbed. I took a step back to run, but the Strikon caught me by the arm. My mouth dropped open as my whole body rebelled, every cell screaming so loudly that I couldn't make a sound. I fell to my knees, unable to breathe. Ben wrapped his arms around me and lifted me from the ground, holding me against his broad chest. His panicked voice yanked me into awareness again, but the pain didn't go away. It wrapped itself around the knife in my chest and pushed the agony deeper, until my bones themselves felt like they were going to shatter.

"What the hell did you do?" Ben shouted. Then he turned to yell at a security guard. "Don't you see this? Help us!"

The guard merely gazed blankly at us and walked on.

Blue Hair waved his hand in front of my face. "I didn't give her that much. It should have faded as soon as I let her go."

"Don't touch her again, Bai," Zhi said. "She doesn't look well." She didn't look that well, either. Her exquisitely beautiful face looked pinched and pale, and I wondered what had happened to her in the months since Zhong had found out she'd helped us find Ben. "Welcome back to Chicago, Mattie. I apologize for the crudeness of our hospitality. Especially because I have been told that you brought us a present."

"Oh, this is awkward," I said between agonized breaths as Ben held me up. "I actually forgot it back at the hotel."

Zhi gave me a pained smile. "We mean you no harm. We only want the magic and the relic, and you will both be free to go."

"Frank Brindle will have something to say about that," Ben said.

Zhi and Tao jumped to their feet, and Bai sidled close enough to make Ben groan. "You work for him?" Bai asked. "What are you? A conduit? Another reliquary?"

"I'm Mattie's fiancé," Ben said. He held me a little tighter, and I forced myself not to squirm to escape. As angry as I was at him, I didn't want to be responsible for his death. Also, I wasn't sure I could stand on my own.

"Oh. This is the brother of Asa Ward," Tao said, his voice flat. "He's not a natural."

"Then he's not useful," said Bai. "Wouldn't it be easier to eliminate him?"

Zhi tilted her head. "That is Zhong's decision to make. He may wish to make a deal with Asa."

I fought the urge to glance around. Asa had said he would be here. He'd said he would back me up. Where was he?

"We'd better get going," said Zhi. "People will soon realize the station is actually open." Her statement made me look around again. A few passengers were trickling in, but their gazes seemed to drift over us as they passed. Somewhere around there, there must have been a Knedas agent. He or she had clearly influenced the guard, who was now chatting up an equally oblivious ticket agent not thirty feet away.

Tao stepped into the aisle and turned toward the exit, then froze. "Wait."

Zhi approached him and rubbed his back, making the rigid set of his shoulders relax. "What is it?"

"Strikon. I . . . over there. Approaching." Stiffly, he turned back toward the concourse. "Moving fast."

"Bai, go with Tao."

We all turned as Tao and Bai headed for the hallway that led to the north and south concourses. Tao was scanning the left side of the hallway, partially hunched over and leaning forward as if he were about to charge. Or fall on his face. He looked a little unsteady. "It's . . . it's . . . there!"

We all stared at the entrance to the men's bathroom, and that was when Gracie charged out of it, sprinting along the hallway toward us with a jangly metal collar fastened around her thick neck, a large heart-shaped pendant dangling in front of her chest. In the moment of stunned silence that followed, Asa leaned out from behind a column only a few feet away from the two agents. He had a straw pressed between his lips. Just as Tao turned around, Asa exhaled forcefully, and a little white projectile flew out of the end of the straw, hitting Tao in the side of the face. He clapped his hand to his face and screamed, which was when Asa nailed him again, this time right in the eye.

"Spitballs?" Ben muttered as Bai whirled around and charged Asa, who calmly raised what appeared to be a water gun and squirted the Strikon right in the face, stopping him in his tracks.

Asa leaned close to Bai and whispered something in the guy's ear, and Bai immediately took off running, straight toward the concourses.

"Please tell me you didn't just tell him to step in front of a train," I said as Asa stalked toward me.

He winked and then looked right past Ben, his gaze settling on Zhi. "Thought we were friends."

"You don't know what he did to me," she said in a choked voice. "You don't know what he'll do."

"I can guess. But you can tell him you had no choice." He walked up to her and squirted her in the face before she could reply. "Go after Bai," he said softly. "He's going to be dancing on a table in the first class lounge, and odds are he will be naked." He held up the water gun and waggled his eyebrows. "This is some seriously good shit."

Zhi set off at a jog, running right past Tao, who was whimpering and rubbing his eye, which had swollen shut. Asa's saliva had been saturated with his magic, which Tao, already filled to the brim with the same kind, was extremely sensitive to. He tried to get to his feet as he saw his comrades abandoning their attempt to capture us, but he was too unsteady to manage it.

Asa gave him a pitying look. "Shake it off, Tao," he said. "Zhong'll have to forgive you. You're too valuable to hurt."

Tao turned his tortured one-eyed gaze on Asa. "Why can't you just kill me?"

"Sorry, Tao. Not my style." His tone sounded genuinely apologetic.

Tao bowed his head, sinking onto all fours. A shriek tore my gaze from the pathetic sight of him, though. It was followed by a chest-deep growl as Gracie dragged a woman out from behind the ticket counter by her pant leg. "Bomb!" screamed the woman—who I assumed was the Knedas agent who had made everyone in the station ignore us—as she waved her arms at us. "They have a bomb!"

This statement had a pretty dramatic effect on the few people in the station, and it would take only one to call the cops. "Come, Gracie!" shouted Asa as he grabbed Ben's sleeve and shoved him toward the exit to the street.

But Ben didn't follow. "You have a bomb?" he yelped as Asa scooted past him. "Mattie, he has a bomb!"

I struggled in his grip. "No, he doesn't! Let me go!"

Asa was already several steps ahead of us. The guard who had ignored us earlier raced forward and started to draw his weapon, but Asa squirted him in the face as he ran by and yelled something about the bomber being in the first class lounge. "Mattie," he shouted, glancing over his shoulder. "Get those little legs—"

"I'm trying!" I reached behind me and slapped Ben hard in the face. "Asa does not have a bomb, Ben," I said, wheezing. "Now get us out of here!"

Ben hustled me toward the exit, firing questions at me about whether Asa might be a terrorist. Gracie easily caught up and moved to run next to Asa, a gray streak beside him. We burst into the hazy glow of dawn in the city and made for Asa's van, which was illegally parked in front of a couple of seriously ticked-off taxi drivers. I worked to regain control of my legs, but my toes were barely brushing the sidewalk as Ben carried me along, his arms like steel cables around my middle, the pressure only ratcheting up the pain. By the time Asa flung open the door, I was whimpering.

"Loosen your grip, asshole," he snapped at Ben. "She's turning blue."

Ben mumbled an apology and clumsily bundled me into the bench seat in the very back.

"Tao'll call in reinforcements," Asa said as he started the van. "Close that door, Ben!"

As soon as Gracie leaped into the back, Ben obeyed. Asa slammed on the gas, shooting us into the sparse Saturday-morning Chicago traffic.

Ben sat on the bench seat and pulled my feet into his lap. His hands were shaking, probably from the adrenaline and chaos of the last few minutes. I didn't particularly want him touching any part of me, but I was too weak to pull away.

"Now that we've established that you don't have a bomb," he said, rubbing his hands over his face as if he were trying to scrub away the confusion, "Mattie told me you're taking us to Joliet."

"Change of plans." Asa glared at his side mirrors. "Zhong is gonna lock down every single conduit in a five-hundred-mile radius. If any of them help us, they'll be in his sights."

I struggled to sit up. "So where—"

"I know a place." Asa's eyes met mine in the rearview mirror. "Settle in back there." His gaze shifted to his younger brother, and his eyes narrowed. "I'm pretty sure this is gonna be the road trip from hell."

CHAPTER NINE

Asa pulled over a few miles down the road and beckoned Gracie into the front seat. She leaped onto it with her hind end wagging but kept still while Asa looped a harness around her body so she could ride safely next to him. Then he unfastened the heavy collar from around her neck. Sweat ran in rivulets down his temples as he gathered the collar with its dangling pendant in a cloth and carried it to the cargo area just behind my seat, where he enclosed it in a padded metal case, which he then tucked into another case, this one with thick walls lined with some kind of dull metallic material. Lead, I wondered? When he saw me looking, he muttered, "Remember what Daeng said about Strikon magic?"

"It covers up the presence of other magic. You put a relic on Gracie so Tao wouldn't notice you creeping up on him."

He nodded, and our eyes caught. I wondered if he was remembering that night when I took down Daeng, the magic sensor of Bangkok, and used a relic to heal the almost-fatal gunshot wound he'd given Asa. *No one's ever fought for me like that,* Asa had said afterward.

"I need a first aid kit," Ben said curtly.

Asa's expression turned stony as he reached back and came up with a soft-sided bag, which he tossed across Ben's lap. "There are antiseptic

re. Bandages, too." He went back up to the front and leaned
kiss Gracie on the top of her head before settling into the
seat again.

have no idea how long Asa drove, only that I huddled on that
ch seat, trying my best not to throw up or scream every time he
it a pothole or bump. Ben busied himself with my feet. He switched
into vet mode, cleaning all my little cuts, covering each with a bandage. The skill and gentle strength I felt in his hands made my throat
constrict.

I must have dozed off, though all I remember is a hazy, throbbing
pain that made breathing a chore instead of a relief. I lurched awake
to a beam of blinding sunlight in my eye. Ben peered out the window.
"Asa went to make a call," he said. "He said he needed to set things up
for tonight."

"Did he say where we were going?"

Ben shook his head. "But we're just south of Toledo. Headed east."

I sat up and looked around. We were at a station, gassing up.
"Where's Gracie?"

"With him." He chuckled. "Asa always had a thing for animals.
Birds with broken wings, stray kittens, one-eyed puppies, you name it.
He related to them better than people. Looks like he still does."

I leaned against the window, closing my eyes at the feeling of sun-
warmed glass against my oddly chilled skin. "Gracie's like his service
animal."

"So she keeps him mentally stable?"

I let out an exasperated sigh. "You make it sound like a bad
thing."

"He cares more about her than about us."

"Can you blame him?"

"A little," Ben said. "He said the cops might be looking for us, so
we had to stay here. But I kind of need a trip to the bathroom. And a
bottle of water. You could use one, too. You're probably dehydrated."

My mouth was like cotton, but I merely sank down into the bench seat again, grimacing as the pain in my chest flared. "He thinks we did it together," I said softly. "He thinks it was my idea."

"Taking the relic to Brindle?"

"Trying to smuggle magic in general."

"And is he mad because you didn't offer him a cut first?"

"I don't know." All I knew was that Asa seemed to hate me, but it wasn't actually *me* he despised. It was some other Mattie he'd built up in his head. Still, it hurt more than I wanted to admit.

"I can talk to him," said Ben. "This is all my fault."

"Don't bother." If it was so easy for Asa to believe I would leap back into the magic business with both feet—and without him—he didn't know me at all.

"Mattie"—Ben cleared his throat—"I've held back on asking you about this for the longest time, maybe because I didn't want to know the answer, but . . . did anything happen between you two last year?"

I let out a slow breath, my nostrils flaring. "What I went through to get that relic we exchanged for your life—it was intense, Ben. Can you get that?"

"Yeah, sure, but—"

"And Asa is the only reason I got through it. Can you get *that*?"

"I do, Mattie, which is why—"

"Stop. Asa and I worked together for one reason—to save you. And then we went our separate ways. If I say his name in my sleep sometimes . . ." I swallowed, and it felt like rubbing two corn husks together. If I said his name in my sleep sometimes, it was probably because the image of him staring at me while he slid his hand into the panties of a barely clad masochist conduit in Bangkok had been haunting my fantasies ever since it had happened. "I'm probably just having nightmares about the transactions. It was pain magic."

"So it hurt more than the Sensilo magic you have in there now."

I rubbed my chest. "Going in, yeah."

"Oh, good," he said with a little smile that made me want to slap him, and he must have read my face. "I get it, Mattie—I do. I know you didn't want to transport the magic. I feel terrible, but I was so panicked, and all I wanted to do was get us to safety."

"I don't need to hear your explanation again."

"But I need your forgiveness! And if telling Asa that all this was all my idea will help, I'll do it."

"Telling Asa doesn't matter," I snapped. "He's obviously willing to help regardless of what he thinks."

"For a price."

"I don't care! I need this magic out of me, and he's the only one I trust. So leave it." I pulled my feet off his lap, drawing my knees to my chest.

"*Do* you want me to leave?" Ben asked softly. "If you can't forgive me, then I could just—I don't know—catch a bus back to Wisconsin."

"I can't get into this with you right now," I mumbled. The pain was all-consuming. "Do whatever you want."

"Okay. I'll stay. I have no idea where Asa's going, anyway. We don't know if it's safe."

"I can almost guarantee it isn't."

I flinched as the van's door slid open. "Got you a disguise," Asa said to Ben. He offered a red T-shirt.

"'Michigan still sucks—go Bucks!'" Ben read. "Do I have to wear this?"

I opened one eye as Asa handed him a trucker's cap. "And this," he said with a wicked smile. "To cover that pretty-boy hair of yours."

"'If I wanted to listen to an a-hole, I'd fart,'" Ben read in a monotone. "You're doing this just for a laugh."

"Asa never does anything just for a laugh," I muttered.

"Damn straight," Asa said, though he seemed pretty pleased with himself. "If you need to piss badly enough, you'll put on the hat like a good boy and keep it low over your eyes."

Ben mumbled under his breath as he hopped out. A moment later I heard the jingle of Gracie's collar and something blocked the sun from my eyes. I opened them, expecting to see her doggy smile, but instead I jerked back—Asa was squatting right next to me, peering at my face like a kid might stare at fresh roadkill.

"I don't want to hear it," I said.

"Serves you right. Maybe you shoulda looked in the mirror a time or two while you went on whatever greed-driven magic-smuggling spree led you to this."

For the second time in the last ten minutes, the desire to slap one of the Ward brothers was almost overpowering. "Do you try to end up sounding like an ignorant bastard, or does that just happen naturally?"

"I've been around for years, honey, and I call it as I see it."

"Right. And you couldn't ever—" I hissed and bowed my head. It felt like a bird of prey had closed its talons around my heart.

Asa's fingertip was warm as he ran it along my cheek, but he drew back quickly. "We'll have this outta you by tonight, okay? You're gonna feel a lot better."

"Can you feel it?" I asked. "Is it leaking?"

"Maybe a tiny bit. Nothing huge."

"Not yet, at least."

"You need to turn off your brain. It's not doing you any favors."

"Easier said than done." I *couldn't*. But he could . . . Suddenly, I wanted him to take me by the throat, to command me to stop thinking about it, to call forth another side of me, one he had created: Eve. He'd done that for me before, and it had felt like the difference between slow suffocation and breathing free.

But the silence stretched between us, and he didn't lean closer or smile or soften. I drew in a shallow breath to try to keep from awakening the agony. Gracie whined from the front seat. "Where are we going?" I finally asked.

"Virginia."

"Can you be more specific?"

"Nope."

"So, just like before, I guess? You're keeping me in the dark so if something happens, I can say I have no idea what's going on?"

Asa's eyes narrowed. "I'm keeping you in the dark because I don't trust you or Ben to keep your fucking mouths shut. You two lovebirds are dangerous to a lot more people than just yourselves now." He turned away to go back up to the front, but I managed to grab his wrist. His jaw clenched.

"Asa, I don't know what I did to piss you off this much, but I'm sorry. And I appreciate that you're helping me."

He looked down at my fingers wrapped over his tanned forearm. "Dammit, Mattie." He pulled out of my grip and headed to the front. After Ben returned, Asa got back on the highway, and I drifted off, still in the fetal position, lulled by the white noise of the road and the unrelenting weight of fatigue.

". . . but she's down to skin and bones and looks fucking terrible. You have any idea what could happen to her if she breaks?" Asa's voice was low but harsh, and its rough edge pulled me up from oblivion. I kept still, though, with my eyes shut, hoping he would give some hint as to what was going on.

"She was sick before," Ben mumbled.

"What?"

"She's looked bad for a while. I mean, not that it's any of your business, but she's had problems ever since we got back to Wisconsin. This transaction, though . . . It would have set us up for life, Asa. It still could."

"Life? What if she's dead by the time that happens? Because you know that could be the result, right?"

"She's supposed to be this überstrong reliquary."

"She *was*. But whatever you two have been up to, it's fucked her up. I can feel that magic inside her without even trying. You're supposed to care about her. And you let her—"

"I've been trying to take care of her for *months*. Taken her to all the specialists, got her any prescription that seemed like it might help. She wouldn't even take the pills."

"You think pills are the answer here? What the fuck is wrong with you?"

"What the fuck is wrong with *you*? You're only here to make money. Do you actually care about Mattie herself, or is she just a useful object to you?"

Yeah, Ben, I could ask you the same question.

Asa was silent. I cracked an eye open to see him basically trying to strangle the steering wheel.

"If I had my choice, she never would have called you," Ben muttered.

"And yet it was probably the smartest decision either of you geniuses have made in a long time."

Ben chuckled. "Do you know how much you sound like Dad sometimes?"

A chill went down my spine as I felt the van swerve. We came to a halt so quickly that I would have fallen off the bench seat if Ben hadn't caught me. I pushed myself up to sitting. Asa slammed the van into park and turned in his seat. "Guess what?" His glare was a knife, slicing through the space between him and his younger brother. "You're taking up space and oxygen that could be spent on someone who actually has the ability to be useful. Get the fuck out of my ride."

I glanced around. We were on a long, empty stretch of highway with forest on one side and farmland on the other. A sign about fifty yards ahead indicated we were thirty-six miles from Hagerstown, Maryland.

Ben's hands closed around my calves, which he'd pulled across his lap again. "You can't be serious."

"Gracie, help Ben out of the van." Asa swept two of his fingers toward his brother, as if giving her permission to attack.

Gracie growled, deep in her chest. Luckily she was still harnessed in the front seat.

"That's irresponsible, Asa," Ben said, using the same voice he did when lecturing pet owners about spaying and neutering. "If the dog bites me, then she'll be put—"

"Threaten Gracie and I'll shove a Strikon relic so far up your ass that you'll choke on it."

Ben's mouth snapped shut, his nostrils flaring. "I'm not leaving Mattie."

Asa's gaze met mine, and I wanted to say so many things, but the storm in his eyes kept me quiet. "My ride, my rules."

"I know," I said quietly. "But we're in the middle of nowhere. Please, Asa."

He ran his tongue over his teeth as he stared at Ben's thumbs stroking my calves. I wanted to scream at Ben to stop, but it felt like one sudden move and Asa would explode. "Fuck this," he muttered, then turned in his seat, shifted the car into drive, and stomped on the gas pedal. We peeled off the shoulder and shot into the lane fast enough to make my stomach swoop.

Ben was smart enough to keep quiet after that, and Asa was clearly in no mood for conversation, either. I pulled my knees to my chest again, curling in on myself. My fists were tucked up under my chin, the diamond from my engagement ring poking at the soft skin beneath my jaw. No part of me didn't hurt, but my heart was the epicenter, a throbbing, raw mess. Broken.

Asa thought this transaction would break me.

But maybe the damage was already done.

Ever since I was a little girl, I had imagined my wedding day. Lace and flowers and so much happiness that I couldn't hold it all in. I had imagined my life—a little house, a few kids, the PTA, lawn parties at my parents' lakeside house. And love. So much love that my days would burst with it. Romance that made my toes curl, adoration that lasted until we took our final breaths. Simple and conventional, yes, but that was what I had craved. It was what I thought I'd had. From the way Ben had clutched at my legs, from the strident desperation in his voice as he'd begged for my forgiveness, it still seemed like that life was on offer.

Except now it was warped. Tarnished. Dented and torn and splintered.

I glanced at Ben, who was dozing with his head tilted back, his mouth half-open. Had he truly panicked in the hotel room? Had he really been thinking only of my safety as Zhong's people closed in? Or had he been thinking of the money he needed so desperately to keep the clinic afloat? Even the clinic, though . . . He'd said he wanted to save it because of me. I'd put pressure on him, told him it was something I needed. Was this whole thing my fault? Had he been driven to this out of a desire to please me, to meet the perfect, fantastic standards and wishes I had happily babbled about as we'd planned out our life together? Had I ever once said, "Love is enough for me"? And if I had, would we have been here right now? Would my grandpa still have been alive?

Asa had been wrong about the details of our failed relic-smuggling operation. But I wasn't sure he had been wrong about the rotten core of it. Shallow desires—a nice house, the clinic, the lifestyle, the dream—had put both Ben and me on this path. I mean, yes, they symbolized other things—security, happiness, love, and success. But couldn't those things be had without the trappings?

I lay awake as the light beyond my closed eyelids turned from pale yellow to dark orange to tar black. I thought about where we were going, and whether I was going to survive what lay ahead. Which begged the question: What was I going to do if I did?

CHAPTER TEN

"Last chance for supplies before we arrive," Asa announced, jerking me from restless sleep full of fractured dreams. I opened my eyes as we passed a Walmart sign.

"I'm good," Ben said sleepily, rubbing at his face.

"Yeah?" Asa hit an overhead light. His crooked profile was etched with contempt as he spoke. "You think your bride there would say the same?"

Ben glanced at me. "You need anything?"

My cheeks were hot. "Honestly? Some clothes that fit me. And clean underwear," I said, then gasped as the shard of pain in my chest flared lava-hot.

Asa winced, and I wondered if he could feel the magic that was tearing me apart inside. "I have to buy a few things for the transaction," he said to Ben. "If you're too tired to get up off your ass and get what she needs, I will. But it'll take longer." He cut me a sidelong glance and quickly looked away. "Doesn't seem like a good idea."

"All right." Ben slid the passenger door open, got out, and closed it again.

The noise and impact of the slam forced me to stifle a groan, but the sound was gone in an instant, engulfing me in quiet. "You felt the magic just now, didn't you?" I murmured as Asa reached for his door handle.

He raised his head and stared out the windshield. "Been feeling it for hours."

"Bad?"

"Definitely not good." He looked over his shoulder, and I caught the sheen of sweat on his brow. "Try to keep still. We'll be back in a sec. Gracie will be right here. She'll eat anyone who tries to bother you."

"Can you undo her harness?"

I needed softness. Uncomplicated love. A tiny bit of joy. Things that only she could give me right now.

"Yeah." He reached over and unfastened Gracie from her perch in the front seat, then bent to whisper something in her barely there ears. She whined and licked his stubbly jaw. "Go ahead," he murmured to her, and then he was gone, shutting the door so gently that the sound was only a soft click.

A moment later she was by my side, licking my hands and laying her large head on my shoulder. I smiled as tears burned my eyes, my fingers curling into the loose skin at her throat. "Thanks, lovely girl," I whispered.

She raised her head and licked my cheek, and I took a deep breath in an effort not to sob. Gracie's doggy smell was laced with the scent of Asa, a mix of soap, sweat, something fruity, something deep and green. It reminded me of all the times I had been close to him, how at first it had been terrifying, how by the end it had felt as necessary as breathing, how when I first got home from our strange odyssey I had tried to imagine this exact scent and failed a million times.

Ben had asked me if anything had happened with Asa, and I had known what he meant. Something simple—had I kissed him? (Yes. Well. He kissed me. And I wasn't really myself at the time. But still.

Wow.) Had I wanted him? (Oh, that was complicated.) But when it came to Asa, nothing was as simple as yes or no, black or white, always or never. My feelings for him were raw and terrifying and impossible. They didn't fit with what I wanted or where I was going. And Asa himself, well, maybe it was just my small-town naïveté, but I had no clue what he would want, what he would demand, what would please him.

"And it's none of my business, is it?" I whispered.

Gracie whined. Then she growled. As the van's door slid open, she let out a ferocious snarl.

"Jesus Christ," yelped Ben.

I laid my hand on Gracie's back. "It's okay, girl."

Gracie growled again, but then she flopped down next to the bench seat. She eyed Ben as he climbed in and sat down, carrying a large Walmart bag. He offered her his hand, which she leaned forward to sniff once before making a doggy *harrumph* and laying her head on her forepaws.

Ben laughed. "She's just like her master, isn't she?" He held up the bag. "Got you some stuff." He closed the door. "The windows are tinted. You can change."

I pawed through the bag and fought back my disappointment as I realized that Ben had gotten me size-six everything, which was the size I was *supposed* to be. Now, though . . .

"Is everything okay? I got exactly what you wanted. I also picked you up some sandals and a bra." He smiled proudly. "Thirty-two C, right?"

Not anymore. I peered at the lacy cups. "Thanks." I turned away from him as I shimmied Daria's loaner panties down my legs, then tore open the underwear package. The panties were loose around my hips, but they were clean, so I wasn't complaining. I tugged a pair of sweats up my legs next and tied the drawstrings tight to make sure they stayed up.

Ben cleared his throat. "I overheard Asa in the hardware department. He was on the phone haggling with someone about a price."

I pulled my dress off and reached for the bra. "So?"

"I know you had some kind of *experience* with him, but what if he plays too rough as he pulls this magic out of you? Asa's always been out for himself."

"People love to believe that about him." My hands pressed the loose cups over my breasts. "But it's total bull, Ben. How can you of all people say that? The night you broke his nose—the only reason he was there was because he brought you home after finding you in a magic den."

"That was one night, Mattie. There were several before when that wasn't how things went. After my dad kicked him out, Asa broke in a few times to steal cash and stuff to sell. He didn't care that we didn't have much money in the first place—whatever we had, Asa felt entitled to it."

"Why did your dad kick him out?"

"Do you really want to know?"

"Yeah," I whispered.

"Dad came home early from work one day and caught Asa fooling around on the couch. With a *guy*." Ben snorted. "The kid who edited the school newspaper, actually."

My shoulders slumped. I had actually suspected something like that. "Poor Asa." He had been only sixteen or seventeen, and I could picture him, skinny and sensitive and trying to figure out who he was—and having the father who was supposed to love and take care of him descend on him like a ton of bricks.

"Poor Asa? My dad nearly died of a heart attack. If it had been a girl, he might have cheered, but a guy?"

"Who cares, as long as they both wanted to be there?"

"Do you have any idea how old-fashioned my dad was?"

I stared out the window. "So old-fashioned that he kicked his own son out on the streets for the crime of wanting someone who didn't fit his narrow preconceived ideas?"

Ben chuckled. "I remember being as confused as hell, because the week before, I'd seen Asa making out behind the arcade with some skater girl. And all of a sudden he was gay? Kind of blew my thirteen-year-old mind."

"I don't think Asa's gay." Like everything about him, Asa's sexuality seemed complicated. Impossible to categorize or pigeonhole. Now I knew for a fact he'd hooked up with guys, but when we had been together, I could have sworn . . . "This isn't actually any of our business."

"You're the one who wanted to know."

I rolled my eyes and yanked the T-shirt over my head. The pain was getting worse, and with even that movement I ended up hunched over. Ben tried to help me up, but I screamed when he put pressure on my skin. Gracie leaped to her feet and started to bark, sharp, percussive bursts of noise that made my head pound. I retched, my ears roaring and my blood shrieking through my veins like hurricane-force winds.

"Mattie, Asa's coming back," Ben said loudly, over the noise of Gracie's growls and my whimpers. "I don't trust him. Just . . . if it comes down to it, we might need to escape quickly, okay?"

I let out a shaky breath as the pain began to subside a little. "Most of Asa's plans end that way."

"I mean *us*, Mattie. We can escape. If we can get away with the relic—"

"No."

"You have no idea where he's taking you, Mattie. You have no idea if he intends to get you out alive."

Gracie barked at Ben, baring her teeth as I turned to him. In the darkness, his eyes glittered with desperation.

"Are you worried about me?" I asked. "Or the money?"

He sat back as if I'd slapped him. "Mattie. I know I've screwed up a billion times, but you can't doubt my feelings. I've spent months listening to you moan my brother's name in your sleep, and I haven't said a word. Because I *love* you. Because I get it—you guys did what you did for me, and who was I to complain? I've spent this whole time hoping you would come back to me. I've worked my ass off to give you the kind of home and life you always said you wanted, all in an attempt to remind you of what we had before I screwed it all up. All of that, everything—I did it for you."

"Why did you do *this* to me, then?"

Right then Asa opened the driver's door and hopped inside. He went still when he saw Ben and me sitting there, our postures tense and our eyes shining with emotion. "Aw. Lovers' quarrel? You guys need a few minutes?"

"Have some decency, Asa. Can't you see Mattie's upset?"

"Yeah, Ben. I see she's upset. I also see that she's a big girl who can speak for herself."

"Shut up, both of you," I said thickly, fighting the nausea.

"I'm sorry, babe," Ben mumbled, running his hand down my back. "You okay? You want me to run in and get you some Advil?"

I pulled away from the touch of his hands on my fragile skin as Asa said, "Advil. Good call. Bet that'll fix her right up."

"Shut up, Asa," Ben snapped.

Gracie barked at him, her lips peeled back from her impressive teeth, which were only a foot or so from Ben's calf. "Can you get her secured up front, please?" he asked Asa. "She seems to think I'm a threat to Mattie."

Asa stared at his brother, then arched one eyebrow.

Ben cursed. "For the love of God, Asa. I want to get Mattie through this as badly as you do!" In a voice trembling with emotion, he added, "More, in fact."

Asa's expression didn't change, but he pointed to the front passenger seat. "Up here, Gracie."

She jumped up and obeyed, then sat with her tongue lolling. She eagerly accepted a treat from Asa. "Thanks for holding down the fort, baby girl." He accepted a lick on the cheek and faced front. "We'll be there in about an hour. I'll make sure we're ready to roll, and then we'll get this done."

I shuddered as the reality hit me—if all went as planned, soon I would have to release this magic and let it flow through a conduit and back into the relic. What if it destroyed me on the way out? I wrapped my arms around myself and stared out the window as Asa pulled back onto the road and turned off after a few miles. I'd seen a sign for Williamsburg, so I knew we must be close to the Atlantic Ocean, but I honestly wasn't an expert in geography. Asa followed one winding gravel road after another. I saw a few signs for a state park, but that was it. Trees thick with late-spring foliage leaned close, and every once in a while the van's headlights would hit a pair of glowing gold eyes in the distance.

The road got bumpy. Asa drove slowly, but every time the van dipped, I felt as if I were going to shatter. I had one hand braced on the window, and the other clamped over Ben's knee. He kept muttering for me to breathe, and when we hit a particularly deep pothole and I cried out, he scooted close and held me, trying to mute the impact of the dips and bumps.

"This kind of feels like we're having a baby," he said with a nervous chuckle. "At least, this is how I imagined it."

New tears pricked my eyes. *Don't,* I wanted to say. *Please don't bring that up now.* Because I had imagined it, too, just another part of my happy little fantasy of how my life would play out, and right now it felt like all of it had been pried away.

"Almost there," Asa said, his voice devoid of the edge it had carried since he'd first walked back into my life. "It's just up ahead."

"Whoa," Ben said as we passed the trees and found ourselves in a huge clearing surrounded by woods and marked by a faded, splintering sign that said, "Carnival Magia." "Is this place for real?" His eyes were wide with wonder.

I squinted into the darkness, where I could just make out concentric circles of campers and trailers in the field to our right, the kind you could hook onto a pickup truck. Along either side of the road were shabbily constructed wooden booths, and another sign marked the area as the "Midway and Festival of Freaks." A few shadowy figures gathered between the booths, watching us as we slowly rolled toward them. On the other side of the midway was a cluster of colorful silk tents lit from inside, their flimsy walls fluttering in the warm night breeze.

"This is amazing," Ben whispered.

Asa bowed his head, his shoulders shaking. "Bet you've never seen anything like this, am I right?"

"What is this place? Why have I never heard of it?"

My brow furrowed. "What are you talking about? This place is—" A dump, straight up.

"That roller coaster is just unbelievable." Ben was peering up at the black starry sky.

"You see it, Mattie?" asked Asa, his voice strained as he tried not to laugh. "Wanna go for a ride later?"

"See what? There's nothing there!" I bowed my head as a terrible cracking sensation ran along the front of my chest.

"Aw. I bet you don't believe in Santa, either—*fuck*. Hang on, Mattie. Just a few more minutes." He pulled to an abrupt stop, and a moment later he was kneeling next to me. "Are you gonna be able to walk?"

"Don't know," I breathed.

"Ben. Relic." Asa held out his hand.

But Ben had his nose pressed to the window. "When does this place open in the morning?"

I waved my hand toward Ben's pants. "It's in his pocket."

Asa jammed his hand in Ben's pocket and came up holding the shining golden locket. Its heavy chain dangled from between his fingers. Ben didn't seem aware he no longer had possession of it, though. "Mattie! They have bumper boats!"

As Asa rolled his eyes, I finally figured it out. "There's some sort of Knedas power over this entire place, isn't there? How is that even possible?"

"They've got relics posted on the road starting about a half mile back, and then all over this field, all projecting the same fantasy."

"Why can't I see it?" I asked weakly.

"Jacks, baby." He nudged my chin up so he could look in my eyes. "I think you're in too much pain to fall for much of anything right now."

"I'm scared."

"I know." He turned to Ben. "Get on out, Ben. But stay close. You can explore tomorrow. I'll buy you some cotton candy and a balloon if you behave."

"I've got my own money for that," Ben said peevishly as he got out of the van, apparently having forgotten all about me.

With Asa hovering close, I slid along the bench seat and started to stand up, but swayed with dizziness as I caught sight of the ground. Asa guided me out of the vehicle, letting me lean on him to stay upright.

Ben was staring out at the ring of shabby campers, his hands limp at his sides, oblivious as a man and a woman approached from between two of the parked vehicles. The man was wearing a backward red baseball cap and dirty overalls with no shirt underneath. His graying brown hair stuck out in unwashed clumps above his ears, and his pale eyes were deep set and piercing. The woman wore floral pants and a voluminous blue smock over her wiry body. She had her white hair up in a perfectly round bun at the very top of her head, and on her neck she sported some kind of winding black tattoo.

"Never thought you'd come out this way again," said the man as he approached Asa, his wide mouth breaking into a snaggletoothed smile that was as ugly as it was uplifting.

"Vernon," Asa said, holding out his arms and hugging the man. "Never thought I would, either."

"You gonna be okay here?" asked the woman, eyeing Asa with concern.

That was when I realized his shirt was rapidly soaking through with sweat. "*Are* you okay?" I whispered.

"Fine," Asa said, his voice clipped. "Mattie, this is Vernon and Betsy Luben." Asa waved his hand toward Ben, who was still staring into the distance, in awe of the fictional Carnival Magia. "That's my brother, Ben. Mattie's his fiancée. Hey. Hey. Ben!"

Ben started and turned around. "What?"

Asa pulled a water pistol from his thigh pocket and squirted Ben square in the face. Ben spluttered and choked, frantically wiping at the liquid. "Ow! What the hell was that for?"

"Very diluted Strikon juice—to clear your head. Look around."

Ben obeyed, and cringed in disgust at what he saw. Betsy stiffened at his expression. "We live how we want out here, you get it? Make a good living, too." Her chin was high, a challenge.

"Oh, I meant no offense, ma'am," said Ben, switching into his smooth customer-service voice. "I was just surprised at how thorough the . . . what's it called? A glamour or something?"

"Call it whatever you want to," Betsy said flatly. "We call it home."

"We're going to get set up," Asa said before Ben could offend the woman further. "Help Mattie walk to the tent, okay? She's a little unsteady."

Ben looked utterly confused for a moment, but then his eyes lit on me, leaning against Asa. "Oh! Oh, damn, Mattie. I'm sorry." He rushed forward and tugged me away from Asa.

I glanced around me. Curtains twitched within a few of the lighted trailers, and a few darkened ones as well. Our arrival had been noted by all. I clung to Ben as Asa released Gracie from the front seat. She sniffed at Vernon and Betsy, gave me a quick lick on the hand in passing, then scampered over to Asa. He pulled a black toolbox out of the van, along with his Walmart supplies, and walked ahead with Vernon and Betsy, talking quietly with them.

"You see what I mean?" Ben whispered, leaning low to talk in my ear. "What if he's made some kind of deal with these hillbillies? These are the kind of people who steal babies to sell on the black market."

"If anyone tries to sell me on the black market, feel free to grab me and jack Asa's van," I said with a groan. "Apart from that, give it a rest, okay?" It took me forever to get the words out, because I was too focused on getting one foot in front of the other. Everything felt wrong, like all my limbs had been pulled out of joint. Finally, my legs just sort of melted away beneath me in a flood of heavy tingling.

"Mattie!" Ben grabbed me before my face hit the ground.

"My legs," I whispered. "They're gone." I drew in a halting breath. "My arms are going, too."

"Asa," shouted Ben, his voice tinged with panic as he pulled me against his chest and strode quickly after his brother.

I heard distant, urgent voices as Ben sped up. My world was oozing red, blood pulsing at the edges of my vision and thumping wetly in my ears. The pain that had been my constant companion for the last few months had evolved into a fanged beast, clawing for release. Then the darkness lifted, and I cried out as harsh light burned my eyes. We had entered one of the silk tents, and this one was lit with a few electric lanterns hanging from the frame above our heads. I writhed in Ben's grip as he laid me down on something soft and low to the ground. A cot. Vernon plopped down next to me and patted my leg. "No worries, darlin', we'll pull it right out. We'll work together." He grinned again, and I stared at the crooked brown mess of his front teeth.

Asa coiled a length of rope around my legs, his expression tight and his movements sharp. "Vernon's a pro, Mattie. You don't have to worry about him."

I looked at Vernon. "This is big. Really big."

"I know, darlin'," he said kindly. "Asa told me. Pretty sure I can take it."

"He's tough as a gator," Betsy said, but I could hear the worry that stained her words.

Asa sank down on my other side. "You're gonna be fine." He glanced down at my arms, which I had forgotten were there. "Do you want them by your sides or tied over your head?"

"I can't feel them, Asa." I swallowed. "Can you just—"

"Got it. I'm in charge."

My eyes fell shut in relief as Asa moved and shifted me, securing me to the cot while the pain devoured me.

"Is all this really necessary?" Ben asked.

Asa paused in his preparations. "How did you get it in there in the first place? This is some of the biggest, baddest magic in the whole fucking world. Didn't she tell you she needed to be secured for the transaction?"

"Um. No. She didn't tell me to secure her." Ben said it haltingly, in the way someone does when he's choosing every word carefully.

Asa picked up on it immediately. "What the fuck aren't you telling me?"

Ben sighed. "She didn't want to do it, okay? She was sick, and she had been for a long time. She didn't want anything to do with magic. She hasn't since last year, after you guys got me back."

"Say that again," Asa said slowly.

"I set it all up. I told her it was a romantic weekend in Chicago, hoping she would get on board when she realized how much money we could make. She didn't budge. But that conduit guy pulled a gun. He threatened to kill me if she didn't go through with it."

"She did it to save you, then?"

"No. I tried to save us both. I fought the guy. But then . . ."

I arched up as pain stabbed straight down my spine, and Asa tightened the ropes. "Spit it out." Each word was a bullet.

"He'd tied her to a massage table. And I hit him, and he just sort of fell on top of her."

"So it happened by accident—"

"Let me finish," Ben said loudly. I opened my eyes, and he gave me a look so intense that it reminded me of why I loved him. "Marcus had just told me that Zhong's people were going to find us, and if the magic wasn't hidden, they'd be able to track us." His mouth twisted, and it looked as if he were choking on his words. "So I made the decision."

Asa went very still. "Did she *agree* with that decision?"

"No," Ben blurted out, his voice clogged with tears. "She begged me not to do it. But I was so scared, and I-I-I . . . I had to decide, Asa. I did it for both of us."

"You did it for *both* of you," Asa said, slow and wooden. "After Mattie begged you not to."

"I know it sounds bad." Ben was pleading.

"She can't control it on the way in. And I'll bet you knew that." Asa's gaze was on my shoulder, but his pupils were dilated. Unfocused. The relic clinked and rattled in his grip. "It forces its way inside whether she wants it or not."

"But you have to understand—"

Asa jabbed his finger at the tent wall. "Wait over there." Then his face was suddenly over mine, and his fingertips traced a delicate path along my throat. "Mattie," he said, his voice firm. "Let me talk to Eve."

"I can't, Asa. I can't do this." It hurt to even think.

He leaned closer. "Who's in charge?"

"You're in charge, sir," I answered automatically, and it was like a lever had been pulled. I looked up at his crooked nose, his honey eyes. "You've got me."

The corner of his mouth twitched upward. "Yeah, baby. I've got you." His fingers went hard over my throat as another bolt of pain went through me. "Hang on for me, okay? Breathe slow and easy. I'm handling this."

I breathed while he pulled my T-shirt up and tied Vernon's hairy arm across my belly.

"Damn," muttered Vernon. "Girl needs to eat."

"She will," said Asa. "When we're done." He leaned over me again. "You're all sweaty, sir," I mumbled.

He chuckled. "No shit. You're killing me."

"It'll be worse for you when the magic is back in the relic." It would hurt him. It would feel like nails being hammered into his skin and heart and mind. "Maybe I shouldn't—"

His smile disappeared. "No. That's *not* for you to think about. Who's in control, Eve? Say it."

"You are, sir."

"Do you get to decide whether or not you release this magic?"

"No, sir."

"Who gets to decide?"

"You get to decide, sir."

"What the hell is this?" asked Ben. "Why are you making her talk like that? Who's Eve?"

Asa didn't take his eyes off me as he pointed to Ben. "Somebody make him shut the fuck up."

"She's my fiancée!"

"She's *mine*," Asa growled, hunched over me like a hungry wolf. I heard Betsy muttering to Ben, but I couldn't make out what she was saying. It hurt too much. The only thing that made sense was Asa. "You're gonna do this now," he said to me. And then he kissed me on the lips, soft and gentle, the most wonderful present in all the world.

"More, sir," I whispered. "Please."

His smile was a knife. "On the other side, baby. You gotta earn it."

I wanted to. I needed to. No future and no past, only this moment and the next, the hope that maybe, maybe I could feel his mouth on mine again. It was worth the risk. I parted my lips and let Asa slide a thick leather belt strap between my teeth. His expression was strained as he nodded at me, and like before, I wasn't sure if he was reassuring me or silently saying good-bye forever. In a daze of agony, I watched him open the locket and take out the knobby lump of gold. He placed it in the palm of Vernon's hand, and Betsy slid a rubber glove on over it, securing the relic to his skin. Already I could feel the pull of it sending fissures along the thin, weakened walls of the vault inside me. If I didn't let it out, it was going to burst right through and shatter me.

"Give it up, baby. Don't wait for it to take control. Open that door and let it out," Asa said, bracing himself above me with his hands on the metal frame of the cot, making sure he was the only thing I could see. "Give it all to me."

Yes, sir.

And I let go.

CHAPTER ELEVEN

I don't remember what happened next. I think maybe my mind simply refused to form a memory of what it felt like to allow the most powerful piece of sensing magic in the history of human existence to go tearing out of my badly weakened body. All I remember was surrendering to Asa, and then his hands on my cheeks and his voice in my ear, pulling me back.

It might have been seconds. It might have been several minutes. I've never tried to find out.

"Breathe for me, baby." The flutter of Asa's lips against my temple made me shiver.

"How'd I do?" My eyelids were too heavy to open, and the rest of me was jelly, completely relaxed but utterly unable to move.

"Fucking incredible," he said with a laugh, but there was something wrong with his voice. Tight. Filed to a point. "Rest here for a minute, okay? I'll come back for you."

"Where are you going?" I tried to open my eyes, but I was too thrashed.

"Gotta take care of something." There was a faint clinking sound, then the snap of Asa's toolbox closing.

"Yes, sir," I whispered. The realization was slowly sinking in—he'd gotten me through. The magic was back in the relic. And I was still *alive*.

A shout made me jerk with surprise and pull at the ropes securing me to the cot. It was immediately followed by the unmistakable sounds of a fight—grunts and shuffling, the dull smack of fists against flesh. Alarm pierced my little post-transaction cocoon of relief and peace, tightening my muscles and allowing me to open my eyes.

I was alone in the tent. Just beyond the gently fluttering silk flap people were yelling and gathering around. I could see flashes of pant legs and skirts and work boots and sandals. Gracie was barking, deep and ferocious.

"Hey!" I shouted feebly. "Someone?" I squirmed, but my wrists were tied together and fastened to the head of the cot. My ankles were fettered in a similar manner at the foot of the cot, and a long length of rope had been wrapped around my body, making it impossible for me to raise more than my head off the musty canvas. "Hey!"

The tent flap lifted, giving me a glimpse of two struggling figures in the grass. They were surrounded by onlookers, some of whom appeared to be cheering, waving their fists. My view of the scene was almost immediately blocked out by Betsy, though, who came bustling forward, rolling her eyes. "We forgot all about you in here, you poor little thing," she muttered, kneeling at my side.

"What's happening?"

Her dark-gray eyes flicked toward the tent flap before returning to me. She began to work the ropes, untying my wrists first. "Did you think he would stand fer that?" She grunted and shook her head. "This is why Vern and I came out here in the first place. Some people's just happy to use us. Don't see us as anything but commodities."

"I'm not following." I winced and rubbed at my wrists. The ropes hadn't been tight, but I must have strained against them during the transaction, because my skin was red and raw. The sight snapped me into the now. "How's Vernon? Is he okay?" This magic had broken so many people, and I didn't want another on my conscience.

Betsy offered a tremulous smile. "Got some of the boys to carry him to our winter trailer, where he could have a real bed fer the night. He's gonna be all right. Like I told you, he's tough as they come. That was some transaction, though." Her chuckle was warped by the tears that glinted in her eyes. "Had me pretty scared there for a minute or two."

I stared up at the ceiling of the tent, listening to the sounds of the brawl outside, as Betsy unwound the rope from my body. "Who's fighting out there?" Misgiving stirred inside my strangely hollow-feeling chest, unsteady and faltering.

Betsy arched one snowy eyebrow. "Maybe you'd like to stay in here and rest like Asa told you."

"Oh, crap." I pushed myself up to standing, and Betsy rose with me, catching me as I nearly toppled backward over the cot. With her at my side, I clumsily pushed my way through the tent flap and squinted between the legs of the people standing in front of me. It confirmed my fear. "No!"

The two people directly in front of me, a gangly red-haired kid who looked like he couldn't be more than seventeen and a middle-aged woman with black hair so long that it nearly reached her knees, turned at the frantic sound of my voice. In the space they created, I caught a full view of the drama playing out in the grass.

Ben was lying on his back, his face a bloody mess. Asa, whose cheek was bruised and whose knuckles were split and bleeding, was straddling him, landing punch after punch. Ben thrashed and tried to block, but Asa was utterly merciless. His face was rigid with rage.

"Stop it," I shrieked. "Asa! *Please!*"

Asa froze midpunch and turned his head. His eyes met mine, and whatever he read in my expression made his jaw clench. He shoved himself off Ben and got to his feet, staggering a little in the thick grass. Then Asa spun around before I had the chance to say anything and pushed his way through the ragtag crowd that had gathered to watch the excitement. Gracie trotted after him. They were out of sight in only a few seconds, sinking into the darkness. My heart hammering, I took a few halting steps toward Ben, who had rolled onto his side and was propped up on an elbow, spitting blood onto the ground.

I stared down at him. "Why?"

Betsy appeared at my shoulder. "Told you why already. Asa weren't going to stand for it. You shouldn't stand for it, neither."

"I'm sorry, Mattie," Ben said thickly.

"Can someone get us some ice or something?" My voice was nearly an octave higher than usual, quavering with horror and the strange unsteadiness inside of me that had replaced the stuffed-to-bursting agony of the Sensilo magic.

The long-haired woman gently shoved the redheaded boy in the shoulder. "Terrence, help the lady. This isn't her fault, and she's one of us. Go fetch some ice and clean cloths if we got 'em."

The boy took off, jogging toward the gathering of trailers across the road from the tents. The rest of the onlookers—to call them an eccentric bunch would be an understatement—were slowly clearing out, tossing me curious looks over their shoulders as they trudged back to their trailers and tents, melting back into the night from which they'd emerged. I shuddered as the wind tossed my hair, and awkwardly sank to my knees next to Ben. "Are you okay?"

"I think he broke my nose," he said with a groan. Blood was indeed flowing freely from the swollen mess at the center of his face. "What the hell, Mattie? He attacked me out of nowhere. I was just defending myself, I swear."

Betsy made a skeptical noise in her throat. "And I'm Hillary Clinton. I practically had to hold you back to keep you from busting in on them during the transaction."

Ben peered up at me with bloodshot eyes. "He kissed you. You asked him to do it again."

Splinter

Heat bloomed across my cheeks. "It was just—"

"Don't you dare feel like you need to explain yourself, darlin'," said Betsy sharply, but then her face relaxed into a kindly smile. "Best sniffer-reliquary work I ever witnessed. Once Vern recovers, I'm sure he'll say the same. That's how it's supposed to be but rarely is."

I had nothing to say to that—I already knew it was true. Whatever Asa and I were, it worked when it came down to business. I offered absolute trust, and in return he offered absolute care.

And now he had disappeared, and his absence was gnawing on my bones. Was he still angry at me, too? Yes, he had put all of that aside when I needed him, but I wasn't foolish enough to believe that everything was settled.

Not when he'd just pulverized his brother, my fiancé . . . I glanced down at my engagement ring, a reminder of the decision I had to make. The stress twisted like a rusty nail in my chest. I frowned and rubbed at the spot.

"You okay, darlin'?" Betsy asked, leaning so she could look at my face. "You need to rest. That kind of transaction'd take the piss out of anyone."

Terrence came running over with a bundle of ice wrapped in a dingy gray dish towel, a few more dishrags clutched in his other fist. I accepted both, but when I moved toward Ben, he put his hand out. "I can do it myself."

"But—"

"Give me some space, for God's sake." He snatched a dishrag from my grip and pressed it to his nose, letting out another strangled groan.

I gritted my teeth and tossed the ice pack in his lap. "Take all the space you want." I pushed myself to my feet and turned to Betsy. "Where did he go?"

"Nearest running water's a stream 'bout two hundred yards into the trees." With a faint smile, she aimed her chin at the woods, then leaned into her tent and grabbed a flashlight, which she tucked into my hand. "Might've wanted to clean himself up."

Or maybe he needed to get as far from the Sensilo relic and the magic of this camp as possible. I set out marching on wobbly legs across the field. My anger toward Ben temporarily tamped down my anxiety about what I was walking toward. Was Ben mad at me, after he had created this situation? I had only done what I had to in order to survive. Yes, I had brought Asa back into our lives, but would Ben have preferred that I die in agony while he watched helplessly? That had been pretty darn close to happening, actually, and still he seemed more miffed about Asa's and my behavior during the transaction.

He hadn't shown any relief that I was alive. But he *had* been bleeding profusely at the time, so maybe that wasn't entirely fair.

I tripped over a clump of grass and nearly fell on my face. "Stupid grass. Stupid Ward brothers," I grumbled as I shone the flashlight ahead of me, where the inky darkness of the woods awaited. Had Asa really gone in there? I paused and turned to look back at the camp, a collection of glowing tents and squares of light within trailer windows, laid out under a bright gibbous moon. I could go back. My entire body was aching. Betsy would give me a place to sleep it off. And if I stayed on this path, I was risking getting my head bitten off by a man who did ornery better than almost anyone I knew.

But I kept trudging between the trees, following a narrow footpath toward the distant glint of moonlight on water. "Asa?" I called as I got closer.

All I got in response was a soft yip from Gracie, but it was enough. I headed toward the noise and ended up on the bank of a swollen creek. Gracie came bounding over, her tongue lolling and her stumpy tail wagging. She pressed her wriggling body against my legs and nosed at my hands until I scratched between her ears. I knelt to give her a hug. "Where is he, girl?"

She licked my neck and set off as soon as I released her, winding her way along a slippery, muddy path, over a few fallen tree trunks and through a few patches of brambles. My bare arms were stinging by the time we reached a place where the trees thinned out. I aimed my flashlight beam at a dark shape rising from the edge of the water but turned off the beam just as quickly.

I had a thing about seeing Asa with his shirt off. It just always felt like too much.

"Didn't take you long to get back on your feet," he said as he wrung out his black T-shirt and pulled it back over his head.

"Well. You know me," I said breezily, then laughed.

Now I was sorry I had turned off the flashlight, because I wanted to see the look on Asa's face. He was staring at the water. "Bet you're gonna feel it tomorrow." He ran his hands through his dripping hair. It looked like he'd dipped the entire upper half of his body in the creek. "But you must've thought coming all the way out here to lecture me was worth the effort, so go ahead." He gave me a sidelong glance. "Let's get this done."

Irritation tore through me, obliterating any concern I had for him. "What the heck, Asa? Why do you always assume the worst of me?" My voice cracked as he turned toward me. "Ever since we met, you've been more interested in your arrogant beliefs about small-town, close-minded Mattie—"

"And you never assumed anything at all about me."

"So, what? Is this payback or something?"

"Everyone makes assumptions. It's what humans do."

My fists balled in my sweaty, mud-streaked baggy T-shirt. "Semantics!" I shrieked.

"Do you know what 'semantics' means?"

"*Argh!* You are such a—" My big finish ended with a strangled sob. I tripped over my own feet as I turned to storm away, and landed with a splat in a muddy patch beside the trail. Expecting to hear a derisive laugh, I began to push myself up, only to feel Asa's arms slide around me and guide me to my feet.

He didn't let go once he'd steadied me. Instead, he pulled my back to his chest, holding me as I struggled halfheartedly, driven more by pride than by an actual desire to get away from him. The truth was, this was the safest I'd felt in hours. The water from Asa's shirt soaked my back as he laid his chin on the top of my head and whispered, "I'm sorry."

I blinked at the darkness as his arms tightened around me. "Say that again."

His chuckle sent a shiver through me. "You heard me."

"Care to elaborate?"

"Not really."

I closed my eyes as his fingers rose to encircle my throat, and I didn't resist as he tipped my head back so it leaned against the hard curve of his shoulder. He looked down at me, his eyes black in the darkness. "It's easier when I can put you in a box," he said. "Can you get that?"

"Yeah. That actually makes perfect sense." I'd done the same to him over the past year, trying to fence him in along with the entire magical underworld. And it had nearly destroyed me.

"Why didn't you tell me what Ben had done to you?" he murmured. "Why did you let me think—"

"Why did I *let* you? Like it's my fault you decided to be a jerkface?"

"I never would have let him in the van with you if I'd known what he did." His voice had gone rough and his body tight, as if he were tempted to go find Ben and start round two.

I gave a weary sigh. "It was just such a mess. I don't even know how to sort it all out."

Asa twisted my engagement ring around my finger. It was loose after all the weight I had lost, ready to slide right off, but he didn't try. "You'll be able to figure it out now that you're not moments away from death," he said wryly.

"Thank you," I whispered. "You saved my life."

"Did you think I was gonna let you die?"

"Not for a moment."

His smile made my stomach swoop. Even in the dark, I could see that it was his rare, sweet smile, the one usually reserved for Gracie and no one else. "*Dammit*, Mattie. I hate apologizing."

"Now there's a shocker."

"But I think I'm gonna have to do it again."

"Why?"

I gasped as his lips descended on mine. This kiss wasn't the soft, sweet touch I had felt in the tent; there was a strength to it, a command, that made me rise to my tiptoes and tilt my head back, offering him more. My fingers curled into his biceps, my fingernails digging into his skin as his tongue slid along mine. His arms were steel around me, one hand on my ribs, one clasping my chin, anchoring our mouths together. He was in charge, and I was totally good with that, because he was totally good at *this*.

When I reached up to slide my fingers into his hair, though, he caught my wrist and pinned it to my body, keeping me wrapped up tight. Contained. Tied up just like he'd tied me to that cot tonight. Under his control. And instead of being disappointing, it was somehow more erotic, frustration and curiosity and trepidation and need all mixing together, melting my insides with its heat. I could feel his growing arousal pressed against my back. I craved each second of it.

I was kissing Asa Ward.

Not Eve. *Me.* Kissing Asa Ward.

Clutching at his arm while the diamond from my engagement ring left its imprint in his skin.

The unsteady feeling inside me suddenly gave way like one of those melting ice shelves in the Arctic. A bright, blinding blade of pain twisted in the new emptiness inside me. I whimpered.

That was nothing compared to Asa's reaction. He tore himself from me and staggered back with a hoarse curse, then turned and retched violently into a bramblebush. I stared as his back arched and his body heaved, as Gracie whined and let out a high-pitched bark. "Asa?"

I pushed away the ridiculous impulse to feel hurt about the fact that kissing me had made Asa throw up in the bushes. Was it an aftereffect of the magic that had been there? Could he still feel it somehow? "Are you okay?"

He held up a finger as he spit on the ground, then walked stiffly over to the creek bank, where he dropped to his knees and brought some water to his mouth in his cupped palm. After spitting again, he slowly got to his feet.

Even in the mostly dark, I could read the horror on his face. "Ben said you had been sick for a while," he said slowly. "I assumed it was because you had been trying to freelance solo, but he said you hadn't touched magic until he—" His fists clenched. "He could have killed you. This almost killed you." He grimaced. "This *still* might kill you," he whispered.

"Asa, you're scaring me."

"How long has it hurt?"

"It's really nothing—"

"How *long*?" he shouted.

"Since I got back from Vegas," I said lamely.

"Why the fuck didn't you call me?"

"I just thought it was . . ." I gave him a sheepish look. "Emotional."

"Fuck." He wiped his sweaty face on his wet sleeve. "This is all my fucking fault."

"Well, if we want to argue semantics—"

"It's been in there this whole time," he muttered, staring at my chest like one might stare at a rattlesnake, which frayed the very last of my nerves.

"Would you please just tell me what you're talking about?"

"The Strikon relic."

"For the last time, it was the Sensilo relic," I snapped, wincing as the knife turned yet again. "Ben took it from my Grandpa and—"

"I felt it when I touched you. I *knew* that's what it was," he continued as if I hadn't said a word. "Shit. I brushed it off. Because . . . *fuck.*" He braced one hand on a tree and ran the other through his hair, which had dried enough to stand on end. "Mattie. We have to fix this."

"I don't want to do anything but sleep." I held on to a tree as I stepped carefully onto the trail, then I stumbled forward, clutching at my head, which felt too full to balance on my shoulders.

He caught up to me, took me by the arms, and shook me a little. "We got the original Sensilo magic out, but that's not the only thing in your vault." He ducked his head, trying to catch my eye, but I stubbornly stared over his shoulder. "Goddammit, look at me! Last summer, when Jack was shot during that transaction . . . it interrupted the flow of the Strikon magic back into its relic, and it must have fractured the magic. There's a splinter of it still inside you." His fingers were bruising my skinny biceps. His face was taut with pain, maybe from the contact with my skin.

"Asa, I'm all right," I said in a high, brittle voice. "Really."

"No, Mattie," he said quietly. "You're dying."

CHAPTER TWELVE

"That can't be true," I said. "You would have known it immediately after Jack was killed. You tried to sense it! You said all of it was out!"

He shook his head. "Do you have any idea how much Strikon magic was in the room that night? This splinter was like a needle poke while I was being run through with a sword or three."

I flinched at the reminder of just how much the magic hurt him. "And once we were at that abandoned mall . . . Reza was there. And you were wearing the relic."

"I never had the chance to figure it out." He left the rest of it unsaid. Because I had refused to go with him. Because I had sent him away. "And because I didn't detect it, that goddamn shard of magic has been snagged inside you ever since." He let me go and turned his face to the sky, his hands clawed at his sides. *"Fuuuuck,"* he roared. He whirled around, his eyes wild.

I stepped between him and the poor, innocent tree he'd drawn back his fist to punch. "Your hands are already pretty torn up."

His fist dropped to his side. "Didn't you wonder?" he snarled, and I realized that by blocking his target, I had *become* his target.

"It didn't once occur to you that magic could be causing your health problems?"

I shrugged. "After seeing a few specialists, I did find a medication that helped a little."

"Yeah? What was it? Some happy pill that numbed you up?"

The longer I had known Asa, the more attractive I had found his angular face, with its crooked nose and deep-set brown eyes, but right then, he seemed so ugly that I had to turn away. "Just because you're mister I-only-eat-fair-trade-organic-vegetables-farmed-by-Tibetan-monks—"

"Better than using pills as a crutch."

"Screw you, Asa." I blundered through the woods toward the camp.

"If you'd just faced what was right in front of you, you could have figured this out months ago," Asa shouted from behind me. In the next instant, Gracie sailed over a tree trunk and landed on the trail in front of me, then slowed down, blocking my path.

"You little traitor," I wailed. "What happened to girls sticking together?"

Asa caught up with me, and we walked silently toward Betsy and Vernon's tent. I had nowhere else to go, really—all I knew was that I wasn't about to ask if I could sleep in Asa's van. On top of that, my sweats were covered in burs, and the front of my T-shirt was splattered with mud. Compared to me, Asa actually looked pretty put together, which made me even more angry. I sped up, but seeing as his legs were about a foot longer than mine, I wasn't presenting him with much of a challenge.

And then I had nowhere to run, because as the wind lifted the tent flap on Vernon and Betsy's silk haven, I caught sight of Ben sitting on the cot, gingerly dabbing blood from the corner of his mouth. I came to a dead halt. "Okay. What now?"

Asa inclined his head toward the trailers and then walked toward them, obviously assuming I would follow. He knocked on the door of one that looked like a giant, rusty steel egg. The door opened just a crack and Betsy's face appeared. The two of them spoke in murmured tones for a few minutes while I fidgeted behind Asa, feeling like a child. Finally, Betsy disappeared back inside and Asa turned to me. "Vernon's out of commission for the night. Betsy's not gonna let him do any conduit work for at least twenty-four hours."

"Are there any other conduits here who could do it?" I was guessing every single person in this camp was a natural.

"Not as strong as he is, and for this, we need the best. Vernon actually has some control over the way magic flows through him, and we'll need it. I want to pull the splinter out of you gradually instead of yanking it out like a superconductor would."

I looked down at my chest, my small breasts hidden by my baggy T-shirt. "Either way, this isn't going to be fun," I said quietly.

He moved closer. "Want me to check on it? Now that I know what I'm looking for . . ."

"Okay."

"I'm gonna stick my hand under your shirt now."

"Wow, what a gentleman. Usually you just do it."

"Yeah, but I figured, after what Ben did . . ." His hands balled into fists for a moment, then relaxed again. "You ready?"

Not really. "Go ahead."

He moved close enough for me to count the beads of sweat along his upper lip, glinting in the light from Betsy and Vernon's trailer window. His fingertips skimmed along my stomach, making it tremble, and straight up the center of me, until he laid his palm between my breasts. I tried to breathe slowly, but his touch made my skin feel supercharged, as if I were about to be struck by lightning. When he bowed his head and closed his eyes, I was glad, because I didn't have to guard my facial expression so carefully. I leaned back against the trailer and let my eyelids fall shut.

"Found you," he whispered. "Nasty little fucker."

"How come it made you nearly puke a little while ago, but now you can be close to me without being sick?"

"Well, the fact that I had my tongue halfway down your throat probably made some difference," he said drily.

"Apart from that," I snapped.

"I think your vault is broken, honey."

"What?"

Asa's hand slid back down my stomach, and maybe I was imagining it, but it really seemed to move slower than it needed to. "Just a theory, but when we were interrupted midtransaction, I think your vault door was still open, and the splinter sort of jammed in there, not letting it close completely. Now the door can't lock, not really."

"So how come I don't feel it all the time?"

His mouth twisted as he thought about it. "You know how sometimes a car door looks closed, but sometimes it's not? It's closed enough to make it hard to tell, but the damn light on the dash keeps flashing red?"

"Yeah. So it closes, but it's not latched."

"And sometimes it swings open. My guess is that it happens when you're stressed, or maybe feeling strong emotions?"

Like just now, when he was kissing me. It had happened the moment I'd focused on my engagement ring, and the guilt had risen hard and fast, knocking me off-kilter. "Maybe. But sometimes it just happens out of the blue. Like when I was having my wedding dress fitted."

Asa bowed his head so I couldn't see his expression. "We won't know if the damage is permanent until we get the magic out of you. And that needs to happen as soon as possible." He reached down and stroked Gracie's neck, and she leaned against him with a weary *grumph*. "But in the meantime, I think we both need to get some sleep."

He sounded as if he were about to collapse. Now that we were out of the darkness of the woods, I could see the purple circles beneath his eyes—and the ugly bruising on his cheek and along his jaw.

"I probably shouldn't ask this, but who threw the first punch?"

Asa began walking toward his van, which was parked at the edge of the midway, in sight of Betsy and Vernon's silk tent. "I did."

"Why?"

"Are you fucking kidding me?"

Asa was better at storming away than I was. I had to jog to keep up. "Were you just ticked that you were wrong about everything, and took it out on him?"

He whirled toward me so fast that I nearly fell on my butt. His face was alight with rage. "I'm *ticked*, Mattie, because my brother is apparently the kind of guy who can listen to the woman he claims to love *begging* him not to force one of the biggest pieces of magic in the world inside of her body, and he can still do it anyway," he shouted.

"Some of us are trying to get some shut-eye," yelled someone in a trailer a few rows away.

Asa's mouth snapped shut, but then his glare landed on me again. "What I want to know is how come *you're* not pissed? I know you want this life, Mattie, but are you really willing to let him rape you to keep it?"

"Ben would never rape me!"

"He violated your body. Not only did he *not* get your permission— he did it while you begged him not to. If that's not rape, it's a close cousin."

I blinked fast as a strange, heavy pressure made it hard to breathe. "I can't think about this right now," I said hoarsely.

"When *will* you think about it?"

"When I'm ready." I took a step backward.

"In other words, never?" He stepped in front of me as I turned to run. "That's kinda your thing, isn't it? Not thinking?"

"I'm not an idiot, Asa!"

"No shit, Mattie. But your head is so deep in the sand that I'm surprised you haven't struck oil."

"Just because I don't constantly mull over every little thing that bothers me—"

"You do, though. That's why you need Eve. You're all in the mix with things you can't control, but when it comes to stuff you might have to make a decision about? The things that might require hard, painful choices? You don't think at all. You just pretend they don't exist."

"And you're still arrogant enough to believe you couldn't possibly be wrong after being *completely* wrong about almost *everything* about this situation!"

"Look me in the face and tell me I'm wrong about this, then. Go ahead."

"Well, I'll give you this—I certainly wasn't thinking a few minutes ago when I kissed you!" I sidestepped him and nearly tripped over Gracie, who had planted herself right next to him.

Asa chuckled, dry and hard. "Right. And my guess is that it came after nine months of trying so hard not to think of kissing me that you probably blamed *that* for the damn chest pains." His eyes widened a bit when he saw my face. "Oh, fuck me, I'm right."

"I hate you, Asa." I pushed past Gracie and headed up the midway lane.

"You gonna go curl up with Ben?" he called after me. "Dream about your minivan and your two-point-five kids and the man who doesn't deserve to fucking say your name, let alone marry you?"

I just kept walking. A moment later, I heard the van door slam, and when I looked over my shoulder, Asa and Gracie were gone. Shaking with sobs I refused to let out, I ducked into one of the little shacks along the midway—the one marked "The Woman Who Ate Baltimore." Inside was an oversized chaise set on a square patch of peeling linoleum laid over the dirt. I shined my flashlight on the chaise. It was made of faded pink velvet that smelled like cheap, flowery perfume, but it looked clean enough, and I was so grateful that I collapsed on it without hesitation.

No way was I crawling back to Asa's van.

And no way was I crawling back to Ben.

So I laid my mud-flecked, tangled head of hair across a gold-tasseled pillow and curled around the shard of pain inside me. I trembled with the bruises Asa had left with his words. I ached with their brutal truth. I flinched at how stupid and childish I felt. I shriveled with the shame of how I could have faced all of this earlier, and yet I hadn't. I was just like my mom, a happy face on all the time, pretending the bad stuff didn't even exist.

Now I had no choice but to take a cold, hard look at it in the light.

"Tomorrow," I whispered. Then I switched off the flashlight and plunged myself into darkness.

CHAPTER THIRTEEN

I awoke with a start and found myself staring into the face of the woman with superlong black hair who had told the redheaded teenager to get Ben some ice. "Good morning," she said.

I peered over her shoulder to see a gray dawn. "Is it?"

"We rise early here. Got to get ready for visitors." She set an honest-to-God tea tray next to me as I sat up, complete with a little pitcher of cream and a plate of toasted english muffins.

"You sure know how to treat them," I murmured.

She grinned, revealing straight white teeth. "I'm Roberta."

"Mattie."

"I know. You're the talk of the camp."

"Already?" I rubbed at my temples. My head was still pounding, and I'd spent the night in a restless doze jam-packed with dreams of Asa and Ben beating the crap out of each other as I lay tied to my grandpa's hospital bed. "I guess we did make quite an entrance."

She snorted and began to butter half of an english muffin. "Not to mention that most of us heard your little lovers' quarrel."

I frowned. "But Ben and I didn't—oh." My cheeks bloomed with heat. "Asa and I aren't involved that way." The kiss in the woods had been a crazy release in the aftermath of an intense transaction, and it was ridiculous to give it more importance or thought than that.

Roberta poured steaming tea into a chipped mug and handed it to me. "None of my business, kiddo. You've obviously been through a lot." She looked over my frizzy hair, my dirty, bur-spangled clothes, the mud-caked shoes I'd slipped off last night. "I've got some extra clothes you can wear if you want to change. Might be a little big, but they're clean."

She was wearing work boots, a long skirt with some kind of kooky parrot print, and a SpongeBob SquarePants T-shirt. And yet, she looked a hell of a lot better than I did. "I'd be grateful."

"Eat up first."

I sipped at the tea and sighed at its warmth, then happily accepted a buttered english muffin. "So, this is a kind of carnival?"

"Yep. We pick up and move every few weeks in the spring, summer, and fall, and in the winter we find a place to bed down. We've been here since December, but we'll be moving on soon."

"And people actually come?"

She gave me a sly smile. "People flock to us. We show them things they could never see anywhere else. We give them an experience. Of course, their memories of it are only a haze afterward. It's a way to make a living without working within the system."

"The regular system, or the magical world?"

"Both. The former is easier than the latter—a bit of Knedas juice works every time we get a nosy sheriff or journalist—but we've managed the latter pretty well. Headsmen more or less leave us alone so long as we don't get too big or loud, and we stick together, which keeps the bosses away. We're stronger than any of us would be out on our own."

"How long have you all been doing this?"

"Oh." She chuckled. "I joined in '86, and it had been going strong for decades before that. We come from all different places, all walks of life." She smiled. "I walked away from a teaching job because this just felt more fulfilling, more fun, more free. Others need to escape whatever hell they've been living. People come and go, but the carnival keeps rolling. Must be nearly two hundred of us right now, but it'll grow through the summer. Shrinks in the winter, of course."

"I was in too much pain last night to see what it looks like, but my fiancé was in awe. It must be a pretty spectacular sight."

"A glamour like no other," she said with a full mouth. "Everyone contributes in their own way. All of us Knedas keep it strong, and we also run the freak show." She gestured at the booth. "I'm the Fat Lady."

I eyed her very ordinary physique. "The one who ate Baltimore?"

"The very same. I'm a luscious eight hundred pounds in custom-made lingerie." She did a little shimmy with her shoulders. "I never get tired of the attention. Or the spending money." She reached under the chaise and pulled out a big urn with the word "Tips" painted on its surface.

"And it really works on people?"

"Every once in a while a little kid'll see through to the real me. But no one believes them when they try to tell Mommy and Daddy that the Fat Lady isn't fat. And besides me, we've got Tom—he's the Three-Headed Man—and Nora, the Lady with Living Tattoos. Doesn't have a single tattoo in reality, but you should see people scream when she makes them see her bird tattoos flapping their wings! Letisha's a fortune-teller—she's not a Knedas, mind you. She's an intention sensor, and you have to see her in action. She's so good at reading a person that anyone with anything to hide in this camp knows better than to pass within twenty feet of her."

I suppressed the urge to ask what Letisha looked like so I could avoid her, too.

"There's also Burt, another Knedas. I'm the Woman Who Ate Baltimore, but he's the Man Who'll Eat *Anything*—he gets people to toss their goods at him, thinking he won't swallow them." She bowed her head to stifle a snicker. "Boy, they howl when they see him eating their iPhones and earrings and wallets!"

"But he doesn't actually?"

"Nah. That's what he makes them see, though."

"I bet people aren't too happy about that. How does he not get beaten up?"

"He warns 'em ahead of time, so they know they've handed over their stuff in spite of that. But we've also got sensors like Terrence and Adrian to pick up when someone's too upset about it, and Ekstazos like Jimmy and Quentin to soothe hurt and angry feelings. Jimmy's head of this camp. General manager, you could say. And with one handshake from him, you'd forgive anyone anything."

I finished my tea and held out my cup for another pour—I was so thirsty. "So people just go home without their wallets and phones?"

She shrugs. "We usually give back the wallets, minus the cash. Can't really use the credit cards and such unless we want to draw attention to ourselves. Phones are a good business, though."

So they were all thieves. I didn't point this out to her—she seemed well aware and pretty at peace with it, plus it felt good to have someone be nice to me. "If it's so lucrative, why do you guys . . ." I took a sizable gulp of searing tea to avoid completing the sentence.

Roberta chuckled. "Why do we live like this? Lots of reasons. Some I already told you."

"To avoid calling too much attention to yourselves."

She nodded. "But also, it means freedom. Who says we have to own a lot of things? Who says we have to live in one place? Those of us who stay—we don't care about that stuff. Who needs a lawn when I've got a whole field of wildflowers to look out on every morning? Who needs a whole house when all I need is a bed and a square of kitchen counter? Who needs running water when I've got a stream that runs crystal clear? Not me, I'll tell you that."

"I guess it does sound kind of freeing."

"Freedom, kiddo, comes in all kinds of forms. We all have to choose which kind is worth fighting for."

I choked down the last of my english muffin. "I never really thought about that."

"Never too late to start." She stood up with the tray, but left a plate behind, complete with a few Smucker's grape jellies and another whole toasted muffin. "My trailer's the one with the herb garden. Come find me when you're ready for a change of clothes."

I took a long time to eat that last english muffin, savoring every bite and the quiet that came with it. My vault door must have been mostly closed, because I could barely feel the splinter of relentlessly powerful Strikon magic buried somewhere in my chest.

Last night, Asa had told me I was dying. That I had been dying since last summer.

And somehow, that felt like the least threatening and disturbing thing he'd said. *This* was a solvable problem. All we had to do was wait until Vernon recovered from last night, and then we could pull the splinter out. I'd be magic-free by midnight, and I could head home and get back to normal.

I bowed my head and squeezed my eyes shut as the knife turned. "Can't be soon enough for me," I whispered through clenched teeth. I picked up my plate and slid my feet into my damp, muddy shoes.

The midway lane was still relatively quiet. A few people were in their booths, setting up, but the rest of the camp was bustling. People were outside their trailers, many grilling breakfast under tattered, sun-faded awnings, others lounging in flimsy lawn chairs and sipping coffee. Laughter and conversation buzzed merrily, and I knew it as soon as I heard it—this was the sound of people living their chosen lifestyles, banded together and free of the judgment of the rest of society.

I scanned the trailers for the one with the herb garden. A long row of at least twenty porta-potties marked the edge of camp. I bit my lip—I'd need a stop there once I had some acceptable clothes on. I was already drawing curious stares as I squished my way past Betsy and Vernon's silk tent. I hoped Ben was still sleeping inside. I wasn't ready to face him.

But because fate seems to hate me sometimes, just as I thought I was in the clear, I heard Ben call, "Mattie" as he stepped out of the tent. His unbuttoned shirt was dotted and smeared with dried blood, as were his khakis. His face was horribly bruised and swollen, and he sported a few butterfly bandages over cuts on his cheeks and just above his left eye.

I stopped walking and turned around with my empty plate. "Oh, hey."

"Hey," he said as he approached. "I was worried about you last night." He looked back at the tent. "I tried to wait up, but I was pretty thrashed."

"I needed to be alone."

"I was actually stupid enough to wonder if you . . . never mind."

I sighed. "You wondered if I was with Asa."

He glanced at my ring finger. "Can you blame me?"

I turned around and kept walking.

He took a few long steps to catch up with me. "Mattie, please. You have no idea how awful I feel about putting you through all this. You have every right to hate me."

"I don't hate you. But I wonder if I should."

"If you did, I would understand. You have to know, though, how much I love you. I'll do anything to make this up to you."

"Then I need you to give me time, because I have a lot to think about." *And I can't think about it yet.* The splinter pricked at my chest wall.

"You can have all the time you want. Once we get back to Sheboygan, I'll move out if you want to, or you can move back to your parents'—"

Just the thought of the mess I'd be facing when I got back was enough to nearly drive me to my knees. "Stop it," I said hoarsely. "I can't deal with this now."

"Mattie, you're going to have to deal with it. If we get an early start, we'll be home by midnight." Ben paused and looked across the field. Unlike last night, he seemed to be seeing it for what it was, maybe because of the lingering pain of his wounds. "This isn't really our kind of scene, is it?"

"They're happier than we are," I murmured, watching Betsy grin as she accepted a heaping plate of bacon from a portly dude sporting the bushiest beard I'd ever seen.

"We were happy, Mattie. Have you forgotten that?"

"Was it real, Ben? Or was it a glamour, like the one that covers this camp?"

"Are you really suggesting our whole relationship was fake?"

I shook my head. "It was real for me."

"I get it. I screwed up so badly that I deserve your worst. We'll have to think of something to tell your parents if we postpone or cancel the wedding, though."

My parents had already sunk thousands into this wedding. Dad had invited all his business associates. It was going to be totally embarrassing to call it all off. It would affect more than just me and Ben. Suddenly I felt as if I were on a speeding train that would be hard to stop. "Ben, I have something I need to take care of here first, and I can't leave until it's done."

"With Asa?" His tone had turned hard.

"Yeah, but . . ."

"No, I trust you, Mattie. And I'm going to earn yours back." He drew himself up and squared his shoulders. "I'm going to prove myself to you." Before I could move away, he planted a firm kiss on my forehead. "Love you."

He walked toward the tent and I hustled over to the trailers, fighting the urge to childishly wipe my forehead. After a quick detour to the porta-potty, I spotted Roberta's trailer almost immediately. It was positioned along the outer ring farthest from the midway, and an overflowing window garden jutted from its side. The camper itself was covered with blue tarps that were strapped to its undercarriage, maybe to shield a leaky roof. Sparing me the effort of knocking, Roberta opened the door and held it wide, allowing me to step inside. She took the dish from me and pointed toward a neatly made bed, upon which sat a pair of denim capris, a belt, and a gray T-shirt that said, "'I saw that.'—Karma."

"Figured you might not want my underwear," she said with the raspy chuckle of a recovering smoker.

"I've actually got a few pairs in the van." As soon as I said it, I realized that fetching them would involve dealing with Asa, and decided to go commando.

"I'll give you some privacy," she said. "We're opening at eleven, so I'm going to help set up." She headed down a set of rickety portable wooden steps, letting the metal screen door swing shut behind her.

I shed my muddy sweats and donned the capris, which were about three sizes too big. The belt was a lifesaver, or else I would have been clutching at my waist all day. After I'd stripped off my muddy T-shirt, I looked down at my scrawny torso, frowning as I ran my fingers along the bumps of my ribs. The magic had been eating me alive for months. Once it was gone, would I be healthy again? I'd forgotten what that even felt like. I had vague memories, sure—I'd always loved my body and what it could do. I'd loved the way Ben had made it feel when we were together. I'd loved pleasure. But when I tried to summon the memory of what it had actually felt like, I couldn't.

I pulled the T-shirt on. Feeling too raw to emerge just yet, I sat on the bed and stared out a window on the other side of the camper, which had an unobstructed view of the vast field beyond the camp.

A tall, lean form was slowly walking across it, a gray dog cavorting beside him. Asa and Gracie. He had probably found a solitary space in which to do his tai chi. I wondered how long he'd been up, and whether the alone time had helped. He was too far away for me to see whether the circles under his eyes were any lighter.

"I shouldn't care," I whispered.

I shifted uncomfortably, realizing that going commando was not all it was cracked up to be, pun intended. "Sadly, this would probably be a good time to fetch my underwear." With yet another exhausted sigh, I gathered up my filthy clothes and carried them out of the camper. I called out my thanks to Roberta and trudged up the road toward Asa's van. He was cutting across the field diagonally and would reach it just before I would. Maybe we could make the interaction brief and painless.

A running figure on the other side of the van drew my eye, and I looked over to see Ben burst from the midway lane and sprint toward the van. He had Asa's black toolbox cradled under his arm like a football. I stumbled to a stop as I watched him run across the road and dive into the back of the van, which shuddered a little as he moved around inside it. I glanced over to Asa, whose head was down as he traversed the thick, knee-high spring grass tangling around his ankles. He hadn't seen Ben.

But Gracie had. She let out a growl that echoed across the field and took off at a dead sprint, racing toward the van as its brake lights flared.

"Oh my God," I whispered as the van lurched into motion. The dirty clothes fell from my limp hands.

"Gracie!" Asa was running, too, now. Screaming her name while he watched her barrel toward the van as it picked up speed.

"Ben," I shrieked, my arms up and waving. I raced up the road behind him, hoping he would see me in his side mirrors.

He didn't slow. Neither did Gracie. There was an ominous thump. Ben didn't stop. Some of the carnies chased him up the road until he rounded a bend and disappeared, but I didn't.

I ran straight for the twitching gray form lying at the side of the road.

CHAPTER FOURTEEN

"Gracie!" Asa's voice was ragged with fear as he completed his sprint across the field. He reached her just before I did and let out a strangled sound that made me want to cry. Instead, I increased my pace, my breath huffing painfully from my lungs as I covered the last few yards.

I dropped to my knees on the other side of her. She was panting, whining with every breath, and bleeding heavily from a deep five-inch gash across her shoulder.

But she was alive. "Asa. Listen to me."

His head was down, his arms around her neck. He was murmuring in her ears. Without moving away from her, he stripped off his shirt and tried to press it to her wound, but she let out a yelp and snapped at his hand, which he yanked out of the way just in time. She struggled to her feet but let out another sharp, agonized yip when she put weight on her right foreleg.

"It's me, girl." Asa inched toward her on his knees as she collapsed on the gravel road. "Please, baby. *Please.*"

"Asa," I said loudly. "I'm a vet tech. I can help her."

"She won't let me touch her," he said in a choked voice.

"Listen to me, okay?" I tried to make my voice steady and soothing, just like I did when people brought their wounded animals to the clinic. No matter how dire the injury, panic and despair never did anyone a bit of good. "I need you to get me a few things. A piece of plywood we can use as a stretcher. A rag or piece of cotton—clean as you can find—and something I can use to make a pressure bandage. Torn strips of cloth, a scarf, something like that. And a blanket." I looked Gracie over. "Because I think she's going into shock."

Asa grabbed my wrist. "Don't let her die."

I put my hand over his. "I won't."

Asa took off running back to camp, pulling his shirt back on as he went, and I scooted slowly toward Gracie. "Hey, girl, it's me. You are such a fierce little lady. That van's going to be aching for days."

And the person driving it? I hoped he would, too. I wasn't sure he'd even known he'd hit her—if he'd been frantic enough, he might have had eyes only for his escape route—but still. I didn't know what Asa would do to him if Gracie didn't survive these injuries, but I was pretty sure it would be brutal, lingering, and creative.

"Need water or anything?" Betsy called as she rushed over. "Oh, that poor sweetheart."

I eyed Gracie's injured foreleg, which was canted awkwardly away from her body. "I need a stick or something I can use to support that leg. And we'll need a vehicle. Maybe a pickup truck or a minivan? We need to get her to a vet as soon as possible."

"Vern and I have a pickup, and you're welcome to it. I'll pull it up."

"Thank you so much."

"Ain't nothin', darlin'." And she was off.

A moment later, Asa was back with the bandages and blanket. "A couple of the guys are bringing the plywood."

"Good." I grimaced as I looked at Gracie's lolling gray tongue, her unfocused eyes, her incredibly sharp teeth. "Asa, we need to muzzle her.

I want to make sure I don't hamper her breathing, but I also don't want her to maul me as I deal with her wound."

Asa examined one of the strips of cloth he'd been given. "I'll do it."

"Just enough to keep her from being able to open her mouth wide enough to bite."

He knelt beside her and did the deed, whispering loving words to her as he slowly tightened the cloth around her broad snout. The look he gave me as I set to work was the most pleading I had ever seen, and I felt it deep in my chest. The next few minutes were pure concentration as I worked first on slowing the bleeding with a pressure bandage, then on supporting her broken leg so it didn't cause her unnecessary pain. As I did, I kept an eye on her respiration, hoping the fact that her breathing sounded dry and unobstructed boded well for her internal organs. Once I had done all for her that I could, I covered her in a blanket, and with the help of a few of the carnies got her safely onto the plywood board. While Asa stood back and laced his fingers behind his head, his body like a live wire, Betsy pulled the pickup truck close, and we got Gracie gently settled in the back. I started to climb up behind her as Betsy tossed the keys to Asa.

"Do you want me to drive?" I asked him. "You could ride back here."

He shook his head. "Will you stay back there with her? She knows and trusts you. And I need to be doing something."

That was Asa, I realized. Control was soothing to him. "No problem. Gracie and I are pals. Take the bumps easy, okay? She needs a smooth ride."

Asa gave me a curt nod, and Betsy went over to his open driver's-side window to give him directions to the nearest emergency vet. Then we were on our way, Asa meticulously avoiding every pothole, and me focused on keeping Gracie comfortable. We made it to the vet in less than half an hour, and fortunately, it seemed to be a competent operation. The vet, Dr. Monahan, was an older woman with short gray hair and deeply tanned skin, and her hands were steady and confident as she checked Gracie out, complimenting our quick thinking with the bandage and improvised splint. I stayed and listened so I could translate for Asa if he needed, but he sounded like a near-expert himself as he reported Gracie's medical history, including the names and dosages of her arthritis medication and eyedrops. I realized that Asa might eschew traditional medications for himself, refusing to take so much as a Tylenol even when he was in intense pain, but he didn't hold that standard with Gracie. He had looked after her like a parent would a child.

When Dr. Monahan said she needed to keep Gracie for evaluation to make sure there was no internal hemorrhaging, Asa looked as if he were going into shock himself. We exited the clinic to face a gloomy day, with clouds hanging low and heavy over the town.

Instead of heading for the truck, Asa sank down on a bench at the edge of the public park across the street from the clinic. The town was a sleepy little three-stoplight place with at least two bait-and-tackle shops, a doughnut shop, the vet clinic, a police outpost, and a library. The park was just a tree-lined square of grass with a statue of some guy on a horse at the center. A farmers' market was in progress on the other side of it. I blinked as I realized it was Sunday—I hadn't been away from home for forty-eight hours yet, but it felt like a year.

I settled hesitantly beside him, his mood hard to read. "Dr. Monahan seemed pretty good. I think Gracie's in good hands."

Asa stared across the street at the clinic. "She looked so bad. And she's getting old, Mattie. She's been with me for nine years. Had to be at least a year old when I found her."

I carefully laid my hand on his shoulder but drew away when he flinched. "She could still have a third of her life in front of her, Asa. This isn't the end."

"What if it is?"

I leaned toward him until I had secured his bloodshot gaze. "I do this for a living, all right? I don't know everything, but I do know that dogs can be incredibly resilient. And Gracie is well loved and healthy, thanks to you. It's a great foundation for healing. That kind of devoted care does wonderful things for an animal, and you love your dog better than any pet owner I've ever met."

He gave me a small, pained smile and then looked away as his eyes took on a sheen. "Thanks for helping her," he said in a strained voice. "And thanks for coming with me. I wouldn't have blamed you for walking away, after some of the stuff I said last night."

I stared at the side of his face. Not coming with him would have been unthinkable. "Gracie's more important to me than hurt feelings."

"Dammit, Mattie," he whispered, keeping his face directed at the Beer, Bait, and Ammo shop across the street.

I glanced over my shoulder at the farmers' market. "Do you want some time to yourself? If you give me some cash, I'll go buy you some stuff to eat. I'm guessing the free-flowing bacon at the camp didn't quite meet your nutritional needs."

"Yeah. Thanks," he murmured, pulling out his wallet and handing it to me.

I held it pressed to my middle. Nearly all of Asa's possessions had just been stolen, but he'd handed me his wallet without hesitation. The warmth of knowing he still trusted me, at least a little, was like a small piece of sunshine inside of me, brightening the day. "I'll be right back."

There was a skip in my step as I headed over to the market. The pain in my chest had faded, and I was actually feeling pretty good. I knew it was temporary; part of it was just the relief of not having the massive Sensilo magic in there anymore, but I suspected it was also that I had been focused on Gracie and Asa, a purpose outside myself that had required all my attention. But I was going to enjoy every agony-free moment I was allowed.

I picked out a fat bunch of carrots, a huge sack of cherry tomatoes, apricots, strawberries, two bunches of kale—Asa *really* seemed to like it—a big sack of raw almonds, a honeydew melon, a jar of organic coconut oil and another of olive oil, and a package of sprouted bread that the lady at the booth swore up and down was suitable for raw diets. She also convinced me to buy a jar of dairy-free pesto. "You must keep enough fat in the diet," she said, eyeing my skinny wrists.

I almost blurted out that it wasn't for me, but then realized it didn't matter. Asa looked like he could use the extra fat in his diet, too. He was bone and muscle and basically nothing else.

I tried not to dwell on how good it felt to do this for him. I was just being a friend. Just a decent human, really. The guy's dog was in the hospital, for God's sake.

By the time I was ready to return to Asa, I was loaded with enough stuff to wish he'd come with me. I skirted the big man-on-horse statue—some Confederate general I'd never heard of—happy that I was almost within hollering distance. I needed some help.

But Asa was gone. I stared at the bench where he'd been. Then I looked up the street to where the pickup had been parked.

It was gone, too.

"You have *got* to be kidding me." Grumbling, I turned around and headed back to the farmers' market, thinking to borrow a phone—and then I realized I didn't have Asa's number. I dropped my bags and rifled through his wallet—his license informed me that his name was Nathan Cockspillier, which made me snort in spite of my irritation. Nothing in there was actually useful, apart from the cool two thousand dollars in hundreds that he happened to be toting.

It had occurred to me once or twice that Asa was probably a pretty wealthy guy, even though most of the time he dressed like he worked at the local army surplus store.

Still, cash wouldn't necessarily help me here. "Why didn't I even suspect you would do something like this?" I said loudly to the overcast sky.

It answered me by way of a few drops of cool rain.

And then about a million of them.

Groaning, I lugged my bags toward the market, where the sellers were rapidly covering their stock and clearing out as the deluge hit. In less than two minutes, the streets were running with water, and I was soaked to the bone and grumpier than a constipated skunk. Planning to shelter in the doughnut shop, I made for the street. One of my paper sacks dissolved, dumping my kale on the ground. Don't ask me why I couldn't have just left it behind, but I scooped it up, carrying one bunch under each armpit. Luckily, most of my other bags were plastic, recycled from a Piggly Wiggly. Limping as my shoes became saturated with mud, I finally made it to the curb—just as a black SUV roared by, splashing me with about fifty gallons of water and nearly knocking me onto my butt. "You see my T-shirt?" I shouted after them. "Karma saw that!"

I was about to step into the street when a pickup rolled up, slow enough not to splash me, thank God. The door creaked open, and there was Asa. "Hop in quick, Mattie. Get those little legs moving."

I glared at him but obeyed quickly, because rainstorm. "What the hell, Asa," I said as he pulled quickly back onto the street.

"I don't want to lose them." He was hunched over the wheel and staring fiercely at the road ahead as the old windshield wipers screamed for mercy.

"About twenty-seven thousand steps behind you." I tugged up the collar of my T-shirt to wipe my dripping face. "Where did you go?"

"I was sitting on the bench when that SUV rolled up to the bait-and-tackle shop across the street."

"Beer, Bait, and Ammo?"

He tapped the tip of his crooked nose without tearing his gaze from the road. "And I recognized the guy who got out of it."

"Who was it?"

"His name's Arkady. Mindfucker with a rep."

"And Russian," I murmured. "Works for Volodya."

"How the *fuck* do you know that?"

"I'll tell you later. Why are we following him?"

Asa gave me a curious sidelong glance and appeared to notice the kale still jammed into my armpits. "This is a new style for you."

"Shut up." I crammed the kale into a sack with the strawberries. "Do you know why a Russian Knedas would be in this tiny town?"

"He's got to be looking for the relic."

It all hit me at once. "His boss thought he had the Sensilo relic all these years, but must have gotten wind that it was in the States."

"He met a black guy who came out of the shop, and they both got back in the SUV."

"Did you recognize the black guy?"

"Didn't get a good look at his face. Could have been anyone. Maybe a spy for Volodya here on the East Coast, maybe a freelance reliquary or conduit. I'd sure like to know where they're going."

"Well, I sure hope that other guy isn't a magic sensor. The relic would lead them right back to the—oh, God."

"What's wrong?" Asa turned to look at me. "Are you okay?"

"Where did you put the Sensilo relic after you and Vernon pulled the magic out of me?"

"In my toolbox."

"The black one?"

"Yeah . . . oh, shit. Ben—"

"He had your black toolbox when he stole your van, Asa. Ben stole the relic."

"That motherfucking—"

"What will they do if they find him?"

"You think I give a shit about what happens to him at this point?"

I folded my arms over my chest, a shield against the sharp tone of his voice. "He said he would regain my trust," I said, dazed. "Not thirty minutes before he stole your van and the relic. I don't get it."

"Greedy little shithead. It would serve him right if Volodya's crew tracks him down and crucifies him. But Zhong's people may find him first. They know what my van looks like."

"What do we do?" The rain was coming down like God had opened a spigot and walked away. I braced myself on the dash as Asa came to a sudden stop.

"Fucking road's washed out." We'd long since left town and had been trailing the SUV far enough behind to render it nothing but a black speck in a sea of green and brown. But now it was out of sight. "They either got through before the flash flood, or they must have chanced it."

"I would think you would, too."

"Not with you in the car," he mumbled. He cursed and turned the truck around.

"I can swim."

"You look like you just escaped a fucking refugee camp, Mattie. You probably couldn't swim your way out of a kiddie pool."

He checked his phone and found a text from the vet saying that it didn't look like Gracie had any internal bleeding, but she still wanted to keep her overnight so she could set the broken leg. Fortunately, that wouldn't require surgery, just mild sedation, so we headed back to the carnival.

"This weather can't be helping business."

"You'd be surprised. Once the Knedas juice hits, people probably don't even notice the rain."

It was tapering by that point, too. Up ahead, the sun had even punched a hole through the cloud cover. "Are you going to try to find out what Arkady's up to?"

Asa nodded. "He's a nasty motherfucker. No one you'd want sneaking up on you—plenty of rumors about how he assassinates via suicide."

I cringed. "He makes people kill themselves?"

"Hard to prove, but that's what I've heard. His power's subtle, too. I was so distracted that I didn't pick it up until he got out of his vehicle." He poked me in the shoulder. "And now I want you to tell me how you know who he worked for."

"My grandpa. He worked as a reliquary for years. Jack was his partner. And they had a run-in with Arkady and Lishka—"

"Arkady's wife. She was killed by Montri's people a few years ago. Revenge—she'd broken one of Montri's daughters. She was a Strikon with some serious juice."

"Well, I guess they were quite a team in their day. They caught my grandpa and Jack at the border as they tried to smuggle something out. They were saved by Volodya's sensor, apparently. A woman named Theresa."

Asa blinked rapidly and pulled over to the side of the road. "What?" he whispered.

"Volodya's sensor," I said slowly. "Her name was Theresa, and she saved them. In return she asked them to help her smuggle the Sensilo relic right out from under Volodya—she was going to replace it with a fake. After the transaction, my grandpa waited for her, but he eventually had to get out. He never saw her again. He never knew what happened to her, and he carried the magic inside him until the day he died."

Until the day Ben had *caused* his death.

"Why did she want the relic?" Asa's face had paled, and his fingers were flexing over the wheel.

"Grandpa didn't know. He knew she wanted to get out from under Volodya, though, and he figured she either wanted to sell it to set herself up or to hand it over to the Headsmen to get some kind of immunity or protection."

"Did he tell you anything else about her?"

"No. Asa, are you okay? What's wrong?"

He turned to me, his bruises standing out garishly on his pallid cheeks. "Maybe it's a coincidence."

"But?" My heart had picked up a cruel, hard rhythm that awakened the splinter of pain inside me.

He swallowed, as if he were afraid to speak his thought aloud. But after several long seconds, he did.

"My mother's name was Theresa."

CHAPTER FIFTEEN

We drove back to the camp in silence. Asa must have been reeling, and based on what I knew of him, he needed alone time to pull himself back together. I'm the opposite usually, though I had come to understand that some things are too overwhelming to talk through.

I wanted to take his hand or give him a hug, anything to offer him a little bit of comfort, but Asa was all sharp edges, and the way he'd grimaced when I put my hand on his shoulder . . . with the splinter inside me, touching him only added to the hurt. I wasn't about to do it again.

Instead, I pulled out the bag of almonds, opened it, and slid it across the seat to him. I did the same with the strawberries. Asa reached over immediately and grabbed a handful of nuts, shoving them in his mouth as if he were starving. By the time we reached the thick forest surrounding the camp, he'd eaten an ungodly amount of almonds and at least two pints of strawberries, along with two carrots and a big hunk of the sprouted bread dipped in pesto. He groaned in pleasure as it hit his tongue, and the sound sent a tingling shiver straight through me. His enjoyment of his food made the ride almost bearable, because even with Asa's careful pothole avoidance, each bump felt like a knife through the lung. My worry about Ben, the stolen relic, and the scary Russian seemed to have awakened the pain.

As we progressed down the winding dirt road that led through the woods to the camp clearing, we began to encounter people parking wherever they could find a shoulder. A steady trickle of men, women, couples, and families was trekking down the road past shabby signs nailed to trees. "Carnival Magia. Experience of a Lifetime."

The way people gasped and pointed every time they saw one, I was guessing they were seeing something much more impressive.

"See that?" Asa pointed at a little mason jar hanging by a rope from a tree branch. "Pure juice right there."

By the way he was sweating, I believed it. "How can you stand it, Asa?"

"You've got enough to worry about already."

That didn't stop me. Without Gracie to ground him, it was going to be that much harder for him to stay healthy. And now he didn't even have his van to retreat to. "Did you have a lot of valuable stuff in your van?"

"Nothing that can't be replaced, except for the relic."

"Are you going to go after him?"

"Not until I get that splinter out of you and get Gracie back from the vet."

"But by then, Zhong might get ahold of it, or some other mob boss might get it. I thought you wanted it. I know it's worth millions."

"You remember what I told you about money?"

"When it doesn't represent freedom or safety, you don't want it."

He tapped the tip of his crooked nose. "It's also not my only priority."

I couldn't imagine it was, what with Arkady the assassin prowling around, his discovery that his long-lost mother might have once belonged to a Russian mob boss and had long since disappeared, and the fact that his brother had stolen all his possessions and nearly killed his dog. "I'm sorry Ben did this."

"Did you know?" He was looking straight ahead, but his voice had taken on an edge.

"I had no idea." My only clue had been how determined he had looked as he had headed back to the silk tent this morning.

"You knew he wanted to end up with the relic."

"Yeah. He kept saying he didn't trust you, that you were only out for yourself."

"And is that what you think?"

"I know you better than he does, Asa."

"I know," he whispered.

He pulled off the road once we reached the clearing, which was now a sea of parked cars and SUVs. "Let's go set this transaction up. I need to get both my girls healthy again."

He grabbed the remaining sacks of food and got out quickly, but I sat there for a second, absorbing what he'd just said, before I hopped out after him. We walked up the crowded lane past people staring at the space above the camp like Ben had the night before, in awe at the magnificent Carnival Magia. "Ugh," I said as my damp denim capris chafed at me. "You may not have had valuables in your van, but I did."

"Your wallet?"

"Underwear. I'll never take it for granted again."

Asa snorted, and for the first time in hours he really did smile, despite the dark circles under his eyes and the rivulets of sweat sliding down his neck. "Dammit, Mattie."

I grinned. Making him smile felt like total triumph. I knew he must be hurting—all the naturals in this camp had their volumes turned up to eleven to please their customers, and Asa was trying to hold his own despite the bombardment.

"Aren't we going back to the tent?" I asked as Asa passed the midway lane, which was packed with people peering into the booths, pointing at the "freaks" inside. Halfway down, a young guy in a University of Richmond hoodie tossed his phone into a booth that must have belonged to Burt, the Man Who'll Eat Anything, because a moment later the guy yelled, "What the actual fuck, dude?"

Red-haired Terrence slid from between two booths, watching the guy intently as his friends laughed and slapped his back. When it looked like the guy was calming down, Terrence melted into the crowd again.

"I need to figure out what we're gonna put this splinter in." Asa sidestepped a group of people gathered around a plump young woman who was presiding over an old cotton candy machine. Judging by people's reactions as they received its output—scrawny wisps of pink spun sugar that didn't look like anything special—they were seeing some kind of fabulous confection. We also passed by an elderly couple accepting five dollars a pop for a single balloon on a string.

"Unbelievable," I muttered, but it turned out it was just an appetizer. After Asa led me through the campers to the field on the other side, we reached a roped-off section of grass within which someone had set up several rows of folding chairs, two in each row. People were excitedly waiting their turn to sit on the chairs, and a woman with thick glasses and thinning shoulder-length brown hair stood just outside the ropes, raising her arms periodically. When she did, the people in the chairs would hold on to the backs of the seats in front of them, their faces pulled tight and their bodies bumping in time, smiles on their faces that turned into screams. All of them threw their arms up and yowled in unison, then leaned abruptly first to one side and then the other.

"Behold, the roller coaster," Asa said, his voice strained. "Goddammit. I can almost see it." He cursed and rubbed at his face.

I hunched my shoulders around the slice of agony inside me. "If you hold my hand, I bet it'll disappear." The pain was enough to clear even the foggiest brain.

"By tomorrow, you'll be having the time of your life. I'll take you on the Tilt-A-Whirl." He pointed across the field at a similar roped-off area with chairs arranged in clusters of four, and then headed along the perimeter of the campers until we reached a newish-looking RV the size of a city bus. When Asa knocked on the door, the guy with the big beard answered. "Hey, Jimmy," Asa said. "Got a few minutes?"

Jimmy pushed the door wider, a stern look on his face. "I was waiting for you both to come back from town. How's the puppy?"

"Alive," Asa said. "Under observation. Vet'll set her leg tomorrow morning."

"Come on in. I've got lemonade."

"I'd prefer to talk out here."

Jimmy grinned and—I am not kidding—twirled the ends of his mustache, which had clearly been waxed. "Scared of me, Mr. Ward?"

"Nah. Respectful."

I thought back to what Roberta had told me about Jimmy, the leader of the camp and manager of the carnival—he was a powerful Ekstazo, maybe like Frank Brindle. Able to influence people with a simple handshake. He didn't seem bothered by Asa's request, though. He stepped ponderously out of his luxury RV. "Would have thought you'd be happy to put a set of walls between yourself and our field of fantasy here."

"Can't say it feels so fantastic to me," Asa said with a dry chuckle. "But I needed to have a word—and a clear head."

"Fair enough." Jimmy turned his twinkling blue eyes on me. "And here's our little wounded bird. Feeling better?"

"Almost," I replied.

"Mattie's got a splinter."

Jimmy's bushy gray eyebrows rose. "You don't say. I'm surprised, Ward. You don't have a rep for sloppy work."

Asa's jaw clenched. "There were extenuating circumstances."

"That's kind of an understatement, actually," I said.

Jimmy nodded and scratched his round belly. "I guess none of us are perfect. What do you need?"

"Something strong enough to hold it."

"Any object should do, shouldn't it?"

Asa bit the inside of his cheek. "Not for this."

"You said it was a splinter."

"It's really more of an ice pick." I rubbed my chest as said ice pick poked at my soft insides.

Jimmy frowned. "May I ask where you acquired this ice pick–size splinter?"

"It might be safer for you and yours if you didn't," Asa said.

"Ah." Jimmy pursed his lips, reached into his pocket, and pulled out a crumpled piece of paper. "That might explain this. Betsy found it in her tent this morning and brought it straight to me. That's why *I* wanted to talk to the two of you."

Asa took the paper and unfolded it. He groaned in exasperation and handed it to me. My stomach dropped as I recognized Ben's handwriting.

Mattie,

I know you're probably thinking the worst of me right now, but I swear I'm not going to try to take the relic to Brindle. Your grandpa told you to take the relic to the Headsmen, and I'm going to find a way to do that. I'm going to give it to the authorities and prove my love to you once and for all. Please come back to me. We have our whole life in front of us. I would be so grateful to have a fresh start with you.

Love, Ben

"I'm going to reveal my ignorance here," I said, looking up from the note and pushing down all the twisty feelings it had inspired—but not well enough, apparently, because the pain in my chest was like a wound torn open. "How easy is it to find a Headsman to hand something like this over to?"

Jimmy guffawed. "Well, when you want to find one, good luck. When you don't? They always seem to show up."

I looked up at Asa. "Can you call Keenan? I'm worried Ben's in over his head."

"Keenan?" Jimmy grunted. "Haven't heard that name in a while. Thought he might have retired."

"Nope. Just risen in the ranks." Asa gave me a baleful look. "You're worried about Ben, and you want me to call Keenan? Do you not remember that he was ready to shoot you just to get his hands on a relic?"

"Only because I was refusing to give it to him."

Asa stared at me and then let out a strained laugh. "You are something else. You'll forgive anyone anything."

"What's that supposed to mean?"

"Children," Jimmy said loudly. "What I'd like to know is whether I can expect outsiders to come sniffing around my camp, and if so, how soon you will be taking your shady business elsewhere."

"*Our* shady business?" I glared at the folding-chair roller coaster. The pain was sending my mood south in a hurry.

Asa took a half step in front of me as Jimmy's eyes narrowed. "What she means is, as soon as Vernon helps us pull the splinter, we're out of here. The show must go on."

"That's better." Jimmy disappeared back into his RV for a moment and came out holding a rusty object, which he handed to Asa. "Give that a try. Hildy, God rest her beautiful soul—" Jimmy crossed himself and kissed his balled fist, right over a thick gold band on his ring finger.

"She pulled off some of the heaviest transactions I
using that. Can hold just about anything."

Asa opened his palm and stared down at the railroad spike, -
inches of rusting iron. "Okay, then. We'll use it. Thank you."

"Repay me with your absence, friend," Jimmy advised. He climbed
back up into his RV and shut the door.

"He's lovely," I said.

"He's responsible for a lot of people. Can't really blame him for
looking out for them. He did us a favor by even taking my call in the
first place. All of them did."

I looked down at the spike. "Who's Hildy?"

"His wife. She was a reliquary, too. I suspect that's why he agreed
to help in the first place. He's got a soft spot for your kind."

"Did she die of magic?"

Asa shook his head. "Cancer. Jimmy kept her going as long as he
could—used his own power and anyone else's he could buy to ease her
pain."

"Oh my God," I whispered. "That's really sad."

"Not as sad as it would have been without his magic."

"Huh. I would have expected you to disapprove of it. Don't you
look down on using magic?"

"Just because I don't use it myself doesn't mean I judge other people
for it."

"You judged Ben."

"I think there's a difference between using magic to control your
fiancée and get yourself off and using it to ease your dying wife's pain.
Don't you?"

"Hard to argue with that." Especially because my own pain had
ratcheted up a few notches, making it hard to breathe.

"Then don't," he said curtly, stalking back toward the center of the
carnival. "Let's go find Vernon and get this done. Seems like we both
have some big decisions to make afterward."

CHAPTER SIXTEEN

Vernon was kind of hard to find. As a conduit, he wasn't responsible for putting on a show like the Knedas "freaks" and "ride" operators or the Sensilo fortune-teller. Instead, we found him wandering the field with a huge sack and a sharp stick, spearing discarded popcorn boxes and cotton-candy cones. Betsy had already told him about the splinter, and he agreed to meet us in the silk tent after the carnival closed at midnight.

Asa was not happy about having to wait that long to do the transaction, but Vernon reminded him that Strikon transactions could be pretty loud and that the silk tent was pulling double duty as a first aid station. Asa backed down with a surly nod of his head. I doubt he wanted to risk having Jimmy rescind our welcome. But by then, my magic sensor was sweating profusely and rubbing his temples like someone had taken a jackhammer to the inside of his skull. I had the same feeling inside my chest, and it was getting worse with each passing hour. Asa said removing the massive Sensilo relic from inside me might have dislodged the splintered Strikon magic and allowed it to rattle around, doing more damage than before.

That pretty much ruined my day. And on top of that, I could tell that even standing next to me was hurting Asa. Every time my pain increased, it was obvious that his did, too.

So I did what my mother would have done: I made him a kale-apple-strawberry smoothie in Roberta's tiny blender and sent him back to town to visit Gracie. I couldn't stand watching him hurt. He left readily and didn't ask if I wanted to come. Probably because he was focused on Gracie, and maybe because he didn't want to watch me hurting, either, especially when there was nothing he could do about it until after midnight. I wrapped my arms around myself as I watched the lights of the pickup disappear around a bend in the road.

The carnival was pretty much packed, so I wandered through the fields, trying to let the incredibly weird sight of people sitting in folding chairs and screaming like they were going sixty miles an hour through a vertical loop distract me from my discomfort. When that didn't work, I headed for the midway.

I stopped and stared at Betsy sitting cross-legged on the floor of a prettily trimmed booth that looked like a gingerbread house. She was the Giraffe Woman. A painted picture on the side of her booth portrayed a dark-haired woman with a neck at least three feet long. And there Betsy was, small and white-haired with a slightly sagging and tattooed but otherwise totally normal neck, waving regally to her awe-struck audience. I hadn't even considered that she was a mind-twister like the others.

Apparently, ever since we'd arrived, I'd been surrounded by people who were capable of bending people's thoughts in amazing ways. And yet, none of them had tried to put the whammy on me so far as I could tell. I was used to Knedas agents who would happily coerce a person into doing what they wanted. And then there were the ones like Arkady, who seemed to have taken it to grisly extremes. I had come to think of people with this power as evil. But these carnies—they were focused on maintaining the glamour of the carnival, but they didn't seem interested in hurting or twisting people up. Yes, what they were up to was ethically questionable, but with the exception of some spent cash and lost iPhones, it didn't seem to be doing any actual harm.

Betsy winked at me when she saw me, and I waved at her and kept walking, not wanting to distract her while she was working. The next booth was the fortune-teller's—Madame Voyant—veiled with heavy velvet curtains almost completely concealing the glow from inside. A couple emerged from the little side door looking shell-shocked, and when the guy reached for the girl's hand, she yanked it away. "I knew you weren't telling the truth about Ashley," she wailed.

"It was just the one time," the guy yelped as he trailed the girl toward the parking lot. Before she reached it, a man blocked her path. He wore jeans, a black T-shirt, and a gray vest. His muscular arms were covered with full-sleeve tattoos, and his dark hair was swept back from his face in a modern pompadour with shaved sides.

He was hot. And the girl seemed to think so, too, because she slowed to a stop right in front of him. He flashed a friendly smile and reached out, running his hand down her arm.

"Hey," said her maybe-ex-boyfriend. "Hands off."

The pompadour guy's smile didn't fade as he pulled the same arm stroke on the boyfriend, and the tension in the boyfriend's body melted away. The couple looked at each other, and then the pompadour guy stepped aside and let them continue on their way, hand in hand.

"That's Quentin," said a rich, mellow voice beside me. I turned to see an African American woman who was probably in her early forties. Her hair was a riot of short braids around her head, and she wore a colorful shawl. "And I'm Letisha."

"A.k.a. Madame Voyant."

She nodded, wearing a sly smile as she watched the couple disappear into the maze of parked cars in the field. "It wasn't just the one time. That boy has been cheating on her for months."

"I thought the point of this place was to make people feel good?"

"Ah, that's overrated. Sometimes it isn't even the best thing for you." Letisha chuckled. "I do my best to keep it light, but some people just piss me off. And hiding the truth does no one any good. I hate when Quentin undoes my good work."

As if he heard her, Quentin turned to look right at us through the meandering crowd of people. He winked at Letisha.

She grunted. "Too much charm on that one for sure."

"I'm Mattie," I said.

"I know."

"I guess that figures."

"Care to have a reading?" She gestured toward the side door of her booth, even as several people waiting in line glared at me mutinously.

"I think *we* were here first," said one college-age girl, waving her hand at her friends. They were all wearing identical sorority sweatshirts.

"Were you? How lovely," said Letisha, completely unruffled. "Perhaps a bit of waiting might be good for your character."

I took a step back. "That's really all right. I don't really want to be told things I already know."

Letisha laughed. "I'm a fortune-teller, dear. Don't you want to know what's coming?"

"You sense intentions, from what I understand," I said quietly. "You can pick up things, but the future isn't one of them. No one can do that."

Her brown eyes glittered with the confidence of known secrets. "You'd be surprised."

And before I could stop her, she had her palms on my cheeks. "So much pain here, not all of it physical."

"Already knew that," I said through goldfish lips.

"You have decisions to make."

"Again with the knowing."

"You know they both want you."

"I—"

"But do you know one of them will kill you?"

She let me go abruptly and I staggered back, my heart beating like a woodpecker sending up a dust of bone chips as it drilled through my rib cage. I doubled over and clamped my eyes shut, unable to keep the tears from leaking out.

"Poor little reliquary," Letisha crooned, helping me upright. "That was cruel. I'm sorry. I couldn't help myself. Some people have such a rich tapestry of wish and drive inside of them. It calls to me."

"Maybe you should let it go to voice mail," I squeaked.

"Sometimes there's enough inside you to make even the unknown future clear. It's a gift and a curse to be able to sift through it." Her fingers were still wrapped firmly around my arms. "But I'm very rarely wrong."

"I need to go . . . over there," I said in a strangled voice, pulling away from her. "Waaaay over there."

"Don't waste a minute, Mattie," she called after me. "Enjoy every one."

Oh my God. Was she trying to scare me to death? I staggered away from the booth, savagely glad to see her line shrink as people who'd observed our encounter decided that maybe they didn't want their fortunes told after all. I wanted to scream at them to run—suddenly this whole place seemed sinister to me, and all my live-and-let-live good vibes toward the carnies disappeared in an avalanche of anxiety and pain.

Do you know one of them will kill you?

Was that what was going to happen tonight? Was Asa going to make a mistake? Was pulling this splinter going to be fatal? Was Letisha telling me I had only hours to live?

I blundered toward the trailers. Jimmy had pointed out an empty camper that they kept for "strays," people who joined the camp for only a season. Come summer, the camper would be occupied, but for now, as the camp emerged from its winter slumber, it was free, and I needed it badly.

"Can I offer you assistance?"

I turned to see Quentin leaning up against a trailer right next to the cotton-candy booth. Bits of spun sugar fine as cobwebs rose into the darkening sky, reflecting glints of orange-and-purple sunset. Quentin smiled as I tore my eyes from it to focus on him again. "I don't think so. I just need some time to myself."

"Letisha is a lovely woman who has the unfortunate quality of enjoying others' discomfort. She really can't help herself."

I rubbed my chest. "And you?"

"I enjoy people's pleasure, of course. I especially like making them feel good myself." He shoved himself off the camper and sauntered toward me. "You look like you could use some pleasure. And maybe a lot of it."

I chuckled weakly and put my hands up. "No, thanks."

His brow furrowed. "Why not? I can tell you're suffering. I could ease that."

I wasn't sure how to explain to him how I had come to hate naturals trying to control my moods and thoughts and body. It bothered me. It made me feel vulnerable. Too much of me had been taken away, and I was scrambling to hoard little bits for myself. "I've had a few bad run-ins, okay? I need to be the one in control of something like this."

Quentin gave me a genuinely kind smile. "Then I know exactly what you need." He reached into the pocket of his jeans and pulled out a small vial of clear liquid. "A gift."

"Why?"

He tilted his head. "Because I feel like offering it?"

I eyed the vial. "That's from you?"

"Plasma-infused oil. Nothing tawdry, I swear. Not strong enough to do you any harm."

"And what am I supposed to do with it?"

"Rub a little of it wherever it hurts. I'm good at relieving pain of all kinds." He looked over to the midway lane, where the sorority sisters had emerged from Letisha's booth on the verge of a full-on catfight. He sighed. "Would you excuse me? Duty calls."

He tossed the vial at me and headed back to the midway, his strides relaxed, smiling at gaping carnival guests who were clearly distracted by how damn good-looking the guy was. I bent down and picked up the vial, which had hit my hollow belly and bounced off. I bit my lip, and my fingers closed around the vial, which was still warm from his body heat. Even holding it dialed the pain back a level, though not nearly enough to allow me to sleep, which was what I really wanted to do, because being awake meant thinking and worrying.

I tromped over to the empty trailer Jimmy had pointed out. There was no lock on the screen door, but everybody in the camp was occupied, so I didn't much care. The space was clean, though it smelled a little mildewy. The air was humid and close beneath the heat of the generator-powered network of overhead lamps that had flickered on as the sun set. Knowing I had some alone time, I examined one of the beds, a simple foam mattress neatly made up with faded flowered sheets. Perfect.

I stripped off my shirt and the desperately uncomfortable oversized denim capris. Clad in only my bra, I slid between the sheets with the vial. It really was a gift—by giving me something I could apply myself, Quentin had taken the control aspect out of the equation and made it a lot easier to accept.

Because I needed the relief. Badly. My head was swimming with thoughts of the pain to come, with knowing Ben was out there somewhere stupidly trying to be noble after causing so much hurt, and with the understanding that Asa was suffering and I couldn't do anything but make it worse. My brain felt as if it were going to ooze out of my ears. It only added to the knife twist somewhere in the area just behind my sternum. I unscrewed the lid on the vial and dribbled a few drops on my chest, then rubbed it in. It smelled like lavender, and I greedily breathed it in. But the pain in my chest didn't disappear as I'd hoped, so I poured a little more onto my skin, painting it in slow swirls across my collarbone and down my belly. Not wanting my bra to get totally greasy, I took it off, too, and slid a little farther under the sheets.

The Ekstazo oil made my skin warm, and the pain beneath my breastbone faded even more, though not completely. I held the vial up to the light filtering in through the horizontal blinds at the window. Only a little bit left.

Ah, well. I might only have hours to live. Why save it?

I dumped the rest out on my torso, rubbing it up over my chest and down my belly, enjoying the feel of my own hands on my skin. It had been so long since I had felt much pleasure at all. My body had become a stranger, an enemy, chipped away to nothing by the fractured magic inside me. But I had always loved it. I didn't want to lose it. I wanted to live.

Slow and loving, I skimmed my hands up and down my arms, taking in the bumps of my wrist bones, the bend in the crook of my elbow, the bony junction of my shoulder, the ridge of my collarbone, the hollow of my throat. I took my time, minutes to cover a few inches. My fingertips circled my breasts as I breathed slowly, noticing that the pain had faded far into the background. I smiled and closed my eyes as I ran my fingers along the curve of my ribs, the flat of my belly, the slight swell of my hips, and then between my legs. My breath whooshed from my lungs as my fingertips came up wet, and I moaned softly at the rush of pleasure that made my whole body tighten.

Oh God, I had missed that feeling, that tingling need that pulled me away from worry and fear straight into bliss. Seeking more, I explored a part of me that I had sorely neglected for months, sliding my fingers up and down, spreading my legs as the promise of ecstasy ebbed and flowed, tantalizing and teasing. I lost myself in the haze of it, the irresistible pull, a path down which I knew I could find myself again, if only I kept going.

"You in here, Mattie?" The screen door swung open, and I gasped, lifting my head from the thin pillow.

Asa stood in the doorway, a plastic Target sack in his hand. For a moment, we just stared at each other. I was too stunned and disoriented to be embarrassed. In fact, my skin tingled with want and compulsion. My fingers were frozen midstroke, my other hand holding the threadbare sheet over my naked body. There was no way I could hide what I was doing.

A normal person would have apologized and backed out of the camper, cheeks hot as a campfire, or maybe snickering at the scene he'd just interrupted.

Asa was not normal.

His gaze traveled slowly up my body until our eyes met. "Don't stop," he whispered. He dropped the sack and let the door close slowly. He pushed it until it latched us both inside. "Don't you dare stop." His voice was low and rough. It was a command, not a request.

And I found I wanted to obey. My head fell back on the pillow and I let go of the sheet, moving my hand to one of my breasts, which I palmed and squeezed. My knees fell wide as I slid my fingers inside, feeling the heat of my own body. I was fully aware of the sheet sliding off of me. Fully aware of Asa tugging on it gently, revealing me inch by inch until I was completely exposed. Fully aware of his scent, and of my need.

Somewhere in the very back of my mind, a tiny voice screamed that this was dangerous, ridiculous, embarrassing.

But at the front of my mind, all I heard was Asa telling me not to stop. All I felt was my body begging me to keep going and the forbidden ecstasy of knowing he was watching.

"Open your eyes," he said quietly.

I did. He was at the foot of the bed, his head bowed beneath the low ceiling. His eyes were on mine, his face unreadable. But the sight of him, the closeness, the tension between us, so taut and electric . . . I traced my fingertips around my most sensitive spot, rubbing quickly, craving friction that was building mercilessly to its crescendo.

"Keep them open," he said as my eyelids fluttered. I had to struggle to comply as the spiraling pleasure threatened to rob my control. But my need to do as he said was just as compelling—it only heightened the tingling, the flush of blood just beneath my skin.

He rewarded me for my obedience almost immediately, by breaking our locked gazes to watch the movement of my fingers. His eyes flickered with raw hunger, unmistakable and searing. He inhaled deeply, and I knew he was smelling my arousal, the lavender oil, the magic. He braced his hands on either side of the narrow trailer and stared down at me writhing on the bed only a few feet away. He was allowing me to see how I was affecting him, and somehow the mere sight of it was as powerful as any touch, any stroke, any kiss I'd ever experienced.

I whimpered as I felt myself reaching the point of no return, and his eyes rose to mine again. "Come for me, Mattie. Let me see you."

It was exactly what I needed. The exquisite twist of pleasure swelled and exploded, and I cried out as my entire body was rocked by it—my first orgasm in months. My fingers were soaked with it, my mind bright with its purity, my limbs flexing with the rush. My eyes clamped shut and I shuddered as the aftershocks began, sweet lightning strikes of ecstasy that made me moan. They wrung me out, and I collapsed, sweating and panting, onto the sheets, floating in the aching glory of the afterglow.

A soft click pulled me back to the present. I raised my head, blinking.

Asa was gone.

CHAPTER SEVENTEEN

I sat up abruptly, still breathing hard, stunned and reeling. "Did I really just do that?" I whispered.

Biting my lip, I rose on shaky legs and pulled the sheet around my body. Asa had left the Target bag on the floor, so I scooped it up and looked inside.

A maxi skirt, size four. A bra, thirty-two B. A tank top and a short-sleeve blouse. A pair of size-six sandals. Lacy underwear small enough not to sag.

And a large package of Twizzlers.

I sank down on the bed as my eyes filled with tears, my reaction and my thoughts multidimensional, complicated. I glanced down at the engagement ring and laid my fingertip over the diamond, remembering the night Ben had put it on my finger. *That* feeling had been simple. Pure happiness I had been sure I would feel for the rest of my life. But here I was, betrayed over and over by the man I had loved, and who still claimed to love me.

Yet though my vision for the future had been fractured, what alternative did I have but to return to my old life? The magical world was a strange and treacherous place, and the man who had been my most reliable guide also happened to be the most complex human being I had ever known. I was drawn to him. Fascinated by him. And I cared about him. A lot. But I wouldn't fool myself into thinking I understood him or what he wanted, or that he really wanted me.

"We're totally wrong for each other," I muttered as I pulled the tags from a pair of underwear. As soon as I said it, I bowed my head and laughed, embarrassed. I was glad Asa couldn't see my thoughts—they made me feel more vulnerable than what I had just done.

Though now that I thought about it, I had lain naked and spread in front of him. I had come while he'd watched. While he'd stayed fully clothed and fully in control, I had literally laid myself bare.

I had to face him again. Soon. How the heck would I look him in the eye?

I groaned and tore the Twizzlers package open, gobbling down a few of the plasticky red ropes, but it only triggered more memories of Asa.

I got dressed, delighted when I found a package of hair scrunchies at the very bottom of the bag. I spent one moment wishing for a mirror and the next deciding that it was probably a mercy that I didn't have one, took a deep breath, and emerged from the camper, half expecting Asa to be waiting outside.

He was nowhere in sight. What was in sight . . . "Whoa," I whispered, staring around me at a field of gingerbread houses, a few of which appeared to belong to elves, who waved cheerfully at me from the windows. An honest-to-God unicorn was contained in a paddock just to my left. It glanced over at me with pale-blue eyes, lifted its tail, and nonchalantly expelled a stream of glitter out its hind end.

In a daze, I walked around the paddock—and came face-to-face with the roller coaster. It flickered as I followed the progression of the cars along a twisting, looping track that rose at least eight stories in the air and seemed to defy the laws of physics. I knew it wasn't there. But I suppose with the pain suppressed, the Knedas glamour over this place was doing a number on my mind.

I had no idea what time it was, but the stars were bright in the ebony sky above, and there was a steady stream of cars pulling out of the parking lot. It must be getting close to midnight.

Which meant it was nearly time to pull the splinter. That thought made the roller coaster flicker and fade even more, though I could still see it. I rubbed my chest, grateful to Quentin for the gift of his magic. It didn't stop the fear from creeping in, though, along with the memory of Letisha's words . . . *Do you know one of them will kill you?*

From somewhere out in the woods came a sharp pop, followed by a second and a third a minute later. I glanced at the sky over the trees. Would there be fireworks? Intrigued, I trudged toward the midway, the entrance to which was marked with a huge lighted archway. A peek down the lane revealed a bizarrely enchanting dark village with a cottage for each "freak," elaborate signs describing the attributes and skills of each one. So different from the shabby wooden booths that flickered faintly beneath the glamour. I nearly bumped into Jimmy as he stood in the middle of the road, peering toward the woods with concern. He glanced over at me and then turned to the midway. "Closing time," he shouted. "Time to go home, folks!"

People obediently flocked toward the field of parked cars, and I waved to Vernon as he walked toward us with his bag of trash. He smiled and opened his mouth to say something, but then his eyes went wide and his expression turned rigid, lips pulling back from gapped teeth.

"Headsmen," he roared. "Headsmen!"

The word had an instant effect not only on the carnies, but also on several of the carnival attendees—just not the kind I would have expected.

I watched in numb disbelief as a group of carnival goers, men and women, suddenly whipped out thick leather gloves and zip ties. Jimmy cursed and shouted, "Evacuate! This is not a drill!"

A few people by the cars screamed. "It's coming down!" shrieked one woman, pointing to the field. "Oh my God, no!"

I spun around to see the roller coaster buckle and crumble, and even though I knew it wasn't really there, I felt the tremors beneath my feet.

"Fire!" a man cried, pointing at the midway. Staggering, I whirled around to see four of the dark cottages become hellish infernos, flame and cinders spiraling into the air. The "smoke" made me cough; it was that real. People howled and scattered, bumping into each other as they ran for their cars. The Knedas folk among the carnies were working hard to create enough chaos to allow their comrades to escape.

But the leather-gloved folks didn't seem fazed. They seemed to see right through the illusion. I turned to run as I watched a guy tackle Quentin and sit on his back. As Quentin tried to reach up and lay hands on his attacker, his wrists were shackled behind his back and his ankles were similarly tied in a matter of seconds. All around me, this same scene was being played out, carnies being tossed to the ground and cuffed. The undercover Headsmen, who had obviously been gathering throughout the evening, posing as regular tourists, were wearing long pants and long sleeves and gloves, keeping their skin covered so they'd be less vulnerable to the effects of the carnies' magic.

I took a few stumbling steps back and darted between the campers where the gingerbread houses had been, thinking to make it to the woods. Where was Asa? Had he already been taken down? I doubted it would be easy, but that made me even more worried for him, especially when I witnessed one Headsman, a young Hispanic guy wearing a Georgetown sweatshirt, shoot a Taser at the bespectacled Knedas lady who had been running the roller coaster. As soon as she went down, the roller coaster vanished, and the people who had been cringing and fleeing from the massive collapsing tangle of metal stopped and stared, brows furrowed in stunned puzzlement.

"Show's over," shouted one woman, holding up what appeared to be a badge that flashed silver under the generator-powered lights. As she did, her sleeve slid up her right arm, revealing a thick silver cuff. "All cars will be searched at the roadblock."

Suddenly I wondered if the popping sound I'd heard had been someone shooting out the Knedas-juice jars that had been hung in the trees, weakening the glamour. I ran along the perimeter of the campers toward the outhouses, hoping to get behind them and sprint to the woods beyond. I grimaced as my heavy breathing awakened the pain in my chest, but I forced myself to keep going. There was nothing I could do to help. My only good option was to try to escape—my last encounter with a Headsman had nearly gotten me killed, and this time Asa wasn't here to strangle my attackers with his suspenders.

But just as I reached the outhouses, two women stepped out from behind them, and one had a Taser pointed right at me. The one with the weapon, a curvy blonde with a ponytail, squinted at my hair, and then her eyes met mine. "Name?"

I put up my hands. "Karen Funkhouse."

Her partner, a slender Asian woman with a sleek black bob, shook her head. "Hang on, Phillips. I think this is her." She pulled out a phone that had been clipped to her belt and peered at the screen, then at me. "She's lost some weight, but it's definitely her."

"Thought so," said the blond Agent Phillips. "Mattie Carver, you're coming with us."

I took a step back but froze when she raised the Taser to keep it centered on my chest. Like the woman with the badge, Phillips had a silver cuff on, too. "Have you ever been hit with one of these?" she asked, tilting the weapon. "We had to do it in our training. You know what fifty thousand volts feels like?"

If she hit me with that thing, who knew what it would do to the splinter inside me? "I don't want to find out," I said.

"Then don't run," said the dark-haired agent. "We've been sent to fetch you."

"What? By who?"

The women moved to stand on either side of me, and each took one of my arms. "Above our pay grade." They marched me back to the road, along which several of the carnies had been lined up, cuffed at the wrists and ankles while casually dressed Headsmen stood over them, taking pictures of their captives with their phones. I gave each of the carnies apologetic looks as I passed, my heart sinking as I saw Vernon trying to scoot on his belly over to Betsy, who was struggling and spitting as a male Headsman dragged her out of her booth.

"You'd better not hurt her," he roared. "Swear to God, I'll kill you if you hurt her."

"Got Ms. Carver," Phillips said as she reached the woman with the badge, a thick-limbed, steel-haired agent who looked as if she was pretty comfortable being in charge.

"Get her loaded up and take her to the station. We'll finish up here. Park, call ahead to tell Winslow to get ready."

Park, the dark-haired agent, nodded and stepped aside with her phone—which was when I noticed she had a silver cuff around her wrist as well.

"What's that?" I asked, pointing to the cuff.

The agent in charge gave me a quick sidelong glance, but instead of answering, she strode over to a group of other agents who were gathered around Jimmy. He was the only one who wasn't cuffed. He had his hands up and was speaking calmly to them, his voice a low rumble. But then the agent in charge parted the crowd, pulled a Taser from her belt, and shot him in the chest. He went down like a sack of concrete, and I cried out at the total injustice of it. "He wasn't hurting anyone," I shrieked. "Who the heck do you people think you are?"

"He was starting to get through the shields," said Phillips to Park, tapping her silver cuff. "That's one powerful Ekstazo. We could use a guy like that."

"What are you going to do to them?" I asked, inclining my head toward the carnies.

"Not your concern," said Phillips, her hand closing around my upper arm.

"Why are you taking me and leaving everyone else? Where are we going?"

Park and Phillips refused to answer any more of my rapid-fire questions and pushed me into the back of a black sedan with a tinted shield between the front and back seats. Once the doors were closed, I realized I couldn't open them. As they pulled back onto the road, I pressed my nose to the window, frantically scanning every face, looking for a familiar crooked profile. But he wasn't among the stream of people rubbing at their eyes and shaking their heads, tossing resentful looks over their shoulders at the campsite. About half a mile up the road, we reached a checkpoint, but when Phillips rolled down the window and held out a badge of her own, the people blocking the road, who looked for all the world like local sheriff's deputies, waved us through.

I leaned back on the headrest and stared at the inky night outside the window as we bumped along the gravel road, and each time Phillips hit a pothole, it hurt a little more. The fear wasn't helping—it was like sandpaper, quickly wearing away any sense of safety or hope I'd had. Confusion was bitter in my throat, and guilt was crushing me. I knew so little about this shadowy branch of magical law enforcement, but what I did know was not encouraging. Though Grandpa had told me to take the empty Sensilo relic to them after he died, he'd also told me to steer clear of the Headsmen whenever possible. And now that I'd seen them in action, I had an even clearer sense of why. Our encounter with Keenan in Bangkok had been just him, one lone agent, but now they'd descended in force and manhandled dozens of carnies. I had no idea if they were going to put them in jail—or worse.

My anxious churning only intensified when we pulled into the parking lot of the New Kent County Sheriff's Office. The two female agents pulled me out of the car and escorted me inside, pulling out their badges, which were simple—and *blank*—silver shields. But the deputy who greeted us at the door looked down at them and nodded. "We've got you guys set up back there."

He pointed past a set of holding cells to a room with a metal door. My stomach dropped. I was so scared that I couldn't even find the wherewithal to try to convince the deputy that these women weren't who he believed them to be. He probably thought their badges said "FBI" or "ATF"—I had no doubt the blank silver shields were Knedas relics.

The women guided me through a quiet office area and down the hall with the holding cells. One contained a guy who reeked of booze and was snoring wetly as he lay sprawled on the floor.

In the other cell, a man was sitting ramrod straight on a bench bolted to the wall. Even though he was surrounded by iron bars and cinder block, his wrists and ankles were shackled. He looked to be in his fifties, with graying brown hair and a sensuous mouth that was pulled into a terrible, twitching grimace. There was a thick silver collar fastened around his neck. As we passed, our eyes met, and his glittered with pain and rage so thick and powerful it was almost palpable. I felt the inexplicable urge to ask the women to unshackle him, to take off the collar, to let him breathe free. But just as I was opening my mouth to ask, we reached the metal door.

"I felt that," Park said with a frown. "Someone needs to turn his collar up."

"I'll get Jack to do it when he gets back," Phillips replied. "I'm not going anywhere near him, cuffed or not."

"Do the deputies know not to approach him?"

Phillips chuckled. "I think we were pretty clear. They'll be pretty relieved when his transport arrives."

"So will I," said Park. "He gives me the creeps."

I wondered who he was and what he'd done. He was clearly a natural—and they were treating him like an animal.

As the two agents guided me down a grim gray hallway and into a room with a mirror along one wall and a metal table and chairs positioned under a bright lamp in the center, I couldn't help but think, how were they going to treat *me*?

CHAPTER EIGHTEEN

"Have a seat." Phillips pointed to one of the metal chairs, and Park pulled it out for me.

My heart beating a thousand miles an hour, the pain increasing by the second, I sank onto the cold surface. "Do I get a phone call?"

"We'll let Agent Winslow decide."

The door slammed, and I sat there, alone. I stared at myself in the mirrored glass. I'd watched enough *Law & Order* to know there was probably a person behind there, watching me.

I'd looked better. My ponytail was crooked, and my hair was tangled and frizzy. My new outfit looked fine enough, but my arms looked like sticks and my cheeks were hollow, my bones sticking out sharp in my face. Asa was right. I *did* look like I'd escaped a refugee camp.

The door clicked, and in walked a short guy, bald on top and gray on the sides, wearing tan suit pants with a mustard stain on the left thigh, a pale-blue button-down stretched over a generous belly that didn't match his wiry limbs, and a plaid bow tie. "Agent Winslow, Ms. Carver," he said in a nasally voice. "Nice to meet you."

"Um . . . hi." He looked and sounded so goofy that my fear faded, leaving only irritation.

He sat down across from me. "You hungry? You want a sandwich? You look like you could eat."

"No, thanks. But I'd love a phone call."

He arched an eyebrow. "Who would you call?"

"Is that your business?"

"We're not the police."

"I'm not sure if that's a threat or a reassurance."

"Consider it both."

"Nice. So can I have a call or not?"

He narrowed his eyes. "You're a tricky one."

"I'm actually pretty straightforward, relatively speaking."

"So maybe you can straightforwardly tell me how you came to be in the company of an infamous group of criminals."

"Criminals?" I blinked at him and prayed he wasn't a sensor. "I'm not sure who you're talking about."

He leaned forward, and I stared at his ridiculous tie. "I'm sure you'd like to go home, Ms. Carver. I'm sure you'd like to see your family again. You can if you cooperate."

Seeing my family again did sound nice . . . then my chest flared. "Oh, for Pete's sake. You're a Knedas."

"Ah. Guilty as charged." He gave me a sheepish smile. "It doesn't make anything I've said untrue."

"What exactly does 'cooperating' entail?"

"I'd like to know everyone you've talked to and been with in the past seventy-two hours."

I rubbed my temples. "Honestly, my head kinda hurts."

He chuckled. "I can see a more blunt approach is required. Let's try this—your fiancé telephoned our central office about twelve hours ago to offer us something very rare."

My fists clenched under the table. "A two-for-one special on neutering?"

Agent Winslow threw back his head and let out a bellowing laugh. "Good one! But no. He offered us a priceless relic that has long been believed to be out of circulation and out of our reach. Imagine our surprise when he described it in detail and offered to hand it over to us."

"So some guy called you out of the blue and claimed to have a priceless relic, and you believed him just because he told you what it looked like? How do you know he didn't look the thing up on Google Images?"

"Some guy?" Winslow's brow furrowed. "Dr. Benjamin Ward is your fiancé, is he not?" He bent to the side and peered at my hand under the table. "Quite a sparkler you've got there." He pulled out his phone and swiped until he got to an image, which he showed me. It was Ben and me two Christmases ago, grinning into the camera, our eyes bright, our cheeks flushed. "And a beautiful couple." He put the phone away.

"We're going through a rough patch."

"He said the same. He's very worried about you, Mattie. And he had quite a story to tell. Would you like to hear it?"

"I'm not sure I can take any more excitement tonight."

"He was willing to exchange the relic for you. It's priceless, and he could have tried to sell it, but instead, the only thing he wanted was our assistance in securing your safe return. He told us the tragic story of how he came to be in possession of it in the first place." He shook his head, drooping with apparent sadness. "I was just a young agent when Howard Carver retired, but he was well respected in our community. I'm sorry to hear of his loss."

"Thanks," I said in a broken whisper. "This wasn't what he wanted, though."

"But Dr. Ward said he wanted us to have the relic. Was Ben lying?"

"I'm sure he thinks he's telling the absolute truth."

"He accepted his share of the responsibility for drawing you into this. He offered to turn himself in and face charges." Winslow snickered. "Like all people not familiar with our world, he assumed we function as the police do."

"You don't care about what he did. You only care about getting ahold of the relic."

"Ms. Carver, you of all people can understand that original relics are incredibly dangerous. Don't you think it best if it doesn't end up in the hands of a mob boss?"

"Only if it ends up in more responsible hands. The verdict's still out on you."

He put a hand to his chest as if I'd wounded him. "We are here to protect innocent people. *All* innocent people—naturals and nonmagicals alike. Especially the vulnerable." He looked me up and down, and I stared mutinously back at him. "Your fiancé was able to describe exactly where you would be and—forgive me for saying so—exactly the shape we would find you in." He waved his hand at my face.

"Hang on a second. What is that supposed to mean?" I had forgotten to be scared for the moment. I was too mad, too hassled, too insulted, too worried, too guilty, and in way, way, *way* too much pain. "Actually, don't tell me. So just because Ben had something you want, and told you to come and get me, that's what you did—even though there was no reason to believe I was really in trouble? Is acting as errand boy for desperate, overcontrolling men something you guys do on the regular?"

"There was every reason to believe you were in trouble. He said you were under the influence of a man well known as a dangerous criminal—Asa Ward is a thief, a smuggler, and possibly even an assassin. Dr. Ward was frantic for your safety."

"Or maybe Ben just wants to punish his brother for breaking his nose last night."

Agent Winslow pushed his chair back and stood up. "Ah . . . excuse me, please." He turned and stared at the mirror. A moment later, the door clicked, and in walked a very tall woman with short black hair and a hawkish nose. "This is Agent Badem." He gave her a raised-eyebrow look. "I'm not making much headway."

"Maybe you need a woman's touch." She held out her hand to shake, and, still reeling from the realization that Ben had betrayed not only me, but also every carnie in the Carnival Magia, I offered mine in return.

The moment our palms touched, a heavy sense of peace shot up my arm and settled in my chest, quelling the stabbing pain. "Nice to meet you," Agent Badem said.

"Hey. Same," I replied, feeling my tongue go loose.

"Asa Ward," Agent Badem said. "Where can we find him?"

"No idea." Although, suddenly the image of the vet clinic popped into my mind. My mouth opened to tell her about Gracie, how much Asa loved her, how stinkin' cute she was, how adorable the two of them were together, how his love and care for her made me want to hug him fiercely and never let go . . . but at the same time, alarm bells inside my head rang loud enough to snap me out of it.

"No freaking idea." I yanked my hand out of the woman's grasp. Her power was different from Quentin's. Both were Ekstazo, but where he emitted pleasure and happiness, she emitted a heavier, mind-numbing kind of contentment.

"Dr. Ward was concerned he'd taken advantage of you. We've certainly seen this kind of Stockholm syndrome in the past, and it would explain why you're protecting him. Have you developed romantic feelings for Mr. Ward?" Agent Badem leaned on the table, looking at me intently.

I smiled as my head lolled back. "Oh, lady, the answer to that is *really* complicated."

"We've got all night." Her grin was full of reassurance and confidence as she placed her warm hand over mine.

"It would take longer than that." I stood up quickly as my head began to swim and my mouth filled with saliva. "Dial it back, lady, or I'm gonna throw up Twizzlers all over your pantsuit."

She looked startled and took a step back from the table. "We just want you to feel comfortable."

"I hate you people," I snapped. "In my book, Knedas and Ekstazos are just as bad as Strikons, if not worse. You use your powers to control people. To make them do things they don't want to. You're just like every mob lackey I ever met."

"We didn't mean to upset you." She put her hands up, giving me a look full of concern. "Are you all right, Mattie?"

"No," I said in a loud voice, swaying where I stood. "I'm not. I've done nothing wrong, and I don't know why I'm here."

"You're here because your fiancé wanted us to ensure your safety in return for handing over the priceless Sensilo relic," said Agent Winslow. "It's really that simple."

"Well, screw you. And screw him."

Agent Badem stepped close to me and closed her long fingers around my wrist. "He was afraid you would be angry with him. But it's obvious he was only doing what he thought was right. He was concerned that his brother was using Knedas magic to keep you at his side, and frankly, we were concerned about the same thing."

A swell of nausea crowded out the relaxed tingling that rolled up my arm. "Oh my God, you people are such hypocrites."

Agent Winslow sighed. "I think it's time for Mattie's phone call."

"Mm," said Agent Badem, who was now rubbing my back. I plopped back into the chair as my legs turned to jelly. I swear, the lady was like walking morphine. I put my head down on the table and groaned.

"Olivia, a lighter touch is called for," said Winslow. "She's clearly a bit fragile. We have to be careful not to overdose her."

"I hayshoo people," I said again, my words slurring.

Agent Badem stopped rubbing my back and instead slid a phone across the table. "Make your call, Mattie."

"Privashee."

"I'm afraid we can't offer you that."

"Shtoopud Headshmen."

"Agent Badem, maybe you should give Ms. Carver some space." Agent Winslow waved Agent Badem from the room. "I'm sorry. I thought it would help to relax you."

I lifted my head and glowered at his blurry form. He pushed the phone a bit closer, deftly avoiding the little puddle of drool I'd left on the table. "Perhaps I can make this easier." He clicked on my photo, and up popped a contact number. He pushed it and initiated a call.

"Hello," said my mother.

"Hello, Mrs. Carver. This is Kyle Winslow from the New Kent County Sheriff's Office. As promised, I've got your daughter here."

"Mattie?" Mom's voice went high and tremulous. "Oh, honey, we've been so worried. Ben called and explained everything."

"Heyyyyy." I shook my head and blinked, grateful for Agent Badem's departure. "What did he explain?"

"He just said he made some mistakes, and one of them was allowing his brother back into his life. We had no idea Ben was related to such a dangerous man. Why didn't you tell us? We've been waiting by the phone to hear from Agent Winslow. He promised to bring you home safe and sound."

I buried my head in my hands. "Mom, I'm fine. I was always fine."

"Oh, honey. They said you might say that." She sniffled. "Come home, Mattie. We got the wedding favors today. They're so cute— you're going to love how they turned out. I never knew Instagram made coasters."

"Instagram didn't make them," I mumbled, suddenly feeling even sicker than when Agent Badem was trying to use her mojo on me.

"Well, your guests are going to adore them. And your dad got fitted for his tux. He's lost five pounds! And—"

"I have to go, Mom." My voice faded as the knife in my chest twisted mercilessly.

"Okay, baby, but promise me you'll call again. We miss you and want you home where you belong."

"Bye, Mom," I whispered. I tapped the phone to end the call and hunched over the pain.

"Mattie, you don't look well."

"I'm so tired of people saying that. As if I was unaware."

"Ben informed us that you're a reliquary. He was concerned that Mr. Ward was going to use you as part of his smuggling operations. It just so happens we have people here who can help you if that's the case."

"No."

"Are you carrying magic? Did Mr. Ward force you to transport magic illegally? You don't have to protect him."

Stupid tears overflowed my eyes, and I angrily swiped at them. "Can you just leave me alone and focus on getting ahold of the grand prize? Will you let me go if Ben gives it to you?"

"Yes. We'll release you as soon as we have the Sensilo relic." But now Agent Winslow was looking at me with a distinctly suspicious glint in his eye. "I hope you won't mind if we assess your health first, though. We're responsible for you while you're in our custody, and we're well equipped to handle smuggled bits of magic." He turned back to the mirror and made a quick gesture at his chest.

The door opened, and in walked a man I hadn't imagined ever seeing again. His black hair was slicked away from his face, and his dark eyes were bright with hatred.

"Daeng." The last time I had seen him, he had been writhing on the ground outside a dingy hotel in Bangkok after I'd kneed him in the crotch, kicked him in the face, and shoved a handful of mud into his mouth—mud soaked with Asa's blood. It had overloaded Daeng's system in a pretty catastrophic way, because he had the same power Asa did.

"My friend," Daeng said softly, malice in every quiet word. "This is a happy coincidence."

"You two know each other?" Winslow asked.

"We only met once," said Daeng. "I had so hoped to see Mattie again someday, however."

I backed up until my shoulder blades hit cinder block. "Aren't you supposed to be on the other side of the ocean?"

"After our encounter, I'm afraid Mr. Montri wasn't very happy with me. But a wonderful Headsman came to my aid. Perhaps you know him. Agent Keenan? He extracted me from that terrible situation and rehabilitated me. I'm very grateful."

I swallowed hard. "Oh, yeah. How is Keenan?"

Daeng smiled. "Very interested to hear how you're faring. Especially if you have information as to Mr. Ward's whereabouts."

"Oh, sure. It's always about him."

He leaned forward slightly. "I'd be happy to make it about you."

A cold chill passed through me.

"I'm wondering if you could tell me if Ms. Carver here is loaded up," said Agent Winslow.

"I can tell you right now that she is," Daeng said. "Strikon. I felt it as soon as I entered the room." He gave me an assessing look. "I shouldn't be able to feel the magic inside you this easily. Are you broken?"

I flinched at the word. "I'm fine. Completely fine. But I've got a heck of a headache. Maybe that's what you're sensing." My heart wouldn't slow down, and I was sweating. The pain throbbed hot and heavy inside me, like I'd swallowed liquid fire.

Daeng didn't look so hot, either—he'd started to sweat, too. He turned to Agent Winslow. "It would be better for her if we remove this magic from her body and get it into a relic we can package up."

"Is it powerful?" asked Winslow, staring at my chest. "Valuable?"

"It's concentrated." Daeng frowned as he sidled closer to me. "Not massive, but extremely potent."

"No!" I said. "I won't let you do this." I had never done an extraction without Asa taking care of me, and in that moment I missed him so terribly that it almost brought me to my knees. And to have Daeng there instead? Horror was choking me. "You can't take anything from me without my permission. I'm a vault."

"Agent Okafor is extremely skilled," Winslow said to Daeng. "He's worked on unwilling reliquaries before."

I gaped at him. "Do you have any idea how *wrong* that sounds?"

"The magic inside her is almost certainly valuable," Daeng said to Winslow. "Once it's out, I might be able to tell you where it came from. It might help you trace Asa Ward."

"It won't tell you anything," I said to Agent Winslow. "And I've done nothing to warrant this kind of treatment. I'm only here because you guys want the Sensilo relic. It doesn't matter what I have inside me—as long as it's not that, right?"

I wasn't about to mention I was holding a different piece of original magic, but it turned out not to matter.

Winslow gave me a sympathetic look. "I'm sorry, Mattie. I think removing the magic is what's best for you."

"Please page your conduit, then." A slow smile spread across Daeng's handsome face. "And fetch me some handcuffs."

CHAPTER NINETEEN

Sometimes, after something terrible happens to a person, especially a woman, other people wonder why she didn't do more to defend herself, to protect herself, to call for help.

I know why. At some point, the terror and the helplessness coil around you so tight that you can't move. It's like ropes twining round your limbs, a blindfold over your eyes, a gag in your mouth.

It smothers and silences, but it doesn't numb.

I mutely slid down the wall and wrapped my arms around my knees as Daeng and Winslow exited the room to page Agent Okafor, the conduit who could apparently overpower reluctant reliquaries. I stared up at the mirror across the room, wordlessly pleading with whoever stood behind it. But I knew they didn't care about me. They wanted what was inside me, no matter the damage they did in acquiring it. I wasn't a person to them. Once again I was just an object—a bargaining chip, a trunk that needed to be opened.

When I had first met Asa, he'd treated me a little like that, too. At some point, though, that had changed. He'd become my rock, my certainty, my safety when the storm hit. And now I needed him. He'd never left me behind. I knew he wouldn't walk away. But he probably had no idea where I was. And Asa could do a lot of things, but breaking into a sheriff's station packed with armed deputies and trained Headsmen who clearly had defenses against mind-twisting magic might be too much to expect.

Yet somehow, I did expect it. My muscles tensed at the sound of every muffled voice outside the door, hoping it might be his. My heart lurched every time a door slammed, wondering if it was the beginning of a rescue. My hope just wouldn't quit.

Until Daeng wheeled the stretcher into the room. It had thick leather cuffs for wrists and ankles, straps for the body. He gestured at it happily. "We borrowed this from the hospital next door. Very convenient. Please take your position."

"Screw you."

"Agent Okafor," Daeng called into the hallway. "I think I might need your assistance to get our reliquary on the table."

In walked a casually dressed African American man in his late twenties, with a broad forehead and a clean-shaven square jaw, good-looking in a solid, staunch kind of way. His black hair was cut in a short crop, thick curls on top and shaved sides. He wasn't that tall, maybe five nine, but he was seriously built, with bulging pecs and biceps that suggested hours spent at a weight bench. He gazed down at me and arched an eyebrow. "Hello, Ms. Carver," he said in a deep, smooth voice. "I'm Jack Okafor."

I blinked at him. "Jack . . . Okafor."

"The *third*," he added, his dark-brown eyes cold. "I believe you knew my grandfather."

"Oh God," I whispered. "You're Jack's grandson."

"And you and Asa Ward left my grandfather on a dingy hotel-room floor with a bullet through his skull."

I grimaced at the memory. "We didn't kill him."

"I didn't say you did. I also didn't say I cared about the distinction. You treated him with as much regard as a sack of meat."

"I'm so sorry. We were running for our lives, and—"

"Really not interested in your excuses."

"I wouldn't have left him like that if I'd had a choice!"

"Ms. Carver actually has a habit of leaving people for dead," said Daeng.

I rose on my knees, anger giving me a temporary surge of strength. "I left *you* after you did your level best to kill me and Asa. Did you honestly expect me to stay and cuddle?"

"Let's get her strapped in," said Daeng, his cheek twitching, his face glistening with perspiration. "I'd like to get this done."

Jack came over to me, and I pressed myself back against the wall, my hands up, my eyes clamped shut, and my face turned away. "Come on, Mattie. Don't be a baby."

His hands closed around my upper arms, and he lifted me up as if I were a puppy. My toes brushed the ground as he briskly carried me over to the stretcher. And here was where I could have struggled. Here was where I could have fought. But the pain and the horror and the absolute helplessness were like a muscle relaxant, sapping me of any fight I had. Jack outweighed me by nearly a hundred pounds, and he had me on that stretcher in an instant.

As he took hold of my wrists to place them in the cuffs, I looked up at his face. "Our grandfathers were good friends. They worked together for years."

"I know. I've heard all the stories." He seemed to be avoiding my gaze.

"What happened to your grandfather was tragic and wrong. But he would never have wanted you to do this. He came to my rescue because he cared about me. He gave his life saving me. He was a great man who made a great sacrifice."

Jack's jaw clenched as he pressed my arms into the cuffs. Daeng quickly buckled them before moving to my ankles. I shuddered as I felt his hands on my legs. "Please, Jack. If you're anything like he was, you won't do this to me."

Jack turned abruptly, grabbed one of the metal chairs, and set it down sharply next to my stretcher with a ringing clang. "*Don't* tell me what kind of man my grandfather was. Don't act like you knew him."

"Look at me and tell me he would approve."

His eyes met mine. "I'm about to remove illegally procured magic from an uncooperative subject. He knew I was a Headsman. He respected my choices."

"You're going to kill me. You don't know what you're dealing with."

He let out an impatient sigh. "I've been a professional conduit for nearly a decade, so I doubt that's true." He glanced at Daeng. "You got the relic we're gonna put this in?"

Daeng produced what appeared to be a solid cube of metal, about three inches on a side. "Winslow gave me this."

Jack nodded. "Made to handle homeless magic. Always does the trick."

I sniffled. "If I die, will you walk away from *me*? Will you treat me like a sack of meat? Is this payback?"

"Look. I'm not here to hurt you. That's not what this is about at all. I'm just here to get a job done."

Daeng fiddled with the cuffs around my ankles. "Your supervisor wants this magic soon."

"My supervisor will get this magic when he gets it," Jack snapped. "I'm not a machine and neither is she."

I blinked. "Thank you."

His nostrils flared and he looked away, the muscles of his neck tensing. It was like he wanted to be hard—but I could tell he had a heart buried under that armor. Maybe he was more like his grandfather than he was letting on. He held out his hand, and Daeng placed the metal cube on his palm. "Mattie, it's gonna work best if you just let this go. Don't fight me."

My need for Asa hit me again, hard and abrupt like a sucker punch. "I'm not sure how." I stared at the ceiling while my tears flowed freely. "I usually have help."

"I'll help you if you let me," he said gently. "I swear I will."

"She's an uncooperative subject," Daeng said. "You're authorized to use whatever force is necessary."

"And if no force is necessary, that's exactly how much I'll use." Jack's voice was thunder in the small room. "If you try to tell me how to do my job one more time, I'm going to show you the door."

"I'm the sensor!"

"And I outrank you, dude, so shut up until I ask you a question."

Daeng's face was a mottled pink, but he didn't reply.

Jack turned back to me. "We're gonna do this together. I'll take it easy, and you let it loose nice and slow. I know it's Strikon, but I've dealt with that shit before."

"You haven't dealt with this."

"Help me, then. And I'll help you."

I shook my head. I wanted so badly to trust him, but though he didn't seem evil, I also knew I wasn't his priority—the magic was. It occurred to me that I should tell him exactly what was inside me, but I was afraid it would only make them more insistent.

"Mattie. I can tell it's hurting you," Jack said, leaning close and speaking in my ear. "You're going to feel so much better once we get this out."

Or I'll be dead, and maybe that would feel better than this. Strapped to a gurney under a harsh fluorescent light, a blade of pain slicing me down the middle. And no Asa. He hadn't come. He couldn't save me from this. He couldn't carry me through.

"Just do it," I said in a strangled whisper. "Do it now."

Jack tucked his palm along the inside of my arm, and immediately the pain increased, as if someone were sawing through my breastbone. I let out a choked gasp and arched back.

"Let it go, girl," said Jack. "Let it go."

I couldn't. I was too terrified, too incapacitated by agony.

But it broke free anyway.

My vision went red and bloody. It was like two hands cracked me down the middle and spread my ribs, presenting my heart and lungs like a buffet just before forks and knives dug in for the feast. I don't know if I made a single sound, but the inside of my skull was one long scream drenched in suffering. My body contracted upward and slammed back. Over and over again until that's all I was, a broken, limp piece of human wreckage.

Then the hurt dimmed a little, replaced by a bubbling sting in my chest and throat. The light beyond my closed eyelids flickered. Hoarse shouting filled the room, penetrating the noise inside my brain.

"Get out of the way, dammit," someone yelled in a nasally voice. "Tell the ER they have incoming."

"What should I tell them about their condition?"

"Aaah, car accident, maybe."

I turned my head as something hot and wet choked me. I coughed, gagging at the metallic taste on my tongue. My eyelids fluttered open. The sheet next to my face was spattered with frothy scarlet blood.

"It's going to be okay, Mattie," said Winslow.

"We're taking you guys to a hospital," Badem added. She had her hand clamped around my wrist, maybe trying to dull the pain.

My eyes rolled in my head as I tried to bring the world into focus. "What . . ." The word gurgled wet from my throat, and I coughed again. My blood splattered onto the sleeve of Winslow's shirt, and he made a face like he was going to be sick. "Magic?" I asked hoarsely. "Is it out?"

"We're not sure," Badem said with a frown. "Daeng lost consciousness after ending the transaction. Jack is right behind us. He's in better shape than you, but . . ."

I cried out as we rolled over some kind of threshold, and then we were rattling across the parking lot, gurney wheels shrieking for oil, me writhing in agony at every crack or dip in the pavement. To say that something had gone wrong seemed like an understatement. "Why hospital?" I gurgled. "This . . . is . . . magic."

"Why didn't that healing relic work?" asked Badem.

"It was dumb to try it. Those things only work on nonmagical injuries—they weren't made for stuff like this."

"What the *hell* was in her?"

"Splinter," I whispered, but it didn't seem like either of them heard me. They were too busy hollering at the medical staff as they rolled me through the doors of the emergency department. Masked faces appeared over me, and something tight was wrapped around my arm just before a needle pierced it.

After that, everything was kinda hazy for a while.

I awoke to the sound of a door closing, my eyes fluttering open to see a room with creamy-yellow walls and a window that overlooked the sheriff's station with the sun sinking behind it—I had been here for the whole day at least. I took a breath and whimpered as it reawakened the animal feasting on my heart and lungs.

"Easy there, girl."

I turned my head toward the sound of Jack's voice. He was sitting in a chair on the other side of the bed, next to the monitors reporting on my heartbeat and blood oxygenation. He looked a little ashen and was wearing scrub pants under a hospital gown. "What happened?" I asked in a weak rasp.

"Fubar, plain and simple."

"Huh?"

"It was bad."

"I'd never have guessed." I glanced down at myself. Wires snaked from my chest to the monitors, and an IV tube extended from the crook of my arm to a bag hanging above the bed.

"They've done a chest scan. Their guess was a pulmonary embolism. You're on some kind of blood thinner." He gestured at the chart hooked to the end of my bed.

"Oh, yeah, feel free to read my confidential medical records."

He chuckled. "Anything to ease a guilty conscience." I turned to look at him again, and he gave me an apologetic shrug. "I thought I'd killed you. I thought I'd killed me, too, for a minute there."

"What happened?"

"I got hit with a bolt of pain like nothing I'd ever felt, but I couldn't get it to flow into the relic no matter how hard I tried. I couldn't control it. So it just zinged back and forth between you and me, slicing and dicing."

"Ouch."

"Daeng pulled me away, so that ended whatever was happening."

"And the magic?"

He let out a heavy sigh. "We had Daeng in here earlier." He gestured to the little table next to my bed, at a small basket with a red teddy bear holding a card with a picture of a cat on it. Below it were the words "Stop being a pussy. Get well soon."

"What a lovely sense of humor. I bet he enjoyed every minute of my agony."

"The guy does seem a little cracked."

"Tell me about it."

"He said the magic's still inside you."

I closed my eyes and let out a shallow, slow breath. "I think I already knew that."

"We should have listened to you."

"I knew that, too."

"Not the best way to start an acquaintance. I think I owe you an apology."

"Yeah. I'd say you do."

"I hate apologizing."

I pressed my lips together as the memory of Asa saying the same thing rose, tightening bands of regret around my chest, making breathing even more of a chore.

"I was angry over what happened to Gramps, okay?" Jack said. "He didn't deserve to go out that way. And I was the one who had to tell my mom and pop, because Headsmen were first on the scene. God, it was a shit show."

"I get it. You don't have to explain."

"It was no excuse to take it out on you. Though if I get my hands on Ward, I'm bringing him to justice. Just a heads-up."

"Good luck with that." If he was saying this to me, it meant Asa had escaped the raid. They didn't know where he was.

"I don't suppose you have any info—"

"Nope. Sorry."

"We don't have to be enemies, Mattie."

My eyes met his. "Then let's not."

He stared at me for a moment, and then his full lips lifted into a smile. I half expected him to go on questioning me, but instead he said, "I got a few stories about our grandfathers. Did yours ever tell you what they got up to?"

I shook my head. "I only found out what he was at the very end of his life. He kept it a secret."

His smile grew, and it was so boyish and excited that it made me smile, too. "There was this one time, down in Rio, when—" He frowned at the sound of funk music emanating from his waist, and reached beneath his gown to retrieve a phone that he'd clipped to his scrub pants.

"Okafor here," he said, his voice dropping into dry professional mode for a split second before rising in alarm. "Say that again? Yes, I turned up the collar! What? How?"

I couldn't hear what the person on the other end was saying, but I caught a frantic note. Jack shot to his feet and strode over to the window, peering at the station. "Stay where you are," he barked. "Do *not* go out there. Do not—shit!"

I heard the gunshot and the scream all the way across the room.

Jack tapped his phone and held it to his ear again. "Pick up, Winslow," he muttered. "Dammit, pick up."

He cursed and ended the call a moment later, probably after it went to voice mail.

"What's going on?"

Jack looked down at his hospital gown, momentarily at a loss. "He got out. I thought we had him fully contained."

I flinched at the muffled sound of gunfire coming from outside. Jack ducked low and pressed himself to the wall as he peered out the window. "Oh my God, that motherfucker is making them kill each other."

"What the heck is going on?"

He turned back to me. "I have to go. He won't affect me." He almost sounded as if he were trying to reassure himself.

"Who are you talking about?"

"Arkady," Jack said as he headed for the door. "And if I don't stop him, more people are gonna die."

CHAPTER TWENTY

Arkady. The man in the silver collar. I wondered if, when Asa had spotted him in town, Jack had been the one meeting him, maybe posing as a freelancer who wanted to help him obtain the Sensilo relic. They'd captured and caged him, but somehow he'd escaped.

And judging from the sounds coming from outside, he was wreaking havoc.

"Code atlas," said a voice over the intercom. "Code atlas." From the hallway, I heard the sound of running feet and urgent voices.

This was bad. But it was also just the chance I needed.

Grimacing, I sat up and tugged the IV from my arm. Blood beaded in the crook of my arm as I pulled the leads off my chest. The machine began to beep loudly, but no one came running in to see if I'd had a heart attack.

I found my clothes in a plastic sack in the bathroom and put them on, pausing to lean against the wall and breathe through the pain every few seconds. My chest felt oddly brittle, like one sharp blow would shatter it. I had to get out of there before the Headsmen were able to do exactly that. Jack might not be willing to go for round two, but I didn't trust them not to bring in someone else to try again.

I slipped my feet into my sandals, grabbed the basket containing the stuffed bear and stupid get-well card, and peeked out the door. I wasn't the only one. The code atlas had a lot of people poking their heads out to see what was going on. But since there was no immediate danger that I could see, I focused on striding toward the elevators as if I were just a visitor delivering a (tasteless) gift for a patient.

"Miss, you can't take the elevators," barked a doctor as he ran down the hall, just as I hit the "Down" button. "We're in lockdown."

"Oh. Where am I supposed to go?"

"Visitors are supposed to go to the cafeteria. First floor. Take the stairs. Go immediately."

"I will!" I followed him to the stairs, letting him widen the gap between us as he rushed down the steps. When I reached the first floor, I slowly opened the door to see staff herding visitors into the cafeteria to my right while medical personnel rushed toward the emergency department to my left.

The exit to the parking lot right in front of me had been barred. If the hospital was in lockdown, that meant no one in or out, but I knew that they had to let emergency responders come and go.

So I headed to my left, wishing I could do what they always do in the movies and somehow steal a pair of scrubs to disguise myself. It turned out not to be necessary, though. I walked through the sliding doors of the emergency department to see that it was in absolute chaos. Uniformed sheriff's deputies lay on almost every gurney, bleeding from gunshot wounds. Against the wall were a few covered bodies—the staff seemed too overwhelmed to handle the DOAs. And peeking out from under one of the sheets was a dangling wrist, a silver cuff fastened around it. A Headsman. And despite what they'd put me through, I felt a pang—of sympathy and of fear.

It appeared that Arkady had single-handedly decimated the sheriff's station, despite their efforts to contain him. The silver collar had looked like some kind of shock device, maybe used to break his concentration so he couldn't influence others. I was betting the silver cuffs did something similar for the Headsmen, supplying just enough pain to enable them to see through Knedas glamours. Apparently neither was foolproof.

I stayed out of the way, keeping my head down as I made my way to the exit. No one seemed all that interested in stopping me—everyone had life-or-death business to attend to. Two frantic medics burst over the threshold shouting, "Self-inflicted gunshot wound to the head, code blue! Code blue!" I took the opportunity to slip outside, averting my eyes from the tragedy on the gurney.

The gunfire seemed to have stopped. The sheriff's station was ringed with New Kent police cars as well as a few Virginia trooper vehicles, along with one black SWAT truck and two fire trucks. Their red and blue lights glowed, brightening the night. I picked my way across the packed hospital parking lot—at least one news van had already arrived—and headed in the opposite direction of the carnage.

I had no idea how to reach Asa. I had no money and no phone. And I was already panting like I'd run a mile at top speed. But I was still alive. I nearly doubled over as the splinter cut its way along my spine, and my body convulsed as I coughed droplets of blood onto the gravel at my feet.

"Okay, mostly alive," I said with a grimace, wishing for a glass of water to wash the awful salt-and-metal taste out of my mouth. I was sure I had crimson teeth. If anyone spotted me, they'd most likely take me right back to the hospital. It was probably where I belonged. But I wasn't about to sit there waiting for someone else, maybe an Ekstazo, maybe a Knedas, to come in and try to work on me again. I was so tired of them trying to control me. I was so tired of feeling like I wasn't the boss of my own body.

I glanced behind me at the chaos of cop cars and other emergency vehicles. I hoped they'd caught the guy now, and that Jack was okay. Magic couldn't affect conduits like it did ordinary people, even other naturals—including reliquaries. It just went right through them, always headed somewhere else. I hadn't thought about it much before, but it must have made them useful as Headsmen. They could see through glamours, shrug off the touch of a Strikon, laugh as an Ekstazo tried to win them over. The only time they felt the effects of magic was when it was passing through them on its way into a reliquary or a relic.

Jack was immune to Arkady's influence. But it didn't mean Arkady couldn't influence someone else to shoot him or run him over.

That grisly thought made me shiver, and I quickened my shuffling steps, hoping for houses around the curve in the road. All I had to do was find someone willing to let me use a phone. If I called my parents, they could wire money or buy me a bus ticket or something. I didn't know what else to do.

I nearly cried with relief and hope as I spotted a house ahead, its windows glowing yellow and warm and safe in the siren-split night. I limped up the driveway, noting the cute little flower garden out front, purple crocuses and hyacinths, clearly carefully tended. Clinging to the porch banister, I dragged myself up the few steps and leaned on the house as I knocked on the door, my breath rattling uncomfortably.

The door opened, revealing a round-faced old lady with glasses and curly white hair. "Can I help you?"

"I was wondering if I could use your phone." I gave her a closed-mouth smile. "I managed to lose mine. My car broke down up the road."

The woman's brow furrowed as she glanced up the road toward the hospital and the sheriff's station. "You involved in that unpleasantness up there? I been in here scared to death."

"No, my car is the other way." I pointed in the opposite direction of the station. "I saw a lot of police cars go by, though."

She nodded, then looked me up and down. "What's your name, dear?"

"Mattie."

"I'm Dolores." She smiled. "You look pretty harmless, but I need to ask my husband if I can let you in."

"Oh. Okay," I said as she closed the door in my face. I peered through the sheer curtains as she walked down a hallway on the other side of the cozy living room, praying that her husband was a nice guy who would let his little wifey assist a forlorn stranger. I braced myself for an old guy to come hobbling down the hall, ready to defend his home, but instead Dolores returned and said, "Come on in. Our phone's right over here." She pointed at a cordless that sat on an end table next to the slipcovered couch.

"Thank you so much," I said, stepping into the house and shedding a tiny bit of the fear I'd been carrying with me since my escape from the hospital. I had done it, pulled free of the craziness of the Headsmen. Now all I had to do was stay free.

"She's in, darling," Dolores called down the hall.

"Thank you, *darling*," answered a Russian-accented voice. "Now please go stand by the door."

A chill zipped through me, and I turned toward the hall as Arkady stepped out of one of the rooms. He looked much more relaxed than he had in his holding cell, shackled and collared. He gave me a smile as he slowly walked toward me, seductive and confident. "Hello, Mattie. I remember you from the station. I saw you going in looking weak and scared. And when I saw you go out, well . . ." He clucked his tongue. "It looked like maybe it would be your final ride. I'm so happy to see you looking—" He narrowed his eyes as he glanced at my mouth. "Hmm. Well, not healthy, exactly."

I reached up and swiped a hand across my mouth, sagging a little as it came away smeared with blood. "I don't think we know each other."

"I feel like I know *you*. I listened to all they said about you." His accent was rich, vibrating along my bones. "But I suppose I should observe the formalities. I am Arkady Igorevich Kalagin." He bowed his head. "I am in the service of Volodya Dimitrievich Zobkov." He brought his head up and met my eyes. "And I am seeking the original Sensilo relic. In this respect I believe you can be helpful to me."

I never thought I'd be truly thankful for the pain the Strikon splinter caused me, but right then, I swear I could feel Arkady's power pressing close around me, caressing my shoulders and throat, my legs and waist—but not sticking. "Actually, I don't think I can. Sorry. It's true that I had it, but as far as I know, it's long gone."

"Dolores." Arkady turned his attention to the old woman, who had moved to stand obediently next to her front door. "Please slam your hand in the door."

"Of course!" She swung the door wide and placed her left hand on the doorframe.

"Don't," I said sharply, walking over and grabbing the door just as she started to slam it shut. Maybe I was weak—or she was surprisingly determined—but she pulled it from my grip and shut the door hard, letting out a whimper as her fingers were crushed.

"Don't let her stop you, Dolores. You know you need to obey me. Now do it again."

Dolores's wrinkled little face radiated frustration as I once again reached for her. "You back off now, dearie, or I'll have to hurt you."

I looked over my shoulder at Arkady, who was leaning against the wall, a smile playing across his lips. "Cut it out, you jerk! She's just an innocent old lady."

"I can't help it, Mattie. You won't give me what I need. I'm in despair." He winked at me.

Dolores elbowed me in the stomach. I staggered backward and landed in a clumsy sprawl on the living room floor. The old woman immediately resumed her project of destroying her left hand. She opened the door wide, her cheeks pulled back in rigid anticipation of the pain to come.

"Stop this and we can talk," I shouted.

"Dolores, hold on a moment," Arkady said. "Actually, just to make this fun, please go into the kitchen and fetch your sharpest knife."

"You bet." She let go of the door and walked to the kitchen, her bruised left hand hanging at her side. I was panting as I stared up at her, horrified that he could so casually destroy a completely innocent woman. Headsmen who had locked him up were one thing—this was entirely another.

Arkady settled himself on the arm of the couch. "Reliquaries aren't usually so skilled at resisting my charms."

"I'm special." I sat up a little straighter. "And I won't help you until you let her go."

He laughed softly. "Oh, you are so amusing."

Dolores emerged from the kitchen with a steak knife in her hand. "Will this do?"

"Do you think you could sever your own jugular with it?"

"My jugular?" She looked down at her belly.

"Your neck, dear."

"Oh!" She squinted at the blade of the knife and touched her throat. "Probably. If I sawed hard enough."

"You're insane," I said in a choked voice.

Arkady scoffed. "That is not accurate at all. People who are insane do not know what is right from what is wrong. I have no problem to recognize that persuading an old woman to cut her own throat is utterly appalling." He shrugged. "But would the fault not be yours? All I ask is that you help me find what was stolen."

I looked back and forth from the old woman to the debonair Russian assassin. If I didn't know full well that he'd just coerced several sheriff's deputies into setting him free and then shooting each other—or themselves—I would have called his bluff. But a woman's life hung in the balance. "What do you want?"

"A mere phone call." He pulled a phone out of his pocket and tapped it, then held it up and showed me the picture of me and Ben.

My stomach dropped. "Is that Agent Winslow's phone?"

"He was most helpful. He told me this man you are to marry is the one who has the relic in his possession, but that he is willing to exchange it for you. So romantic."

I stared at the phone. "He told you all that? But . . . he's a Knedas."

"Yet I, my dear, am a better one." He smoothed his hand over his dark hair, revealing his widow's peak. "I particularly love dealing with the people like him. So used to being the chess master. Imagine his surprise when he became the pawn."

"Did you kill him?" I whispered.

"Oh, no." He grinned. "Agent Badem did that for me. Just before she took her own life."

"I think I'm going to be sick."

He stood up. "Why should you not be glad? You and I, we are not so different. We were both at their mercy. The Headsmen." His full lips curled with disgust. "They fashion themselves as the good guys, the white hats as you say. But look at how they treat their fellow naturals." He gestured back and forth between us. "We have no rights—even here in America! They lock us up. Torture us. Worse than KGB on their very cruelest day."

"So basically, they're like you?"

"No, not like me. You see, I never claimed to be a good guy."

I shuddered as I looked down at the image of Ben and me on the screen of the phone he had clutched in his hand. "Fair point."

"Ah. I see that you can be reasoned with. This is hopeful. But just in case, one moment—Dolores, do you have a knife sharpener?"

"I think I do."

"Please use it. Test the blade on your palm to make sure it cuts the flesh like it was butter."

"Happy to!"

I groaned, tears stinging my eyes. "Please don't hurt her."

"Again, that is entirely up to you. Are you ready to talk to your Benjamin?"

I winced at the sound of metal on stone. "Yes."

He wiped a tear off my cheek. "This will not do, Mattie. You must not sound frightened when you speak with him. I would have to make Dolores bleed by her own hand if you did that."

"What do you want me to say?"

"I will make the call from Winslow's phone. Tell him you are with the agent who rescued you from the carnival. Tell him that you are no longer under the influence of Asa Ward." Our eyes met as he said Asa's name. "I only know Mr. Ward by reputation, but I would love to hear more."

"You and everyone else."

"Well, now I am even more intrigued. Where is Mr. Ward now?"

"That's the twentieth time in recent memory that someone's asked me that question. But I swear, I don't know." And even if I did, the pain in my chest was jagged enough to enable me to keep my mouth shut.

He sighed. "We will come back to that later. Priorities." He held out the phone. "Shall we call Benjamin Ward? Are you ready to convince him?"

"What am I convincing him of, exactly?"

"Tell him to bring the relic and meet us outside Fleeger's Tavern in Barrett's Corner at midnight."

"Where?"

He rolled his eyes. "Dolores . . ."

"Okay! Call him! I'll do it!"

He gave me a tight smile and called Ben's number and set it to speaker as Dolores came out of the kitchen with her knife gleaming—and her palm dripping blood from a three-inch gash. I stifled a sob as I heard Ben say, "Hello? Agent Winslow?"

"It's me." I rubbed my face and desperately tried to pull myself together.

"Mattie, thank God. I've been dying, just waiting to hear your voice again."

"You made quite an exit from the carnival." I cleared my throat, trying to knock away the terrified tremor.

"I had to risk it. Nothing is as important to me as you are."

I swallowed hard. "I can see that."

"I'll hand the relic over whenever. Wherever. As long as you come home with me."

I told Ben where the "agent" wanted him to meet us, even as a dark fear stirred inside of me. I glanced at Dolores, who was standing placidly as she bled onto the living room carpet. "We can just drop the relic and get going." I looked at Arkady, pleading. "Right?"

He nodded and smiled.

"Sounds perfect to me," said Ben. "I want you to know, Mattie— I'm going to leave Asa's van where he can find it. He thinks I'm guilty of a lot of other stuff—I don't want stealing his ride to be one of them."

"Okay. That'll be good."

Arkady looked somewhat intrigued by the mention of Asa's van, but he gestured for me to wrap up the call. "I guess I'll see you at midnight," I said, wishing dread allowed my words to flow a little more easily.

"You okay, babe? I know you've been through so much. But I swear, we're almost through it."

"I'm fine," I mumbled, rubbing my chest. "I'll see you soon."

Arkady ended the call, then looked at his watch. "We have three hours until our meeting. What do you say to some dinner? Should we have Dolores make us a home-cooked meal?"

I looked up at him in horror, and then at Dolores. Arkady plucked the bloody knife from her hand and laid it on the counter. "Say no more," he said. "Let us go out."

CHAPTER
TWENTY-ONE

We ended up in a little roadside bar with hunting trophies all over the walls—leaping fish, staring deer, and one snarling bobcat—and slipped into a booth with a gummy tabletop presided over by a shriveled red fox whose plastic eyes were so round and big that it looked terrified.

I probably wore a similar expression as Arkady settled himself across from me. My pain was the only thing keeping me from Dolores's blank-eyed fate, but I knew too well that everyone around me was in danger as a result—and that meant that I had to be very careful about any escape plans. A waitress immediately came over like she'd been yanked by a hook, and he ordered a vodka and a reuben. I wasn't hungry but had barely eaten in days, so I ordered an orange juice and some toast with peanut butter.

"Come. This calls for a drink." Arkady made a dismissive gesture at the waitress. "Fetch my friend a vodka as well."

"Be back in two shakes of a lamb's tail," said the young woman.

I smiled at her and didn't contradict him. I was afraid that if I turned down his gift of vodka, he'd have her stab herself in the eye with a fork. It was a relief when she disappeared into the kitchen—but of course that meant I was alone with him. "So . . . have you traveled to the States a lot?" I asked, hoping to keep the conversation shallow while my mind raced to figure out a plan.

"Several times." He laid his arm along the back of the booth and gave the terrified fox an amused look. "This is a rather silly country, but you do have many nice things. And the things you people do with magic?" He chuckled and kissed the tips of his fingers. "Very creative."

I thought of Asa and the improvised magical weaponry he carried in his pockets, badly wishing he were here right now. "I'm not really into the magical world, so I wouldn't know. I just want to go home."

"Home to Sheboygan, Wisconsin?" He said the name of my home state in that exaggerated American accent, wrapping his lips around the second syllable as if it were trying to escape. But even though it sounded funny, it still felt like a threat.

"Does it matter? We're going to give you the relic, and then *you* can go home."

"Yes, my boss is fairly eager to have his relic back." He accepted a shot of vodka from the waitress and downed it in one swallow, then eyed the one she'd set in front of me.

I pushed it toward him. "I don't really drink."

He tossed that one back as well. "I would love to hear how one of the original four relics ended up in the hands of a young couple from this state of Wisconsin. Especially since all this time, we believed *we* had possession of it."

I took a sip of my orange juice. "It's really not that interesting."

Our waitress returned with our food, but once she'd set it on the table, she merely stood there. Arkady patted the back of her hand as he looked into my eyes, and I let out a shaky breath. "Message received." For two seconds, I considered lying, but then realized that if he saw through it, our waitress would pay the price. "My grandfather was a reliquary. My last name is Carver." At least I knew he couldn't hurt my grandpa.

Arkady's eyes widened for an instant. "You are the granddaughter of Howard Carver?" He threw back his head and laughed. "It seems I am doomed to be haunted by the progeny of colleagues past."

He was talking about Jack the Third, I was sure. "Colleagues? Is that what you call the people you captured and threatened to torture?"

"Jack Okafor and Howard Carver were intruders and thieves. They came to Russia to plunder and profit. It is my job to protect the interests of my master." His hand gripped the back of the booth. "Even when he does not have his own best interests in mind."

"Well, I guess I won't argue with the thief part, since they stole the Sensilo relic right out from under you."

"But what I don't understand is *how*—" Arkady's face hardened, and his eyes became slits. "Theresa," he growled.

I stayed very still. Jack and Grandpa were dead, but I had no idea if Theresa the sensor was, and I didn't want to do or say anything to put her in danger—especially if she happened to be Asa and Ben's mom. "Um. Who's Theresa?"

"A traitor! On this I bet my life," he said through clenched teeth, then glanced at our waitress, who was still standing at our table.

She looked down at him. "I'll be right back with that vodka, sir," she said and rushed away from the table.

With shaking hands, I spread peanut butter on my toast. "And you think she had something to do with the theft of the relic?"

"It explains so much." He ran his hands over his face, looking suddenly weary. "This will break Volodya's heart. All these years, he has refused to believe she would betray him. He punished anyone who even suggested it. He sent us to the edges of the world to search for her. He has held on to the belief that she was taken from him, and now he will have to face the terrible truth—she *took* from him."

"So she disappeared?"

He nodded. "Perhaps fifteen years ago. Soon after my final encounter with your grandfather and Mr. Okafor. Now I realize it must have been around that time she helped them to acquire the Sensilo relic. No one but her could have recognized the false relic she left behind. Only a very powerful sensor could detect the difference." He slammed his fist down on the table. "If I ever find her . . ."

A tight knot inside me loosened slightly—she was out of his reach. "Did you know her well?"

He took the third vodka shot from the waitress's tray before she had a chance to put it on the table. After he drained it, the stiff line of his shoulders softened, and I wondered if maybe the vodka was my best ally at the moment.

"I doubt anyone really knew her," he said, "though my master would have done anything for her. She was precious to him." He grunted. "She found me distasteful. My Lishka as well." He muttered something to himself and reached into the collar of his shirt, pulling out a gold chain from which hung a wedding ring. "My late wife was a beautiful woman, you know. But she was poisonous." He smiled sadly and stared at his reflection in the narrow band. "Theresa could not stand to be in the room with us. I was glad when she was gone, because while she was at Volodya's side, he exiled my Lishka and me to the very edges of his territory. But soon I realized Theresa was not really gone. Volodya was consumed with her. She escaped him once, but despite that, he could not fathom why she would do it again."

"What do you mean, she escaped him once?"

"Well, she was American, you know. And they met young, just as he was gathering power. It was the height of the Soviet Union. He was the son of a party official, but he is also a gifted sensor. Not magic—emotion. It is nearly impossible to lie to this man." Arkady smacked his lips and accepted a fourth shot as it arrived. My hope grew as he downed it.

"If he's such a powerful emotion sensor, though, couldn't he tell what she was feeling?"

"Not with her. And he found it intriguing." He rolled his eyes. "That must be it, as she was no great beauty. She had a strong face. A strong presence. But she was not like my Lishka." He smiled wistfully.

"If she was American and he was Russian, how did they meet?"

"He caught her trying to steal from him, of course, little thief. She tried to leave East Germany with a powerful Knedas relic. He could have had her shot." His eyes shone. "He could have called *me*. I would have taken care of her. But my master has a tender heart. Instead of punishing her, he took her under his protection."

"Magic sensors *are* pretty valuable," I muttered.

"She was his jewel. With her at his side, he rose in power, collecting the most powerful and valuable relics and artifacts in the world, acquiring the best people to work for him, building his juicing operations and infrastructure for the sale of the product, bribing all the right people and blackmailing the others. And then, just as they had the world at their feet, the little bitch ran away."

"When was this?" I was frantically trying to build a timeline to see if the pieces fit.

"She could not have picked a better time. It was Christmas of 1982, when our two countries were on the brink of war. Even for people like us, crossing borders became more difficult. I think Volodya did not realize how much he had come to depend on her. We needed her talents in order to *find* her, this you understand?"

"Yeah." I forced myself to take a bite of my peanut butter toast even though my chest was blazing and my stomach was off. "So how did he get her back?"

"He sent me and Lishka to search. Many others, too. Theresa covered her tracks very well, and like I said, the travel was not so easy. Headsmen were vicious in those days—I think perhaps your president Reagan had them targeting the Soviets. Who knows how much he paid them. But eventually, we narrowed our search to the middle of your country. And then, just as we believed we might be close to finding her, she appeared in Thailand."

"How long had she been gone?" I took another drink of orange juice—it felt like the toast was caught in my throat.

"She was gone maybe four years, I think? So much time, and yet my master welcomed her back with open arms. She claimed that she had been captured by the boss of Chicago, and that she had finally escaped. Volodya has been quietly at war with Zhong Lei ever since."

So Theresa had disappeared at the end of 1982 and had returned in 1987. The timeline was eerily accurate. Asa was about two years older than Ben, who was thirty-one and had been born in 1985. She could have returned to the United States, married their father, had the boys, and then . . .

"What was she like when she returned?"

"She was so happy to be back. When we found her, she presented the Sensilo relic to Volodya as a gift. It was good—until she disappeared again thirteen years later. And this time, she was gone for good. Volodya went after Zhong with much brutality. He thought maybe he had stolen his precious magic sensor yet again. But Zhong did not have her. He had a sensor of his own."

I thought of poor Tao on his hands and knees in Union Station, practically begging Asa to kill him. "So what does Volodya think happened to her?"

"A few years ago his grief pulled him under. That is when things began to fall apart. He is not the same man he was . . ." He slapped the table, now cluttered with five shot glasses. "He was a man without hope. Until a few days ago."

"When you heard that the Sensilo relic was here."

He nodded, his mouth full of sandwich. Bits of corned beef fell from his lips as he chewed sloppily, clearly an effect of the alcohol. "Marcus Franko contacted one of our operatives to see if we wanted to make a bid for it. At first we did not believe him. Then he sent us a picture." He smiled as dressing dribbled from the corner of his mouth. "A picture taken by the seller, Benjamin Ward."

I closed my eyes, the betrayal crashing down on me yet again. "But didn't you think it might be a counterfeit?"

"Of course. People do this all the time, amateurs who try to sell fake original relics. But this one . . . it was so perfect. It looked exactly like the one in Volodya's collection. And we do not have a reliable sensor, sadly, so we had to determine its authenticity another way. We did a little experiment. Here I will tell you a secret about original relics." He downed a sixth vodka and leaned forward conspiratorially. "The magic will go into a reliquary, assuming it doesn't break them. But to get it out . . . ?" He clucked his tongue.

The splinter inside me jabbed mercilessly in time with the hammering beat of my heart. "Yeah?"

"That magic is not like any other magic."

"No kidding. And? How *do* you get it out?"

"Volodya was able to transfer the magic in his golden relic—a lump of gold said to encase a piece of the original sorcerer's body—into another relic. And that was when we knew it was not authentic."

"How? What happened? Would original magic not have transferred? How do you get original magic out of a reliquary, then?"

The frantic edge in my voice seemed to sharpen his suspicion. "You are very inquisitive little person." He put his head in his hands. "And giving me a headache."

Defeat and frustration twisted the knife deeper. I had been so close to what I needed to know. "I think I need the restroom. Do you mind if I go?"

He absently waved to the bar, as if that were the location of the toilet. "By all means."

I slid out of the booth and headed for the back, wondering if I could find myself an exit and run. But just as I reached a hallway at the rear of the room, our waitress caught up with me.

She held up a metal mallet—a meat tenderizer. "I'm going to smash myself in the face with this if you try to get away," she said cheerfully. "He said I shouldn't stop until I couldn't breathe anymore." She was shifting from foot to foot, looking kind of excited at the prospect.

"Give me the mallet." I held out my hand.

"He said if you asked for it, I should do this." And she hit herself square in the mouth with the mallet. Blood spurted from between her lips and gushed down her face, and I cried out. No one in the bar even turned to look. Arkady was influencing them, too.

I held up my hands and took a few steps back. "Okay. I'll be right out. I won't try to escape."

She nodded and grinned, revealing a broken front tooth.

I walked into the bathroom and barfed up orange juice and peanut butter.

Shaking badly from weakness and pain, I rinsed out my mouth, gave the back exit one last, longing look, and headed into the bar, walking past our bleeding waitress without looking at her face.

Arkady had gotten me a glass of water, as if he'd known I was going to be sick. He smiled and pushed it toward me, and I glared at him as I gulped it down gratefully. I sighed and leaned back as the water sailed down my throat. Nothing had ever tasted so good. And suddenly, the pain in my chest ebbed, like a fire being extinguished. I groaned with relief.

"It seems as if you are feeling better."

"So much better," I said, and meant it.

"Perfect. I think it is about time for us to go. But do you think we should leave a calling card for this little town, just to make sure the authorities are properly engaged?"

Something approving stirred inside me, but it was quelled by a throb of panic behind my breastbone. I glanced at the empty water glass and then up at Arkady, who was watching me intently.

"It really is less bothersome if I influence you directly."

"You . . . you put . . ." I rubbed my chest. The pain was gone. And so was my defense against his influence.

"I availed myself of the stores of Ekstazo juice when I was keeping company with the Headsmen, this is true. Thank you for giving me the opportunity to slip it into your drink. I would have hated to force it down your throat."

"Yeah," I said. "That would have sucked! This was so much better."

No. Don't let him do this to you. The voice was so quiet I could barely hear it. And frankly, kind of annoying.

He stood up, swaying only slightly as he offered me his arm. "Shall we?"

I got to my feet and took his arm. "Let's blow this joint."

His eyes glittered with intrigue. "Yes. Let's." He glanced over at the bartender and smiled, then handed me the car keys. "You drive. I am little bit—how do you say? Tipsy."

"No problem."

We walked out to the parking lot. I got behind the wheel, and he gave directions. I hadn't gone more than a quarter mile when my rear-view mirror lit up orange and yellow, tongues of fire spinning into the night sky as the bar went up in flames.

CHAPTER
TWENTY-TWO

"Tell me about you and your fiancé," Arkady said as I drove up the two-lane country road that would take us to our meetup with Ben.

Don't tell him, whispered the tiny voice that seemed to be emanating from somewhere in the vicinity of my heart. "We worked together. He's a veterinarian."

"He is not a natural?"

"Nope." I pulled over to the side of the road as two fire trucks, a police car, and an ambulance sped by in the opposite direction, sirens screaming.

"And you? When did you learn of your special abilities? Did your grandfather tell you?"

"Well, it started about a year ago, when Ben was kidnapped by Frank Brindle, and I went looking for him—"

"Ah, Frank Brindle," said Arkady, his voice turning gravelly. "Here is one who likes to pretend nice, but in action he is as ruthless as any Strikon."

"Yeah. I kind of got that vibe. Anyway, in the process of trying to figure out where Ben was, I fell—no, *literally* fell—onto a conduit and ruined one of Asa's transactions by absorbing the magic. He's the one who first told me what I was."

"Benjamin and Asa are brothers?"

I fidgeted in my seat. *Don't tell him don't tell him.* But it felt so good to talk this whole complicated mess through. "Yes, but they're not close. I think things were always hard for Asa. Ben had it easier. He fit with what his dad expected of him. He fit with what society expected of him. Asa didn't." I told Arkady about how Ben had broken Asa's nose at his father's command, and how Asa had gone to jail for a year after they lied and claimed he'd tried to rob them.

Arkady grunted. "And Asa could not defend himself from his younger brother?" He sounded contemptuous. "Perhaps what I have heard about him is an exaggeration."

"That was fifteen years ago. Asa's all grown up now."

I could feel Arkady staring at me from the passenger seat. "You admire him," he said quietly.

"It's more than that." My fingers tightened over the steering wheel.

"How much more?"

Don't tell him don't tell him don't tell him. "I'm still trying to figure it out."

"How intriguing," Arkady murmured. "And how does he feel about you?"

"I don't know. We have a . . . thing."

"A thing."

"Yeah, a thing. I mean, I know he likes me. Sometimes. And when we're doing a transaction . . ." I leaned on the headrest. "He's just . . . I don't even know. He's hard and ruthless, and then a minute later he's the most gentle . . ." *Don't tell him don't tell him.* "Somehow, he knows how to take care of me better than anyone else. Knows what I need before I do, even. And when I do something good for him, just little things, it feels like I've really accomplished something major." I chuckled. "And every once in a while he says, '*Dammit*, Mattie' in this certain kind of way, like I've gotten to him. It feels rare, I guess. Special."

I was totally rambling, finally saying aloud the thoughts I'd been trying to ignore for months. And my conversation partner was a freaking assassin controlling my brain. It just figured.

"So Asa must hate his brother, if you are to marry him." Arkady's voice was sharp with curiosity.

"No. I think he *wants* to hate Ben, and sometimes he's mad at himself because he can't quite manage it."

"This is fascinating. Asa Ward is very sought after as a sensor and ignores offers of millions of your dollars from those looking to employ him. He is very hard to find and refuses to make any deal for his services if he is not in charge. These stories have begun to defy belief. And yet, suddenly he has been revealed to me as a man like any other. With weaknesses like any other."

"Eh. That's kind of oversimplifying it."

"I am a man. I understand men's hearts."

I glanced over. "Okay. Maybe you could explain them to me, because—"

"This is going to be marvelous," Arkady said quietly, a smile playing across his lips.

I steered Dolores's car into a parking lot behind a dark building with a sign outside that said "Fleeger's." Asa's van was parked right in the middle of the gravel expanse, under one of the bright overhead lights.

"Pull the car over here." Arkady pointed to a spot about twenty feet from the van.

I obeyed and handed Arkady the keys to the car. We were in the middle of freaking nowhere, surrounded by thick woods on all sides.

"Ah, here he is," said Arkady. "Are you ready, my dear?"

I looked over and saw Ben get out of the driver's seat of the van and close the door behind him. He had the Sensilo relic clutched in his hand. His face was mottled with bruises from his fight with Asa, including two black eyes, and he had a bandage over the bridge of his nose. He looked nervous as heck, his gaze shifting from us to the surrounding woods to the building and back again.

We got out of Dolores's car, and Arkady came over to stand beside me. "Hello, Dr. Ward," Arkady said, not trying to conceal his Russian accent.

Ben frowned. "You're not Agent Winslow."

"How astute. But aren't you glad to see your lovely fiancée again?"

Ben's expression smoothed over. "*So* glad."

Arkady turned to me. "And you, Mattie. Aren't you overwhelmed with joy at seeing your Benjamin again?"

Happiness tingled inside of me. "That's an understatement."

Arkady smiled. "I think a passionate reunion is called for."

No sooner had he said it than I was running to Ben. He met me in the middle, scooping me up. My legs were around his waist, and my arms were around his neck in an instant. Our mouths melded with a ferocity that left me breathless. His hands were on my rear, holding me against him, the relic locket clanking as it dangled from his grasp.

"I missed you so much," he murmured as he nuzzled my throat.

I tangled my fingers in his wavy hair. "Not as much as I missed you."

"Carry her to the van, Ben."

Ben obeyed immediately, opening the sliding side door with one hand as he held me up with the other, kissing me hungrily the whole time. My body was on fire, desperate to feel his skin on mine.

"Hand me the relic and lay her down."

Ben shoved the locket at Arkady and laid me on the floor between the front seats and the rear bench.

"Mattie, unbutton his shirt."

Oh, yes. My fingers tore at the buttons while he pressed his hips between my legs. I moaned and pulled his shirt open, then yanked up his undershirt to feel his abs.

Arkady chuckled. "This is beautiful." A glimmer over Ben's shoulder caught my eye. Arkady had pulled out a gleaming knife from a sheath beneath his shirt. "Ben, you will make love to Mattie one last time. And after that, we will leave something very special for your brother to find when he retrieves his vehicle."

"Sounds perfect," Ben said, sliding his hand up my leg, pushing up the hem of my skirt.

I thought so, too. I pulled him down on top of me, needing his mouth on mine again. Ben groaned and thrust against me. Hard. I winced at the pain. *Stop this, Mattie. This is bad bad bad,* whispered the voice inside me. My fingers froze, curled into the collar of Ben's shirt, grabbing at awareness before it sank beneath the surface again.

"Harder," I said.

Ben's hands turned to steel on my thighs. He ground against me, pressing my back against the unforgiving floor of the van, making my bones feel like they were about to snap.

"You feel it, Benjamin—do you not?" Arkady said silkily. "That she has not been completely faithful to you. Perhaps you want to punish her a little bit."

Ben lowered his head and bit my shoulder, not hard enough to break skin, but hard enough to clear my head even more.

"I think your brother is never far from her thoughts. You want to erase him from her memory. Only then will she be yours."

Ben kissed me savagely as I struggled beneath him, unable to breathe.

"Tell him, Mattie. Tell him how you've thought about Asa."

The pain had erased Arkady's control over me, but I couldn't let him know my mind was my own again. Tears sprung to my eyes. "I've thought about Asa," I whispered.

Ben's fingers closed over mine, and he nearly crushed my hand as he raised it, shaking it as he glared at my engagement ring. "Doesn't this mean anything to you?" he shouted.

"It does. It always has." I placed my free hand on his cheek. "Come here."

He collapsed on me again, his mouth ravenous, his hips bucking, and I squeezed my eyes shut. "Let me be on top, okay? I want to show you how much I love you."

I was surprised and grateful when he obeyed. As he did, I did my best to give Arkady a look drenched with lust and longing, even though I was screaming on the inside. He grinned, twirling the knife. "By all means, Mattie. Show him." He inched closer, leaning on the van's doorframe, obviously enjoying the show.

I reached for Ben's belt. He lay on his back, his hands on my hips, rocking against me while I unfastened the buckle and pulled the strip of leather free inch by inch. His brown eyes were on me, so full of adoration that it made me want to sob. "Tell me you love me, Mattie," he murmured. "I've been so scared you didn't, not anymore. I've been so scared that I'd lost you."

"I love you." I pulled the belt free. Leaving the buckle hanging, I wrapped the very end around my hand. "Part of me always will."

I pivoted and swung the buckle at Arkady, hitting him square in the face. He went stumbling back and lost his footing, shouting and cursing as he hit the ground. Without losing momentum, I swung the buckle down at Ben, leaving a dark red mark on his face. "Snap out of it," I screamed, trying to free myself from his grip. "He's going to kill us!"

"You little bitch," Arkady roared. Gravel crunched as he lurched to his feet. With Ben still blinking in shock beneath me, I turned to see Arkady's blade slice through the air.

I had no way of defending myself. I couldn't get the belt up fast enough. I opened my mouth to scream, but a dark blur tackled Arkady, and the blade passed within inches of my chest. The two men landed in the parking lot, a tangle of hatred. I stared, my mouth literally hanging open. "Asa?"

He was bleeding from a gash on his arm, but the knife was lying several feet away, knocked clear by the impact of his collision with the Russian assassin. Arkady was whispering to him as he elbowed Asa and tried to grab his arms. Asa gritted his teeth as he kneed the older man in the side.

I moved to help but found I was cemented in place. Ben's hands were still clamped over my hips as I straddled him. "He wants me to kill you now," he said in a calm voice. "He wants me to show your dead body to Asa."

I slapped at him with the belt, but he caught it on the downswing and yanked it out of my hand. "Thank you. This will work just fine."

Terror exploded inside me, no longer a whimper but an inferno. "Ben, let me go."

"We could have sex first if you want," he offered. "It would be quick. I'm pretty turned on."

I smacked him in the face. "Wake up," I shrieked, fighting his one-handed grip. "Think about what you're doing."

He glanced at the belt. "I don't think it's all that complicated. A simple loop should do. Like a noose."

"Asa," I screamed, but the only sounds from outside were the grunts and thuds of a fierce struggle.

"Stop calling his name," Ben yelled. As he sat up and reached for my wrists, I slammed my palm against his bruised, tender nose. He fell back with a shout, and I dove over the bench seat, landing on a bunch of toolboxes. As Ben shouted obscenities at me, I wrenched open the first box I could reach and found a rainbow array of water pistols like the one I'd seen Asa pull in Union Station. I had no idea what was in them, but as Ben lunged over the bench seat, I grabbed a red one and squirted him in the face with it.

Unfortunately, he was so close to me that some of it splattered on me. It felt like my face had been set on fire. As Ben started to howl, so did I, fumbling blindly for the handle to open the back doors so I could escape. With tears and snot streaming down my face, I fell out of the van and nearly landed on Arkady and Asa. The older man was on top of him, and Asa was gasping, his eyes bright as Arkady murmured to him. But as I landed in an awkward sprawl, Asa turned his head, and our eyes met. His flared with defiance as he faced Arkady again. "Shut the fuck *up*," he snarled.

He yanked his arm out of the Russian assassin's grip and jabbed his fist into Arkady's throat. The Russian's eyes bulged as he choked. My own eyes still burning, I scrambled to my feet and squirted Arkady in the face with Asa's water pistol. He had the same reaction Ben did.

Asa looped his arm around my waist and dragged me back to the van, closing the rear doors as he passed. Briskly, steady despite the blood smeared all over the side of his face and down his left arm, he yanked the side door shut and dumped me in the front passenger seat. He stripped the pistol from my grasp as Ben, growling with rage, lunged up from the back. Asa squirted his brother in the face, causing Ben to fall backward yet again. Then Asa calmly went to the driver's seat and twisted the keys that were in the ignition.

Gravel flew as the wheels spun, but then we shot forward.

"You're just going to leave him there?" I asked, stunned. One glance in the side mirror showed Arkady rising from the ground, the knife in his hand, his face a mask of pain and fury.

"Yep," said Asa. He swung a wide turn at the edge of the parking lot and shot around the front, picking up speed. But instead of pulling onto the road, he zoomed past the bar and turned when he reached the other side of the building. "I am."

Arkady took a few unsteady steps back when he saw the van barrel into the parking lot again. He started shouting something, but Asa switched the radio on, cranking up the white noise, blood dripping lazily down his neck and onto his shirt. Arkady took off running, heading for the woods behind the bar.

He didn't make it. I closed my eyes as I heard a scream and a few heavy thumps. When I opened them, Asa was pulling onto the road. He turned off the radio and took a deep breath.

"I don't know about you," he said, "but I think he mighta had that coming."

CHAPTER TWENTY-THREE

"Are you okay?" I looked Asa over as he sped down the road. He had a deep cut along his forearm and a gash above his cheekbone, and he was sweating like crazy.

"Fine. But Arkady was laying down some serious shit out there." Asa waggled his arm at me. "I had to do a number on myself to break free of it."

"You did that yourself?" Ben asked.

"I couldn't shake it off otherwise. It was like a heavy weight, just keeping me where I was. Watching everything that was happening."

Including me and Ben and our "passionate reunion," as Arkady had called it. I swallowed the hard lump of freak-out that had lodged in my throat. "Like the people in the bar tonight," I said. "They sat back as this waitress hit herself in the face with a meat tenderizer. No one looked at us sideways."

"We thought you were coming with Headsmen," Asa said. "I was hiding in the woods until Ben handed over the relic, just to make sure they respected the bargain they'd made."

"Wait, what?"

"He found me, Mattie," Ben said. "He was with me when you called earlier."

"We could tell you were scared, but after what you saw them do to the carnies . . ." Asa shook his head. "I knew you would be upset."

My chest had started to ache again. "But how did you find Ben?"

"That part wasn't hard," said Asa, rolling his eyes. "He had my van and he had the Sensilo relic with him. Unpackaged. Lucky someone else didn't find him first."

"Oh no! We left the relic behind with Arkady," I said.

"Nope." He pulled it from his pocket and handed it back to Ben. "There are lead wrappers in the back in a gray toolbox. Cover it up and then get it into one of the thicker metal boxes on the floor under the seat."

Ben took the relic and did as Asa said. "I had already called the Headsmen to offer them the relic when Asa tracked me down. And they had already raided the camp. So we decided to play it out, hoping they would keep their word."

Having packaged the relic, Ben dropped heavily onto the bench, staring down at his belt, which lay on the floor. "I remember everything that happened just now, but . . . Oh, Mattie." He looked up at me with black despair in his eyes.

I shuddered. "It wasn't your fault. I was out of control for a while there as well."

"I was so happy that you wanted me," he whispered.

Asa kept his gaze anchored out the front window. "Arkady is one of the most powerful Knedas naturals in the world. If he wants you to do something, chances are you're gonna do it."

"Mattie fought back," Ben said. "She hit him."

"Mattie is in constant pain. It lets her shake off the influence."

"He dosed me up with Ekstazo juice." My fingers dug into my arms as I watched the black woods go by. "It's wearing off now, but—"

"Fuck," Asa whispered, rubbing his chest. "You're right. How the hell did you manage to defy him?"

"I didn't do it fast enough. For a while I was completely caught. I said, 'Let's blow this joint' before we walked out of a bar, and I guess Arkady took what I said literally and made the bartender—" I stifled a sob. "I saw the fire. I *know* people died."

"Stop that," Asa snapped. "It wasn't your fault, and whatever happened in here before I managed to get Arkady wasn't either of your faults. This is what he's known for. He gets off on it." Asa looked over at me. "He made sure to tell me as much."

I remembered how Arkady was whispering to him while they struggled. "Was he trying to get you to hurt yourself?"

"No. He was trying to get me to hurt *you*."

And then we were all quiet. Asa drove briefly on a state road and then turned off, finally following a series of signs for Lake Doherty's Family Cabins and Campgrounds. As we bumped down the road, any remaining effects of the Ekstazo juice peeled off in strips, my pain rising with every second. By the time Asa pulled into a gravel parking lot at the front of a set of lighted trails with signs that indicated the lake was straight ahead, I had my knees to my chest and my head bowed.

"Ben, help her out."

Ben opened my passenger door a minute later. "Can I carry you, or do you want to walk?"

"I'm not sure I can."

His arms slid behind my back and under my knees, and he pulled me snug to his chest. I tucked my head into the crook of his neck. "I've got you."

He carried me along a trail, up an incline, and then up a set of steps, his shoes clunking on wood as he carried me to the door.

"Got her," Asa said to someone as a screen door screeched open and a light switched on.

Splinter

"He got her!" said a familiar voice, and the announcement was followed by excited exclamations from others. I opened my eyes to see Vernon's snaggletoothed smile, with Betsy standing just behind him. Jimmy stood near the window, looking out on the path as if he expected someone to be following us, and Letisha sat in the corner, her lap covered in an elaborate knitting project.

"Knew he would," she said casually.

"Do you have somewhere she can rest?" Asa asked.

"Right back here," called a voice I recognized as Roberta's. "She can have my bed."

Ben carried me down a hall as I blinked at my new surroundings. It was a rustic cabin, very plain, a few pictures of fishing scenes on the walls but little else. Ben laid me down on a bed with clean sheets and a crocheted afghan, and I immediately curled onto my side. It felt safer and better to be huddled in a ball instead of stretched out and vulnerable.

Ben sat down at the foot of the bed, and Asa knelt next to me. "We're gonna pull that splinter now, Mattie."

"What? No!" I said.

Asa sat back. "No? I've got Vernon here, and we've got something strong enough—"

"No. Asa, they tried to pull it when I was at the sheriff's station." I told him everything that had happened, that Daeng was there, who Jack was, and how the whole thing had ended with me coughing up blood. "I can't do that again. I think it would kill me."

Asa ran his hands through his hair. "We can't leave it in there. That'll kill you, too."

"So what are we supposed to do?" asked Ben. "Should we take her to a hospital?"

"Won't help," said Jimmy. "Maybe I could give her some of my juice, and then you could try."

"I said *no*," I shouted, but the effort made me cough. I got my arm up to cover my mouth, but it came away speckled with blood. Roberta made a distressed noise and disappeared down the hall. I avoided everyone's gazes as my head sank to the pillow. My skin felt clammy and chilled, and I shivered. Asa pulled the afghan up over my shoulders.

"Arkady told me how Volodya realized that his Sensilo relic was a fake," I said weakly. I let out a raspy cough and opened my eyes as Roberta set a glass of water on the bedside table. Asa moved out of the way as she gently used a warm, wet cloth to clean my bloody arm. "You should take care of Asa, too."

He waved her off. "I want to hear what Arkady said."

"He said they knew it was fake when the magic in what they thought was the original could be transferred into another relic."

"Did he say what kind of relic?"

"No. And he wouldn't tell me more. He just said original magic isn't like other magic."

"I believe we knew that already," said Jimmy.

"Original magic isn't like other magic," Asa said slowly. "And we know it's a fake if we can transfer it into another relic." He stood up. "I have to go make some calls."

"So we're not doing this tonight?" asked Vernon.

"We're not making another move until we know what the fuck we're actually doing." Asa turned and walked down the hall without a backward glance.

Ben gave me a sad, guilty look. "I'm going to go get cleaned up," he mumbled. "I'll call your parents and let them know you're okay."

He left, too, and Jimmy, Vernon, and Betsy followed him out.

Roberta sat down on the floor next to my bed, pulling her extraordinarily long hair out from under her bottom, twisting it around, and laying it in her lap like a pet. "They're all feeling helpless and scared to death."

"I am, too."

"Yes, but you can't run from it."

"You could."

She gave me a kindly smile. "But then you'd be in here all by yourself, and that just seems unfair." She patted my hand. "What a crazy few days, huh? I thought I'd be in some underground cell the rest of my life. I thought those Headsmen were going to disappear us all."

"Why didn't they?"

She grunted out a laugh. "Things started exploding."

"The Headsmen had defenses against Knedas magic."

"Oh, this wasn't magic. Asa rigged a few of our generators to blow. Fire shooting into the sky, smoke, *boom*. Ooh, boy, those Headsmen were running around like headless chickens. They thought the only thing they had to worry about was magic. And then, just as the fires got bad and the agents had scattered to figure out what was going on, Asa comes roaring up in Jimmy's RV, jumps out, and tackles the head agent lady. Shot her with her own Taser. He cut a few of us free, and then it was pretty chaotic there for a while. I think we got everyone out, but only a few of us wanted to stick together." She shrugged. "That's probably good, since the Headsmen might still be looking for us."

"I think they've been kinda busy." My guess was that a bunch of small-time carnies was on the bottom of their list of priorities right now after the wide swath of murder and mayhem Arkady had left in his wake.

"Well, either way, it's just a few of us now. We haven't decided what to do, but we figured we owed Asa for what he did for us. And the one thing he asked for in return was help in getting you whole again."

"Thanks for agreeing to his terms."

She smiled, then helped me sit up and sip some more water. "It was a pleasure, sweetheart. Can I get you anything else?" She turned as Asa appeared in the doorway, his bruised face pale, a butterfly bandage over the cut on his cheek and another wrapped over the gash on his arm. "What's wrong?"

"I need a minute with Mattie."

She left the room, and Asa sank down on the floor to take her place. "Hey," he said gently. "How are you?"

"Good."

"Liar." He touched the center of his chest. "Right here. Like a fucking knife."

"Then why did you ask me how I am?" I took in the shine of sweat on his brow. "I hate that it hurts you."

"I can deal with it."

"How's Gracie?"

"She's good. Her leg's set. Dr. Monahan agreed to keep her a few more days so I could take care of things. I didn't want her in the line of fire."

"Does Ben know what he did?"

Asa shook his head, and when he saw my raised eyebrows, he said, "I needed him to focus, Mattie. We can deal with it later."

"Thank you for coming after me."

"Did you think I was gonna leave you behind?"

"Not for a minute."

He gave me a sweet smile that faded almost instantly. "We have to talk. I think I know what Arkady meant about original magic. You're not gonna like it. I sure as hell don't."

"Tell me."

"I think original magic won't just flow into any vessel, no matter how strong it is, no matter how good the conduit. I think it'll only enter the *original* vessel. The original relic."

A shiver shook me to the bone. "So this splinter . . . it has to be united with the rest of the magic, in the Strikon bone relic."

Asa winced as the splinter jabbed at my chest wall. "We could try to get it into another reliquary, but—"

"I'd *never* ask someone else to take this," I said through clenched teeth.

"I know." He looked pained as he reached up to touch a stray curl that had fallen across my face. "I know you wouldn't. But I was about to say that I didn't think it would work anyway. It's pretty likely that the magic will only flow out of the relic and into a reliquary, or out of a reliquary and into the relic, not from person to person. Even if we were willing to try, it might kill you."

"So we have no choice."

We stared at each other for a long moment. "No, I don't think we do," he finally said.

A drop of sweat trickled down Asa's cheek as he laced his fingers with mine, and we both hung on tight. I knew I was hurting him, but he'd said he could take it, and I was counting on that.

If we wanted to succeed, if I wanted to have any chance of surviving, we were going to have to seek help from the person who possessed the bone relic—the magic boss of the West Coast, the man who had brutally kidnapped Ben last year just to lure Asa into his web . . . and who had expected Ben to deliver the Sensilo relic to him a few days ago. Frank Brindle.

CHAPTER TWENTY-FOUR

The smell of coffee and bacon pulled me from my cocoon of pain. I hadn't slept much, just tossed and turned, trying not to scream. What few moments of sleep I did get were full of fire and meat tenderizers and Ben telling me he loved me before pulling his belt tight around my throat.

Not exactly the most restful night.

Needing the bathroom, I braced myself on the bedside table and slowly rose on shaking limbs. The last few days had almost completely sapped my strength, and each step felt like a risk, like my bones might crumble each time I put weight on them. I was halfway down the hall when Letisha came rushing up the hallway toward me, her brown eyes wide. "I could hear you from two rooms away!"

I leaned on her as she put her arm around my waist. "I wasn't making noise, was I?"

She shook her head. "Your determination—and your fear that you won't make it. I can hear it, loud and clear."

She gave me a few minutes of privacy in the bathroom but hovered outside the door. I could hear her talking to someone in low, urgent tones. I grabbed a washcloth and cleaned the tearstains from my face. When I opened the bathroom door again, Quentin had joined Letisha in the hallway.

"I got in late last night," he said. "It's all over the news—the New Kent Sheriff's Office was attacked yesterday, and then there was a major fire in—"

"I know already," I whispered, holding my hand up to stop him.

"Jimmy told me the rest," he said, looking somber. "He said you were in bad shape."

"I'll be fine." I leaned against the wall, hoping I wouldn't slide to the floor. The greasy smells coming from the kitchen turned my stomach upside down.

Asa picked that moment to emerge from the kitchen with a green smoothie in his hand. He looked back and forth from me to Quentin as he sipped his drink.

"I can help," Quentin said, taking a step closer to me.

I turned my face away from all of them. "No."

He held out his hand in front of me, another small vial full of clear liquid sitting on his palm. "For whenever you need it or want it."

"Thanks, but no." I began to shuffle down the hall, my whole body shaking. I couldn't get away from him fast enough.

Letisha helped me back into bed and I focused on breathing, once again getting lost in a haze of nightmare and memory. I woke to the sound of arguing. The door to my bedroom was mostly closed, but I recognized Ben's and Asa's voices immediately.

"I know you don't like it," Asa said. "But if you love her—if you *really* love her—you're gonna let me help her in whatever form that takes."

"It's like you want me to write you a blank check," Ben replied.

"If that's how you want to think about it."

"And how do I know you're not just helping *yourself*?"

"Mattie is dying," Asa said, his voice dropping to a savage whisper. "And I'm the one who's gonna keep that from happening."

"Brindle has people who can—"

"Brindle and his people see her as a fucking alligator handbag, Ben. They want what she's got inside. And I want . . ."

"What? What were you going to say?"

"Nothing."

There was a thump, like one of them had hit the wall, and all my muscles went rigid. "Why can't you just be honest, Asa?"

"Get your fucking hands off me."

"She's *not* yours," Ben said quietly.

"I know that."

"Yeah? That's not what you said when you were about to pull that magic out of her."

"I wasn't talking about Mattie."

"Huh?"

"It's complicated. But I know full well Mattie doesn't belong to me and never will. I also know she'll never belong to you."

"She does belong to me, though. She's my—"

"What the fuck, Ben? She belongs to *herself*. Nobody else gets to decide. But right now, she's sick, and she's hurting, and she's weak. She's gonna break if she's not handled the right way."

"Because of me." Ben sounded like he was fighting back tears, and the sorrow of it had the same effect on me.

"Because of both of us. So both of us are responsible for fixing it. Just let me help her. When this is all over, I'll go my own way and you guys can work out whatever shit's between you. But for now, I'm her anchor, and anything you do to interfere with that connection hurts her. And I'm not going to let you hurt her anymore. Stay. Out. Of. My. Way."

After a long, fraught moment of quiet, the door swung open quickly and I clamped my eyes shut. Soft footsteps coming toward me contrasted with heavy stomping ones headed up the hall. "Stop playing dead," Asa said. "I know you were listening to every word."

I opened my eyes and stared at his pant legs, all those pockets. His fingers dipped into one over his thigh, and he set a clear vial on the bedside table. I stared at it, recognizing it from earlier. My cheeks grew hot. "Not really up for putting on another show for you right now," I muttered.

"What the actual fuck, Mattie."

"I don't want Quentin's magic."

"Because of what happened in the camper? You want me to apologize or something? Listen, you need the relief. There's no reason for you to be hurting this much."

"I'd rather be hurting than out of control."

Asa's brow furrowed. "Quentin's magic doesn't—"

"I hate all of it. I can't defend myself. Everybody just *does* things to me." My sobs were convulsing my entire body, magnifying the pain. "And even when I try to take control, I . . ." I flailed my arm between the two of us.

"That was different."

"How? I've never done anything like that, Asa. It wasn't me."

"It was. You just don't want to own it, because it scares you."

"You're darn right it scares me! It's freaking humiliating! And if Ben knew—"

"Fuck Ben."

"Asa, for God's sake. This whole thing is out of control."

"You're wrong, honey. But until you pull your head out of the sand, you're not gonna be able to see it."

"Get out," I whispered.

"No." He sat down on the floor next to the bed. "There are a few things you need to understand."

I bowed my head and covered my face with my hands. "You're making this harder."

"*You're* making this harder, Mattie. I know you've been through hell. And I know a lot of it has been forced on you. You've been violated in too many ways, and I don't blame you for being scared, or for wanting control."

I exhaled a shaky breath, still unable to open my eyes. But the razor edge of his voice had dulled, and it allowed my heart to slow a bit.

"But you can't always be in control," he continued. "Sometimes you have to hand it over. And that's okay. Better than okay."

"I can't. Not anymore. People slipping things into my drinks and tying me down and telling me what to do—"

"Do you understand the difference between those things and how you and I work together?"

"Is there a difference? In both cases I'm tied up and taking orders," I said bitterly.

"They couldn't be more different, Mattie. Ben *took* your control when he forced that magic into you. Arkady *took* your control when he slipped the Ekstazo juice into your drink and made it impossible for you to resist his influence. They stole something from you. It made you feel powerless and weak."

They had. And it had happened over and over. I pulled my knees even tighter to my chest.

"Look at me," Asa said. "I'm gonna sit here until you do."

I obeyed. His gaze was so intense that I felt something inside me give.

"When we're together," he said, "you *give* me control. You *let* me be in charge. You might surrender, but this isn't war, baby. You're not admitting defeat—you're offering a gift. And every time I take over, I understand how absolutely fucking sacred that trust is. It's the opposite of weakness."

I blinked at him, and a tear slipped across my cheek. He smoothed his thumb over it, then let his fingers slide into my hair. I closed my eyes and leaned forward, and our foreheads touched. "Sometimes it's almost as scary," I whispered.

"I know," he murmured. "Good thing you're brave as hell and stronger than anyone I've ever met."

"Do you really believe that?"

His fingers tightened in my curls. "It would be a lot easier on me if I didn't." He scooped the vial from the bedside table and pressed it into my palm. "Use this. You need to rest. You need to eat. You need to be ready for what's coming."

I pulled away from his sweaty face. "Hey. I talked to Arkady about Theresa. If you want—"

"Tell me everything."

"Okay." And I did, eager to offer him something, anything, after what he'd just given to me. I told him that she was American, and how she had met Volodya when he caught her stealing a relic. I told him how she had run away from him—and when.

"My mom and dad got married in February of 1983," Asa said slowly. "Later, after she was gone, he would talk about her while he was drunk. They knew each other as kids. He'd always had a crush on her, but she dropped out and took off when they were in high school. Then, a few years later, she showed up at some New Year's party he was at, like something out of a dream. They reconnected like she'd never been gone. Only two months later, it was a shotgun wedding. She had me in August."

I did the mental math, a tingling sense of possibility rolling across my skin. "That would mean she got pregnant in the fall of—"

"No, it doesn't. I was born early. My dad always said maybe that explained what was wrong with me. 'Didn't have enough time to cook.'"

I'd never heard of that phrase being used in such a cruel way. "Do you remember her?"

"Yeah. Not much, though."

"Do you want to tell me?" The stark line of his shoulders had hunched, and he'd drawn his knees up. I knew that position so well—when you're hurting, you try to protect your most vulnerable spots.

"I was kind of an anxious kid. Had a lot of nightmares. Nothing specific, really. I was just always waking up with this feeling of . . . I don't know. Dread. My dad would shout at me when I went into their room, but Mom would take me back to my bed. She'd stay there with me for a while."

"It's nice that she comforted you."

"But she didn't." His voice was hushed and I strained to hear. "She'd ask me what I felt, and when I told her it was like bugs crawling across my skin, or like sandpaper rubbed all over me, or like someone was poking me right in my brain with a sharp stick, she didn't say it wasn't real. She told me I had to be brave. She told me I had to learn to keep my fear inside."

"You were just a baby."

"I remember that I just wanted her to tell me it was okay," he whispered. "She never said it was okay."

"Asa . . ."

He rubbed his hands over his face and let them drop into his lap. "She was right, though. It was never okay. At least she told me the truth."

"Do you remember when she left?"

"At first it was quiet, my dad just making a bunch of phone calls, smoking cigarette after cigarette. But then . . . I don't know if she called him or if he found a note or whatever, but after that it was things smashed against the wall and me hiding with Ben in the closet."

"Ben doesn't remember her."

"He was barely walking when she left."

"Theresa showed up in Thailand with the Sensilo relic in 1987. Does that match?"

"My mom disappeared on August 13, 1987," he said in a dead voice. "The day after my fourth birthday. There were still balloons taped to the wall."

I winced. "I'm so sorry."

"The Theresa that Arkady told you about had to be her. It all fits. My dad had no juice. Ben doesn't, either. But she—she had to have been a sensor. Fucking look at me." He raised his arms and let them flop back into his lap. "But she *knew* I was like her." He let out a choked noise. "She knew. And she left me there."

"Maybe she didn't know, though. Maybe she only—"

"She could have *sensed* it, Mattie. Think about it. She might have known before I was even born."

God, what a heavy burden to bear, to know your child was going to suffer in this world because of something you'd passed down to him. "You don't know why she left."

"I don't care." The tension had returned to his body. "She knew what I was, and she *left* me. Maybe Dad knew, too, because he blamed me," Asa said, his voice trembling. "He was all I had, and he fucking hated me."

"I'm so sorry, Asa." I hated myself for bringing this up. I hated that Asa was hurting. And more than that, I hated that I couldn't do anything for him. Maybe that was why my hand closed over his shoulder. I was desperate to give him just a tiny bit of comfort.

He wrenched out of my grasp and rose to his feet. His eyes were red. He wasn't crying, but the look on his face was so terrible, so drenched with pain, that it was almost worse. "Don't touch me."

"I'm sorry. You held my hand earlier and—"

"That was different."

"How?"

"*We're* different, Mattie."

"What about Eve? You told Ben she was yours. Is any part of you hers? Could *she* touch you? Could she reach you?"

"You really don't get it."

"We're both human, Asa. Don't pretend you don't need anyone else."

"I *can't*," he said, his voice rising. "And especially not you." He took a few steps backward, headed for the door. "I'm gonna go try to arrange this transaction with Brindle. I'll let you know when everything's set up."

"Asa, please—"

"I'll talk to you later." He stalked down the hall, letting the door swing shut behind him.

I sank back into the bed, shaking with sadness and frustration. How freaking hard could it be to accept a darn hug every once in a while? Asa had acted as if my touch were poisonous, even though he'd been touching me just a few minutes before. "Stupid control freak," I whispered, replaying everything he'd said.

As I did, a dim, dark understanding penetrated all my angry thoughts, my helpless frustration at not being able to do something for him.

We're different. That was true in so many ways, but the one that mattered most stared me hard in the face, merciless and bleak. I had people in my life who loved me. I *knew* I was loved. I had been loved so well by my parents, in fact, that I took it for granted.

Asa didn't. He couldn't. And because of that, he'd learned that relying on himself was the only safe option. Accepting comfort felt *dangerous* to him. And needing someone?

I can't, he'd said. *And especially not you.*

I sniffled. He was right.

Because when this was over, we were going our separate ways, off to live our separate lives.

Worlds apart.

CHAPTER
TWENTY-FIVE

Several hours later, having availed myself of Quentin's magic, taken a shower, and changed into some clothes Betsy had picked up for me, I was bundled in a blanket on a chaise down by the lake. The carnies were having a barbecue on the shore. Because I was feeling almost no pain, I could see that Betsy and Roberta had put up a glamour complete with signs saying the campsite was closed until June. We had the place to ourselves.

The sun was setting, and Quentin had rolled his truck close enough that we could listen to the local country station. Jimmy brought me a plate of corn on the cob and grilled chicken, and then pulled up a chair beside me. "How's our little wounded bird?"

"Feeling pretty darn good at the moment, thanks to Quentin."

Quentin turned and winked before returning to some argument with Letisha about fatalism. She was gesturing at him with a corncob.

"I've never seen a group of people who are so different fit together so well."

"That's the beauty of it," said Jimmy, looking a bit wistful. "I hope we can rebuild. We've been a haven for naturals for decades. My father led the carnival before I did. I'd hate to think this is the end."

"Where will you go next?"

"Somewhere far from here."

"I'm sorry we brought all this chaos to your doorstep."

"I can't say I'm happy about it. But you're one of us. So is Asa. It would have been wrong to turn you away." He took a huge bite out of his corncob, leaving little yellow bits embedded in his bushy gray beard.

"You said your dad led the carnival. Does that mean you've always been a part of it? Did you ever live in the—"

"The real world? The normal world?"

I chuckled. "I guess."

"What's real and normal for others is oppressive and destructive for some of us. I gave it a try in my twenties. Rebelled. Went off to get a normal job. It wasn't hard—I got the first position I applied for with a simple handshake."

"I bet you did."

He gave me a mischievous smile. "You would think people like me and Quentin would have no problem getting along. But it doesn't always feel right when you've gotta wonder if someone likes you because of *you*, or if they just like you because you accidentally gave them a jolt of your magic. Here, you don't wonder. People know you're doing it and accept it. They tell you to knock it off if they don't like it. There's a sense of trust and an expectation of honesty. And we all work together to create this beautiful thing . . ."

"So you don't have to hide what you are. You can be up front about it, and people accept you."

"That's it. For the sensors like Letisha, we understand when she needs time to herself. We don't think she's moody or get down on her for withdrawing. For the Knedas like Betsy and Roberta, they don't have to apologize for being what they are. Instead, we appreciate their creativity. We all respect each other."

"Do you have any Strikon?"

He picked a bit of corn out of his teeth. "We find they don't seek us out near as often as others do. Also not sure what role they'd play."

"Might be helpful at closing time," said Vernon from over by the grill. "Give everyone a headache and send 'em home!"

We all laughed, except for Quentin. "I think my way is better," he said, waggling his eyebrows at Letisha.

"How many babies do you think owe their post-carnival conception to good ol' Quentin here?" asked Betsy, slapping him on the behind as she walked by.

"Enough to drive repeat business for generations to come," said Roberta with a sly smile. She had her hair in a braid that hung down to midthigh, and she twirled it girlishly while cocking her hip.

"You want me to take that for you?" Ben asked about an hour later, as the sun was setting and the carnies were gathered around a bonfire they'd built. He gestured at my empty plate. "It's great that you're finally eating."

"Where have you been?"

He sat down in Jimmy's vacated chair. "I just wanted to give you some space."

"Because Asa told you to?"

"Maybe." He gave me a nervous smile. "I know I've apologized a lot, but I want to do it again."

"There's no need, Ben."

"About Asa."

I looked over at him. His fair hair was tousled, boyish. He was sporting two days' worth of stubble and wearing his Ohio State T-shirt and a pair of jeans, along with some flip-flops. Suddenly the simple familiarity of him, of seeing him dressed like this on Saturday afternoons as he tooled around the house, hit me so hard that I could barely breathe. "What about him?" I murmured.

"I don't know if I can ever fix stuff between me and my brother. But I know I was wrong about him."

I stayed very still, letting the words hang in the air.

"I've always made Asa the bad guy," Ben continued. "It made it easier to sleep at night, I guess, because then I didn't have to think about what I'd done to him."

"Ben, your dad was responsible for that."

"I wasn't a child. I could have stood up to him. I could have stood up for my brother."

I pulled the blanket a little tighter around myself. "He needed you to."

"I know. I've always known that. And, Mattie, it's just so goddamn painful that the only way to live through it was to convince myself that Asa deserved it."

"But now you know you were wrong."

"More than that. Now I know *I* was the bad guy. And that I still am." He rubbed his eyes. "Christ. I had a heart attack when I stepped out of my hotel and found him leaning on the van in the parking lot. I thought he was going to kill me. And you know what he said?"

"What?"

"'Next time you steal a relic, fucking package it up or you'll get yourself killed.' It . . . God, it took me back in time. That night he pulled me out of that nectar den, he was the same way. Angry, but at the same time—"

"Caring about you."

"Yeah. I didn't deserve it. There are so many things I don't deserve." He hesitantly reached for my hand, and I let him take it. "Not least of which is you."

My chest throbbed dully. "Ben, I'm not sure I can—"

"The things I did to you last night. I can't get them out of my head."

"That definitely wasn't your fault." But I couldn't suppress my shudder.

"You and Asa shook off that guy's influence. I couldn't."

"Asa and I have our reasons for being able to do what we did. You were far, *far* from the only person last night who couldn't resist Arkady, Ben. Trust me. I'm just glad we made it out alive."

"I guess. You know, Dad always said Asa was weak. He used to pick on him all the time. He called him a pussy and a fag. The drunker Dad was, the meaner he was, and as the years went by, he drank more and more. He wanted Asa to man up. Grow some balls. It used to scare me. I hated when Dad said those things to him. But eventually, I blamed Asa for being the kind of person who drew that fire, you know?"

I pressed my lips together, the pain in my chest intensifying as I thought once again of what Asa had gone through growing up. No wonder he couldn't trust anyone. No wonder he never felt safe.

"I thought Asa was the weak one," Ben said quietly. "It's only now I realize how strong he had to be to survive all of that. I'm not sure I could have. And now I see that I was the weak one. Still am. But you know the kicker?"

I turned my head to look at him.

"I still want to be strong for you. I've never been more willing to face what's coming and deal with it head-on. Mattie—I came clean to your parents when I talked to them on the phone this morning. I told them everything."

"What?"

"I told them we were about to lose the clinic. I told them I'd tried to do something foolish and illegal to get the money, and that was why you were in trouble. Your dad threatened to drown me in the lake"— Ben chuckled—"and I told him I would let him. But only after I got you home safe."

"Wow."

"I did more than that. I asked them for a loan to save the clinic."

"And what did they say?"

"They'd do anything for their little girl. Once I made sure they understood how much it meant to you, they jumped on it. I was so stupid to let my pride get in the way. But I fixed it, Mattie. As soon as we get back, your dad and I are going to the bank to set it up. We can keep the clinic open. We can grow it together."

"I have to get through this first, Ben."

"I just want you to know that even if you don't want to be my wife, we can be business partners. No strings attached."

I stared into his eyes, thinking of all the happy days I'd had in that clinic. The wet kisses of puppies, the heart-melting softness of affectionate cats, the way ears would perk and a tail would wag when each animal heard the one voice that meant home. "Thank you."

"Thank your mom and dad, Mattie. I couldn't have made it happen without them. They love you more than anything, and they just want you home. They miss you."

My parents. They'd just lost Grandpa. What would it do to them if I didn't make it through this transaction? "I miss them, too." And I prayed I wasn't about to break their hearts.

"Hey! Here she is," called Roberta. "Need some help?"

I turned to see Asa walking slowly up the trail from the parking lot with Gracie in his arms. Her right front leg was in a cast, and her shoulder and chest were wrapped in a thick bandage. She had her head on his shoulder. I could hear her whining with each breath and felt complete sympathy.

"If someone could fetch her shiny new cage from the van, I'd be grateful," Asa said, frowning.

"What the heck happened to her?" asked Ben.

Silence fell over the shore as we all looked back and forth between Asa and Ben.

"Hit-and-run," Asa said in a flat voice.

"When?"

"Ben—"

"Oh my God," he whispered. "Please tell me I didn't do this."

This time the silence was flinty, full of condemnation.

Asa stared at his younger brother for one long moment. "The ride was kind of hard on her," he finally said. "Will you take a look at her stitches?"

Ben rushed over to help Asa get Gracie into the house. A few of the others hiked up to the van to gather the cage and the supplies Asa had gotten from the vet. The rest went back to the house, carrying our dishes.

I sat there, looking out on the moon's reflection in the water, listening to the chirps and moans of crickets and frogs, wondering if it was possible for Ben and Asa to truly be brothers again.

I looked over my shoulder when I heard footsteps. Asa was coming down from the house, a steaming mug in his hand. "Letisha wants you to drink this."

"Is there a secret ingredient?" I asked warily.

Asa sniffed at it. "Yep. Rum."

I snorted. "Hand it over."

"You took my advice about the magic."

"Yeah." I took a sip of the hot cider-rum mixture and sighed as it burned my throat. "It's been a pretty okay night as a result. So, thanks. How's Gracie?"

"The doc said she should heal completely, but it's gonna take about six weeks—and that's *if* I can keep her off that leg. She has to spend a lot of time in the cage so she doesn't run around like the crazy lady she is. It's not gonna be easy. She hates that motherfucking cage. And I hate putting her in it." His hands were clenched around the arms of his chair.

I knew better than to try to touch him, though God, how I wanted to put my hand over his. "Once you get her through this next few weeks, you can toss it in a Dumpster and walk away."

"I might have to run over it with the van first."

"Some things just have it coming."

"Dammit, Mattie," he said with a sigh.

I bowed my head into my afghan to hide my grin.

"I got through to Brindle's people."

"And?"

"We're working some things out. We have a location. Atlanta. Neutral ground—the Grand Hyatt in Buckhead. Nice hotel. Right now we're looking at Saturday. The only thing is they want to supply the conduit. So far I can't budge them."

"I would think they'd give us whatever we want. Don't they want the Strikon relic whole? It's not as valuable if it's fractured, right?"

He nodded. "But they know we want *you* whole, so they have some leverage."

"If I die, the magic dies with me."

"I know. That's our leverage. That and the Sensilo relic. It's like a two-for-one."

"But you. Are you worried Brindle's going to try to trap you and keep you for himself?"

"Nah." Asa grinned. "He gave me three days to plan, baby. That's like a lifetime."

I smiled back, but my guilt and fear didn't subside. Frank Brindle had given Asa three days to plan. He'd also given himself three days to lay the perfect trap.

CHAPTER
TWENTY-SIX

Asa had been right—three days *was* like a lifetime.

On Friday morning, he announced we'd be leaving after lunch. After he and Ben disappeared into a back room, they emerged and Asa said that Ben would stay to take care of Gracie, and that if all went well, we'd be back by Sunday morning at the latest. They actually shook hands, and I should have been happy about that. Instead, it made me feel worse. Asa had been cool to me for days, and had just spent longer talking to the brother he claimed to despise than he had to me since Tuesday. Then he walked right past me and got into his van without so much as a glance.

Ben kissed me on the forehead when it came time to go, telling me that we'd talk when I got back, that whatever I decided was okay. Jimmy announced that the carnies might be hitting the road later that day—he'd found a possible new carnival site at an abandoned amusement park down in Louisiana, and they wanted to get going. So we shared hugs and good-byes, and I felt even sadder than before at the thought of not seeing them again.

Ben helped me get into the van. It was easier to get around with Quentin's magic on board—he'd given me two vials to take on the trip—but I'd become pretty weak. Jimmy had asked if it wouldn't be more prudent to fly instead of making the eight-hour-plus car trip, but Asa had said even if they did let me on a plane (he seemed to think I looked crappy enough that they might not), it would take nearly as long end-to-end and wouldn't be nearly as safe, given the risk of ambush.

He was already sweating as he drove away from the campground. "Do you want me to go sit in the back?" I asked.

"Doesn't matter," he said curtly. And then we rode in silence for hours, the quiet cranking me tighter with every mile. What had started out as a beautiful late-spring day turned dark and ugly the farther south we got, matching my mood. By the time the sun set as we reached the outskirts of Atlanta, it was pouring.

"Where are we staying tonight?" I asked.

"Hotel in Midtown. About fifteen minutes from the Hyatt. I didn't want to be too close. I'm gonna drop you off and then go scout it."

"I'd like to come with you."

"You'd slow me down."

Annoyance zipped through me. "I want to see what I'm dealing with, okay?"

"What are you gonna see, exactly? It's just a nice hotel in a nice part of town. I need to go figure out if Brindle's got his people positioned there. I'd feel them in an instant, and I know how to avoid them. But you—"

"I'm part of this," I snapped. "I'm not just a—how did you put it?—an alligator handbag."

"I thought you trusted me." He took an exit for Buckhead.

"I did."

"And now suddenly you don't? Your timing sucks."

A few days ago, I would have done anything he asked, but then he'd left me alone with my fear and uncertainty after telling Ben he would take care of me, that he'd do whatever it took.

We didn't speak until he pulled into a spot just off Peachtree Road. He tore the keys from the ignition and pushed past me to get to the back. I listened to toolboxes opening and slamming shut for a few minutes. "Come on, then," he said in a hard voice as he jumped out the side door and pulled it closed.

I pushed my door open and winced as the rain began to pelt my legs. My skin felt oddly sensitive and thin. "I don't suppose you have an umbrella."

Asa was standing on the sidewalk, his dark, wet hair shining under the streetlight, drops streaming down his angular face. "Does it look like it?"

I turned toward the main road and looked up at a black skyscraper up ahead. "Is that it?"

He let out a brusque laugh. "Nope. It's about seven blocks thataway." He jabbed his finger to the right as he began to walk toward Peachtree.

I swallowed back a whine and followed him, but I nearly had to jog to keep up. The rain drenched me to the bone within a few minutes. My hair hung down my back in tangled clumps, and my shoes squished with every step. My teeth were chattering so hard that it felt like a woodpecker had taken up residence in my skull, and each breath was coming out as a harsh, painful rasp.

And finally, I just couldn't. I wrapped one arm around the narrow trunk of a fledgling tree planted along the sidewalk. My tears were washed away instantly by the downpour, so I let them come.

Asa kept walking for a few steps, then spun around. "Come on, Mattie. You want to see it for yourself, and it's still three blocks up."

"You parked this far away on purpose," I said, panting. "Are you trying to prove a point?"

"No, I'm trying to keep us out of trouble. I'm not exactly going to pull up right in front of the damn building and get out before I know what's waiting for me. Nor do I want to stand here in the middle of the fucking sidewalk as a stationary target for whatever comes along. So let's go."

"I can't."

"This is what you wanted."

His cold tone twisted inside me, finding its ally in the Strikon splinter. I whimpered, and Asa cursed, probably feeling just how bad it was. He strode toward me and scooped me up just as I started to pitch forward. "This is stupid," he snapped.

I began to struggle to get down again, but he only held me tighter, cradling me against his chest as he stalked up the sidewalk. "Let me translate for you," I said. "You think *I'm* stupid."

"We're heading into the most dangerous, tricky transaction ever, and you're picking a fight with me?"

"Maybe I am! If we're fighting, at least you're forced to acknowledge that I exist."

"And you don't think I'm aware of that every single goddamn minute of every goddamn day already?" When we reached the van, he let my legs drop and my feet hit the ground, but he kept hold of my arms. "I'll drive you to our hotel."

"No."

"What the *fuck*, Mattie." He groaned. "I'm not Ben. I'm not gonna play little head games with you—"

"You said you would take care of me," I wailed. "You said you weren't going to let me hurt anymore! And I *believed* you. I trusted it completely! Do you have any idea what the last few days have been like for me? You just disappeared!"

He stared down at me, his face in shadow, and his silence made me want to kick him in the shins.

"You told Ben I would break if I wasn't handled the right way. Well, here I am." I held out my scrawny arms, knowing how pathetic I looked. "You were right."

And still, Asa just stood there.

"Now we're back to the silent treatment?" I asked, my voice cracking, my entire body trembling. "Great. You want to know something? All your talk about how strong and brave it is to give up control—it's bullshit, Asa. You don't even believe it yourself, and I get that. It's smart. Because as soon as you trust someone to hold you up, they *walk away*. They start pretending you don't exist. They start treating you like a stranger."

I planted my hands on his chest and feebly shoved him. He let me go, and I leaned on the van to stay upright. Rain was coming down in sheets, blurring my vision and raising goose bumps. "So yeah. I *am* stupid. I should never have bought into it."

"You're not stupid."

"I let myself need you! It's not like I want to." I covered my mouth to hold in a sob. "I've tried really hard not to. And yeah, I buried my head in the sand since last summer, but I was just trying to survive, okay? Then you were back, and even though things have been scary, and even though you've been kind of an ass, I knew you would never leave me behind. Until these last few days, when that's exactly what you did." I wrapped my arms around my body, trying and failing to hold myself together. "I know I made you angry. I understand why you didn't want me to touch you, and I shouldn't have tried. But I don't think I deserve this. Especially not now."

His jaw went rigid.

"I guess you're going to yell at me," I squeaked. "Tell me all the ways I've got it wrong."

"No, I'm not."

"Why not, dammit? Why are you being so freaking cold right when I need you most? How did I manage to lose you just by caring about you?"

"Because I'm a fucking coward," he said.

I blinked up at him. "What's that supposed to mean?"

He ran his hands through his wet hair. "Can't we just . . ." His arms fell limply to his sides. He sucked in a sharp breath and blew it out. "Okay. I can fix this. I can handle this." It sounded like he was trying to convince himself. "Twenty-four hours tops, and then we're done. Then I'm gone."

That comment hit me right in the heart, sinking the Strikon splinter deeper. I tensed and put my hands up as he moved closer. Slowly—but very firmly—he laced his fingers with mine and pulled me against him. Tension vibrated through every fiber of his body, like a billion live wires bundled together, impersonating muscle and bone. "What are you doing?"

"Giving you what you need," he said in a strained voice as he put his hand on the back of my head and held it to his chest. His heart was thumping fast and fierce, as if it were trying to escape from its cage. "I can handle this."

"Is it hurting you?"

"Yeah," he whispered. "More than I ever thought it could."

I pushed against him, but he held me tight. I hadn't had any idea it was this bad. "But I don't want to hurt you." And I had been so selfish, expecting him to hang around close to me when it probably drained every bit of his strength. He needed all of it for tomorrow, and I should never have begrudged him his space. "That's the opposite of what I want."

"I know, Mattie." He kissed the top of my head.

"Asa, I'm so sorry."

"Me too, baby. Me too." His fingers tightened in my hair. "Come on. I'm taking you back to the hotel."

He helped me into the van. I stared at Asa's crooked profile as he drove down the rainy streets, just aching. He checked us in. One room. He carried our stuff up, obviously not willing to trust the bellboy with an original relic—no matter that it was thickly packaged in lead and tucked into a locked case. I sat in the lobby, shivering, while the two young women at the reception desk kept giving me anxious looks. "Could we page the hotel doctor for you, ma'am?" one of them finally asked. "We have one on call."

I shook my head. "Nothing they could do for me."

Their eyes went wide, and that's when Asa stepped out of the elevator. He lifted me from the chair, and I leaned my head on his shoulder. The reception ladies gave us this *awwww* look.

Asa carried me all the way to our room. He got me set up for a shower, and when I was through, he helped me to the bed. He handed me one of the vials of Quentin's magic, and I spread it over my skin, grateful for the relief—and knowing it would make things easier for Asa, too.

After taking a quick shower of his own and emerging in track pants and a T-shirt, Asa settled on the bed next to me and held his arm out, inviting me close. I wasn't about to turn that invitation down. But . . . "Is it better with Quentin's magic?"

"Either way, I can handle it. Get over here."

I did, because selfish or not, I needed this. I laid my head on his chest and clung to him.

He threaded his fingers through my damp hair. "Are you scared?"

"Yes." But . . . not of Brindle or the transaction. For some crazy reason, it felt like the least of my worries, a speed bump as I raced toward the edge of a cliff. I didn't want to explain that to him, though. Doing that would mean I'd have to say it all out loud.

"It's them or us now. And it's gonna be us."

"Really?"

"I am gonna make absolutely sure you get back to Ben and your family."

I pressed my cheek to his chest. He didn't control everything. I had to control some of it myself.

I clamped my eyes shut and counted the beats of Asa's heart. He held me close as we both drifted. I don't know how much he slept, but I remember briefly regaining consciousness to feel his arms heavy and loose around me, his breathing slow and even. Grateful it wasn't over yet, I sank back into rest, dreading the morning.

It came anyway, though. Asa nudged me awake as sunbeams sliced through a crack in the blackout curtains. "I want you to eat some breakfast," he said, already showered and fully dressed. "I ordered room service."

A knock came at the door a minute later, just as I was standing up from the bed. Asa peered out the peephole, his collapsible baton nestled in his hand, which he held behind his back. Apparently satisfied, he opened the door. The server, dressed in the hotel livery complete with a cap, rolled the cart in, his head down.

And as he raised it, I gasped. "Jack."

There was a click as Asa extended his baton, but Jack had a gun pointed at Asa's chest before he could raise it. "Drop it, Ward," he said sharply.

Asa cursed and obeyed. He glanced at me before glaring at our uninvited guest again. "I'm guessing you're Jack's grandson. The Headsman."

Jack smiled. "How are you two? Big day, huh?" He arched an eyebrow as he took in my messy hair and the one bed in the room. "Wait, I thought you were engaged to the brother?"

"What the fuck do you want?" snapped Asa.

"Breakfast, for starters." Jack's grin didn't fade. "And then we're gonna talk about how today's transaction is gonna go."

CHAPTER
TWENTY-SEVEN

"Not that you care, but Mattie's life is on the line for this one," Asa said. "You want to fuck with one of my other transactions, go ahead. But—"

Jack put his hands up, finger away from the trigger. "I know she's in bad shape." He gave me a regretful look. "Some of that is probably my fault."

"Then get the fuck out and come after me another time." Asa's fists clenched.

The conduit shook his head. "I'm here to offer a deal."

"You have nothing I want."

Jack's eyes met mine. "I'm going to be your conduit today."

"You're a fucking Headsman. Brindle would shoot you on sight."

"I've been undercover for the last seven years, man. Very few people know I'm not a freelancer. Sunday was the first time I'd surfaced in four years."

"When you brought Arkady in," I said. "But he knew after you captured him, obviously. He could have told someone after he escaped."

"Arkady wasn't loose for long, and now he's back in our custody." Jack's brows lowered. "And his social life's not very active right now, seeing as he's in a coma."

"Shit," said Asa. "He survived."

"Can I take that as an admission that you're the one who ran him over, Mr. Ward?"

"Fuck yeah."

Jack let out a hard laugh and shook his head. "You're exactly like I thought you'd be. No regard for human life. No remorse."

"That's not fair," I said. "The only reason I didn't run Arkady over myself is because Asa never lets me drive."

Asa arched an eyebrow. "We've already talked about this. The screaming is a nonstarter."

"I demand a rematch," I grumbled.

Asa's smirk disappeared as he turned to Jack. "Look, man. We've gotten off on the wrong foot. Your grandpa was a good guy, and I had a lot of respect for him. I'm sorry about what happened, but he understood the risks and decided to save our asses anyway. And if it helps at all, his killer probably didn't make it outta that parking lot."

I cringed, remembering how Asa had unleashed the power of the Strikon relic on Zhong's assassins who'd come to steal it.

"Yeah, you left quite a mess behind," said Jack. But was that begrudging admiration in his tone?

"Not like I had much of a choice."

"You could have called in the Headsmen."

Asa laughed. "Like, for actual help? Right."

"From what I understand, you nearly became one of us."

My mouth dropped open. "Huh?"

"Ancient history," Asa said, all his humor gone.

"The guild has a long memory." Jack holstered his weapon behind his back and kicked Asa's baton behind him. "But for now, let's focus on today."

Asa's eyes narrowed. "Unless you've got a fuckload of conduit and reliquary agents with you, you came by yourself. I don't sense any naturals nearby."

"I'm here on my own. It's my fault Arkady got loose. He caused the deaths of eleven of my colleagues and eighteen other innocent people, not to mention dozens of injured and maimed." Jack slid the cap off his head and tossed it on the bed, then squared his muscular shoulders. "Some redemption is in order, and from what I understand, there are two original relics in play today. I plan to take both off the street."

Asa gave Jack an appraising look. "And what do we get? If Brindle ends up empty-handed, he's coming after us. Maybe even Mattie's family. But that would be just like the Headsmen, am I right? *Who* has no regard for human life?"

Asa's hand twitched toward one of his thigh pockets, but Jack had his gun drawn again with a speed and fluidity born of years of practice and experience. "I will personally make sure the blowback doesn't land on you."

Asa put his hands up with a look of pure exasperation on his angular face. "Brindle's been insisting on his own conduit for the transaction, so your cute little plan is irrelevant."

Jack's smile was slow and assured. "Who do you think he called to do the deal? The best on the East Coast."

"You?" I asked in a weak voice.

He winked. "I got a certain rep."

"Oh, fuck," said Asa. "You're Jack Winchester, aren't you? The one all the foreign bosses like to use stateside. And it's all a cover."

"One my organization would kill to maintain," Jack said, the threat clear. But then he grinned. "Thought you mighta heard of me."

"So why did you come to us first?" I asked.

"Couldn't have you blowing my cover when we meet for the first time, could I?"

Asa turned to me. "Was he good to you at the station? How did he treat you?"

I glanced at Jack and sank down on the bed, my stomach turning at the memory of that transaction. "Um . . . he could have been harder on me than he was. Daeng was trying to get him to force me. To yank it out of me." I folded my arms over my middle. "Jack threatened to kick him out of the room."

I looked up as I felt Asa's stare. Somehow it was both bleak and saturated with absolute fury. After several long seconds, he turned back to Jack. "Daeng," he said, his voice clipped and harsh.

"Didn't make it out of the sheriff's station," Jack replied. "Someone set it on fire. They were still pulling bodies out when I took off."

"I want confirmation."

Jack gave a stiff nod.

"Mattie?" Asa's voice gentled. "We're not moving forward until you give the okay."

"Do I have a choice?"

Asa came over and squatted in front of me. "I can't always determine which options you have, but I am here to make *sure* you have a choice."

He might have pulled away earlier in the week, but now he was back, solid and certain, ferocious in his protection of me. The difference was dizzying, once again driving home just how much I needed him. Want and wish and terror were a storm inside me.

"Okay. Right now Jack seems like the best choice."

Asa stroked his thumb over my cheek and stood up. "All right, then. Let's talk about how this is gonna go down."

A few hours later, at three o'clock on the dot, Asa and I entered the lobby of the Grand Hyatt, no longer looking like refugees from some natural disaster. At some point earlier in the week, Asa had gone shopping for me again. To my shock, he'd gotten me makeup, and I was so relieved and happy when he pulled out the bag that I almost kissed him. Of course, then he ruined it by saying, "I don't want to draw unnecessary attention."

Meaning I looked bad enough that people would notice me.

I forgave him because he'd also bought me antifrizz gel that smelled frankly amazing.

And then there were the clothes. It was a strange feeling not to have a say in my wardrobe, but I'd learned in Bangkok that Asa actually had a pretty keen sense of style—though it showed only in certain situations—and for whatever reason, he liked choosing what I wore. Today's outfit consisted of deceptively comfortable platform sandals, crisp navy-blue twill shorts—a little shorter than my usual—and a flowy peachy-pink blouse. It had a deep V-neck and a zipper that offered the possibility of making that *V* even deeper—and made the possibility of a bra basically *im*possible. When I'd walked out of the bathroom with it on and arched an eyebrow, Asa had simply said, "I need access to your chest."

In any other circumstance, I might have been offended. Or, *okay*, turned on.

Today, I understood that he was talking about being able to quickly hook me up to a defibrillator if it came down to that.

Now we stood in the marble lobby of this fancy hotel. Asa looked casual in dark-gray cargo pants and a light-gray crew neck, but the slim fit and slick black boots made him look surprisingly elegant. We could have been a hot young couple here for a romantic weekend, except our only luggage was the black metal toolbox Asa carried. With my hand in his, he led me past the front desk toward the elevators, his stride unhurried. My gaze snagged on a group of young women wearing long lavender dresses hurrying toward the grand staircase, each with a small bouquet in her hand complete with trailing ribbons. Bridesmaids. It was a Saturday in late spring—there must be a wedding reception taking place in the ballroom. A strange sadness washed over me, and I looked away as they descended the stairs to the sprawling level just below the lobby.

"Do you feel anything?" I asked Asa, trying to keep my mind on the task at hand.

"Yeah. They're up there." He turned his eyes to the ceiling. "Knedas. Ekstazo."

"Can you sense the bone relic?"

His brow furrowed. "Yeah. It's faint, though. They must have it packaged incredibly well."

"But no Reza?"

"No Reza. And no one giving off anything nearly as powerful."

"This is good, though, right? We can just go up there, do this transaction, and leave."

"I tried to plan for every outcome, but here's hoping," Asa murmured as he punched the button next to the elevator. The doors opened, and we were greeted by mirrors all around. Asa's eyes met mine in the reflection as we stepped aboard. "You look good."

"I don't look like myself." And my legs felt like they were about to buckle. My walk across the lobby had left me winded. I was *so* tired of this. "I haven't looked or felt like myself in months."

"But you still *are* you." He put his arm around my shoulders and let me lean against him. "Somehow, no matter how bad you feel, you always manage it."

I didn't know what to say to that, so I simply held on to him as he pressed the button for the twenty-fourth floor. "This isn't happening in a regular hotel room, is it?"

"Nope. Only one exit from a typical room. We're doing this in one of the boardrooms."

"Good."

He winked. "And after we're done, I'm taking you out to dinner."

"Will there be french fries?"

"A whole fucking mountain of them, baby."

I closed my eyes and pressed my forehead to his chest. *Please let it be that easy. Please let this be easy.*

"What the . . ." Asa frowned as the elevator dinged and stopped at the twentieth floor. "Oh, shit." He shoved me behind him as the doors slid open.

I peeked around Asa to see a slim, sleekly dressed Asian man with killer cheekbones standing in front of the doors. Next to him was a statuesque Asian woman with crimson lips. It was Ho-Jun and Maew—and they worked for an entirely different boss than the one we'd sold the Strikon relic to in exchange for Ben's freedom last year.

Ho-Jun smiled. "Hello. Mr. Montri would like his property back."

CHAPTER
TWENTY-EIGHT

Ho-Jun started to step aboard, but Asa slammed his foot into the guy's middle. But the Knedas henchman caught his boot and wrenched it forward, and Asa went tumbling out of the elevator, toolbox and all. I fell against the mirrored wall as Ho-Jun and Asa collided outside in the carpeted alcove between the elevators. Maew jumped inside, agile despite her skintight cocktail dress. Her long black hair shimmered around her shoulders as she pressed her hand—tipped with long blood-red fingernails—against my shoulder, pinning me to the wall while she swiped some sort of keycard through the elevator's control panel.

"Going down," she said in her crisp British accent.

"Mattie!" yelled Asa.

I struggled against Maew as Asa punched Ho-Jun and lunged for the elevator. But Ho-Jun tackled him just as the doors began to close, and he fell to the floor with Ho-Jun on his back.

"I'm sorry," Asa gasped. He wrenched his hand up from one of his pockets and hurled a small object into the elevator just before the doors shut completely.

Maew and I both blinked down at what looked like a tan wad of chewed gum.

Is that . . . Silly Putty?

It was my last thought before the thing exploded and my ears filled with the shrieking of metal against metal. The floor fell out from under me. Maew screamed. I was too breathless and shocked to make a sound. Mirrors shattered all around me as the elevator rumbled and plunged. I curled into a ball and covered my head with my arms.

When you know death is only seconds away, your thoughts can get pretty weird.

Mine were, in chronological order:

Didn't he just promise me french fries?

I'm sorry, Mom and Dad.

At least now I won't have to choose.

And: *Shouldn't we have hit bottom by now?*

No sooner had I thought it than I felt a sharp pain in my wrist and opened my eyes as Asa dragged me out of the elevator, back into the carpeted alcove. He'd clamped one of the Headsmen's silver cuff bracelets around my wrist, and it was emitting needle-prick shocks strong enough to clear the fog of terror from my mind. The elevator door was still open, and Maew was on her knees, screaming, her eyes rolling in terror. Asa calmly leaned in, pressed a button for a lower floor, and let the doors close. We listened to Maew's shrieks fade. "That oughta keep folks busy down in the lobby for a while."

Asa took the cuff off my wrist and tucked it into his toolbox, then picked it up and steered me toward the stairwell, past Ho-Jun, who was lying on his back, laughing as he pointed up at the ceiling, oblivious to our presence. Obviously yet another victim of the contents of Asa's pockets.

"You okay?" Asa asked. "Hated to do that while you were in there."

"It's all right," I said breathlessly, feeling strangely elated now that I'd survived that kind of disaster, even if it had been completely fake. "That was some trick."

"Showed Betsy some video of the elevators in this place on YouTube. That woman has an amazing and terrifying imagination. Worked up a sweet little glamour for me, and Vernon helped me get it into the putty. Just in case."

"Do you think of everything?"

"I hope to God I did. But I'm thinking we need to steer clear of the elevators for now." He held the door of the stairwell open as I followed him in. He gazed up the stairs, then knelt at the base of them. "All aboard, Mattie. Four floors to go."

I wrapped my arms around his neck and climbed onto his back, and he looped his free arm beneath one of my legs, helping me secure them around his waist. My chin pressed to his sweaty temple as he began to climb. "Thank you, Asa," I said quietly.

"That's my job."

"You've ruined me for anyone else." I pressed my lips together as the words escaped me, as their truth echoed in the stairwell around us.

Asa paused halfway up a flight. His fingers closed around my bare calf. The silence made my heart speed. But then he laughed. "That's what they all say, baby."

I rolled my eyes as he resumed climbing, part of me relieved he'd let it pass . . . part of me disappointed for the same reason. *I don't want to choose. I'm not ready for this to end.*

That was my silent chant as Asa reached the twenty-third floor, as he turned to keep climbing. I know he felt differently, having to huff up four flights of stairs carrying a heavy toolbox and a person on his back—not to mention the painful magic that had to be wearing on him—but I wanted it to go on forever. Me clinging to him for dear life, him solid and steady, fearless and lethal, practically immortal.

Asa reached the landing of the twenty-fourth floor, and I slid off his back. He leaned against the wall to catch his breath, but he kept his fingers entwined with mine. "It's gonna be us, Mattie. Remember that."

"Promise."

He looked down at me. "I will if you will."

My cheeks burned and my stomach dropped. Asa smiled and squeezed my hand, shaking it playfully. "Just kidding. Let's go."

He swung open the door and led the way, and I rubbed my chest as it started to ache again. "Do you feel anything?"

"The relic is in the boardroom, but I don't sense naturals."

The floor was virtually deserted, which I thought was really strange until we passed the elevators, where easels had been posted with signs on them that said, "Floor Closed for a Private Function. We Apologize for the Inconvenience."

We followed signs for the Regency Club Boardroom, which was tucked away down a corridor opposite a path that led to an enclosed bridge connecting the two wings of the hotel. Asa's grip on my hand grew firmer the farther we walked. His palm was clammy. I could tell he was feeling the Strikon relic, and it made me want to pull him back toward the stairwell. But then we were right there, and the door to the boardroom opened before he had a chance to reach for the handle.

The guy standing in the doorway had to be at least six and a half feet tall. His black hair was cut high and tight, and with his prominent forehead and lantern jaw, he looked like my mental picture of those Special Forces guys in the military. He wore a navy-blue suit and carried a briefcase. "Mr. Ward? Ms. Carver?" He grinned. "I'm Sean Hernandez, one of Mr. Brindle's representatives for this transaction. Come on in."

Asa shook his hand, frowning. Sean's grip was hard as he shook mine and then stepped aside. Two other men were waiting on the other side of the room. One was middle-aged and thickly built, his skin leathery and tattoos marking the backs of his hands and the sides of his neck, ruining the effect of the suit he wore. And the other was Jack, who was dressed casually in slacks and a black T-shirt that clung to his broad, muscular chest. He didn't smile as we approached.

Sean introduced us. We acted as if it were the first time we'd met Jack. I was suddenly glad he and Asa had done most of their planning while I was in the shower—I had no idea what exactly was going to happen, so I couldn't give it away. The other guy was named Rob, another representative of Brindle's. "We're just here to ensure everything goes smoothly," said Rob, his voice a gravelly growl.

Asa set his toolbox on the table and opened it, pulling out the metal box in which he'd packaged the Sensilo relic. "That's our payment for Mr. Brindle."

Rob briskly opened the case, opened the lead wrapper, and peered at the spherical locket inside. He opened the clasp, whipped out his phone, and took a picture of the gold-plated relic. "Getting verification. Hang on." Less than thirty seconds later, his phone chimed, and he nodded as he looked down at the screen. "We're good to go." He pointed at Sean.

"We've brought the Strikon relic." Sean set the briefcase on the table next to Asa's toolbox.

Asa winced as he opened the case. Inside was another case, this one dull and gray—lead. "Hold it right there for a minute, okay? I need to get Mattie settled."

Sean complied, giving me a lingering once-over. "Where are we putting her?"

"My eyes are up here, buddy," I snapped as he stared at my (braless, *argh*) chest.

He gave me a cocky smile and slowly complied. "Yes, Ms. Carver?"

"I will put *myself* over there," I said, pointing to half of the boardroom table. I gave Asa a quick glance and he nodded, the corner of his mouth twitching upward. With as much strength and grace as I could muster, I walked to the end of the table. Asa helped me up but let me do most of it myself, which I was grateful for. I was in a room full of men who were all staring, and suddenly I felt really exposed, conscious of my hard nipples chilled by fear and nerves and overefficient air-conditioning, of my bare legs, of the fact that I was laying myself out on a table like a buffet.

Jack settled himself in a chair next to me as I blinked up at the chandelier. "Slow and easy, right?"

"Yeah," I whispered. "Be gentle."

He reached over and squeezed my upper arm. "You got it, Ms. Carver."

Asa gave him an assessing look before busying himself securing me to the table. Instead of going with ropes this time, he had padded cuffs, which he connected to the table legs. They looked uncomfortably like the ones that I'd been drawn to at this magical sex-toy shop we'd been at in Bangkok, but fortunately, though the leather was soft and supple, it didn't seem to be coated with Ekstazo magic.

Asa bent over me. Jack was on my other side. My heart was beating like a jackhammer, driving my pain deeper with every beat. "We're gonna pull it slow," he said to the two of us. "Jack, I'll be giving you signals. You're gonna have to stay alert."

"Not a problem." Jack had his game face on, his dark-brown eyes stern.

Asa pulled a pair of surgical gloves from his pocket and tugged them on. He yanked his toolbox over and pulled out one of the trays, revealing his defibrillator and other various tools. "Slide that relic over here."

Rob pushed the briefcase along the table until it was within Asa's reach.

And then he pulled a gun and aimed it at Asa's head. Sean did the same, and I found myself looking up at its long black barrel. A silencer was screwed onto the end of it.

"Mr. Brindle was pretty clear," Rob growled to Asa. "You try to turn on us with that pain relic, we shoot. You somehow try to reverse the transaction and drain the relic, we shoot. We might not be magical fairies like you people, but we're both former Delta Force, Mr. Ward. Believe me when I tell you that you *cannot* move faster than we can."

"I knew they were Special Forces," I mumbled.

"Fucking mercenaries is what they are," Asa said. "You got any other demands before we get started?"

"Only one." Sean smiled as he lowered his weapon and leveled it at my head. "When this transaction is done, you're coming with us—or we kill the reliquary."

CHAPTER
TWENTY-NINE

Asa's jaw clenched. "That was *not* the deal."

"Mr. Brindle is a powerful man, Mr. Ward," said Sean. "Better just give him what he wants. He paid me enough to be willing to shoot this pretty lady here. He can pay you enough to make you happy."

I turned to Jack, expecting him to say something, but he just shook his head. "Let's just get this done, man."

"Yeah. Just get it done," said Rob.

Jack's eyes met mine, and he arched one eyebrow, as if challenging me to question him.

What if he was on their side? What if he let them take Asa? I already knew he resented him. And he wanted only the relics.

I stared up at my sensor, my body starting to tremble. "It's okay, Asa." I couldn't make myself tell him to walk away and let them shoot me, but I could never live with being the reason he was caught.

He bowed his head and stared at the center of my chest. Unlike Sean's leer, which had made my stomach turn, Asa's stare made me feel as if I were rising off the table. It wasn't a sexual thing. But it was definitely a *thing*, just part of the thing we had, the thing I could never explain or unpack. It just *was*, and as his eyes rose to mine, I was waiting. "It's okay," I said again, hoping he would understand. *Do whatever you need to do.*

He glanced over his shoulder at the weapons aimed at us, and then he seemed to make some sort of decision. He climbed up on the table and stretched out next to me, his mouth curved into a seductive half smile. "Hey there."

I snorted, even though my eyes were stinging with tears. "Hey."

"You're gonna be okay, Mattie. You know that, right?" He leaned over me on one elbow and caught a tear as it slipped from my eye.

"As soon as I let this go, they're going to take you away," I whispered.

He touched his forehead to mine. "Don't think about that right now."

"I can't help it."

"Do you want to be Eve?"

I let out a shuddery breath, completely torn. Part of me, maybe Eve, screamed *yes*. It was simpler. It was easier. There was no guilt there, because everything was in the moment. It didn't leave a mark.

But the rest of me was roaring *no*. If these were my last minutes with Asa, I didn't want to give them up, no matter what came after. "I want me to be me. And I want you to be you."

He moved close enough so that I could feel the pace of his breath. "Then do you trust me, Mattie?"

"With my life."

"Will you do everything I tell you to do without questioning it?"

"Yeah."

"Will you let go when I tell you to?"

But . . . letting this go meant letting *him* go.

He gave me a stern look when I paused. "Mattie . . ."

"I . . . I'll let go when you tell me to."

He nodded. And then he sat up and used tongs to open up the relic and hand it to Jack. When he returned to my side, his brow was beaded with sweat, and his muscles were twitching. He tugged off one of his gloves with his teeth and slid his bare palm under my shirt, up my stomach, between my breasts. Behind him, I heard Sean muttering something in a suggestive tone that drew me tight, made me wish I could curl up in a ball.

"Ignore him," Asa said. "Look at me. Jack and I are the only ones here. You're gonna listen to my voice and let it guide you. You see my eyes? You keep looking at them."

"Ready," said Jack. He wrapped his fingers around my upper arm. Immediately I felt the pressure, the brittle cracking, the danger.

But I wasn't ready for this part to end yet. "What, no gag?"

Asa chuckled. "I got one if you're feeling kinky, but I don't think you need it this time. We're gonna go slow and easy." He leaned down and whispered in my ear, "Not that I'd mind seeing it on you again."

A hot shiver went down my spine, melting some of the tightness. If we actually had been the only two people in that room, I think I would have taken him up on it. But we were doing this for an audience, and I didn't want to give Sean the satisfaction. Asa may have seen the conflict in my eyes, because his flared with amusement. "Are you remembering that first time?" he murmured.

"Are you, *sir*?"

"Well, I am *now*."

"Any day," grumbled Jack.

But the playfulness had unknotted me, stolen some of the terror. How did Asa know *exactly* what I needed every single time? I looked up into his eyes. "I don't know what to do about you, Asa Ward."

He laughed. "Ditto, honey." His smile was soft, full of light despite the sweat trickling down his cheek. "Let's figure that out after we get this done, okay?"

"You're in charge."

He closed his eyes, and I ached. When he opened them, he began to press on my chest. "I feel it right there. I want you to let go of it little by little. Don't just let loose."

I let my eyes go unfocused, seeing only the honey tint of his eyes as the center of my attention shifted lower and deeper. Quentin's magic had dulled the pain, but now, as I imagined what lay inside me, the hurt rose up, twisting and jabbing, like a missile in search of a target. I gasped as it stabbed, half expecting to look down and see it protruding from my chest. My thoughts turned dark and twisty, and my vision went red.

"Oh, no, no, no," Asa said quickly. "Jack, I know it hurts, but don't pull that hard." Asa kept murmuring instructions, to Jack and to me, all the while keeping his hand anchored on my chest. I know it must have hurt like hell, but he didn't even flinch.

I moaned through gritted teeth. "It feels like it's breaking," I said in a quavering voice after one particularly awful stab that sent agony radiating along my limbs.

"It's just coming loose. It's been in there a long time."

I grimaced as something burned in my throat, and Asa looked down at my lips. I watched his Adam's apple move as he swallowed hard, but then a moment later he was pressing something soft to the corner of my mouth. I caught a flash of red as he pulled it away.

"Is she gonna make it?" I heard Sean say through my haze of pain.

"There's no one else here," Asa said to me, drowning Sean out. "It's just you and me and Jack." He muttered some more instructions to Jack, and the pain ratcheted up even higher, making my back arch as I cried out. Suddenly I was made of the pain. It bled through every part of me, liquid fire. Asa's voice became an echo, but I couldn't understand what he was saying. His voice rose and fell, but his words were lost in my storm.

I couldn't scream. I couldn't ask for help. All I felt was hurt.

And . . . Asa's hand on my chest. Warm and real, heavy and constant. I couldn't hear him now, but I knew he was there. I knew he hadn't left. I knew he wouldn't abandon me. I clung to that touch, the only sliver of my awareness that wasn't alight with agony. Even as it burned brighter, even as my muscles locked, even as it felt as if I were being torn right down the middle, I knew Asa was still with me. Still fighting for me. His hand over my heart.

Don't let me go. My mind started to flicker, everything going black. *Please don't let me go.* My body went numb. Was he still there? Oh God, had I lost him?

"Don't let go," I whispered. "Please don't let me go."

"I'm right here," he said in my ear, his voice a harsh rasp.

"Don't let me go."

"You did it."

"Please. Don't let go."

"Mattie, open your eyes." He smacked lightly at my cheeks. "Come on. Let me see those baby blues."

My eyelids blinked open. "Are we done?"

His eyes were bloodshot, and there were dark circles beneath them. "Are you hurting?"

I took a deep breath, amazed at how easy it was. "No."

He grinned. "Then we're done." His thumb stroked over the top of my chest. His fingers were still spread over me, his palm still pressing. "I don't feel a thing in there except your beating heart."

I took in his face, his crooked nose, his high cheekbones, his knife-like smile.

I loved the view.

His smile faded as he took in my spacey, adoring stare. "Are you sure you're okay?"

"Yeah," I whispered, feeling tears starting in my eyes, but for a completely new reason. I blinked fast, trying to push the new, fearful truth from the front of my mind. "And Jack?" I turned my head. He wasn't in his chair.

"He's fine."

"Actually fine, right? Not dead fine?"

He chuckled. "Yes, he's actually fine. He's walking it off right over there." He inclined his head toward the hallway. And then he abruptly leaned down and kissed me, fast and firm, maybe impulse, maybe sheer relief. When he raised his head, we just blinked at each other.

More. It almost came out of my mouth.

But then Asa glanced at something over his shoulder and cleared his throat. "I'm gonna untie you now, okay?"

I nodded, stunned, glancing around to see a bloody cloth next to my face. "What the—"

"It got a little dicey there for a minute." He whipped the cloth out of sight. "You scared the shit out of me. But it stopped as soon as we got all the magic back in the relic."

"And it's time to go, Mr. Ward," said a voice that jerked me out of my dazed, floaty reverie.

"No," I said, abruptly remembering Sean and Rob and what they were about to do.

Asa took my hand and pulled me up. "It's gonna be okay, Mattie."

"No." My feet hit the floor, and I wobbled over to Sean, who was standing in the doorway. Behind him, out in the hallway, I could see Rob leaning nonchalantly against the wall, texting as Jack paced. Our conduit looked ashen in the wake of our transaction, but his strides were steady.

Sean watched me with amusement as I approached. He was holding the briefcase they had brought the Strikon relic in. "Looking better already, Ms. Carver."

"Frank Brindle is getting two original relics today, including the Sensilo. Why would he need Asa when he has that?"

"Not really my job to figure that out. I just follow orders."

"You are *not* taking him," I said shrilly.

"You gonna stop me?" He checked his watch and then leaned forward to look down my shirt before I could reel back. "I guess that could be kind of fun."

"She's not gonna do anything." Asa slid his arm around my waist. He turned me around and took me by the shoulders. He looked sick, his cheeks hollow, sweat dripping from his chin. "Eat some french fries for me tonight, all right? And take good care of Gracie. Tell her I love her."

I glanced down at his pockets, praying he had a secret weapon stashed in there. "Tell me what to do," I whispered.

Asa glanced at Sean, who had one hand tucked behind his back—probably on whatever weapon he had holstered back there. "Be good," he said as he turned back to me. He started to reach into his pocket but had a gun shoved against the back of his head in the next second.

"Seriously?" snapped Sean. "Now you're just pissing me off."

"You *are* fast," Asa said lightly. "But I was actually just reaching for my car keys." He bounced on his heels, and his hip pocket jingled. "Slowly."

Asa reached into his pocket, and I held my breath. But all he removed were the keys. "Once we're gone, drive straight back to Ben."

I pocketed the keys and focused on the words, trying to decode whatever secret plan he had. I was *sure* he had one. Asa laughed when he saw me mouthing what he'd just said, my forehead squinched in concentration. "Oh my God, Mattie." He pulled me into his arms, hugging me tightly. "I'm gonna miss you so fucking much."

"Please, Asa." *Don't let this happen.*

He planted a fierce kiss on the top of my head. "Stay here, all right?" He took my face in his hands and tipped my chin up so that I had to look in his eyes, full of warning. "Stay right here."

"Okay," I said in a choked voice.

"Time to go." Sean grabbed Asa by the arm and tugged him backward, the barrel of his weapon pointed at me, maybe to dissuade Asa from fighting back. And he didn't. He just let Sean tow him out into the hallway, and I watched helplessly as Jack, Rob, and Sean surrounded him.

In that moment, as they disappeared around a corner, I silently vowed that I would get Jack back for betraying us like this. I wrapped my arms around myself and hugged, hard, unable to believe I'd just let Asa go like that. I couldn't breathe. Every fiber of my body was rebelling.

No. I wasn't just going to let him go.

I glanced around the room, looking for a weapon. Anything I could use. The only real option was a phone sitting at one end of the conference table. I yanked its long, thin cable from the wall and hooked my fingers under the back of it as I stalked to the door.

Yes, I *knew* no one was going to be intimidated by a skinny woman wielding a conference phone. But my heart, newly freed from the tyranny of the Strikon splinter, impulsive as ever, beat with absolute determination.

As soon as I stepped into the hallway, I heard a heavy thump and a sharp snap followed by something shattering. And then a man screaming, plaintive and pathetic and terrified. I ran to the end of the hall and peeked out. Jack and Rob were grappling on the floor, both men trying to control the mercenary's gun. Asa was standing over Sean, who was sitting with his back against the wall, his fingers scrabbling at something wrapped around his neck. I squinted at it as Sean clawed at it feebly, wheezing now. It was a green yo-yo.

I ducked back into the hall, trying to stay out of sight as Asa strode away from Sean and approached Rob and Jack, who were still locked together, limbs tangled.

"Need some help?"

"Got it under control," Jack said through clenched teeth as he locked his legs around Rob's waist. He slid an arm around the mercenary's throat while the other guy punched at him.

"Are you sure?" Asa pointed at Sean. "Because I got him taken care of and—"

"I'm fine," Jack said with a grunt.

"Can I at least take his gun?"

"Brindle's gonna hunt you down," Rob wheezed, his face turning purple.

"Yeah, yeah," Asa said, sounding bored.

Rob went limp in Jack's arms. "See?" Jack said to Asa. "I told you."

"My way was faster."

Jack rolled his eyes. "We better tie these guys up."

"Mattie can help."

"You wanna go get her?"

"Nah, she's standing in the hallway." Asa turned and locked eyes with mine. "And she's brought some cord with her."

My cheeks burning, I trudged into the open, carrying my phone, the thin gray cord dragging on the floor behind me. "What exactly were you gonna do with that?" Asa asked as I reached him and Jack.

I looked down at the phone and then tucked it behind my back, my fingers clawed around it in a sweaty grip. "Why didn't you tell me?"

"You wanted me to tell you what I was about to do while the guy I was about to do it to was standing right behind me with a gun aimed at my skull?"

"You could have given me a signal!"

Asa sighed. "But if you had been cool with me leaving, Sean would have picked it up. You know that."

"You scared me," I wailed.

"Better than having you caught in the crossfire," Asa yelled, pointing across the carpeted space to a giant vase that had been standing in a corner, filled with stalks of a slender, leafy plant. Now it was cracked, a bullet hole through its front. "They had orders to shoot you if I fought back, and I wasn't gonna . . ." His brow furrowed and he looked around, his gaze darting to the massive wall of windows that lined one side of the twenty-fourth-floor atrium. "What the fuck," he whispered, whirling to face Jack. "Are they yours?"

Jack had Rob's gun in his hand. "You're feeling them, aren't you?"

"What the fuck, Jack."

"I can't just let you go, Ward. You're wanted on just about every continent, and after you assaulted one of our bureau chiefs last year—"

"What the *fuck*, Jack." Asa stalked toward the Headsman, who began to raise the weapon.

I slammed my conference phone into the side of Jack's head. He staggered to the side, and Asa was on him in a second. He whipped a small syringe from his back pocket, uncapped it, and sank the needle into the bulge of Jack's shoulder. He'd depressed the plunger and stepped back before Jack seemed to register what had happened.

Jack steadied himself and looked at the syringe sticking out of his shoulder. He pulled the syringe out and tossed it aside, then raised the gun again and aimed it at Asa. Smirking, he said, "So was that Strikon or Knedas? Ekstazo, maybe?" He chuckled. "You must be off your game, Ward. I'm a conduit. None of that shit affects me."

"Oops," said Asa. "My bad."

I looked up at him in confusion. It wasn't the type of mistake I'd have expected him to make.

Jack rubbed the side of his head and gave me a resentful look. "And I should charge *you* with assaulting a Headsman."

I held up the phone and rattled it at Asa. "*That's* what I would do with it."

Asa snorted. "*Dammit*, Mattie."

"Asa, what did you pick up on?"

"At least twenty naturals coming our way. They're within a block of us. We need to get the fuck out of here."

"Wait, twenty?" Jack swayed a little, looking surprised.

Asa gestured for me to head for the stairwell.

"Whoa . . . hey . . . you're not going any-anywheres." Jack's voice was thick, his words slurring together. "What the hell," he mumbled, looking down at his hands as the gun fell to the ground. He wiggled his fingers. "Magic doesn't affect me." He raised his head and peered at Asa, looking bewildered. "Magic doesn't affect me!"

"It wasn't magic, you double-crossing motherfucker," Asa said as Jack sank to his knees. The Headsman's mouth was slack, and his eyes were sliding out of focus. "It was ketamine."

CHAPTER THIRTY

"You shot him up with a doggie sedative?" I asked as Asa grabbed Jack under the shoulders and dragged the drooling Headsman to a room marked "Employees Only."

"I stole some from the clinic, and Ben told me how much to use. I told you I was going to be prepared." Asa opened the door and pulled Jack inside. "Grab that briefcase, will you?"

He took the case from me and pulled one of the relics out. As Jack groaned and mumbled something unintelligible, Asa set the packaged relic on Jack's lap.

"What are you doing?"

"Giving him half of what he came for. He was good during your transaction. Without his cooperation and skill, that splinter could have really torn you up. I owe him for that. And for helping me take down the mercenaries. Plus, I feel bad about what happened to his grandpa."

"Which one are you giving him?"

"Strikon. I'd rather not leave that in the hands of a boss. Not that the Headsmen are much better, but they seem less likely to hurt innocent people with it."

Asa shooed me out of the room and shut the door behind him. "He'll come around in a few hours, and until then, he should be safe from what's coming."

"I thought what was coming was Headsmen."

"Did you see the look on his face when I said there were twenty? He was shocked." Asa took my hand and led me toward the stairs. "Headsmen are the least of our concerns."

"Brindle's people?"

Asa swiped his sweaty face across his shoulder. "There's a powerful Strikon with them."

"Reza?"

"Probably."

My stomach turned. "And we're surrounded?"

Asa stopped in front of Sean, who was still passed out with the yo-yo around his neck. Rob was weakly stirring about twenty feet away. Asa pulled a pair of gloves from a pocket along his calf and tugged them on, then unwrapped the string of the yo-yo from Sean's neck.

"What was that?"

"Knedas. He thought there was a hungry boa constrictor around his neck."

"Yipes."

He gave me one of his knifelike smiles. "Fast is good. Sneaky is better." He looped the yo-yo string around one of his fingers and then snapped it back, and the thing recoiled into his palm, the string wrapped neatly around its center.

We jogged toward the stairwell, leaving the mercenaries behind. I followed him as he moved quickly down the stairs, and though it was easier than it had been, my legs were jelly as we approached the lobby floor. "Can you still feel the naturals?" I asked.

"They're closer," Asa said, slowing down. "Fuck. They're in the lobby already."

I grabbed the railing and stopped. "Do we go back up?"

"Only if we want to get cornered." He beckoned to me, his face sheening with sweat. "Down, Mattie. Quick as you can."

My heart was hammering as we reached the lower lobby floor, but for the first time in months, it was a pain-free experience. Instead of feeling frightened and tortured, I felt exhilarated. Alive. Determined. We emerged from the stairwell, and I ran right into Asa's back.

"They're down here." His fingers were white-knuckled around the case that held the Sensilo relic.

"Reza?"

"Still above us." He pulled me away from the door. "Three coming down the stairs."

From the ballroom I could hear thumping music, and I recognized the tune—"YMCA." "Let's get lost, then," I said, and slid my hand along the wall as I made for the wedding reception. I glanced down at my clothes. It was a Saturday-afternoon wedding. Probably semiformal. Asa and I looked more suited to a trendy club than this kind of event, but with gangsters and Headsmen converging on us, I couldn't think of a better place to hide than on a dance floor. "Can you get rid of that briefcase?"

Without slowing down, Asa whipped it open, grabbed the smaller box containing the relic from inside, and tucked the empty briefcase behind a planter as we moved toward the ballroom. The lower lobby was partially open to the upper level via the grand staircase, and several people were descending quickly and purposefully, their gazes already scanning the area. I picked up my pace, practically running the last ten yards. Guests were milling around in the open doorway, which was marked by a sign that said, "Rollings-Getchell Wedding."

Asa put his arm around me, his grip sweaty, leaning on me more than should have been necessary. I knew he was suffering under whatever vibes the approaching naturals were giving off. They probably knew it would affect him and no one else. Forcing myself not to glance behind me to see if we'd been spotted, I wrapped my arm around Asa's waist and snatched a wedding favor—an etched champagne flute with dangling silver ribbons—from one of the tables arrayed outside the room.

A guy in a tuxedo frowned as we approached. "Invitations?"

"Oh, hang on," said Asa, reaching in his pocket. "Right here." He drew a small spritzer bottle and squirted the tux guy in the face. "We're friends of the bride."

The guy grinned. "Welcome!" He nodded at the box tucked under Asa's arm. "Gift table's on the right."

"Thanks," Asa said quickly, swinging me inside. The tables were decorated with lavender and creamy linens. It was a huge wedding, three hundred guests at least, and nearly half of them appeared to be flailing around on the dance floor, with the bride and groom in the center, their grins huge and their eyes bright.

"They're coming," Asa muttered, looking behind us. "I think they saw us. We have to find the back . . ." He looked toward the rear of the room as two people emerged from a door in the corner, just behind the table where the wedding cake was on display. They wore stark, serious looks out of sync with the guests' smiling faces—and they had silver cuffs on their wrists.

"Headsmen. And they've got defenses against—"

"Those cuffs won't save them from me." Asa yanked my arm and pulled me onto the dance floor. We got a few odd looks from the suit-and-tie crowd, but I jumped into a line of women in cocktail dresses and did my best YMCA, craning my neck to see if the approaching Headsmen had spotted us. Asa dropped to his knees next to my feet, and at first I thought he was sick.

Then I realized he'd opened the case holding the Sensilo relic.

I grabbed his shoulder. "Not here! Asa, this is their wedding reception." I had stopped dancing and was leaning over him.

"Is he okay?" asked a guy in a tan suit with a lavender tie. Probably one of the groomsmen.

"Just catching his breath." I grinned at him, and he grinned back. "Quite the party."

"Long time coming, though, right?" He waved his arm at the bride and groom, who had paused in their dancing to kiss while those around them cheered.

"I know—*finally.*" I was still wearing a smile, but my throat was tight. I so did not want to ruin this couple's perfect day. I turned to check on Asa and locked eyes with someone else who looked just as out of place. One of the Headsmen, a woman with blond pixie-cut hair and pale skin, was already on the dance floor, bouncing to the music as she wound her way through the dancers toward us. My fingers closed tight over Asa's shoulder, tugging him up.

Asa rose to his feet, the relic around his neck, his eyes shiny and bloodshot and wild. "Hang on to me, or else it'll get you, too."

"Let's just run," I said desperately. "We can't hurt these—"

He stumbled back as someone yanked on his shirt. "Asa Ward," said a sharp voice, "you're coming with us—"

Asa jerked his foot backward, catching his captor in the knee, and staggered toward me as a few of the guests screamed. His hands rose to the golden locket around his neck and wrenched it open. His fist clenched around the relic inside.

The most amazing feeling suddenly swelled inside me as I stared at him, so exquisite that I thought my heart would shatter with it. My lips parted as my body and brain lit up. I grinned as Asa reached for me.

"I love you so much," I said. It felt so good to say it out loud, like taking a breath of air after too long underwater. How had I been able to contain this adoration before now? How had I been able to hide it? And why had I wanted to? "I love you, Asa."

"Yeah. Thanks," he said drily as his hand closed around my arm, and it was like he'd pressed the "Mute" button on my heart. The world came back into focus, the lens widening to include more than just him. I glanced around to see people embracing, kissing, laughing as they held each other's faces, gazing into each other's eyes like they couldn't get enough. The bride and groom were hugging each other so tightly that they were shaking. Tears were running down their faces, but they didn't look sad. They looked ecstatic.

Every single person in the reception had someone—including the Headsmen, who were happily fondling each other—and this beautiful feeling filled the room to the ceiling. We were swimming in it. Drowning in it.

Asa looked pallid and sick, though, his jaw clenched as he steered me toward the back of the room. The knobby gold relic was clutched tightly in his other hand, which he held over his head in what looked like a gesture of defiance. But he wasn't inflicting pain or sadness or rage or confusion on the wedding guests and the Headsmen who had come to take him away.

He was using love.

Asa half dragged me to the exit. He wrenched the door open—and his head snapped back as someone drove a fist into his chin.

I caught him but barely managed to slow his fall. A lean, clean-cut guy with brown skin and black hair charged through the door with eyes only for Asa. The relic fell to the floor, the chain clanking softly around Asa's neck as he tried to regain his footing. As the Headsman drew a Taser, I scooped the lump of gold from the ground and lunged between him and Asa. I clutched the relic in my palm, wishing I had some idea how to use the stupid thing. My entire body was jangling with the aftereffects of the magic, and my only coherent thought was that I needed to protect Asa.

I thrust out my hand as the Headsman aimed the Taser at my chest. A powerful pulse vibrated up my wrist and arm, and the Headsman's mouth dropped open. His arms went slack and he fell backward, landing on his butt right next to the wedding-cake table. He stared at me as if in awe.

"Damn, Mattie," Asa said in a choked voice.

Reeling with confusion, near panic, I dropped to my knees next to Asa and shoved the relic back into the locket, then snapped it shut. With shaking hands, I pulled him to his feet and helped him to the door. We dove through it, and Asa twisted a dead bolt before pushing me up the steps. "What just happened?" I asked as I climbed.

"You turned it on him." Asa's breaths were coming heavy and jagged. "You made him sense what you were feeling. It was . . . overwhelming."

I swallowed hard and gave him a sidelong glance. Had he sensed it, too? I didn't have time to ponder it, because Asa stopped dead on the stairs, his whole body trembling.

"Asa, we have to keep going. Those Headsmen down there are probably snapping out of it. They'll be right behind us."

"And the lobby is full of Brindle's people. They're everywhere." Asa looked like he was about to keel over. If he used the Sensilo relic again, I was afraid he wouldn't be walking out of here.

I began to head for the door to the lobby. "Tell me what to do."

He grabbed my wrist. "I'm not letting you go out there."

"Is there another way out?"

Asa looked down the stairs just as the door began to rattle. "Not anymore."

I snatched the necklace and lifted it over his head, then put it over mine. The heavy locket rattled as it bounced against my belly. "I can distract them, and you can get out."

He grimaced. "Do you honestly think I'm gonna let you parade in front of Reza—"

"*Let* me?" I poked him in the shoulder. "We're a team, you jerk! Just because I let you boss me around sometimes doesn't mean you're actually the boss."

He drew in a strained breath, then his hands fell to his sides. "You've got to hold his attention." His eyes met mine. "But he's gonna hurt you. Try to break you."

Fear curled inside me, a snake ready to strike. But if this meant Asa would get out, if I could give him this chance—I forced a smile. "I've just carried a giant splinter of original Strikon magic around inside my body for months. You think I don't know how to deal with pain?"

He stared at me for a second, then reached up and wrapped his hand around the back of my neck, bringing our faces close. "I fucking love you, Mattie Carver," he said in a ragged whisper. And then we were kissing, and I have no idea who started it, only that it was desperate and hot, clenched fists and harsh breaths and me determined never to let go, knowing it would hurt like hell when I did. But the sound of crunching, buckling metal from below wrenched us apart. "One minute," Asa murmured against my lips. "I swear. Hang on for me."

"Here I go." I tore myself away from Asa. My hands fumbled to open the locket's latch, my plan forming at the speed of light. With a quick prayer, I plunged through the doorway to the lobby. "I need to talk to whoever's in charge—" I started to shout.

The words died in my throat. People were cowering against the walls, their arms over their heads. Whimpering. Somewhere beyond the elevator banks, someone was shrieking, the noise saturated with agony.

I glanced behind me as the door clicked shut, no idea whether Asa had emerged and skirted the elevator banks or was still in the stairwell. But he'd asked for a minute, and that's what I was going to give him. My right fist clenched tightly, my palm sweating. This had to work. It had to.

The locket clanking against the zipper over my belly, I walked past the elevators and the cowering people who had sought shelter against the wall, then turned as I reached the soaring atrium. Here were more terrified people huddled on couches and in corners, a few of them crying, their eyes all focused on the concierge, who was writhing on the eight-pointed star set into the polished marble floor. The front doors were maybe fifty feet away, but I could already see the way was blocked with agents. Given the man who was standing in the middle of the lobby like he owned the place, I was guessing they belonged to Brindle.

"Hello, Mattie," said Reza, taking his eyes off the contorted body of the concierge, who immediately went limp. "Have you been making mischief again?"

I blinked at him for a moment, taking in ebony hair slicked away from the most exquisitely handsome face I'd ever beheld. "I was just trying to give you guys back the rest of your relic. You're the ones who had to try and hijack Asa."

He gave me a sad smile. "We were certain the splintered magic would have taken its toll, maybe even damaged you permanently. We did our best to spare you."

"You're so full of crap. Your stupid mercenaries had orders to use me as leverage."

He chuckled, looking over my shoulder toward the elevators. "And where *is* Asa?"

"Long gone."

"I don't believe you." His dark-brown eyes settled on my face. "But let's find out, shall we?"

Suddenly it felt as if he were tracing a red-hot knife right down my middle, from my throat, between my breasts, down my stomach, all the way to the apex of my thighs. The agony wrenched a scream up from my depths, but I clamped my teeth down on it, not wanting Asa to hear, not wanting to distract him from whatever he was doing. I glared at Reza as my legs buckled and I fell to my knees. But I kept my right fist clenched, determination holding my fingers closed.

Reza smiled pleasantly as he strolled toward me, as his gaze traced over my belly and I felt the pain inside, something rending and tearing.

"I'll take that." He lifted the locket from around my neck.

Now, a distant voice cried from beneath the pain.

Still smiling, Reza opened the locket. And then the smirk melted from his face. "This is empty. Where is the relic?"

"Right here, you asshole." I shoved my fist upward, opening my fingers to press the knobby lump of gold against his stomach.

Reza screamed, his arms flailing as he reeled backward. I lunged up with him, one hand wrapped around my middle, the other balled in the front of his shirt, keeping the relic close to him as I projected all the pain I was feeling onto him. It was like a deadly loop between us, him lashing out to protect himself, using all the painful power he possessed, and me taking it in and pushing it back out through the original relic, making him sense all the pain he was causing me. He tripped over his own feet and fell backward, and I landed on top of him. The pain whited out my thoughts, just like it had when Asa pulled the splinter. Only this time, Asa wasn't here to anchor me, his hand on my chest, warm and steady. This time I was alone.

But I wasn't empty. Inside me I carried wishes and wants and hopes so big and fierce and tangled that they couldn't be eroded by the mad rush of hurt roaring through me. Hands shoved and punched at me, but I clung like a freaking barnacle, determined to give Reza back every last ounce of bitter magic he dished out.

My back slammed against the floor, knocking the breath and intent right out of me. My muscles twitched, but the pain was gone, having evaporated as soon as I'd let go of Reza. Gasping and confused, I stared up at the ceiling. A man in a suit glared down at me. On his wrist was a silver cuff. He was blond, ruggedly handsome.

It was Keenan, the Headsman Asa had nearly strangled with a pair of suspenders in Bangkok.

He knelt down and scooped me up as I struggled feebly, swatting at him with empty hands. The relic was gone. I'd lost it. My ears ringing, I looked around to see the lobby full of Headsmen, tackling anyone who ran, tasing resisters, zip-tying the wrists of their captives.

I kicked at Keenan, then pitched forward so forcefully that he nearly lost his grip. My gaze snagged on a discarded plastic spoon sticking up from the dirt in a planter near the wall, and I grabbed at it, thinking to use it as a weapon.

"Stop," he snapped, trying to corral me as I clawed for it. "Calm down."

"Screw you, buddy." I smacked at his face as he bundled me toward the door. The Brindle agents who had been by the hotel entrance, probably keeping people away, were gone, and the circular drive beyond the doors was scattered with Headsmen, their cars blocking incoming taxis and limos. I peered over his shoulder to see Reza crawling on all fours, pale with the echo of the pain I'd inflicted and looking as confused and terrified as I felt, scrambling to get behind the front desk and away from the marauding Headsmen. "You're taking me but letting Reza Tavana get away?"

"Fuck him." Keenan's grip on me was steel, but his hands were clammy, and his face was shining with sweat as he carried me, struggling like a speared fish, out of the hotel.

"Help," I shrieked.

He clamped his hand over my mouth. "Mattie, it's going to be okay. Stop struggling. I know you're scared, but you have to stop. We're almost there."

But I couldn't stop. Asa was somewhere in that hotel, and the place was full of people who wanted to cage him. I thrashed and writhed, trying to get my feet back on the ground, and Keenan barely managed to contain me as he got us out from under the massive hotel awning. He stepped over another plastic spoon that had been planted upright at the edge of a flower bed.

"Look at me," he said as I drew back to slap him again.

I gasped, my upraised palm frozen midair. "Asa?"

He gave me a smile that managed to be seductive despite the black circles under his eyes and the sweat pouring off his body. "Not bad, am I right?" He turned me to face the hotel.

"How did you do this?" This was no boa constrictor. It was more than the size of an elevator—it was the size of a city block.

He pointed to the spoon. "Like the carnival. I had to lay them around the perimeter. After what they experienced with the Headsmen, it wasn't hard to get Betsy and Roberta to put together something realistic, but I had to surround the whole area. I went as fast as I could, but there were agents everywhere. I couldn't have done it if Reza hadn't been completely distracted."

I peered through the glass doors and into the hotel lobby, where I could still see Headsmen swarming in and out, could still hear shouts and screams. "I can't tell what's real and what's not."

"Exactly. Here's hoping the actual Headsmen are competent enough to call in their cleanup crew before Reza and his minions crawl away."

"You let him go."

"I had to prioritize." He put his arm around my waist as we limped toward the street. "Besides, you hurt him worse than I ever could."

"But I lost the relic."

"You were still holding it when I pried you off him. Got it in my pocket."

No wonder he looked so bad. "Let me take it."

"Not this time."

"Why not?"

"You getting power hungry on me, Mattie?"

"Are you serious?"

He squeezed my shoulders as we limped up the block toward his van. "You were fucking incredible," he said as we reached it.

I turned and looked up at him. "You weren't so bad yourself."

His eyes searched mine, and he smoothed a stray curl away from my face. "We're a good team, yeah?" He gave me a faltering, stunningly vulnerable smile. "Do you think—"

He arched away from me with a cry of pain, his limbs locked and his muscles taut to the snapping point as he hit the sidewalk. I staggered back as his assailant raised a second weapon, and I had a split second to register his face before my world lit up in yet another explosion of bright-white pain.

CHAPTER
THIRTY-ONE

By the time the shock stopped, I was in Asa's van. So was Asa. We were in the very back, packed so tightly that I was half on top of him. Like me, he was lying on his stomach, wrists and ankles zip-tied.

I raised my head and looked down at his face, his closed eyes. "Asa?"

"Yeah," he said with a moan. He didn't open his eyes.

"It's Daeng."

"I know. I can feel him now."

"Why couldn't you before?"

"Sensilo relic was in my pocket." His voice was ragged with exhaustion. "Dwarfed any magic of that kind in the area."

We shifted as the van made a tight turn. "Where do you think he's taking us?"

"Probably to whatever headquarters they've got set up . . ."

We both got quiet as the van braked and we heard gravel popping beneath the tires. The van rolled to a stop, and the engine went silent. I winced as a train's horn blasted somewhere nearby, followed by the clack of wheels on rails.

"Near a rail yard," mumbled Asa as footsteps approached. "Fuck. We're not in Buckhead anymore."

The door swung open, and Daeng smiled down at us. He had a long wound on the side of his face, clumsily stitched, as if he had done it himself. "Hello, my friends," he said, his voice soft but filled with cold menace. "I thought it important that we have a talk."

He grabbed me first and dragged me through a small parking lot toward a shop with boarded windows and a shabby sign out front that said, "Abby's Wholesale Bridal."

"Oh, the irony," I said, too weak from all the punishment I'd taken to put up a good fight.

Daeng hauled me through an open doorway and into a warehouse room with a few overturned mannequins piled in the center. In front of them were two chairs, facing each other. Daeng plopped me down in one and deftly fastened my wrists to the chair, followed by my ankles. "I'll be right back."

I sneezed from the dust he'd kicked up, my stomach tight with dread. This place in no way resembled the sheriff's station where the Headsmen had set themselves up last time.

A minute later, Daeng was dragging Asa across the floor. Asa wasn't struggling, but it was clear he wasn't giving Daeng any help. He was totally limp, and Daeng was sweaty and grunting as he heaved Asa onto a chair.

"The more uncooperative you are, the more I hurt her," Daeng said gently.

Asa sat up quickly and glanced down at his pockets. Daeng clucked his tongue. "I emptied them before I stopped the shock."

"Where's the rest of your crew?" I asked. "Aren't you a Headsman now?"

"I was. But then most of my colleagues killed themselves, and I killed those who were left." His fists clenched convulsively. "I decided I needed to pursue my enemies on my own. Fortunately, Mr. Okafor put out a call for assistance, conveniently letting me know where to find you."

Asa's jaw was rigid. "What the fuck do you want?"

"A measure of justice. There's so little of it in this world."

"No shit," said Asa. "I'd figured that out by the time I was four."

Daeng sighed as he stepped back to survey his handiwork. "I understand you, Mr. Ward. I feel as if we are kindred spirits, perhaps."

"Do you make a habit of tasing and tying up kindred spirits?" I tried to sound calm. "That's no way to treat your friends, Daeng."

Daeng chuckled as he turned to me, his eyes glittering with hatred. "Better than I'm going to treat you." He strode over to a metal cart covered by a cloth and ceremoniously uncovered it, then rolled the squeaky-wheeled contraption closer. On its surface were arrayed a few syringes with scary-long needles, metal picks, tongs, a corkscrew, and a scalpel.

"You're not even in the same league with me," Asa snarled as he glared at the cart. "You'll never be even half as good."

Daeng stiffened, his fingers positioned over one of the syringes. "Good . . . how do we gauge that? Results? Because now I have the Sensilo relic." He patted a bulky round lump in his breast pocket. He'd obviously wrapped it in something to try to shield himself from its effects. "And by the time the day is out, I will also have the Strikon. You will tell me where it is."

"Unlikely." Asa's lip was curled with contempt.

Daeng plucked a syringe from the tray. "You met Arkady," he said, turning away from Asa to stand over me. He ran a finger along the side of his face, next to the poorly stitched gash. "So did I."

"Then you should realize that people like him are your real enemies."

"Are you not my enemy, Mattie?" He examined the syringe in the gray light filtering in through a few unboarded windows. "You were as cruel to me as Arkady was."

"That's nothing compared to what I would do to you," Asa said, his voice echoing in the room.

Daeng smiled. "If you had the chance. But you haven't. The last time we met, your little reliquary had to save you. And this time? You will watch as I punish her for it. Who is the more powerful one between us, Mr. Ward?"

I stared at a clear drop oozing from the tip of the needle. "What is that?"

"Are you afraid of pain, Mattie?" Daeng asked.

"It's not exactly my favorite thing."

"Ah. But you're not afraid of it. I can tell." He tilted his head. "I know what you *are* afraid of, though. I watched you in that sheriff's station. You are afraid of being controlled." Sweat dripped from his chin, and his cheek was twitching.

A hard chill rolled through me as he wrenched up the sleeve of my blouse.

"You pathetic little worm," Asa shouted. "I'm the one you're gonna have to deal with! I'm the one who's gonna make you sorry you were born!"

"You can't provoke me into hurting you instead of her," Daeng said dreamily. "So stop trying." He aimed the needle at my upper arm. "They juiced Arkady as soon as they brought him into custody." He looked over his shoulder at Asa. "Do you think that I should make her cut off her ears first, or her lips? The pain won't clear her mind, not when Arkady's magic has invaded her veins."

I whimpered, and Asa's eyes flashed with rage—and unmistakable fear. "I'll get you the original Strikon relic," he said quickly. "Today."

Daeng laughed. "Oh, yes. And I'm sure I can trust you."

"Then I'll tell you where, and you can go find it." Asa was looking back and forth between the needle and my arm.

Daeng dug his thumb into my skin, and I grimaced. I was fighting tears, determined not to shed even a single one for this maniac. "The night I first saw you," he said to me, "I was struck by how vibrant you were. I was at that party, thinking nothing could bring me pleasure. It's hard for men like us to find, you know. Hard because we're so sensitive to it, hard because too much makes us prisoners. We can never trust it. But you . . . I watched you dancing, and I thought . . . there is joy. Real and natural and . . ."

He wiped his face on the sleeve of his black button-down shirt. "I couldn't wait to meet you. I was so eager to experience some of that joy for myself." He leaned down so that his mouth was right next to my ear. "I wanted to taste it."

Asa's chair scraped against the floor as his body jerked. I glanced over to see him leaning forward, his face contorted with fury and helplessness. His expression only heightened my dread and fear, and I closed my eyes. "I never intended to hurt you," I said softly. "I could tell it hadn't been easy for you."

"I thought, for once, here is someone who is no more than she seems. Here is someone who is simple and sweet. I had no idea you would cause me so much agony."

"You did it to yourself, asshole." Asa was straining so hard against the handcuffs that I was afraid he was going to break his wrists. "Every ounce of pain Mattie inflicted? You brought it on yourself."

"Could I say the same to you, Mr. Ward?" Daeng asked, his thumb stroking up and down my arm as he held the syringe only a few inches from my skin. "Have you brought this on yourself? Did you make the same mistake I did? Were you foolish enough to crave her?"

He brought the needle closer and Asa roared, the sound so loud it made my ears ring with his frustration and rage. But then his head bowed abruptly, and he started to laugh, half-hysterical, his shoulders shaking. Both Daeng and I stared at him, though I still had half my attention on the needle that hovered only an inch from my arm.

Daeng frowned. "What's so funny?" He sounded peeved that he'd been deprived of Asa's horror and fear.

Asa was laughing so hard that a tear streaked out of the corner of his eye. "Oh, man. Daeng, you have the worst luck."

"What?" Daeng forced out a stiff giggle. "You're the one who is tied up."

"And you're the one with the relic in your pocket," Asa said loudly. "Guess who's gonna pay?"

Daeng whirled around and his eyes went wide. I turned to see three men standing just inside the doorway, and my eyes went wide, too.

Zhong's people had found us. Tao strode forward, his strides a little clumsy but his hands steady as he pointed his weapon at Daeng. Shan and Bai were at his sides.

"Put the syringe on the cart," Tao said, drawing in a deep breath as his brow beaded with sweat. His eyes zeroed in on Daeng's breast pocket, where the Sensilo relic lay.

"This is kind of an interesting scene," said Shan, looking over the contents of the cart and then at me. "Couldn't we have let it play out?"

"Zhong wants the relic secured as soon as possible," Tao said, his voice stern.

"We can do a deal," offered Daeng, dropping the syringe on the cart before raising his hands in the air. "Such an esteemed man as Mr. Lei . . . a good price . . ."

"Unnecessary." Tao glanced at Asa and then looked over the cart again, his weary, melancholy features hardening with dislike. "It is best to keep this simple."

He raised his weapon abruptly and shot Daeng between the eyes. Daeng fell backward, and Tao immediately removed the Sensilo relic from the dead sensor's pocket.

I tensed as he rose to his feet, and my eyes found Asa's. My sensor was staring steadily at me, no longer laughing. Shan and Bai had moved over to the cart. "Tao, get over here and tell us what's what," said Shan. "We can have a little fun before we go."

"Oh, for fuck's sake," Asa muttered.

"I might be a sniffer, Shan," Tao said, raising his weapon again. "But I am finished being your trained dog."

And as the two henchmen turned to him, surprise etched on their features, Tao promptly shot them, too. I screamed as Shan dropped right between me and the cart, his eyes still wide open.

Asa tilted his head back and let out a long, relieved sigh. "Took you long enough."

Tao holstered his weapon. "The Buckhead area is swarming with Headsmen. It was hard to pick up the scent at first." He held up the relic, which was wrapped in one of Asa's lead-padded pouches. "And he had it packaged, albeit carelessly."

"Wait a second," I said, trying to inch my chair away from the growing pool of blood near my feet. "You guys planned this?"

"Not Daeng," said Asa. "He was a nasty surprise."

"Asa called me a few days ago. He was kind enough to offer me an opportunity." Tao fastidiously covered the cart of torture instruments as if he couldn't stand the sight of them, yet left the three men he'd just killed lying where they'd fallen. "He requested my aid and backup in exchange for the Sensilo relic."

"You can buy your freedom with that," Asa said.

"And I intend to. I am in your debt." He offered Asa a quick bow of his head.

"So could you maybe find the key for these cuffs?" I asked.

He smiled. "Oh, no. I don't trust either of you quite that much."

"Tao," Asa yelled as the other man started to walk away. "Hey, Tao! A little help, please."

"Sorry, Asa. Not my style," he called as he walked out the door, and for the first time since I'd encountered him, his voice was full of laughter.

CHAPTER
THIRTY-TWO

I sat across from Asa in the diner booth, fidgeting. It had taken us a long, painful hour to free ourselves from the handcuffs, and it had involved us both getting much closer than desired to Daeng's dead body. But we'd worked together, and here we were, free and clear. We'd hightailed it out of Atlanta and hadn't stopped until we'd crossed into North Carolina. Now we'd exchanged our blood- and sweat-stained clothes for cleaner, more casual duds, and Asa had just ordered me a "Hungry Man's Platter" of french fries.

"How does it feel?" he asked as our waitress bustled up to our table, a salad in one hand and my trough of fries in the other. She promptly set those down in front of Asa and offered me the salad, then blinked at us in surprise as we exchanged dishes.

I took a deep, pain-free breath and smiled. "Fucking incredible."

Asa, who had been taking a drink of water, began to cough. "Dammit, Mattie."

Every time he said that to me, it made me feel like I could fly. *Dammit, Asa.*

My stomach growled, and I started in on my french fries. Attending to them was less painful than thinking about what was coming. "You ended up without any of the relics," I said after a few minutes of silence. "I thought you were going to keep one of them as payment."

"I did. I just spent it quickly." He winked.

"I think we made a lot of enemies today."

"You'll be okay, Mattie. I'll make sure you're safe."

Frustration zipped through me. I hadn't been asking for his protection or reassurance. I wasn't worried about myself, though maybe I should have been. I was worried about him. "Thanks," I mumbled.

He gave me a quick, detached smile and stared out the window at the interstate, watching trucks speeding by. Now that he was out of reach of powerful magic, he looked like himself again. I smiled as I stared at his crooked profile.

We really had been a good team.

My smile faded. Who was I kidding? We had been more than that. *I fucking love you, Mattie Carver,* he had said, and then we had kissed, and again, it had been just me and him, no excuses.

Had he meant it, or had that just been the aftereffects of the magic he'd unleashed on the wedding reception? Or the heat of the moment, the threat of impending pain and death?

I wanted to ask. I needed to ask. *We have to figure this out. We—*

"So when's the big day?" Asa asked, his eyes still directed out the window.

I twisted my engagement ring around my skinny finger. "Three weeks from today."

"I'll be sure to send a gift," he said, and went back to eating his salad. I picked at my french fries, but I had lost my appetite. I had nothing to hide behind now. No more burying my head in the sand. I needed to face what had happened and decide what to do—about Ben, and about Asa.

I had loved Ben for years, almost since the day we'd met.

I thought he truly loved me, too.

But he had hurt me. More than anyone had ever hurt me. I had trusted him without question. I had believed in him. And he had used those things as a weapon against me. He had left scars on my heart.

And yet, I craved the life he represented. The solid certainty of my family's love and support, my small town, my friends. Plus, I dreaded the idea of disappointing people. I hated the idea of giving up. I had committed to Ben when he had put that ring on my finger. He had accused me of thinking it was meaningless, but he couldn't have been more wrong.

That dread nearly choked me as Asa paid the check and we hit the road again. As the highway lights lit our path, I mulled over everything between me and Asa. It would have been easy to let him be Ben's foil, the opposite of my fiancé. Forcing him into that box didn't do him justice, though. I needed to think about him separately, sort my feelings out separately, and give both room enough to be whatever they actually were.

I kept waiting for Asa to say something, to tell me to come with him, to tell me to leave Ben, to be defiant and angry and forceful—to make it easy. To make the decision *for* me. But he didn't. He just drove, and stared out the windshield, and left me all alone with my thoughts.

The time passed agonizingly slowly as I wrestled with feelings bigger and more complicated than I'd ever wanted to acknowledge. And then, all of a sudden, Asa was pulling into the campground, and there was a light on in the cabin at the end of the trail, and that was that.

My heart picked up a brutal cadence as I hopped out of the van. I could hear Gracie barking in the distance. "I think our presence has been noted."

Asa smiled. "She sounds good. Strong."

"She does."

"I guess we'd better get up there."

"Yeah." But I just stood there, looking up at him, his face lit in profile by the warm light from the cabin. The sight of him made me ache. But it didn't matter, because we had run out of time. "Yeah," I said again, then turned and marched up the trail.

He fell into step next to me as we hiked the trail to the cabin, but we stopped again just before we reached the porch. "Where will you go from here?" I asked, desperate to prolong our time together, trying to decipher the unsteady feeling inside my chest. It felt different from magic, but it was no less powerful.

He shrugged. "I was thinking—"

The door swung open, and there was Ben, wearing a nervous smile. "I was starting to worry that you'd run away."

"I—"

"Oh, Mattie," wailed my mother, charging past Ben.

"M-Mom," I stammered as she enfolded me in a hug, but then my surprise melted and I put my head on her shoulder, treasuring the safety and certainty of her embrace. My dad wrapped his long arms around us a moment later, and there I was, encased in my parents' love, and it felt like nothing in the world could reach me or harm me. It felt amazing, and I stood there for at least a minute, just letting them hold me tight.

"We've been so worried," said my dad, loosening his grip. "We flew down last night after Ben called."

My parents released me, and I looked into the cabin to see Asa hunched over Gracie, letting her frantically lick his face as his hands smoothed over her wiggly body. "I take it this is Ben's brother," Dad said. The kindness had disappeared from his voice, replaced by stern disapproval.

Asa didn't look up from Gracie, but I saw his body stiffen.

"Mom and Dad, this is Asa," I said loudly, stepping into the cabin. "He's saved my life more times than I can count. If it weren't for him, I'm pretty sure I'd be dead or insane."

I narrowed my eyes at my dad, who cleared his throat. "Well, then," he said.

"I'm gonna go get Gracie loaded up." Asa didn't meet my eyes as he lifted her from the floor.

"I'll get the crate for you," my dad said gruffly.

Asa gave him a wary look and then headed out the door. My mom hustled out a moment later, carrying a bag of dog food and the duffel Asa had left behind, full of Gracie's medicines and supplies. My heart beat really fast as I watched them trudge down the trail single file.

"So, it went okay?" Ben asked.

"Yeah," I said huskily. "I guess so, in that we both made it out alive."

"I haven't slept. I've thought about you every minute."

I turned to him. "I've thought about you a lot, too." I stepped into his arms and gave him a fierce hug.

"Oh, Mattie," he whispered, holding me close. "I swear I'm going to make you so happy."

"I think maybe you would have," I said quietly, pulling away from his embrace. "But things have changed, Ben. I've changed." With shaking hands, I pulled my engagement ring from my finger and held it out. "I can't marry you."

Ben paled a little as he looked down at the ring. "But—"

"I wish you all the best. I really do. I hope you learn to be strong and brave like you want to be. I think you have it in you."

"I could do it, if you were with me!"

I shook my head, blinking away tears. "I think that's something you need to do for yourself."

"Well, he's all packed up, and he looked pretty eager to get out of here," my dad said as he strode back into the cabin, then froze as he saw the scene in front of him. "Oh no, what's going on here, sweetheart?"

I grabbed Ben's hand and pressed the ring into his palm. "I'm not getting married next month, Daddy. I'm sorry."

My mom, who had walked in just as I spoke, braced herself against the wall. "Oh, Mattie, are you sure?"

I looked up at Ben and then turned to her. "Yeah. Completely sure."

She opened her arms and I walked into them, wishing my heart would slow down. It was kicking against my breastbone, hard enough to fracture it. "I told you that whatever you decided was okay," she murmured. "We'll take you home. You can have your old room. We'll take care of you."

Her words hit me sideways, knocking the wind out of me. "No, Mom." I glanced over her shoulder, out the door, panic rising in my veins. "I need to take care of myself." I disentangled myself from her embrace as my decision slid into place like a slab of iron, unavoidable and certain. "And I need to go, okay?"

"What?" yelped my dad and Ben at the same time.

"I have to go." I moved toward the door as my mother clung to my arm. My eyes met hers. "Mom, I'm not a little girl anymore. I'll never be happy if I don't explore what's out there for me. I have to do this now."

My mom's eyes were wide and shiny with tears.

"Let me go, Mom," I said gently. "I'll be okay."

She pressed her lips together and nodded.

And then she let go of my arm.

Without a backward glance, I took off running, terrified that I was too late. I sprinted down the trail toward the parking lot, crying out as Asa's headlights lit the darkness. He was already rolling toward the road leading away from the campground.

"Wait," I shrieked. "Asa, wait!" My feet pounded the dirt, and my hope sang in my veins. "Please!" I waved my arms as I burst from the trees and into the parking lot.

Asa's brake lights flared red, and I let out a strangled laugh of relief as the van came to a stop. The driver's-side door opened, and he stepped out, looking cautious. "I was trying to avoid an awkward good-bye," he said warily.

"Do you think you could use a reliquary on any of your upcoming jobs?" I asked, panting.

He looked up the trail toward the cabin. "Mattie . . ."

"Take me with you." Nervousness coiled like a viper in my belly—he hadn't asked me to go with him this time. He hadn't made it easy, hadn't made the decision for me, and I couldn't blame him. But now I had to put myself out there and risk him turning me down. "Please, Asa. Take me with you. I can earn my way. You know I can."

"I'm not going to help you run away from your problems."

"I'm not running away. I made a decision." I leaned on the van, trying to catch my breath.

He looked down at my bare left hand. "You're sure?"

I put my hands on my hips. "Do you trust me?"

His gaze met mine as the corner of his mouth lifted in a sly half smile. "I guess maybe I do."

"Then tell me honestly if you don't want me as a partner. I'll go find my own way. But I'm not going back to Sheboygan."

"A . . . partner."

I lifted my chin. "A business partner."

Here's the thing—I was done with Ben. I think I had been done for a while. And Asa loomed large, casting a shadow over my heart. Denying it would have been stupid at that point. But I wasn't about to jump right out of one relationship and into another—especially one as complicated as anything with Asa was bound to be. Plus, everything about the man in front of me screamed *heartbreaker*, and mine had already been cracked a few times.

Didn't mean he wasn't tempting as hell.

"*Strictly* professional," I added.

"*Strictly?*"

"Strictly." I folded my arms over my chest.

He pursed his lips and looked me up and down. "Hmm." He reached forward and slid the side door open. "What do you think, Gracie? Room for one more?"

Gracie yipped, her stub of a tail wagging madly as she pressed her nose against the side of her crate, her bandaged leg sticking up in the air. I offered my fingers and she licked at them frantically, her best effort at a kiss.

"Okay. I suppose we could swing this." Asa gestured toward the passenger seat. "All aboard, partner."

I stifled a nervous grin as I jogged around the back of the van and got in on the other side. "So . . . where are we going?"

Asa threw the van in gear. "I'm thinking Bali."

"What's in Bali?"

"A vacation. I need one."

A vacation in Bali. This would surely involve Asa with his shirt off. "Oh," I said in a choked voice.

"There might be a certain relic there that I'd like to swipe."

"Oh!" That sounded less dangerous.

"But any reliquary working with me has to be healthy." He reached over and jiggled one of my skinny arms. "We're going to put some meat on those bones before we ask your body for any more than it's already given."

"Good plan. Will there be french fries?"

"A whole island of french fries, baby."

"Right. Okay. Good. Wait!"

"Yeah?"

"Asa, I don't have a passport."

He reached into his center console and removed a ziplock bag, which he tossed onto my lap.

I blinked down at the bag, then slowly pulled out its contents. Two passports—one for a Mr. Kenneth Doubledee, a dark-haired man with a knifelike smile and a crooked nose. And another for a Mrs. Griselda

Doubledee, who happened to be wearing my face. "When did you get these?"

"I told you I was gonna plan for every outcome."

I smacked his arm with Griselda's passport. "Are we married?"

He smirked. "Do you wanna be?"

I rolled my eyes and laughed. "Asa, I meant it when I said I needed this to stay professional. I have some things to sort out." I waved over my shoulder at all I'd left behind.

"I know you do." His smile was wicked. "But you're gonna want to try me out sooner or later. I can tell you're curious."

"Once again, you think you have me pegged."

"Well, not yet, but . . ." He waggled his eyebrows.

"Time," I said, even as my body drew tight. "I need time."

"Take all the time you want, baby. We'll see how long you can hold out."

"Game on, *sir*."

"Dammit, Mattie." He was grinning as he turned onto a state road and hit the gas. "This is gonna be fun."

I covered my mouth to hide my own giddy smile. I was headed into the unknown, about to write my story all over that vast blank slate that had terrified me for so long.

And I wasn't about to admit it, but I was pretty sure Asa was right.

ACKNOWLEDGMENTS

A huge thank-you to my team at 47North. I am so grateful for the unwavering support I've received for this book and these characters. I'm most grateful to Jason Kirk for wrangling all the priorities, deadlines, players, and details, providing leadership and vision, and for being the champion for this series. Thanks as well to Courtney Miller and Britt Rogers for additional enthusiasm, management, and the occasional lovely surprise in my mailbox. More gratitude goes to Janice Lee for excellent and thorough copyediting and to Jill Taplin for ushering the book through production.

Once again, thank you to my developmental editor, Leslie "Lam" Miller. You give me so much more than excellent revision guidance. I am so utterly grateful for your patience, wit, savvy, flexibility, creativity, and general awesomeness.

Kathleen Ortiz, my agent, has been my advocate for over five years now. KO, we have come so far, and I am so lucky to have you as my partner in this journey—you're the one who ensures that I don't wander off the trail and drown in a bog or get myself eaten by a bear. And to the rest of the team at New Leaf Literary & Media, thank you for all that you do.

A special thank-you goes to Amber Lynn Natusch for her incredible cheerleading throughout this series. I am so fortunate to have had that fuel and inspiration as I let the tale unfurl. And thanks to both Amber and Shannon Morton for providing early reads and insightful feedback.

Lydia Kang and Brigid Kemmerer . . . you ladies are such dear friends. Thank you for being there for me this past year, for listening, for your wisdom, for GIFs of screaming goats, for being the green dots I most look forward to seeing, for being such amazing, strong women. I adore you both.

For Paul, Liz, Jim, Susanne, Claudine, Sue, and Craig, thank you for providing me with a haven whenever I needed it, for laughter and drinks, and for making absolutely sure I always knew I was cared about.

To my parents, thank you isn't really enough. You know what you've done for me, and I hope you know how grateful I am. And to Asher and Alma, thank you for being my reason, day and night and always.

ABOUT THE AUTHOR

Photo © 2012 Rebecca Skinner

Sarah Fine is a clinical psychologist and the author of the Servants of Fate and Guards of the Shadowlands series. She was born on the West Coast, was raised in the Midwest, and is now firmly entrenched on the East Coast.